UNCONQUERED

UNCONQUERED

A Novel

Johnny Neil Smith

SANTA FE

Sunstone books may be purchased for educational, business, or sales promotional use. For information please write: Special Markets Department, Sunstone Press, P.O. Box 2321, Santa Fe, New Mexico 87504-2321.

Book design ≈ Vicki Ahl
Typeface ≈ Chaparral Pro
Printed on acid free paper

Library of Congress Cataloging-in-Publication Data

Smith, Johnny Neil, 1939-
 Unconquered : a novel / by Johnny Neil Smith.
   p. cm.
 ISBN 978-0-86534-515-7 (softcover : alk. paper)
 1. United States--History--Civil War, 1861-1865--Influence--Fiction. 2. Southern States--Social conditions--1865-1945--Fiction. 3. Southern States--Race relations--Fiction. I. Title.

PS3569.M5375514U63 2008
813'.54--dc22

                    2007046320

WWW.SUNSTONEPRESS.COM
SUNSTONE PRESS / POST OFFICE BOX 2321 / SANTA FE, NM 87504-2321 /USA
(505) 988-4418 / ORDERS ONLY (800) 243-5644 / FAX (505) 988-1025

DEDICATED TO MY THREE WONDERFUL CHILDREN:
Christopher, Richard, and Jami.
Truly, a blessing from above.

PROLOGUE

THE BATTLE FLAGS HAD BEEN FURLED. THE HILLS, MEADOWS and woodlands where men once struggled in bloody conflict and brought a new country to its knees, was now peaceful. The brutal sound of clashing armies was now replaced by the soft whisper of birds and breezes. Only the torn and shattered trunks of trees and an occasional row of lonely graves confirmed the terrible sacrifice that had been made. The battles had ended, but other conflicts lay ahead, conflicts that would test the inner soul of a young democracy. The year was 1866.

§§

The nineteenth century had brought flourishing change to the United States. Waves of immigrants flooding the cities along the eastern seacoast surrendered their family ties to venture into a new country. They brought with them their hopes and dreams of finding a better life; a life where a man could acquire his own piece of land and build a home for his wife and children; a life where personal freedom was guaranteed, for himself and his posterity.

In the northeastern United States, the Industrial Revolution begun in Europe was now prevalent throughout the region. Newcomers seeking work could find jobs in factories, but pay there was little and the working conditions often deplorable. These jobs were stumbling blocks for those trying to obtain enough money to make dreams of land and a home a reality. Factory workers who were not able to accumulate enough became enslaved economically to the system.

Strangely enough, however it was this very system that produced an abundance of war materials that in the hands of the Union soldiers brought the American Civil War to an end and gave freedom to thousands of African slaves. These freed men also had hopes of a promised parcel of land and mule and dreams of a good life for their families. Would this government that had waged such a costly war in terms of expense and loss of human life, and in the end granted these slaves freedom, forsake them now that they stood on the brink of a new era? Would the highly revered Constitution of this great young democracy stand by all of its citizens, no matter what race or gender?

Meanwhile gold had been discovered in California and people had flocked to the West Coast seeking their fortune along the abundant streams and rivers in this beautiful and enchanting land. Many did strike it rich, but most people abandoned the gold fields for other interests such as farming, lumbering, and the raising of livestock. Once word spread to the eastern shores about the vast wealth of California and Oregon, people aggressively sought ways to reach this land of wonder. The dream of land drove them relentlessly. To those unprepared for the journey, disaster lay ahead. Their dream would become their nightmare.

Throughout the eastern United States, most of the Native Americans had been removed and placed on reservations located west of the Mississippi River, land not particularly of value. But in contrast, during the 1860's the Indians of the American plains were still living on their tribal lands in much the same way as their ancestors. But with the completion of the transcontinental railroad, change and rapid development of these sacred grounds was inevitable. The dreams of these people, dreams of being left alone to live their lives on grounds guaranteed by treaties signed with the United States government, were threatened. Would the United States protect their rights and grant their children the freedom they had experienced for generations on lands of their ancestors?

Following the American Civil War, the South outwardly appeared prostrate as defeated armies were disbanded, and tired and ragged soldiers made their way home. Once home, they found themselves under military rule with little self-government. As the Southern states began their reorganization, many former representatives and congressmen were chosen to return to Washington only to be denied their seats by the predominant Republican-led congress. With the rejection of these men, the Southern States had to find others to represent them. In many cases, newly freed Negroes, citizens from the North who had come south to seek their fortune and white men who had not supported the Southern cause, filled the vacancies.

Outwardly, the South appeared a conquered country. Its armies had been driven from the field. Its white supremacy government no longer existed. Many of its farms and plantations lay in disrepair. The economy was depleted.

Their rifles had been stacked and uniforms exchanged for plain clothes. These warriors of the South were now mere men trying to rebuild their lives and fortunes. The South appeared in submission. But underneath, its pride, spirit, and sense of loyalty to its cause were still alive. The white South dreamed of reclaiming its identity and freedom.

But would the Negro be integrated into this new Southern culture. They were given no land at the end of the War as they had hoped, and with no education, what would they do? Who would protect their new grant of freedom?

Who would come forward and lead the South? Out of the ashes of war would someone with vision, mercy, and a feeling of justice for all step forward? Did the South have men such as these and would they be allowed to serve their country during these difficult times?

1

A GLIMPSE IN TIME

WITH A LOUD BACKFIRE, THE 1930 BLACK T MODEL FORD came to a sliding halt sending a cloud of dust swirling through the air and across the porch of Herrington's General store in Little Rock, Mississippi.

"Whoaa, Popee! We almost ran into the steps," exclaimed the young boy staring over at his great grandfather.

Twisting in his seat to peer over the hood and evaluate the situation, the old man replied, "Didn't even come close, Andy. I got plenty of room and do you have to call me by that name?"

"I like the name Popee and I already have a Papa and a Grandpaw. I guess I'm just running out of names," the young lad said smiling.

"Well, I've been called a lot worse during my lifetime. I guess I can live with it," laughed the old man as he reached for the door handle. "Let's go get us a cool soda, Andy. This heat is beginning to get to me."

The boy reached for the old man's hand. "This store is kinda run down. Where are we anyway? This place looks too small to be a town."

Once again the man chuckled as he slowly stepped down from the automobile. "Town, no, it's too small for that, maybe a village. It's had several names through the years. Some called it Riversville and others Coontail, but it finally just became Little Rock."

Satisfied with the explanation, the lad jumped down from the automobile and bounded up the steps that led to the entrance of the store. While opening the door, the boy paused and looked back. "Watch those steps, Popee. And you did almost hit the porch. Mama says you're getting too old to be driving one of these things."

Reaching for the handrail, the man grumbled, "I'm doing just fine and your mama talks too much." Reaching the top step, he stopped to get his breath and continued, "and don't call me that name so loud. There's folks around."

The boy laughed and hurried inside.

Standing there in the warm July sunshine, the old man paused and carefully scanned the area. Up the street he saw a large frame church with a tall steeple which brought back memories of throngs of people filing out of the large entrance way, shaking hands, laughing, and enjoying each other's company as they shared their past week's experiences with friends and neighbors. Children scampered here and there chasing one another, making the horses and mules harnessed to the buggies and wagons nervous.

Turning his attention to the other side of the village he saw the old blacksmith shop across the street much as he had remembered. Down near the creek the water-powered mill lay in ruins. Progress had taken its toll.

Looking closer, he found that many new homes had been built in the village and the railroad had finally reached this little remote community. Along with the homes, there were now a cotton gin, a barbershop and several other stores along the main street.

The dusty road awakened the image of a time when the stagecoach from Meridian would roll into town carrying travelers, goods and family mail; he remembered the excitement of possible visitors or hoped-for letters. It all seemed so long ago.

Breaking the silence, a small voice echoed from inside. "Popee, you ought to see all this stuff! They have everything in this old dump."

Hurrying inside the old man found the boy standing in awe in the middle of the floor. Canned goods of every kind were stacked in shelves that rose to the ceiling and clothing on long racks ran the length of the building. Exposed beams were covered with smoked hams and sausages, and support braces holding up the roof were loaded with saddles, harnesses, bridles and every imaginable item needed for working animals.

"Shuu.., not so loud," said the old man grabbing the boy by the hand and leading him toward the counter at the back of the store.

"But Popee, I ain't never seen so much stuff like this. They have everything in the world in here. Look back there! They even got guns for sale," the boy said pulling his great grandfather's hand and leading him to the gun rack. "Will you buy me one of those? I bet I could shoot it. Mama said you were in the war and did a lot of shooting. Said you shot a bunch of Yankees. Can I hold one of 'em?"

Frowning down at the boy and leading him away from the rack the old man replied, "You're too young to be thinking about owning a rifle and as for me in a war, I try to forget those days. Killing other human beings just ain't right—downright ungodly. When you get older your father will probably teach you how to handle one of these and there isn't anything more fun than a good squirrel huntin'. Your time will come, lad."

"Then how about that cool soda?"

"Sounds good to me," he replied leading the boy to the counter.

The clerk who had been busy restocking a cracker barrel pushed his glasses up and carefully studied the two eagerly awaiting his service. "Well, I hope you don't think I have intentionally been ignoring ya. I seen you was a havin' a good time looking over the old place and it did give me time to catch up on some chores. Can I help ya?"

The boy yanked at the old man's sleeve and motioned for him to bend down.

"Popee, they talk funny down here. I bet it's Choctaw ain't it," he whispered. With a loud burst of laughter the old man exclaimed, "Choctaw? We're in Miss'sippi, Andy. They talk southern down here."

"You folks ain't from here 'bouts, are you?" the clerk asked, wondering what had brought this unusual pair into his establishment. "Say you want a soda?"

"Coldest you got," said the old man reaching into his pocket for some change. "We're hot and might near worn to a frazzle. By the way, how's the times down here in Little Rock treating you young man?"

Placing two cold sodas on the counter, the clerk paused and wiped his brow. "They says a depression is hittin' the country. I says we has always had hard times down here. The old folks say that it ain't been the same since the Yankees took us apart back years ago. Now where's you folks from?"

Andy opened his drink and began to gulp down big swallows. As he stopped to take a breath, he answered, "I'm from Maryland and my Pops is from everywhere."

"Everywhere?" the clerk said. "That's hard to imagine."

The old man chuckled. "What he means is that I have lived in a lot of places. You know, I ain't a spring chicken."

Giving the old man his change, the clerk asked. "How old are ya? If you don't mind tellin' me, sir."

"Well," he replied, scratching his head. "I'm might near eighty-five, I guess. Eighty-five will do."

The clerk shook his head. "Ain't many of you fellows left 'round here. You go back a spell."

Just then the screen door opened and a group of women came in and approached the clerk.

The old man led his great grandson outside to a bench on the shady side of the porch.

"What do you think of the town, Andy?" the old man asked reaching down and patting the boy on the back.

"I thought you said this place was a village," the boy answered, more interested in the soda than conversation. In a moment he continued. "I think the store is great."

The old man smiled. "You see that bridge down yonder? I'd like to go down there and look around the creek. Might even see some fish or maybe a turtle. Who knows, we might even find one of those Choctaw arrowheads."

"Arrowheads?" exclaimed Andy. "Let's go" Andy jumped up and pulled on his great grandfather's shirt sleeve.

"Not so fast, boy. You'll pull me down if you don't be careful. You run on ahead. I'll catch up with you. Just don't go near the water 'till I get there. You hear me?"

"I hear you. Don't get in the water," the boy said over his shoulder as he sprinted for the creek.

Standing on the shady bank, Andy was mesmerized by his surroundings and the waters below. He could imagine a party of fierce Choctaw warriors as they stopped to rest and wash their wounds after a bloody clash with the north Mississippi Chickasaws. He imagined a deer easing to the edge of the water and then trying to escape before he could shoot an arrow at him.

"Well, what do you propose to do, Son," questioned the old man as he looked down from the bridge.

Andy shook his head. "Popee, I rightly don't know but I think it would be fun to wade out in the water and maybe see if I could find one of those arrowheads."

The old man eased down and found a comfortable place to rest on the edge of the bridge., "Well, go ahead and get on in there. There ain't no gators round here."

Andy looked up at his great grandfather in uncertainty. "But I can't swim very well. What if I fall and get drowned."

"Drowned! The water ain't knee deep. This used to be the place where wagons crossed heading in and out of Little Rock. Get those shoes and socks off and get on in there, Boy."

The lad hesitated. "But, what if I get my clothes wet. Mama will sure get mad with me."

"Mad? Your mother is too straight laced. She needs to let you be a boy sometimes. We're visiting down here. It's time to have some fun. She's gonna make a softy out of you. Now if you want to get in that water, then get at it and if you don't that's also fine with me. Just make up your mind."

Looking down at the cool, clear water, Andy could wait no longer. He sat down and hurriedly took off his shoes and socks, rolled up his britches legs and waded out into the stream.

For the first few moments, Andy splashed around enjoying the cold water and a new experience in this wilderness, and then he began studying everything in and around the creek. Every small rock became an arrowhead for his great grandfather to see, but finding out that his arrowheads were only small rocks, he would race down the steep bank in search of another.

The afternoon passed quickly as the two enjoyed the quest.

Tiring from too many trips up and down the creek bank, Andy scrambled once more down to the water. In his haste, his feet slid out from under him, and he sailed into the creek, head first.

Emerging as quickly as he had entered and giving a loud snort, the boy quickly regained his balance. Andy looked down at his muddy, wet clothing and then slowly looked up at his great grandfather. " Popee, Mama's gonna tan my hide I know. If she don't , Aunt Betty sure will."

The old man smiled down at the boy. "You didn't drown did you?"

"No Sir, I'm still alive, I reckon."

"Then you wash the clay off your clothes and then come on up here. I think you need to rest a spell."

"You ain't mad at me, Popee?"

"Heavens no, child. I been waiting on you to get in that water and I've been disappointed that it's taken you this long to get soaked. You come on up here and we'll go get us another one of those sodas."

"What about Mama, Popee?"

Placing his arm around the boy the man replied, "Your clothes will dry and this will just have to be our secret. That all right with you?"

"Yes sir. I wish I could stay with you all the time. You're a lot of fun."

Entering the store again, the two found the clerk in a rocking chair sound asleep. Hearing the floor creak, the clerk aroused from his slumber, adjusted his glasses and muttered, "May I help ya?" Recognizing the two, he continued, " I thought y'all might be long gone by now."

"Been down to the creek hunting for arrowheads and I kinda fell in the water. Need another one of those cold sodas, Sir."

The old man smiled down at the lad. "It's getting pretty hot out there. By the way, where is everyone? Looks like you ought to have more business than this."

"Most folks is out in the fields this time of the year and it's hotter than four hells out there today. Ain't nobody stirring 'round here, except maybe folks like you who is from everywhere. Here's your soda. Just leave yore money on the counter. I'm going back to my chair."

The old man and the boy decided it was time for them to leave the clerk in peace so they quietly made their way back out to the bench on the porch.

Sitting there in the shade, Andy stretched out on the bench and rested his head on his great grandfather's lap. "World looks different down here looking up, Popee. Kinda hard to see up through your fuzzy white beard though. It looks like a briarpatch and your nose holes resembles some tunnels where trains come through puffing and clanking."

Pushing the boy's hair out of his face, the old man replied. "You have some kind of imagination, boy. I used to like to daydream too."

Growing sleepy, Andy gazed up at the sky and pointed. "Popee, I can see all kind of things up there in those clouds. I think I see an elephant. No, it's just an old bear, maybe."

Eyes closing, he mumbled, "Popee, would you tell me one of those stories about when you were a young man? One of those about the big war you fought in?"

"Your Mama don't like for me to tell about the war," he replied, but thinking back he began to reminisce. "My life has been good in many ways, but there are things I want to forget. Things too painful to think about, much less speak about."

Glancing back down at Andy, he saw that the boy was sleeping soundly. "Sleep on young man. Chase your dreams, harness the rainbow, fight your battles and enjoy the life the good Lord has given you."

Looking up at the clouds, he could see himself as a youngster lying on a sandy creek bank listening to the water ripple across the rocks bringing fantasies tempting him to another kind of life. Shutting his eyes, it seemed that time had played a trick on him. The same sky full of puffy clouds had not changed at all. The sun was still up there laughing at him, tempting his patience. Thinking harder, he could vividly remember his days as a young man returning from a war that should have taken his life, only to find that his older brother had died up in Virginia and another had deserted the army and fled to the West. He remembered the pain of loosing the woman he had worshiped since childhood and finding his country devastated by four years of struggle for survival against overwhelming forces.

It was a perilous time for the South. Home government was a thing of the past. The South lay conquered. The year was 1866.

2

HOPE IN DESPAIR

The late March winds gently nudged the tops of the trees creating an eerie sound as it whistled around the corners of the stately home located on the outskirts of Richmond, Virginia. Inside, a man wrapped in a dark red housecoat stood with arms crossed, staring out a large window.

Hearing the door open behind him, he turned and muttered, "Come on in, Joshua. I know it's about time."

An old Negro man dressed in a dark suit entered, holding a bottle in one hand and a spoon in the other. He nodded politely. "Mas' Stephen, it shore is some kind of cold out da'er and dat wind will cut 'chu in half."

"You can drop the Mas' Stephen, Joshua. Those days are over," replied Robert Stephens as he reached for the spoon.

"I always called you dat, sir. Ever since I can remember. What you wants me to call you?"

Smiling over at the old man standing patiently in front of him, Stephens replied, "Well, you can call me Mister Stephens or I guess maybe, Senator. Some folks still use the term."

Nodding his approval, Joshua said, "I thinks I'll call you Mister Senator. I'll never forget them days we spent up da'er in Washington. You with all them high f'luting folks, and I'll never forget you being invited to dine with the Pres'dent. Them was some days to behold."

Pouring the medicine into his spoon, Stephens nodded in agreement and pointed back to where a fire was burning in a fireplace located at the back of the room.

"Joshua, sit a spell with me. I get a little lonesome, especially this time of the year. She left me about this time two years ago."

Not accustomed to socializing, Joshua dropped his head and replied, "You shore you wants me to sit with you."

Making himself comfortable, Stephens continued, "Joshua, I've known you all my life. You served my father when he was alive; you took care of me when I was a youngster and when the war ended and the slaves were freed, you wouldn't leave us. You go ahead and have a seat."

"Yes Sir, Mister Senator, I ain't never left you. You is the only family I got. You know, Mister Lincoln sho enough freed us, but he didn't tell us where to go or what we 'spose to do," easing into the chair next to Stephens. "I decided I'd just stay right here with you, if'n you'd have me."

Trying to refrain from coughing, Stephens grabbed his chest. "If I don't hurry up and get over this ailment that danged ole medicine is gonna put me in the ground. Maybe that's where I need to be anyway. The hope of the South, the Confed'racy, was crushed without mercy, our armies driven from the field and worst still, my beloved wife of more than twenty years passed away leaving me all alone. Some men have children. We never could."

Placing his hand on Stephen's arm, Joshua whispered, "Don't talk like dat, Sir. You still got ole Joshua and before long the cold winds will be gone and Mister Sunshine is gonna pick you up and send you right back to ole happiness. You jest wait and see. You never was a winter man."

At that moment there was a light tap on the front door, but the two men ignored the rapping sound thinking that it was probably no more than the wind.

"Sir, I think someone is out front," Joshua said, getting out of his chair. "Yes Sir, that is a knock."

Keeping his seat, Stephens said, "It's might near dark. Be some kind of a fool to come out on a day like this. Unless it's someone special, tell 'em I'm not here."

"Yes Suh, I'll do just dat."

A few moments passed and by the sound of voices conferring downstairs, Stephens felt that it was probably just one of Joshua's friends who on occasions would drop by to chat with him. I'll try one more dose of this medicine, Stephens thought, and if I don't get some relief then it's gonna be left up to the Lord Almighty to do what he wants with me. Suddenly the sound of people making their way to his room caused him to put down his spoon and pick up the glasses that were lying on the table beside his chair.

The door slowly opened and Joshua whispered, "Mister Senator, I thinks you might want to see this gentleman, he says —"

"He says what?" Stephens interrupted, clearing his throat. "It better be good"

A tall man wearing a gray overcoat and a scarf wrapped snugly around his neck replied, "Well sir, you sure are in a foul mood tonight. I thought I'd just come by to see if you would like to make a charitable donation toward one of our local houses of ill repute."

"Ill repute! What in tarnations are you talking about?" Stephens answered, adjusting his glasses.

Unwrapping his scarf, the intruder began to chuckle. "Robert, I know we're getting a little old, but I didn't know you'd be blind as a bat."

Hearing a familiar voice, Stephens peered closely at the man standing by the door. "You're Jack Hudson. Good gracious man, I haven't seen you in years. What in the world are you doing here in Richmond?"

Extending his hand, Hudson replied, "Good to see you Robert. It's been a few years since you and I were cadets at the institute. I was passing through here and I thought I'd better stop by to see you."

Happy to see his old friend, the two embraced. After a hard pat on the back, Robert said, "What's it been, thirty years or so? Come on in here by the fire. We've got a lot of catching up to do. Joshua, take Mister Hudson's coat and prepare the guest bedroom."

"I can't impose on your hospitality, Robert, and you may not feel like puttin' up with an old fool like me. Joshua told me you've been sick for a spell. I can stay downtown."

"Downtown! There ain't much left downtown since the Yankees burnt us out. You're staying here with us," Robert insisted toward Joshua. "Go do what I told you and go to my study and get me a bottle of scotch. You haven't stopped drinking, have you, Jack?"

"I've been known to sip a little on special occasions."

"Well this here is one of them occasions, and if you'll stay with me, we might just make a night of it," Robert said, feeling better.

Joshua stood quietly for a moment. "Mister Senator, you know what the doctor told you 'bout that dranking. He said if'n you didn't quit, it'll most near kill ya."

"Kill me," Robert exclaimed. "That medicine he prescribed for me is gonna kill me. No sir, tonight we're going to do some serious drinking and if it kills me, you're gonna be one rich Richmond Darkie."

"What you mean by that, Mister Senator?"

"Joshua, my kin folks don't give a tinkers damn about me. They only come to see me when they want something. So Mister Joshua, I've left everything I own to you when I die. You'll have one of finest houses in the city and a little bit of money that'll last you if you're careful. The only problem you're gonna have is all them women that'll be after you. You know you ain't as spry as you used to be. They might take advantage of you."

Joshua laughed, "Mister Senator, you joshing me, ain't cha and if'n you ain't, Ole Josh is more spry than you thinks. Yes Suh, I'll bring you a bottle. I'll brang you two of 'em."

The two men laughed, then settled themselves before the fire. Joshua soon returned with the Scotch and two clean glasses, asking to be excused as he quietly closed the door.

Jack and Robert reminisced over times at the Virginia Military Institute and laughed at the senseless youthful capers that had often sent them to detention hall. They also remembered their last farewell and promises at graduation to spend the next Christmas with each other. Through the years they had exchanged numerous letters, but until this evening they never had seen each other.

Standing up to stretch, Jack moved over to the window and stared out into the darkness and then as speaking to himself, he whispered, "You know Robert, our lives certainly moved in different directions after the institute. I accepted a commission as a second lieutenant in the United States Army and spent twenty years out west chasing Indians and you went into politics and should have become our president."

"President, did I hear you say president," Robert questioned, leaning over to hear him better.

Jack returned to his chair. "That's right, I said president. I followed your career up there in Washington and you were outstanding. You were honest, clever, and I must say you helped make some laws that were beneficial to all of us here in the South. If we hadn't seceded from the Union, I believe you'd be in the White House by now."

"White House, I made more enemies up there than you know about, and when the state of Virginia sent me back up there after the war, what happened? They wouldn't accept me. They sent me and a lot of others like me right back home. They said that since we served in the Confed'rate Congress, we weren't eligible. Ain't that a hell of a note."

Jack poured another drink and replied, "It weren't right. You're suppose to represent the state that elected you. You ought to be up there right now. What are you going to do with yourself now?"

Robert got up, leaned against the mantle and stared into the low burning fire. "I'll hang up my shingle and start practicing law again. Folks always gonna be getting into trouble. I'll do all right. I'm still a cadet at heart. I'll survive."

"Survive," Jack stammered. "Looking out into that darkness a few minutes ago, I wondered if the South is gonna survive. They drove our armies from the field; the military has control of our government; our economy is in shambles and a lot of us that could add stability to the situation can't even vote or hold office. It's just like that wall of darkness outside your window, we can't see out there. We don't know what's in store for us and if we could, we can't control any of it."

"Jack, I think your liquor is talking for you. Unless you've changed, it always got you down when you got two sheets in the wind," Robert said, swirling the scotch around in the bottom of his glass. "First thing, you and I are both alive and you survived more battles than a man could expect. And another thing, they taught us at school, no matter what, there will always be problems and to every problem, there is a solution. There ain't no denying, we've got one heck of a problem, and it's gonna be left up to someone to solve it. We're just gonna have to get control of the South again, that's all."

"That's all," Jack exclaimed, feeling a little tipsy. "You think we ought to put our men in arms again. You think we could drive them out? That's ridiculous. Our war is over."

"I'm not talking about raising new armies. I'm talking about taking control of our government again," Robert explained. "The military won't always be stationed here and when they're gone, we've got to place our men in every elected seat of government in every southern state. Whoever makes the laws, controls the action of its citizens. Our job is to form an organization now that will place our eligible candidates on the ticket come election time and find ways to get the Negroes, sorry Whites, and those Northern scavengers who are now holding office, back to where they belong. That's what we need to do."

Jack laughed. "I think the scotch is getting to your head now. You think all those so called undesirables will graciously give up their seats? We don't even hold a majority vote. What we gonna do? Run 'em off with sticks. How 'bout killing the devils? Is that what you intend?"

Robert peered over the top of his glasses and nodded "I state once again. We select our candidates and then do whatever is necessary to eliminate the competition. There are ways that this can be done, and yes, if it takes violence, then let it be. You know the old saying, 'The end justifies the means.'"

"You think someone could do this?"

"We've just got to find someone to lead the movement. Someone the South will follow, someone the soldiers respect. Our troops have put down their rifles, but I promise you, they still have the fight in 'em. It'll just be a little different kind of warring. Our Southern soldiers will follow the right man. How about you? I followed your career during the war and you were one of the best division commanders the South had."

"Not me old friend, I might have had a good military reputation but I paid the price for it. I got shot eleven times and there are times that even now I have numbness in my left leg and at other times I can hardly catch my breath."

Jack thought for a moment. "How about Hood? I'm on the way to New Orleans right now for a job he has lined up for me. He was some kind of Gen'ral."

"Don't think so. He all but destroyed one of our armies up there at Franklin. Lot of the men lost faith in him. We need someone they idolize. We need a real fire-eating fighter. It's got to be someone special."

Jack walked about the room for a few moments, then said, "I know the man that will get the job done."

§§

On an August day in 1867, in the Little Rock community located in rural east central Mississippi, slightly past mid-day, a young woman suddenly slammed open her front door, angrily picked up her sagebroom and scurried out on her front porch where two of her husband's hounds were curled up sleeping. Loose chicken feathers surrounding the dogs revealed the plight of the flock.

"You sorry devils!" she screamed. "My husband said he thought the foxes or hawks been eating 'em, but now we know," she said taking a swing at the nearest dog. "You're the culprits cleaning out the hen house, and I'll tell you one thing. I'm fixin' to beat the living sin out of both of you." She struck one of the dogs so hard it knocked him off the side of the porch as he tried to run toward the steps.

"Not only that, the next time my husband is gone for a few days, you two devils gonna come up amiss. I'll take that shootin' iron of his and for all he knows, the panthers got you. That's what I'm gonna do."

Howling to the top of their lungs, the hounds ran for protection under the house. A few wandering chickens flapped their wings in flight to the nearest tree limb. Meanwhile the angry woman hadn't noticed the visitor who had ridden to the edge of the yard.

"Say you gonna kill 'em, Sister," the man called out.

Startled by the sound of a voice, the woman spun around and saw a man she had known all of her life sitting there calmly on his horse rolling a smoke.

The woman threw down her broom and placed her hands defiantly on her hips as she scowled, "Timothy Johnson, how long you been sitting there?"

With a smurkish smile, he replied, "Long enough to see you beat the hell out of James' dogs, and I do believe you're gonna sure 'nough kill 'em first chance you get. I do believe that Mister James has up and married him a dog killer."

"Dog Killer! I barely hit 'em and they have been killing my birds," Sister said, as she went down the steps.

"Yes Ma'am, I saw what you done to James' prize hounds," Timothy said, lighting his smoke. "And just wait 'til I tell the preacher how you been cussing right out in public. Yes ma'am, Sister Wilson, you are one violent woman."

No sooner had he finished his statement, than Sister reached for her broom and with one swing, and to her own surprise, knocked Timothy from his horse onto the ground. Startled by the unexpected attack, Timothy's horse bolted across the yard into a field and in the confusion, Timothy's smoke went sailing into the air landing right in Sister's hair. Sister could envision her hair aflame and began screaming and shaking her head in all directions.

As she frantically tried to get the smoke out of her hair, Timothy sat there on the ground laughing as hard as he could, enjoying every minute of Sister's dilemma.

Seeing the smoke fall to the ground and knowing that she was no longer in trouble, Sister quickly regained her composure.

Through the years, Timothy, one of her older brother's best friends, and she had delighted in tormenting each other with pranks and verbal comments. Sister had always loved to antagonize Timothy but had a difficult time when she was the one being teased. Often parents had to intervene when the arguments got out of hand. Her seeming appearance of dislike masked the fact that she had found him both attractive and somewhat dashing. Timothy's lack of parental discipline and his stories of devilish and adventurous exploits intrigued her. Even though she knew his stories were exaggerated, they still managed to excite her. One thing was certain, when they were together, sparks were going to fly.

Smoothing her hair, she glanced over at Timothy. "I know what you're trying to do and it ain't gonna work. You're not getting me upset, Mister Timothy Johnson."

He, pulling himself up, replied, "Too late, Sister. You done made a fool out of yourself, and you might near killed me in the process. That fall almost broke my wood leg." He had lost the lower part of his right leg during the war and was very protective of his artificial limb.

Hobbling to get his horse he continued, "Come sundown, me and that brother of yores is going to a revival down near Hickory."

"Revival! You ain't going to no church meeting," Sister exclaimed. "You ain't been in a church since your daddy died more than a year ago, and my brother don't need to be going nowheres with the likes of you."

Mounting his horse, Timothy replied, "Then where in blazes do you think I intend to carry him, Miss Know-it-all."

By that time Sister had gone back to the house and begun sweeping the feathers off the porch. "Knowing you, you will try to talk John into going to Meridian with you for a night of drinking, gambling, and you know what else."

"What do you mean by, you know what else," Timothy asked.

"The only thing you is fit for is whoring. Timothy Johnson you are nothing but a sinning whoremonger, and my brother won't be going to Meridian with you. He's got a pretty young lady who thinks the world of him. He don't need yore whores. Why do you think that wife of yores run off with that visiting preacher? Cause of your constant carousing and staying away from home for weeks at a time. That's why she left you. You just go on to Meridian by yoreself."

Before the Civil War, Meridian, a bustling rail center, was the largest town in Mississippi. When General Sherman sacked and burned the town on his raid across the state, many feared it would never prosper again, but as soon as his troops had left the area, its people began to rebuild. Now Meridian was once again thriving and prosperous. It was filled with merchandise, and its nightlife attracted people from all parts of the state. Gambling houses were in operation twenty-four hours a day and for those who wanted the company of the opposite sex, the red district was rivaled by none.

Timothy was in the process of leaving when he caught the remark about his ex-wife and he sharply brought his horse to a stop and turned in the saddle. "Sister, we may get into some squabbles sometimes and most of the time it don't mean nothing, but you better never say anything about Sally. That's none of yore business what happened to us, and I'll tell you one more thing, least I didn't up and marry a damned Yankee."

During the war when Sherman made his raid through Little Rock, some of his soldiers were foraging for food when they came upon the Wilson's house. Making their way inside, they knocked Sister's father unconscious and were trying to force themselves on Sister and her mother when suddenly a federal officer, Lieutenant James Robinson, rode up and intervened. In the scuffle that followed, Robinson killed one of his soldiers and wounded the other. Following the war, he was assigned to the Newton county area as part of the military controlled government and began to stop by the Wilson's on a fairly regular basis. Eventually, Sister and he began to see each other socially and after a ten-month courtship, they were married.

Knowing she had probably gone too far, Sister stood motionless, fearing to say anything else.

Heading down the road, Timothy stopped and shouted back to her. "You think I'm nothing but a whoremonger, but you know what your are,

Lucretia Wilson? You're the biggest gossip and hypocrite in Newton County and for your information, we ain't going to Meridian, I think."

Calming down as he rode off, Timothy couldn't help but feel a fondness for Sister. Even with her quick lip and spunky attitude, she could be delightful at times. Glancing back, he noticed how attractive she had become, standing well over five feet six inches tall with long flowing blond hair and blue eyes. She was certainly a striking figure on the porch. Without thinking, he raised his hand and waved.

Without hesitating, she smiled and returned the gesture.

§§

Because Sister and James had built their home on a plot of lower Wilson land, it didn't take Tim long to reach Sister's parents' place. Riding up, he could see Mrs. Wilson sitting on her front porch churning butter and singing a familiar church tune.

At that moment she stopped churning and peered over the top of her glasses. "Timothy Johnson, you sure are dressed to kill. You must be on your way to see some pretty little thing. Get down and come on in."

Tim dismounted and politely tipped his hat. To him, the Wilsons were his second family. They had always accepted him no matter what he had done, and Mrs. Wilson always encouraged him to try to do better. He felt that his own parents never cared enough about him to even correct him or give him encouragement.

Making his way up the steps, he said, "Good to see you Mrs. Wilson, mind if'n I give you a hug."

"I'd be disappointed if you didn't, young man," smiled Mrs. Wilson.

After a hug and a kiss on the cheek, she said, "How's your mama doing these days?"

"She's fine. She's been doing a lot of garden work lately and putting up with me keeps her pretty busy," he replied. "Is John in?"

Mrs. Wilson pointed to the back of the house. "He finished his chores early today. You'll find him back there in his room, probably reading. Sometimes I think he spends too much time in them books." Pausing a moment she continued, "I bet you boys gonna do some courting tonight. That's why you're so dressed up. That's it, ain't it?"

"Pretty close, Mrs. Wilson. I've come over to invite John to a meeting. A kind of revival meeting," he replied.

"A revival meeting. I ain't heard of any such meeting around here. You sure 'bout that?"

"Yes Ma'am, there's gonna be one down near Hickory Station. A shore 'nough big 'un."

Tim made his way down the open hall toward John's room.

Easing the door open Tim began to sing, "Shall we gather at the river, the beautiful, the beautiful river down near Hickory."

"Come on in Tim, I could recognize your voice anywhere. And by the way, you can't carry a tune and your lyrics border on being sacrilegious. No wonder they never encouraged you to sing in the church choir."

Lying across the bed with a pillow folded under his neck and a book across his lap was Tim's best friend, John Wilson. They had attended the same church and had been classmates in school until Tim quit in the eighth grade. Although Tim and John were total opposites, they had a special bond of friendship. John was serious and believed that honest hard work was the way to success and that education would open the doors of opportunity to those who persevered. John's reputation of being the best student the local school had ever produced was a promise for his future, but the war and the effects it had upon his family had kept him at home and away from his dreams. Tim, in contrast, lived only for the day. As a youth he never cared for farming and the loss of his leg during the war made farming impossible. Instead, Tim loved to gamble, drink and carouse and had become so skilled at the cards that he made more than a meager living.

Even as different as they were, they were inseparable. Since they had joined the same regiment during the war and had experienced the same horror and trials of combat, they had drawn even closer.

Easing down in a chair next to John, Tim reached over and glanced at the cover of the book. "Thought you might be reading some of that ole Shakespeare the professor used to try to cram down our throats. You used to like that stuff, didn't you?"

"You know I never cared for that," John replied, closing the book. "I'm reading about the Greek way of life. It's fascinating to see how they formed their government. You know, their system is part of the foundation of how we operate today."

"Greeks," Tim exclaimed, grabbing the book. "Let me see what you got yourself in to."

In a few minutes Tim handed the book back "Don't look too interesting to me. Them folks been gone for a thousand years."

"Thousand years," John replied. "Been longer than that and what do you like to read, nothing I bet."

Feeling somewhat offended, Tim responded, "I do read sometimes. I read the newspapers when I get a chance and things posted around on walls and I've read some of the Bible. So you see, I ain't as illiterate as you think."

"Read anything in the last month," John asked.

Tim was silent for a moment and then replied, "You been to bed with any good-looking women in the last month, Mister Socrates."

John shook his head in disbelief and thought, here I am trying to show him the importance of reading and he completely turned the table on me.

"No, I ain't been to bed with any woman. How about you?" John asked.

"Me neither," laughed Tim. "I thought that might be a good way to shut you up. Now back to them Greeks. Why do you like reading that stuff?"

John sat up on the side of the bed and after stretching answered, "Governments and law systems are what control the lives of people. Without law and order no one's rights would be protected. We'd live in total chaos. Without our governments it would be a kill or be killed society."

"Well, I guess that kinda falls in line with what I came by to tell you," Tim said. "You see there's gonna be a special, secret meeting down near Hickory tonight and you and me has been invited."

With a question on his face, John asked, "What do you mean a secret meeting?"

"You can't tell a soul about what I'm gonna tell you, John, especially if'n you decide to go with me."

"You know me better than that, Tim."

"Well, there's gonna be a get together down there tonight and there's gonna be a high ranking confed'rate gen'ral who's suppose to talk to us."

"Gen'ral!" John exclaimed. "What in tarnation about?"

"Well, if'n you'll shut up, I'll tell you about it. Now as I was saying, this here meeting is the beginning of a movement to take our government back."

"Government back!" John said. "What kind of hair-brained joke you trying to play on me."

"It ain't no joke," Tim replied. "Folks here in the South is tired of them Northerners, sorry white Southerners and Negroes running things. We're tired of the treatment they dishing out to us. Things fixing to change around here, Mister John Wilson and if'n you want to help us, you got an invitation."

John shook his head in disbelief. "Tim, the military gov'ment ain't always gonna be around here. There's gonna be a time when we'll get our chance to run things. How do you think this group is planning to take over the government? You know there's no way we can fight the Federal troops. We been through that before and I must say we didn't and don't have the men and resources to do it again. You'll not get me in trouble this time. I won't be going with you, and who is this person who wants us at the meeting anyway? "

"Frank Olliver and 'Fessor Hendon wants you there tonight, that's who," Tim answered.

"Frank Olliver! That's enough for me. If Frankie's involved, there's got to be trouble connected. You can go, but you can count me out."

"Wait a minute, John. There was a time when you two was closer than two straws in a broom. Frankie don't mean you no trouble."

"That was a long time ago. He's changed a lot these past few years. We speak to one another, but that's about it. If Frankie's involved, you can bet trouble ain't far behind," John said.

"You know why you're on the outs with Frankie," Tim replied. "You ain't ever forgive him for not showing up down at Newton Station and when he up and married—"

"Stop it right there, Tim. You don't know what you talking about. Don't ever mention her name to me. That's a part of my life that just don't exist no more, you hear me."

"Sorry, I was just trying to tell you that they wanted you there for some reason and if'n you don't care much for Frankie, then you know the 'Fessor means you no harm."

Professor Hendon was the only teacher John and Tim had ever had and even though he could be eccentric at times and had a reputation of being a ladies man, he had the men's respect. To John, this was the man who opened his eyes to learning and always challenged him to never accept mediocrity.

"The Professor," John said, regaining interest. "He really wants me there?"

I can't believe that he wants me to go with him tonight, John thought. It seems like I should still be just a student to him, listening to him lecture about the poets, the art of speaking and politics. Politics, that's what he enjoyed the most. No wonder he is interested in this meeting. Politics was always his first love.

"If'n 'Fessor Hendon will be going, then I might just tag along with you," John said, changing his mind. "It might be interesting just to see what this group is up to, but y'all better not get me into any kind of trouble with the law."

"Won't be no trouble, John. If'n you don't like what you hear then you can quietly bow out, and I'm sorry about what I almost said. I know'd it was a ticklish subject."

"Don't worry about it, and I was a little too hard on Frankie too. I'm suppose to go over to see Suzanne tomorrow, and her mother ain't never been nothing but nice to me. Mrs. Olliver can't help that she's got a son like Frankie."

A large smile crossed Tim's face. "I must say, that Suzanne is one beautiful woman. With that long black hair streaming down her back, those dark brown eyes, long legs and a figure that would even catch Preacher Gilmor's fancy, I swear I don't have but one good leg, but I'll tell you one thing Mister John Wilson, I'd give ever bit of that good leg of mine fer one glance of that woman in the raw."

John immediately reached for his pillow and sailed it across the room so fast it almost unseated his friend. "It's just like you Tim Johnson, always got your mind where it ought not to be. If'n you'd behave yourself, you could find yourself a good woman, but all you like is those women who let you have your way."

Tim laughed. "Why don't you go ahead and say it? I like the whores. I can have a night of passion and fun and when the sun comes up, I go my way. No commitment, no marriage, and no nagging wife to hound me twenty-four hours a day. That's what you thinking, ain't it?"

"I'm just saying that you have a lot to offer some woman if'n you'd just work on it a bit. You ain't that bad," John said.

"Talking about marriage, folks around here is saying that you and Suzanne would make a fine couple. They say y'all been doing some heavy courting and figure won't be long 'til Miss Suzanne and you will set up house."

"Set up house, that's ridiculous," John replied getting up to retrieve his pillow. "I agree she is a fine looking woman but like Daddy always said, when you marry a woman, you also marry her family and that Olliver family is a strange lot."

"Well, John, I don't see how you could beat her. As I said, she is some kind of looker and her mother and Frankie own a large chunk of Newton County. Some say they is among the richest folks in Miss'sippi."

"That's part of the problem, Tim. I know how they got their wealth and it ain't honorable. To my family's disgust, Frank Senior was one of the first to bring slaves into the county. His father-in-law gave him ten or twelve to get him started and then he cheated many a poor Choctaw and white alike out of their land along the way. My daddy still believes Frank Senior was in on getting my Uncle Jake killed and that was all about land that the Choctaw Land Company wanted. Yeah, they got plenty of money but the way I see it, it's blood money. Marriage, I don't think so."

"Well," Tim said leaning back in his chair and resting his good leg on the edge of John's bed, "I'd marry her in the twinkle of the eye. With her money, Ole Tim wouldn't ever have to hit a lick at nothing. I'd just sit back, drink my mint juleps and just observe that woman from morning to night and when the ole hoot owl starts his screaching, I'd be in glory land."

"Well, you can be in your glory land if'n you want but if'n we're to be at Hickory tonight, I need to go get washed up."

It wasn't long before John returned clean-shaven, hair brushed back as well as his curls would allow and wearing the only suit he owned. As they were about to leave, Mrs. Wilson stopped him on the porch. "John Wilson, you better wait up a second and let me look you over. You got to pass my inspection before you two go gallivanting."

Embarrassed, John replied, "Mama, we been going through this ordeal ever since I was a young 'un. Don't you think I'm a little too old for this?"

"Not as long as you live under my roof and have a mother that cares about you like I do. Now stand up straight," Mrs. Wilson ordered.

With Tim snickering in the background, John stood erect and then smiled down at his mother. "May I go now?"

"Not until you give an old woman a kiss."

John bent down, gave his mother a hug and a kiss and then bounded down the steps to where his father, who had figured they were going off for a good time, had his horse saddled and waiting. John's father, Lott, had been among the first white men to enter what was now Newton County, and he was instrumental in the organization and settlement of the Little Rock community. Lott was noted for his honesty and hard work and his reputation was beyond reproach. With his thick curly white hair, piercing blue eyes and stocky build, his presence still demanded respect.

Handing John the reigns, Mister Wilson said, "Mother said you two was going down to Hickory to some kind of a meeting. That's a pretty far piece. What time will you be getting home?"

"I'm not sure, Papa," John replied.

"Mister Wilson, since our place is closer to Hickory and if'n it's alright with you, John can spend the night with me and come on home in the morning," Tim said.

Mister Wilson nodded. "John you get on back before too late tomorrow. We got some planning to do for next week."

While John sat in the saddle waiting for Tim to mount, Mrs. Wilson couldn't help but admire her son. John stood over six feet tall, broad shoulders and with a frame much like his father's when he was a young man. His hair was soot black with a trace of premature graying across his temples. Sitting tall in the saddle, she thought, some folks say he's the most handsome man in these parts, but I say he looks like his father and that's good enough for me. Don't see why some pretty little thing ain't grabbed him, but John hasn't been the same since he returned from the war.

At the end of the war, the Confederate officials and some of the soldiers in John's company had thought he'd been killed in battle. Mrs. Wilson never believed them and on a cold, snowy night John had quietly rapped on the door and fell into her arms half frozen. She knew the Lord had brought John home to her. Even though he had recovered outwardly, inwardly he was not at peace. He didn't enjoy socializing with other young people like he once did and he spent too much time to himself and with his books. Mrs. Wilson was surprised to see him ride off with Tim tonight. Even though much time had passed since the war, he still seemed to have dreams that haunted him, and he would often wake up screaming. He would hardly ever talk about it. Something terrible had happened to him up there, something John had buried deep inside himself.

John and Tim waved goodbye, and when they were out of hearing range, John exclaimed, "I heard you laughing back there on the porch. I wish she'd stop that inspection routine; it's embarrassing."

Tim glanced over at John. "I might have laughed a little, but I'd give anything in the world if'n my mother would ever tell me she cares for me. Seeing the way you two feel about each other made me sort of jealous."

"Tim, your mother loves you just like mine does. I can tell by the way she looks at you. She just doesn't know how to show her feelings. Some folks are just like that."

As the two continued their way, John had no idea of the movement that was well underway throughout the South and certainly had no idea of what lay in store for him. The events that followed the meeting at Hickory Station would forever change the structure of politics in Newton County. The lives that would be shattered were never envisioned by John Wilson on that hot August afternoon.

3

THE MEETINGS

Western Pennsylvania

THE RUSHING WATER RIPPLED OVER THE STONES AND bubbled toward a large pool forming in the bend of the stream. The limbs of a large willow tree sloshed up and down as the current rhythmically nudged them. Even though the sun had been up for over two hours, a haze of misty fog hovered in the heights of the nearby hills. It was a beautiful morning.

Downstream where the water rushed from the pool and across another shallow run, a short, stout man with bare feet and trouser legs rolled up, gently reeled in his fishing line a soft tug at a time. After retrieving it, he pulled the brim of his hat down on his forehead keeping the glaring sun out of his eyes, then adjusted his glasses and made another cast out into the rapids.

Knee-deep in the stream, the man chewing a large wad of tobacco mumbled to himself, "You're gonna get caught this morning, Big Daddy, and I bet you'll weigh might near ten pounds, if you weigh an ounce."

Studying the water across the way, he continued, "If you're not under that ole willow branch, then you'll probably be over near that big boulder, but I'm gonna get you. I hung you a few years back and let you get away, but no more."

"Papa, say you're gonna catch him? How many times have I heard you say that? I bet a hundred," came a voice from far up on the bank.

"You heard me right daughter and when I do, I'm gonna carry him all over town and show him off. You just wait and see. Those folks down there will know that ole Doc Caulder can do more than just dish out the medicine."

Lamar Caulder was indeed more than a rural medical doctor. Although he had finished at the top of his class, he chose not to practice in the larger cities where his potential for financial success was practically guaranteed. Instead, he moved to the rural western part of Pennsylvania where he was needed. Even in the small town of Gettysburg, he had earned the reputation of being an excellent doctor and his surgical skills were unsurpassed. People would come from hundreds of miles away when surgery was needed.

No sooner had he finished speaking, when he leaned forward to make another cast, stepped on a slippery stone, and lost his balance. In an attempt to steady himself, he took several awkward steps but fell headfirst into the water. Drenched and his hat disappearing downstream, he regained his balance and then just sat there in disgust.

His daughter, Lucretia, couldn't help but laugh. "Papa, are you trying to scare the fish to death or are you just trying to baptize yourself? You know we're Methodist, don't you?"

Refusing to face his daughter, Doc Caulder remained in his sitting position. "Daughter, you better not tell anybody about what I just did to myself. I just stepped on a slippery rock. Anybody could have done it. Now run down there and get my hat before it gets in that deeper water."

Lucretia closed the book she had been reading and after retrieving his hat, edged her way down the stream and extended her hand to her father.

Dripping wet, Doc Caulder, with the help of Lucretia, crawled up the creek bank to their blanket.

"Here Papa, wrap up for a spell," Lucretia said placing the blanket around his shoulders. "It won't take long to dry you out and at least your shoes and socks are dry, and I won't tell a soul about what happened to you, except maybe Mother."

Wiping the water from his eyes and straightening the few hairs that he kept neatly combed across his balding head, he exclaimed. "You better not tell her. She doesn't much like me going fishing, anyway. She thinks I'm getting too old. That's why she wants you to go with me, to keep an eye on me."

Lucretia pulled the blanket closer around his neck and with a tight hug replied, "Mother doesn't make me go. I love spending time with you. And you certainly can be entertaining," Lucretia replied with a smile.

At that moment a brisk wind above ruffled the treetops enough to let a glint of sunlight filter to the ground where Lucretia was sitting. As its rays illuminated the rock and sparkled through her hair, Doc Caulder realized what a beautiful woman Lucretia had become. She stood a little over five feet tall with curly blond hair and large emerald eyes that glowed with warmth and excitement. She normally carried a smile on her face and her quick humor made her presence a joy.

"Father, you sure do have a strange look on your face. Is something wrong with me?"

"Wrong. Nothing's wrong with you. It's just the opposite. You ought to be married by now," he said.

"Married," she replied. "I'm only seventeen and who do you think I should marry?"

Doc Caulder reached in his pocket, pulled out a twist of tobacco and after biting off a wad continued, "You're going on eighteen and your mother feels that Robert would make a fine husband for you. He's smart as a whip, well mannered and, I must say, he's going to make one fine surgeon. No telling where that young man will end up. He's far ahead of where I was when I was his age, and you know the ladies around here think he's kinda handsome too."

Robert Townsley had finished at the top of his class in medical school and instead of remaining on the east coast for his apprenticeship, he choose to study under Doctor Caulder whose reputation was well known throughout the medical circle.

Surprised at his remarks, Lucretia exclaimed, "What you're saying is that Robert has a promising future and would be a good provider for me. What about love? You didn't mention that, Father."

Seeing that he had upset his daughter, Doc Caulder squirmed uneasily under his blanket and muttered, "You know you need to love the person you plan to spend your lifetime with. What I meant is that if you two do fall in love, then it would be fine with me."

Lucretia, with a twinkle in her eyes, replied, "I'm glad to hear that, because Mother and I had the same conversation the other day. Only difference is that she says that with all that he has to offer, that if I don't love him right now, I would probably grow to love him with time. Kind of like what happened between you two."

"Like what happened between me and your mother!" her father stammered slinging his blanket. "Did she actually say that she learned to love me?"

"Well, in a way she kinda insinuated that."

"Well let me set you straight right now, Miss Lucretia Caulder. I was in my senior year at college and we were having our spring ball. The orchestra was playing and the young men all dressed in their best were twirling the girls around and around on the dance floor. Being a little bashful, I was over near the punch bowl, when all of a sudden the door opened and the most beautiful woman that I had ever seen in my life appeared. I couldn't keep my eyes off her as she removed her wrap and then looked around the room as if she were unescorted."

"What did you do Papa?" Lucretia asked, moving closer to her father.

"Well, I dropped my glass like a fool, got up the nerve and hurried over there as fast as these little short legs could carry me. Several other boys had the same idea, but I got there first, introduced myself and had her on the dance floor before she had time to say no."

"Could she dance well?"

"No matter how tired I became, I stayed on the floor with her and wouldn't allow anyone to break in on us. Finally she asked me if I would care to escort her outside to the terrace to get some fresh air. Well, we walked a spell and talked a lot and the whole time I was thinking of nothing but trying to steal a kiss. I kept waiting for the right time and I just couldn't get up the nerve. Finally, with only a few minutes left before the dance ended, I asked her if I could please kiss her and to my astonishment she consented."

"Papa, you're embarrassing me talking about you and Mama and all that kissing stuff."

"Well, I've got a point to make daughter and that is when our lips touched I broke out in a cold sweat and your mother got so limp I thought she was going to faint on me. For the next few moments, I thought I was in heaven and when we finished, she stood there speechless. Finally, she straightened herself and then invited me to her home for dinner. Yes ma'am, Lucretia, we were in love and I did say 'we.' I dated your mother for about three months and to her father's objection, we were married."

"Why did he object to your marriage?" Lucretia asked.

"Said that we needed a longer courtship and that no respectable woman would marry someone she had only recently met."

"What happened then?"

Doc Caulder smiled. "She told her father that she was going to marry me whether he approved or not, and within the month, we were married."

"Why are you telling me this now, Papa?"

"Lucretia, your mother and I fell in love with each other the first night we met and when I kissed her, I knew I'd found the woman that I'd always dreamed off. And no matter what she said, she felt the same about me. It wasn't any growing in love."

Lucretia wrapped her arms around her father and said, "I knew you two didn't just grow in love. I was just teasing you. I just hope that I can find the kind of love that you and Mother have for each other. It's getting late and dinner will be on the table before long. You're about dry, and here, let me help you with your shoes."

"First, go down and get what few fish I caught. I didn't catch the one I wanted, but we do have a good mess for supper," Doc Caulder said, pointing to the stream.

Walking hand in hand across a flowered field where they had left their buggy, Lucretia said, "Papa, what you were saying is that I need to love the man that I marry and then marriage will be something right and special."

Smiling down at Lucretia he replied, "That's exactly what I said and nothing less."

"How will I know when I fall in love with someone?"

"Well daughter, you'll just know. And remember, you have got to like the person like you would a best friend, and you've got to love spending time with him, and he's got to feel the same about you. And one more thing, when the two of you kiss, something special has to come over you. Have you kissed many boys, yet?"

Blushing, she said, "Papa, that's a personal question."

"Well, that's one way to find out."

Later that night Lucretia lay awake in bed thinking over all her father had shared and when she thought about the special kiss he described, her mind began to wander. She had kissed several boys including Robert whom she found very attractive, but the only kiss that seemed special was the first kiss she had ever received. She was only thirteen and the boy was maybe seventeen. He was a wounded Southern soldier her family was keeping until he was well enough to be transferred to a Federal prison. After several months of care, the two had become friends. She remembered sitting on the front porch watching the golden leaves of fall flutter to the ground under a full November moon. Since the moment she met him she had wanted to hold him close and had dreamed how it would feel when their lips met. Knowing that he would be leaving the following morning, she finally got up the nerve to ask him for a goodbye kiss. It had been over four years since he left, but she could still feel the warm touch of his body, and the memory of the touch of his lips made her blush even in the stillness of her room. It had been so long ago, she thought, and the experience of any young girl's first kiss would be impressionable, but still, she could not erase the feeling that she had experienced with the young soldier.

Since that night, she had learned through several letters that he survived the war and prison, but something had happened to him. He no longer returned her letters, and the last note that she had received had come from his sister, not him.

§§

It took little more than an hour for John and Tim to reach Professor Hendon's house and once there, they were amazed at the commotion in the front yard. Two young boys had taken refuge behind a large oak tree while another was hurling sticks and rocks at them as fast as he could pick them up.

Throwing one stone so hard that it bounced back toward John and Tim, scaring their horses, the boy shouted, "Damn you, Robert Earl! I'm tired of you not playing fair. All you do is find a way to cheat."

"I ain't cheatin'! Lay down them rocks and we'll come out and fight you like a man," came the reply from one of the boys behind the tree.

No sooner had the boy dropped his rock than the two behind the tree raced after him and all John and Tim could see were fists slinging and dust flying as the three boys tumbled in the yard.

Hearing the ruckus, the Professor adjusted his suspenders, tucked in his shirt, and stepped out on the front porch to shout, "Boys, stop that fighting right now and I better not hear any more out of you! You know better than that!"

The boys didn't hear a word he said and continued fighting.

The Professor then reached for the limb he kept near the doorway and headed down to the boys and without asking any questions, he began to thrash the lot. In a matter of seconds he had them separated and howling with pain, as they ran for the safety of the house.

Seeing his guests, he apologized, "Sorry about that, boys. Sometimes I think I'm rearing a bunch of savages. The problem is, I just got too many children. Let me finish getting dressed and we'll be on our way."

Glancing back toward John, he said, "Good to see you with us, John. I wasn't sure Tim could get you away from the house."

Professor Hendon was over forty when he married the widow Langford and the rumor was that he had been secretly seeing her before her husband passed away. Many a suspecting husband breathed a breath of relief when the preacher pronounced them husband and wife. Since that time his wife had born him four sons and three daughters.

Tim, still on his horse, commented, "See why I ain't gettin' married. I couldn't stand all that racket with them children."

John nodded in agreement. "At his age, he's just got too many."

"Too many of 'em," Tim replied. "He's got more children than this. He's probably got a half dozen more around these here parts that folks don't know about."

"You saying what I think you're saying, Tim?"

"Exactly, John. He's got a bundle of bastards."

"That's a terrible thing to say about a man. How do you know what you've heard is true? Could be all lies."

Tim reached into his pocket and checked the time on his watch, then continued, "You know I spend a lot of time gambling and when men gamble, they also drink a lot and when they drink, they get loose tongues. I've heard more than one man who happened up on the Professor down near the river with one of his women and they weren't just parleying."

No sooner than Tim had finished his statement than the Professor stepped out on his porch again, dressed in his best. Even though he was now in his late fifties, he was still a handsome man, tall with long graying hair kept neatly combed and a short cropped beard. He was also impeccably dressed and possessed a dignified and stately manner. When addressing a lady, he would usually talk in a soft and almost feminine tone that often brought him the desired results. In contrast, some men judging him to be somewhat of a softy, had confronted him about his evening endeavors only to find that his fists were too fast for them. Afterwards he usually informed them that he was a champion boxer while in college.

As the Professor made his way down the steps, his wife came to the door to wish him goodbye. Standing there in the doorway with two small girls peering from behind her skirt, the woman carefully studied the men out front. Although Mrs. Hendon was years younger than her husband, her children and household chores had taken their toll. Short and fairly plump, she stood on the porch with her hands on her hips watching her husband make his departure. As the Professor was about to mount his horse, she called out, "That you out there, John Wilson?"

"Yes, Ma'am," came the reply.

"Don't you let Mister Hendon do no drinking tonight. If'n he gits to drinking, he don't know when to stop. Last time he went on a binge, he didn't come home fer 'bout a week. You hear me? "

"Yes, Ma'am. I hear you Mrs. Hendon."

"And don't let him fool with none of them pretty young skirts, neither," she teased.

"Ain't suppose to be none there, Mrs. Hendon, but if'n there is, I'll keep 'em off of 'em," Tim said with a smile.

"Tim Johnson, you're worse than Mister Hendon. I know all about yore shenanigans," she replied.

"John, you do what I said, now. Take care of him for me."

Knowing he had no control over her husband, John said, "Mrs. Hendon, your husband is a grown man. I'll do what I can. Can't promise you nothing."

Ignoring his wife's remarks, the Professor directed his horse through his front gateway and as they rode away, he laughed and called out, "If I'm not back later tonight, I'll see you sometimes next week, darling, and don't let them children kill each other."

"You better be back here tonight or you might just find me and the children gone," she replied.

"Won't anyone want all those children but me," the Professor said. "Let's get on our way, boys, time's a-wasting."

Mrs. Hendon was well aware of her husband's numerous affairs, but her love for him caused her to overlook his fondness for feminine companionship. Throughout their marriage he had been drunk on numerous occasions, but he had always come home to her. She also had noticed that with age, he was appearing to be slowing down in his pursuit of the opposite sex and like he had said, "Who would have all of them, anyway?"

The men hurried down the road leading to Hickory. Passing a farmhouse, John spotted a young man about his age sitting on the front porch swing with his wife cuddled close to him. That should be me out there on a porch of my own home, with my wife by my side, he thought, trying not to stare at the couple. "Life sure hasn't been fair," he mumbled to himself.

"What'd you say, John?" Tim asked.

"Nothing, just thinking."

As they neared a stream, the Professor led his horse out into the water. "Better give 'em a rest now. We still have a way to go."

For a few moments the men made small talk as they dismounted and rested on the creek bank. As they rose to mount, the Professor said, "John, wasn't sure you'd come with us tonight. You need to get away from the place more often. You need to be more sociable."

"Got a farm to work, Fessor. The Yanks almost put us under. Time I get the work done, ain't much time left for others," John said.

"You going with the best looking woman in the county. If'n she was my woman, I'd stay over there from daylight to dark. I bet you don't see her once a month," Tim said, wading out to his horse.

"She is a looker, John," the Professor agreed, stepping up in the stirrups.

"What exactly am I getting into tonight?" John asked, not caring to discuss his relationship with Suzanne.

"Tim told you about all that I know," the Professor replied, bringing his horse to a cantor. "We're tired of the way the government's been run since the war ended. We think we can change some things. Something's got to happen to give us some relief."

Having no idea about what he had in mind and wondering if it was legal, John said, "Is this going to get someone in trouble with the law?"

"Not for sure, John. I don't know much more than you do, but I do know a building is going to get torched over near the Decatur courthouse tonight. That should keep the Federal men occupied for the evening," Hendon replied.

"Torched," John exclaimed, wondering if he had made a wise decision in going with the group. "I'm not sure I like the sound of that."

"The building is vacant. Won't be nobody hurt. It'll give us some privacy," Tim said.

Nearing the small rail town of Hickory, John was apprehensive about the evening and he felt that the Professor and Tim knew more than they had shared with him.

As they entered the town, the Professor pulled his horse to a stop in front of a store near the tracks and told the boys to remain mounted and he would be back in a moment.

John and Tim noticed a steady stream of horsemen and occasionally a buggy moving east down the main street, and it was no doubt that the meeting place was somewhere in that direction.

The professor soon returned, remounted his horse and pointed east. "It's about a mile down the tracks; can't miss it."

Making a turn in the road that ran parallel with the tracks, the men saw a large warehouse built next to the tracks so cotton could be loaded easily on the train. Everywhere they looked, they saw horses and buggies tied to makeshift hitching posts and in some cases young boys were left outside to watch over the horses. The men dismounted and tied their horses to some tree branches and hurriedly made their way through a steady flow of men toward the warehouse. Nearing the building, the Professor recognized several of the men and waved.

As he approached, one called out, "'Bout time you got here, Hendon. Thought Little Rock weren't gonna be represented. The General ain't here, yet."

"General," John said. "Who are they talking about?"

No one replied as they moved through the crowd. At the entrance, John saw two men checking everyone as they entered the building. When Professor Hendon, Tim, and John reached the doorway, one of the men put out his hand to Hendon and said, "Good to see you Ernest. Thought you might not be coming. Who you got with you?"

Turning to John and Tim, the Professor replied, "This young man is Timothy Johnson and the other is John Wilson. I've known them all their life. In fact, I taught them both. They can be trusted."

Looking over at John one of the men said, "You any kin to Jake and Lott Wilson?"

"Jake was my uncle and Lott's my father."

"Jake and I used to run some together, that is before he got himself kilt. How's Lott doing?" one of the men asked.

"He's not in the best of health but he's doing all right," John answered.

"Well, if'n you're anything like them, you're the kind of man we're looking for. Now y'all better get on inside. It's about time to get things started. Our guest is running a little late. The train from Meridian is behind time."

The kind of man we're looking for, thought John. What do they mean by that?

The Professor remained outside talking with the men while John and Tim worked their way inside the crowded building. The large crowd of over two hundred made the August heat almost unbearable. John and Tim immediately removed their coats and tried to get closer to the platform that had been built at the far end of the gin. The air was filled with tobacco smoke, and the sound of men talking and laughing made normal conversation difficult. As they edged their way forward, they heard someone behind them call out, "Tim Johnson! John Wilson! Back here!"

Turning, they spotted Frankie Olliver pushing his way toward them. "I'd 'bout given you two up. Thought you were gonna miss out on this here get together," Frankie said, extending his hand. "You won't believe who's gonna be here tonight."

Before John and Tim could question him, someone called out, "Frank Olliver, we need you up front. Right now!"

John and Tim looked at each other, astonished at why someone wanted to see Frankie.

"What in the world?" Tim exclaimed.

At that moment a very dignified looking man made his way up on the platform and a hush came over the crowd.

Stepping up behind the podium the man said, "Gentlemen, I'm Daniel McWorthan from over at Meridian. I run a business there and some of you may know me. Before I begin I want to thank all of you for coming out and before this thing's over tonight, I think you'll be glad you came. I've got a few questions to ask you before I introduce our special guest. First, how many of you like the way this here Federal Government is treating you?"

A roar of disgust erupted.

"How you like the taxes they put on ya?" the man continued.

Once again nothing but shouting and hissing could be heard as excitement filled the air.

Stepping out from behind the podium and pointing toward the crowd the man continued, "Well, how about this? You know anyone who's lost their place? Lost their home and farm that they've worked hard for?"

Before the crowd could respond, a man yelled out, "Damned shore do! I lost my farm five days ago. Some son-of-a-bitch from up North bought it up 'fore I could raise the money."

Immediately several other men called out that they also had lost their land.

The speaker reached inside his coat and pulled a pistol out and waved it above his head. "Now don't you think it's about time we done something about it? Don't you think it's time we take the South back before it happens to more of us?"

At that, the crowd roared and screams and gunshots rang out.

The speaker then beckoned to Frankie who was standing near the back of the platform. "Mister Olliver, I think we got 'em ready for him. You can bring him on in now."

A tall well-dressed man with graying black hair, a mustache, and goatee stepped up on the platform and walked toward the podium. A complete silence covered the room for a moment, then someone, recognizing the man, exclaimed, "It's Forrest, It's Gen'ral Forrest!"

Once again murmuring rippled over the men assembled and then what began as one man chanting, spread instantly through the group. "Forrest! Forrest! Forrest!" Over and over the men called his name until finally the guest raised his hand and all became quiet.

"Gentlemen, Sons of the South, Soldiers of the Grand Confed'racy, it's indeed a pleasure to stand before you tonight," Forrest said. "Any of you men ride with me during the war?"

Several of the men raised their hand and a round of applause filled the building.

"God bless you for the sacrifice. How many of you served in the field for us?" Forrest continued.

Most of the men raised their hand and gave a yell that years earlier had sent chills through Union soldiers as they awaited the waves of gray and butternut clad Confederates in battle formation.

Forrest continued, "Men, things ain't going too good for us since the Yankees run us off the fields. I always felt that we could've fought 'em longer. We could've made 'em pay a heavier price. We quit the war too soon for me."

With that statement a roar of agreement sounded and one man in the back of the building screamed out, "You want us to take up arms again, Gen'ral? We can raise another army!"

Forrest raised his hand for quiet and said, "Appreciate your dedication sir, but we ain't exactly wanting to raise another army of that kind. What we do plan to do is to raise an army of loyal Southerners to get control of our government. We want you Miss'sippians to take the Governor's seat, all the legislators' seats, all the way down to your justices of the peace. When you get control of your government then you'll have control of what happens in this state. The war is over and there won't be no return of slavery, but we can seize what is rightfully ours. We can stop them rascals from making a mockery of our society, and we shore as hell can stop 'em from taking our homes away from us."

"How can we do that Gen'ral? Some of us ain't even eligible to vote nor hold office," a man called out.

"Good question," Forrest answered. "The group that's sitting over there at Jackson is sorry Northerners who come down here to take advantage of the situation, turncoat Southerners loyal to the Yankee dollar and them illiterate Negroes that can't even read nor write. What we got to do is simply find us some young men who are eligible to run for office and put our total support and financial backing behind them."

"But, with some of us not able to vote, we probably won't have no majority in most of the counties," Frankie said, standing next to the platform.

Forrest looked down at Frankie and replied, "Son, your job is to get every man you can to the polls on voting day and a little bit of money and whiskey in the right place can do wonders for an election."

"What if we are still outnumbered," Frankie replied.

Forrest reached inside of his jacket, pulled a revolver out and raised it arms length above his head. "You then persuade them bastards to stay home on election day. As I have often said, 'You get 'em scared and you keep the scare on 'em.'"

With that he discharged his pistol overhead, causing a state of pandemonium.

After order was restored Tim called out, "Gen'ral, how far do we go with the scare!"

Returning his pistol to its holster, Forrest replied, "To get Miss'sippi back ain't gonna be no easy task and it's gonna take a lot of sacrifice on all of you. Some folks could get killed and some of you men right here tonight might have to pay the price. Just depends on how bad you want freedom."

Instantly the group began shouting, "Freedom! Freedom! Freedom!" as several men discharged their pistols.

Professor Hendon then called out, "Sir, we can't do this without some help, some kind of organization."

Mister McWorthan, sitting near the podium leaned over to Forrest and said, "You got 'em General, finish it off."

"Men, what I'm gonna tell you is confidential and for us to be successful you got to keep it quiet. All over the South there are meetings just like this one going on and we don't plan to only get Miss'sippi back, but we plan to take control of all the South and we do indeed have a organization that'll do the job. An organization like folks have never seen."

"What's it called, General?" someone yelled out.

"It's called the Ku Klux Klan, Gentlemen," Forrest answered.

"Who's running this here Klan and how do we join it?" Frankie asked, raising his hand to get Forrest's attention.

"Men, you know all you need to know for right now, but you will be contacted 'fore long. There will be men in every county and community assigned to lead you, but before we close our meeting I just want to know if'n you approve of what's going on here tonight."

With the shaking of fist and shouting in support, there was no doubt in Forrest's mind that the Klan had arrived in Newton County.

As Forrest sat down, McWorthan returned to the podium and began reading a list of names of men Forrest wanted to see as soon as the meeting closed. Among the names called, to the surprise of John and Tim, were the names Ernest Hendon and Frank Olliver.

As the group dispersed, John and Tim waited outside for the Professor, wondering what Forrest wanted with him and Frankie. After about half an hour Hendon apppeared.

"Big night boys, wasn't it?" Hendon asked as he approached. "Haven't got much time. Frankie and I are going over to Meridian tonight to meet with some men. John, just tie my horse up in the gin by the water barrel and tell my wife I'm out on business and be sure she knows I'm not chasing any skirts, strictly business. I'll get my horse in the morning."

John assured the Professor he would take care of the matter and as the train was leaving for Meridian, Tim decided he would go with Hendon and Frankie to spend a little time in the city. The lure of city life with its gambling opportunities, drinking and women of the evening was too much for Tim to resist.

As the train pulled out Tim leaned out the window. "John, you can still spend the night at my place. It's a long way to Little Rock at this time of the night. Tie my horse up with Fessor's."

John waved, then saddled his horse and headed for home. It was good of Tim to offer to let him stay at his place but since there was a full moon and a cool evening breeze, John decided home was best. As he made his way down the road, John could hear the occasional cry of hoot owls and at times the lonely sound of the whippoorwill. A feeling of loneliness overcame him and as he stopped at a stream to water his horse, he rethought all that he had heard and observed that night at the warehouse. The statements about how the Klan would restore power to the people and that someone could be hurt, bothered John. A period of uncertainty prevailed over the South, and it was not a time when people were thinking rationally. He knew that Mississippi was a conquered land and that people, both black and white, were being mistreated, but he also felt that with time, law and order, and the justice promised by the Constitution, freedom could be restored if only people would have faith and patience.

4

CHRISTMAS TIME

NEAR CHUNKY CREEK, THUNDERING HOOVES AND SHOUTING men interrupted the silent afternoon. Two horsemen galloped down an old track that had, years earlier, hosted the best of country racing where spectators once cheered riders on to victory and substantial betting money changed hands. This track now lay in decayed ruin. The high platform that enabled the judge to declare the winner was still standing, but vines and small saplings suffocated the structure. The track still visible between the thick interwoven weeds tempted riders to test their skill and horses' speed in an afternoon race. Such a moment brought John Wilson and his Negro friend, Andy, to the track.

As the riders sped around the far end of the track, birds nesting in the low branches fluttered away to safety while squirrels scurrying around on the ground scampered up the trees.

"Heahhh! Heahhh!" shouted John as he leaned down near his horse's neck while glancing back at Andy less than a half-length behind him. "Push 'em! Push 'em hard!"

The horses rolled up dust as they raced down the backstretch like a storm out of control; nothing could stop them. Making the north turn of the track, Andy called out, "Gonna take you this time, Mist' John. We're gonna outrun ya!"

With both men leaning low and forward on their mounts, they made the last turn and came galloping down the final stretch, the horses' manes thrashing their faces as they raced toward the finish line.

"I'm gonna kick 'em," Andy shouted as their horses were now even.

"Do it!" came the reply.

With a loud scream and a kick in the flanks, Andy edged forward and crossed the finish line. Knowing he had just triumphed over the finest rider in the county, Andy raised his arms in celebration and cantered his horse around the track once more. John followed closely behind him. As they approached the starting point, they pulled their horses to a stop and dismounted.

John extending his hand and exclaimed, "Dadgummed good ride Andy. That buckskin can sure 'nough run, can't he?"

Andy shaking John's hand and smiling from ear to ear replied, "Well, you gave me the best hoss, what'd you expect?"

"I thought I could still beat you. I thought I could still out ride you but I sure couldn't," John answered.

"Let's take 'em down to the creek and let 'em cool off a bit before we head for the house."

The two men led their horses across a wooded area that bordered the track, worked their way down the steep bank that led to the creek, then turned them loose to water. As the horses wandered around in the creek, they knelt down to dip up water in their hands and after washing off their faces, they also quenched their thirst.

"Touch of fall in the air, Andy," John said, looking west to where the sun was setting. "Can't believe the summer's about gone.

"Shore 'nough is, Mist' John. We've had a good one too."

With the horses watered, they remounted and made their way up the bank toward home. As they leisurely rode through the woods Andy said, "You think these here hosses is as good as them your daddy and Mist' Jake used to run?"

John thought for a moment then replied, "They ran pretty good today but it's hard to say. You know when Sherman came through here, they stole most of the herd. We only saved a couple of 'em and those were some fine animals them Yanks took."

"They pay you for 'em?" Andy asked.

"Pay for 'em," laughed John. "I just told you they stole 'em."

The two rode quietly for a few moments, occasionally glancing up in awe at the huge branches of the massive oak trees that had covered the woodlands for centuries. Then Andy said, "You know that war done a lot to us folks. Mister Lincoln went and freed all of us but he shore didn't tell us what we s'pose to do or where we s'pose to live. I heard tell he was gonna give us a piece of land and a mule, but I ain't seen none of it. I feel mighty good though. You and Mister Wilson up and give my family eighty acres of land and a fine house to live in. Yes sir, we done just fine thanks to your kindness, and for Mister Lincoln, I ain't seen nothing he promised us."

John ducked his head as a low limb of a dogwood tree almost took his hat and replied, "The president got killed. If'n he'd lived you might have seen some of those promises come true, and we didn't just up and give you the land. You worked for it. We didn't have money to pay anybody and we needed workers. We told your daddy that if'n you would work for us for two seasons where we could hopefully get back on our feet again, then we'd give you the land. We got the farm back in good shape and y'all earned your land; we didn't give it to you."

Pulling his horse closer to John, Andy said, "Mist' John, you Wilsons is good, God-fearing folks. I'm just glad you took us in. Some white folks ain't so kind to us, but I did hear that an outfit called the Freedsman Bunch is trying to help us. They s'pose to be trying to settle some of us on land and even maybe start us a school. Lord have mercy, John, I might even learn to read one of these days."

"It's the Freedman's Bureau," John replied. "I've heard a little about that, but I ain't heard nothing about any schooling."

Spurring his horse across a rippling stream, Andy said, "You know I've also heard that there is even some colored over in Jackson sitting in the Capital. Is that true?"

John nodded. "That's right, they's over there making laws for the state of Mississippi right now."

"Great heaven to mercy, I can't believe what all's happening with my people. There they is sitting in there and making laws and weren't long ago we was all nothing but slaves for the master. Mist' John, why don't you go over there and make the laws. You'd be a good 'un."

John smiled over at Andy. "I've read a lot about the law system but I don't think that's for me. You know, my parents ain't as young as they used to be, and I've got the responsibility of taking care of 'em. You know, I get by just fine working the place and enjoying every day the good Lord gives me."

John hesitated for a moment, pulled his horse to a stop and motioned for Andy to stop. "Andy, there's things that happened to me during the war I can't explain."

"What's you talking about Mist' John?" Andy asked, adjusting himself in the saddle and wondering what John had on his mind.

"Andy, it might not make sense to you, but something happened to me up in Pennsylvania."

John thought for a moment and continued, "I feel that I got killed there during that terrible battle and by some strange means, I'm alive."

Disturbed by what John had shared with him, Andy shuddered. "Mist' John, I'm not sure I want to hear no more 'bout that story. Sounds like you believe you is a haunt or sump'n."

Afraid that he had upset Andy, he reached over and patted him on the back. "I ain't no haunt, Andy. I'm just saying something happened to me up there that I can't understand. I still have dreams that bother me, and it's always the same one over and over that troubles me. I just can't free myself from it and until I can, I can't seem to be able to get on with my life."

Thinking back, John could still hear the clash of arms, the loud screams of horror, the smell of burnt gunpowder and the pleas of men gasping for life. Disturbed with his thoughts, John quickly forced his mind back to Andy's suggestion and said, "I think I could be a good politician, but it'll never happen to me. Nobody is gonna elect me to any office."

Andy gave him a serious look. "I'd vote for you and I know a lot more folks that would too, black and white. I just wish I could do the voting."

"Andy, the government's given you the right to vote. You can be a voter. That is, as soon as the state accepts the amendment and makes it a part of the state constitution."

"I don't know nothing 'bout no constitution but someday I want to do some voting." Andy exclaimed. "You shore 'bout that, Mist' John?"

"I'm sure you can," John replied as he pushed his horse forward and reined it toward the road up ahead.

"Then I want you to help me do it. You got to promise me," replied Andy.

"That I'll do, Andy. That I'll surely do."

§§

December 23rd, Philadelphia, Pennsylvania

The spectators were silent as the curtain fell and the last chord from the orchestra faded away. A grand performance had the people spellbound. Then one man began to clap and suddenly the entire room was filled with applause as the people rose for a standing ovation.

A young man pointed toward the orchestra pit and said, "Weren't they something, Lucretia! Bravo! Bravo!"

In awe, she replied, "The play was wonderful but the music, I've never heard anything so beautiful before. The trumpets, violins and all those other instruments."

"Here take my hand. It will take a while to fight through this crowd," Robert Townsley, Lucretia's escort for the evening said. "Nothing like this in the country."

Lucretia had been to church musicals and school plays but none was like the entertainment she had savored that evening. Taking his hand and following closely behind, she couldn't help but admire him. Robert was dressed in a black tuxedo, closely shaven and there was not a hair out of place. Although he was somewhat on the thin side, he carried himself in a dignified manner and had a slight air to him. There was no doubt that someday this young man with his confidence would be an exceptional doctor.

Finally reaching the lobby, Robert told Lucretia to wait for him a moment while he collected their wraps. Returning, he helped her with her coat and said, "I told you that Christmas in the city was something to behold. Let's hurry on and beat this crowd to the hotel restaurant for a late dinner."

As Robert was helping Lucretia with her coat a voice out front called out, "That you, Robert Townsley? Didn't know you were back in town."

Turning, he recognized Alex Hillman, a college classmate and friend making his way through the crowd toward them.

"Alex, you ole rascal, I thought you were in New York. What are you doing here in Philadelphia?" Robert exclaimed, reaching out to shake his hand.

"I'm here visiting an uncle for the holidays and he said that I shouldn't miss the show," Alex replied.

Glancing at the young woman clasping Robert's arm, he was immediately astonished by her beauty. Speechless for a moment, he blurted out, "Robert, where in the world did you meet this young lady. Is she from Philadelphia?"

Laughing, Robert turned to Lucretia. "Lucretia Caulder, this is Alex Hillman, a friend of mine."

"Where in the world did you two meet?" Alex asked, still spellbound by the young woman.

Jokingly Robert pushed him away. "Just back off ole friend; she's taken for the evening and hopefully a lot of evenings to come."

Quickly reaching out to Alex to keep him from bumping into a couple edging by, Robert continued, "Seriously, her father is the doctor I've been studying under for the past year. We met in Gettysburg."

"Well, Robert, I think I might have to start venturing out a little more into the country. We just don't have women like this around here."

"Alex, your remarks are too kind," Lucretia said. "I'm sure there are plenty of pretty girls here in Philadelphia. See that young lady over there, I bet she'd like to meet you. You want me to call her over," Lucretia joked.

Being more bashful than was apparent, Alex blushed and whispered, "Lucretia, don't do that. She's probably got an escort for the evening or she might even be married."

Robert began to laugh. "Alex, you haven't changed a bit. How in the world are you going to meet women if you can't stand the introduction process?"

"Shh," whispered Alex. "How about us getting out of here?"

"That's exactly what we had in mind. You want to join us?"

"You sure?" Alex asked, with a sheepish grin forming on his face.

"Sure. We're staying down the street a couple of blocks with my parents at the Grand Hotel. They have an excellent restaurant there."

The city at this time of year was beautiful with each lamp pole wrapped in season greenery and the store windows alive with Christmas decorations. As they hurried along in the evening cold, a few snowflakes began to flutter about, giving them a warm sense of holiday spirit. In a few moments they reached the hotel and soon were seated in the restaurant next to a large window overlooking the city.

Tugging on Robert's sleeve, Lucretia said with a smile, "We've got the best table here. You must have paid the waiter well."

"I'd say very well, young lady, but I figured you're certainly worth the cost," Robert admitted.

After a delicious meal, the three sat there watching the people outside hurrying to get out of the snow. In a few moments Alex turned to Lucretia. "Well, Miss Caulder, what do you think about the city? Have you ever been here before?"

Teasingly she answered, "You must think I'm just an ignorant backwoods girl that's never left her parents' side. Do I look the part?"

Taking her seriously, Alex blushed and apologized, "I didn't mean that, at all. Since you seemed to be so fascinated with Philadelphia and its attractions, I just assumed this was your first trip."

Robert slapped him on the back and laughed. "Alex, this woman has traveled all over the east coast with her parents and even spent some time in Europe. In fact, she is teaching school and making quite an excellent reputation for a first year teacher."

Seeing how uncomfortable Robert's remarks had made Alex, Lucretia leaned over and gave him light kiss on the cheek. "We're treating you horribly, Alex. This teasing has got to stop. Robert and I only tease people we like and I do think you are a charming young man."

Satisfied that he had been accepted and forgiven by Lucretia, Alex smiled.

"To answer your question, Alex, I have been to a lot of places but I've never had the pleasure of attending an opera and I've never been to Philadelphia during Christmas. This has all been fascinating to me. I've never had so much fun," Lucretia said.

"If you stay with me, this will be only the beginning of things to come," Robert said, taking Lucretia's hand and giving it a gentle kiss.

For a moment the trio was silent as they watched the snow outside flutter down in large flakes. Then a solemn expression came over Alex. "I guess you heard about my father."

"What are you talking about?" Robert asked.

Alex cleared his throat and in a low voice replied, "He was killed during the war. Somewhere down in Georgia. Somewhere called Kennesaw."

Lucretia reached over and clasped his hand. "I'm sorry, Alex. That war was a dreadful thing. It should have never happened. Too many fathers and sons were sacrificed."

"I had no idea, Alex," Robert said. "How's the family holding up?"

"We're doing fine. My mother already knew more about the family business than Dad. But the reason I didn't go to New York was because we couldn't afford the expense of college."

"What are you doing now?" Robert asked.

"I'm working in the business and maybe one day I'll be able to go back to school."

Robert was quiet for a moment, then exclaimed, "I wish they'd shot Davis, Lee and the whole damned Rebel army after the surrender. Those people down there with their slave holdings aren't nothing but animals. They should have killed them all."

An older man at the next table who was obviously intoxicated replied, "Young man, I tried my best and I killed more than I can count on my fingers and toes. Never took a prisoner after I heard that them devils killed one of my sons. Hell's gonna be full on them gray-clad devils."

Extending his hand toward Robert he muttered, "I'm Amos Jones. Captain Amos Jones formally of the fourth New York Infantry."

Surprised at the remarks that had been made, Lucretia stammered, "There are good people in both the North and South. It's the politicians that should be held responsible for the bloodshed. They start the wars and the common citizen pays the cost. It's those politicians who ought to burn in hell. Those southern boys were no different from ours. And, most southerners don't even hold slaves."

Stumbling out of his chair Jones raised his glass and getting the attention of those around, he exclaimed, "Well folks, it appears we have a Southern sympathizer with us here tonight. I'd like to make a toast to the pretty Southern Belle. I guess she comes from Georgia or perhaps Alabama."

Robert immediately rose to his feet and with clinched fist said. "Sir, this woman is no Southern sympathizer and in fact she served as a nurse to our soldiers after the battle of Gettysburg. You will apologize to her."

With a smurk on his face the drunk replied, "You sure are a mighty scrawny twirp to be talking so big. I bet you never served in the army, did you? "

Alex got to his feet. "He might be scrawny but there are at least two of us who'll shut your filthy mouth."

No sooner had Alex finished, than the hotel manager and a policeman entered the room and hurried over to where they stood. Pushing the drunk away from Robert, he said, "Mister, you've had too much to drink and for you two young men, there won't be any fist a cuffs in this establishment. It's getting late and I think it's time for all of you to retire for the evening."

Robert took Lucretia by the arm, relieved that he did not have to tangle with the man. "We were not bothering anyone until he insulted Miss Caulder. I owe no apologies for my behavior. Lucretia, you and Alex wait here while I take care of dinner."

Standing there at the window, watching the snow floating and swirling in all directions, Lucretia thought how proud she was of the way Robert had defended her. The man, much older and stronger, would have probably beaten both Robert and Alex. There was so much to admire in Robert. A girl would be foolish not to marry him, she reasoned. Then seeing a lone man standing outside waiting in the cold, her mind wondered back to the war years. They were boys just like ours except they were far from home, not knowing if they would ever see their love ones again, she thought. The man turned toward her and seeing her gaze, smiled and gave her a faint wave. For a moment she imagined him to be the boy she had met years before. She could see that dark curly hair, sparkling blue eyes and sheepish smile, as she told the young soldier that she was fourteen, and standing there on the tips of her toes, she received her first kiss.

§§

Phoenix Hotel, Meridian, Mississippi, January, 1869

The men hushed their talk when they heard two taps on the door followed by a harder knock. During the evening they could hear loud talking, cursing and occasionally a gunshot from outside. This was a typical Saturday night in Meridian.

"Ralph, check the door. It sounds like one of ours."

"Yes sir," came the reply.

Ralph eased the door open and, recognizing the men standing in the hall, motioned them in whispering, "Anybody see you come in?"

"Not on your life, Ralph. There's too much of a ruckus going on in the streets tonight for anyone to pay any attention to the likes of me and Frank.

The troops have got their hands full with some drunks up the street. One of 'em got shot."

Inside the smoke-filled hotel room were eleven well-dressed men who by appearance looked to be men of means and power. Hendon began shaking hands and introducing Frank and himself.

In a few moments one of the men, Daniel McWorthan, who had earlier conducted the meeting in Hickory, asked the men to have a seat and said, "Men, I apologize for calling this meeting on Saturday night, but as you can tell from all that is going on outside, we certainly won't be bothered. Also, we have reserved rooms for all of you for the night. If you care for a drink, we have a small bar set up for you over by the window. Hendon, we're glad you and Mister Olliver could be with us."

"Thank you Sir," Hendon replied, settling himself in a chair.

"Now to get to the point, this here is Jonathan Curry from over at Birmingham," McWorthan said, glancing over to the man sitting next to him. "Even though you've met him, you don't know what he wants to share with us and at this time, I'm turning the meeting over to him. Mister Curry."

Curry, a heavy set man with a bulging stomach that completely covered his belt, short stout arms and a bushy unkempt beard, started to stand, then realizing this was only a small group, he settled himself back into his seat. For a moment he quietly looked each man in the face as they sat there wondering what he had in store for them.

Finally he said, "Men, you know from the meeting in Hickory, what we intend to do and if it's not clear, let me refresh your memory. We believe that some things are gonna happen later this year that's gonna open the political doors in this here State of Miss'sippi and when it does, we're taking this state back. We plan to place our handpicked men in every elected office in each southern state. We plan to get every Negro and undesirable white out of office and we will go to whatever means it takes to accomplish this goal. Nothing is going to stop us."

One of the men interrupted, "This ain't gonna be easy, especially with all them Yankee troops here."

"I didn't say anything about being easy, Sir. Right the opposite. We will be highly organized in all that we do and secrecy will be mandated. Some of us will probably lose our lives in the struggle, but in the end we will prevail. We will get Miss'sippi back. We will be in control of what happens to us and our children to come. Our organization is becoming more powerful by the day."

At that, the men nodded their approval and softly applauded.

McWorthan then spoke. "There are secret meetings going on all over the South just like what's happening here tonight to organize each state county by county. As you look around here you see men from Lauderdale, Kemper, Neshoba, Newton, Jasper and Clarke counties. You men and your counties will represent district nine of our organization. Each one of you will be in charge of selecting your candidates, raising election funds and running the program."

"What program are you talking about?" Frank asked, excited at what he was hearing.

"Young man, I'm talking about the Klan. You are to enlist men in Newton County, hold your own meetings, conduct your business and do whatever it takes to secure Newton County in the new South. You will be the head of the Klan in your county."

Then looking over at Hendon he said, "People over in Little Rock know you as a teacher, but I also know how involved you've always been in politics. If you'll take the position, we'd like for you to take Newton County for us."

Hendon remained quiet for a moment thinking about his demanding duties as a teacher, his family responsibilities, and the possibility of becoming in trouble with the government and thought, I might not be the best husband in the world, but I do care for my children. If I end up dead or in prison, who'll take care of them? But the thought of leading others in the struggle for recapturing Mississippi and the power that could come from such a movement was certainly a dream of his.

"I can do what you propose, Sir," he said. "I don't know much about the Klan, but politically, I'll work for Newton County. I know a lot of men over there who'll do what is necessary."

"That's good, Hendon. For a moment I thought we'd picked the wrong man. And for you Mister Olliver, we feel like you'll be a good assistant for him. You're young, energetic and from what we hear, own a large amount of Miss'sippi land. Think you can help us?"

Without thinking Frank blurted out, "We can do it, Sir. You can put Newton County in your pocket right now."

At this point, neither Frank nor Professor Hendon had any idea what the group intended to do.

"That sounds good," Curry said. Turning toward McWorthan he said, "McWorthan will be in charge of the district and it will be him who'll be meeting and leading y'all, and before we leave here tonight, I want to know who you have in mind that might represent you as a legislator come fall election. You need someone who's young that'll be there for a spell and patriotic to the cause. Most of the older politicians aren't even eligible to run but that's all right. We'll get our men in there."

Starting with the Kemper county representative, each man gave Curry the name of a prospective person they felt was popular enough to carry their county. Finally it came time for Hendon to make his selection. "There are a lot of fine young men in Newton County, but I just don't know. Let me think a moment."

"How 'bout Mister Olliver there," one of the men from Jasper County said. "With his money, he could buy the whole state of Miss'sippi."

Even though the men were trying to be as quiet as possible, they couldn't help but laugh at his suggestion.

"How about it Mister Olliver," Curry said, taking a draw from his cigar and tilting his head backwards and blowing a gust of smoke high above his head.

There was nothing Frank had rather do than represent Newton County in the state legislature. All his life he had dreamed of being in a position of power where people would have to look up to him. This would give him a chance to show what he could do. When he was growing up, it had always been someone else in school elected as a class officer or chosen to lead in a community project, never Frank Olliver.

He won't get the job done. You can't depend on Frank. He's nothing but a weakling, resounded through Frank's mind. But I showed them. My father and I did it to them. I can buy and sell every one of them now. I might even become governor one day if I really set my mind to it.

But then he remembered, there are things in my past that if brought up, could be detrimental to me and my family. There are a few people who not only could stop my election but could also place me behind bars. There's no way I can take the chance.

Finally Frank shook his head. "That's not for me. I'll help Professor

Hendon but I have other responsibilities. You can depend on my means come election time. As I just said, we'll carry Newton County."

"Sorry to hear you won't run, Mister Olliver. How about it Hendon, you know someone else?" Curry asked.

All of a sudden, Hendon's eyes brightened. "I'd like to run John Wilson. He was a student of mine and I must say one of my best. He's smart, hardworking, honest as the day's long and he fought for us during the war. Got shot up pretty bad at Gettysburg. Yes Sir, he's the best we have to offer."

"How about it, Mister Olliver? How about this John Wilson?" McWorthan asked.

Frank thought for a second. Growing up, John had been his closest friend, the brother he had never had and many a time John had stood up for him when no one else would. If it hadn't been for Rebecca, they would probably still be friends. When he was listed as killed, Rebecca was finally his and as the law goes, she was.

But John knows too much about me and my family, Frank thought. What he knows is placing me in my own prison. If it weren't for him and a couple of others, Mississippi might well could be mine.

"Mister Olliver. How about this Wilson?"

Frank looked over at Hendon. "He'll do fine, that is if you can get him to run. He ain't been too sociable since he came home. War affects people in strange ways. He'll do."

After the meeting Hendon and Frank decided to go downstairs for a late drink and possibly a little female companionship. Sitting next to a roaring fire and enjoying a refreshing drink of Kentucky bourbon, the men began to reflect on all that had transpired that evening.

"Fessor, think this thing can be pulled off?"

Putting his glass down and scratching his head as he often did when thinking, Hendon replied, "We don't have a choice. Things couldn't be any worse than they are now and somebody has got to take a stand. Might as well be us."

"Yeah, but what if'n we're standing out there by ourselves. We could end up in big trouble," Frank replied.

Taking a sip from his glass, Hendon said, "We won't be by ourselves. There are plenty of men ready to do what it takes. As I taught you in school, revolutions are always carried on by a minority. The vast majority don't want to get involved, especially if it becomes violent. We'll get the men."

"What about John, Fessor? You think he'll run?"

"I'll have to talk to him. I'm not sure he'll go along with the Klan. I think he's a good man, maybe too honest for his own good and you know he's always been idealistic. If he'll run, he'll win. How about you talking to him about it or better still get your sister to speak with him? They have been seeing each other a lot."

"I don't know, Fessor. Me and John speak, but we're not close like we used to be."

"You boys have got to forget what happened between you. Time's passed and there's nothing you can do about it. You need to make amends."

"Easy to say but I don't think it'll ever happen. I guess the breech is just too wide. Suzanne will be the one to convince him if anybody can. She adores the ground he walks on," Frank said. "She'd marry him tomorrow if'n he'd consent. Heck, she's probably sleeping with him now. She may be my sister, but she's one beautiful woman and he's human, ain't he?"

"Frank, you know as well as I do that John isn't doing any sleeping with her, but to change the subject, do you think he'd leave his parents' farm?"

"The Wilsons ain't nothing but small time farmers. Suzanne's been trying to talk him into expanding or coming to work for us. He could be our foreman or bookkeeper. Who cares, all she wants is a man in her bed and a father for her children. He could marry her and do nothing. We got more money than we'll ever spend in my lifetime and with me investing into the railroad business, I need someone I can trust to help me run things."

"He probably won't do it, will he Frank?"

"I'm not sure, Fessor. He says that he won't work for no Olliver and he won't be no puppet on a string. He just says that he'd rather be a smalltime farmer. You know what I say? I say that his pride is keeping him from being one wealthy man. I think he's crazy as hell. What do you think?"

"I think he does things his own way, and I also think he would make the state of Miss'sippi one hell'ova politician if we can get him to run and teach him the art of compromise somewhere along the way."

All of a sudden the Professor noticed two women making their way down the stairs toward the bar. "Frank, you see that tall red-headed woman who just came in? I was hoping I wouldn't run into her tonight. That is one fine woman. I could turn down most, but sir, I will not neglect her. I'll see you in the morning or sometime next week. Lord forgive my sins."

5

COURTSHIP OF A POLITICIAN

January, 1869

SEVERAL WEEKS AFTER THE MEETING IN MERIDIAN, JOHN'S parents were enjoying a late afternoon, relaxing and reading in front of a warm fire while John and his brother-in-law, James Robinson, were down behind the barn working.

During the winter months farmers in east central Mississippi had less work than during the growing season. They would maintain and repair farm equipment, take care of their livestock and split wood for fence rails and fireplaces.

Mrs. Wilson, hearing an approaching rider, eased the curtain back and peered outside. "Looks like John's got a visitor, Lott. A pretty one, too."

Rising from his chair, Lott replied, "You talking about Suzanne?"

Grabbing their wraps, the two made their way down the open hall to the front porch to welcome the young woman.

"Afternoon, Suzanne," Mister Wilson said. "What brings you out on a cold afternoon like this?"

Smiling she replied, "I'm just out riding and I thought I'd better check on John. He hasn't been over to see me lately and I was getting anxious to see him."

Mrs. Wilson, feeling Suzanne was a little too forward, responded, "I don't rightly know what John's been up to lately but I'm sure he tries to see you when he can.

Suzanne sensed Mrs. Wilson's disapproval and replied, "I'm sure John's been working hard, but I really do need to see him."

Suzanne thought, need to see him is an understatement. If determination and willpower can prevail, I will marry that young man. And if I have my way, my husband will serve in the Mississippi legislature come next year. He won't be doing any more farming around here.

For the next few minutes, Suzanne and the Wilsons shared small talk and since they seldom left home during the winter, Suzanne informed them of all that had happened lately in the county. Before long the conversation turned to politics and Suzanne told them that Frank was hosting a dinner at their home and some prominent politicians were to be present. She invited them to attend.

Lott couldn't believe they had been asked to the Olliver home. He had known the family for over thirty years and had never set foot on their property. He and Frank Senior had come to the Mississippi territory as young men and Frank had done some things Lott knew were illegal and immoral. It seemed that Frank and he had been at odds about one thing or another as long as they had known each other. When Frank got killed, Lott felt for the family, but it certainly made life easier for him. Lott knew Frank Olliver was behind his brother Jake's death, and even though he could not tolerate the man, he never let his feelings stop his children from associating with the Ollivers.

"You sure you want us to come?" Lott asked.

"We certainly do and I think we have a little surprise for that son of yours. Where can I find him?"

Lott pointed down to the barn. "He and James are down there splitting wood. Go on down if you like."

Suzanne kicked her horse in the flank. "Good seeing you. Remember, Saturday week, six o'clock."

As Lott watched Suzanne leave with her long black hair flowing behind her, he remembered a time when his brother returned after several days with the most beautiful Choctaw woman he had ever seen sitting behind him. Her eyes were almost as dark as her hair and her long bare legs took his breath away. In many ways, Suzanne reminded him of her. Enough of that, he thought.

"She's a pretty girl, ain't she, Lott," Mrs. Wilson said, looking over at her husband. "She reminds you of Hatta, don't she?"

Turning, he placed his arms around her. "Woman, you been living with me too long; you even read my mind."

"You loved her, didn't you," she whispered, watching Suzanne as she rode toward the barn.

Lott squeezed her tightly. "She was my brother's wife and I cared for her like a sister. Hatta was an unusual and attractive woman, but you stole my heart. Sarah, I loved you the minute I saw you and with the depths of my heart. Don't you ever doubt my feelings."

She stretched up on her toes and gently kissed her husband. "I've never doubted your love for me, Lott."

Down at the barn, Suzanne dismounted and tied her horse, and eased around the side of the building.

"Let the ax do the work, James," John was saying. "It'll kill your back if you don't."

With a hard swing, James struck the piece of wood near its center splitting it in half. "How about that, John?"

Stopping for a moment to wipe the sweat from his brow and looking at the large stack piled to the side, he exclaimed, "Don't you think we've got enough for the rest of the winter?"

John, sitting on the ground resting, replied, "You can tell you don't know nothing about roughing it down here in the South. That pile might last a month if'n we're lucky."

As James was placing another piece of wood on the splitting block, he noticed Suzanne gently easing up behind John. She motioned for him to be quiet. As she placed her hands over John's eyes, he swirled around, pulling her down into his lap.

"What do you think you're doing?" she laughed.

John began to chuckle. "Who do you think you're fooling with? I heard you ride up and I've been watching you out of the corner of my eye as you attacked me."

"I was just having some fun. Let me up before I call your mother on you."

John held her tightly, "You sure you want me to let you go?"

Pretending to be angry she replied, "I was just teasing you and what did you do? You just pulled me down like some common woman. Isn't that right, James?"

Amused, James went back to work. "When you two get through playing, we might get this job done."

Suzanne then pulled herself up and began brushing the grass from her riding skirt. "You didn't see me Mister Smarty Pants. How'd you know I was there?"

John, still sitting on the ground casually answered, "I've hunted all my life and I heard every step you took and I could smell your perfume."

Standing in front of him she sighed, "You didn't say anything about my new riding outfit. Don't you think it becomes me?"

John sat there for a moment and then replied, "You got a new one every time I see you and they all look fine to me."

Disgusted, she turned to James, pulled back her shoulders displaying her full figure and asked, "Do I look fine to you, James?"

James blushed and looked away. "Yes Ma'am, you look just fine. Just fine."

"Now Suzanne, leave James out of it," John said. "You rode a far piece. What do you want?"

"What do I want!" she said reaching down and pulling him to his feet. "That's certainly not a gentleman's response to a lady's visit. You could have said, 'I'm glad to see you or what a pleasant surprise to see you,' but the only thing that crossed your mind was, 'What do you want?'"

John smiled. "You just startled me. I wasn't expecting you, and you do look striking in that outfit."

Taking her by the hand, he said, "Come on. Let's go down and see the horses."

Occasionally James could hear them laugh at something down at the corral, and before long they returned hand in hand.

Realizing that it was getting late, Suzanne said, "John, remember, Saturday week. We have a surprise for you and we want your parents there too."

As she rode off she called back, "You better be there. I'll make it worth your while."

"Ain't promising you!"

Watching in wonder, James muttered, "What was that all about?"

John, reaching for his coat, replied, "Some kind of a danged dinner they say they're planning. A surprise. They even want Mama and Papa there. That'll be the day when Mister Lott Wilson sets foot on Olliver property. You've heard of hell freezing over, ain't ya? Get your coat, we're calling it a day."

Walking back toward the house James said, "John, that woman's got her eye on you. When you had her on the ground, I think you could have done anything you wanted to her, and I'll tell you something else, when she was standing there with those shoulders back, some wayward thoughts went through my mind. Not many men could keep turning her down like you do."

John smiled, reached over and placed his arm on James' shoulder. "I hope my sister don't hear you talking like that. You might be sleeping out on the porch with them hounds of yours."

James pushed his arm away. "Well, brother-in-law, what I'm saying is that you'd be a fool not to pursue a relationship with that woman."

"You may have hit the nail on the head," John replied, laughing. "But I'm gonna have to think a little more about that dinner. Let's just put it like this, if'n my parents will set foot in the Olliver house, then I might just tag along too."

⌇⌇

John reined his horse to a stop and gently patted him on the neck. The horse shook his head and snorted. It was barely dusk, and a full moon was bringing light to what could be a dark winter night. A light breeze shuffled the fallen leaves about on the ground, and John noticed small puffs of clouds dancing across the sky. The chill of the night caused him to button the top of his jacket and adjust his wrap snugly around his neck. Up ahead, he saw a long straight road bordered with large oak trees which, during summer, created a green lush canopy overhead, but now appeared as large skeletons with thin arms reaching out to grasp and devour wanderers invading their territory. Accepting the challenge, John kicked his horse in the flank and galloped up the road, dodging the bare oak limbs overhead.

Located on the crest of a large hill overlooking a creek bottom that had produced some of the finest cotton in the county, the Olliver's large lighted two-story mansion dominated the skies. The four massive brick columns supporting the roof looked like sentinels standing guard.

John reined in his horse and thought back to the time when as a youngster he had enjoyed many visits to the Olliver's. They were full of fun and foolishness as he and Frank created new adventures. All the hunting trips, camping, horse racing or playing hide and seek in the spacious barn seemed to melt away the exhaustion from the daily toil and labor which occupied his every waking moment at his father's farm.

To John this was his home away from home, but that was years ago. In a way, he still had the same warm feeling about the place, but the relationship with Frank had changed through the years. The Frank Olliver he had known as a boy no longer existed.

A shuffling sound on the porch caught John's attention, and looking closer, he saw the figure of a man rising from a chair behind one of the columns. At the same time he was aware of the sound of people inside the house enjoying the evening.

As the man made his way to the front steps, he stopped and peered into the darkness. "Who's out there?"

"It's John, John Wilson."

"'Bout time you got here. You by yoreself? Where's yore folks?"

"They ain't coming. Papa said he didn't like eating late and that late hours is for young folks," John answered, knowing the real reason couldn't be revealed.

"That you, Sammy?"

Easing down the steps Sammy tottered over to where John was saddled and reached up for the reins. "Let me take yore hoss, Mist' John and yes suh, this is what's left of Sammy. I ain't as spry as I used to be."

Sitting there looking down at the old colored man, John could see that the outcome of the war had changed nothing for the man. As a boy, Sammy was always there to meet him when he rode up. He would ask about his parents, make a comment about the weather, and then lead John's horse off to the barn where he would feed and water the animal and brush him down before placing him in a stable. Although the war had freed the slaves, here stood Sammy taking the reins.

"You can get down now, Mist' John. I'll shore 'nough take care of yore hoss."

Hesitating, John said, "Sammy, you know Mister Lincoln freed all of you. Why are you doing the same things for the Ollivers that you did when you were a slave?"

Sammy began to chuckle. "I ain't no slave no more, Mist' John. The Ollivers give me a place to live and food for the table and when I needs some clothing, I can go down to Walker's Store and charge what I needs. I did try to go off but they says that since I didn't have no job, I have to go back to Mast' Olliver."

Surprised by his logic, John said, "Sammy when you were a slave, the Ollivers gave you quarters, fed and clothed you. I can't see anything's changed at all for you. Appears to me that you're still in bondage."

Not understanding what John really meant, Sammy said, "I just works here, that's all. By the way, ain't it shore 'nough a cold night."

At that moment, the front door burst open and Suzanne whirled out on the porch and down the steps. Dressed in a black velvet dress with a high-necked white laced blouse and with her long black hair pulled back and pinned behind each ear, she smiled up at John.

For a moment, John sat there mystified.

"You're late young man. The party is awaiting you."

With the sound of screeching leather, John brought his right leg over the saddle and effortless dismounted, standing so close to Suzanne that he could feel the warm touch of her breath against his face.

John was dressed in a dark gray woolen suit that had belonged to his older brother who died during the war, and it was a little snug. The tightness of the fit revealed the strong body that John had acquired while laboring in the field, and nothing could have aroused Suzanne more. Not worrying about what Sammy might think, Suzanne reached out and pulled him close as she whispered, "Tonight is going be something special for you and I hope you'll stay over. I promise you it'll be worth your while."

Without thinking, John leaned down and kissed her. "We'll see. I'm not sure I'm ready for any of your surprises, but I must say you do look enchanting."

Sammy led the horse away and began to laugh. "I must say you two shore does make a good match, and I thinks ole Sammy better get on to the barn and leave you two be."

Suzanne took John by the hand and led him up the steps and into the house. "Where is your mother and father? I thought they would be coming."

John didn't reply, but thought, you know good and well why they didn't come. And for our relationship, Mother is apprehensive and Papa knows how difficult it is for a young man to resist the temptations of a beautiful woman.

Walking down the hall toward the parlor, John could hear what seemed to be a large number of men chatting and laughing. He was unable to identify any familiar voice. A haze of tobacco smoke filled the air as he and Suzanne entered and the group stopped talking.

To John's surprise, Professor Hendon and Frank were sitting over near the fireplace having an evening smoke and next to Frank, John recognized Daniel McWorthan from the Hickory meeting. At his left was a short, well-dressed man in his late fifties standing next to the roughest looking man John had ever seen. The man was taller than John and was dressed in a brown cotton shirt with black trousers tucked into his knee length boots. He wore red suspenders that pulled his pants high above his waist line, making him appear even taller. The man's hair was combed and greased straight back revealing a wide scar that began above his left ear and ran down across his cheek to his nose.

Frank quickly got out of his chair, walked over to John and Suzanne and extended his hand. "Good to see you John. I'm glad you made it. There's some folks here I want you to meet."

Frank was dressed in his best for the evening. He wore a light beige suit with a ruffled brown shirt and dark brown tie. He stood slightly taller than John with long well groomed hair combed straight back. He was clean-shaven and thin and still appeared younger than his age. Even with a somewhat feminine appearance, Frank was unusually handsome.

John could think of no reason why he would be meeting with such an unusual group of men. Glancing over at Suzanne, he felt she must be behind whatever was going on and he became very uncomfortable.

Motioning John in, Frank began to make introductions. "Gentleman, this is John Wilson, the man we've been telling you about. Of course you know the Professor."

Hendon nodded and a wide smile crossed his face as he extended his hand.

"And I think you remember Mister McWorthan from over at Meridian," Frank continued.

McWorthan carefully examined John with the care of an officer inspecting his troops and then reached with the weakest handshake John could ever remember. Thinking back to his father words, "A hardy handshake reveals a man's inner strength," John became suspicious.

But John cordially shook his hand and replied, "I remember seeing you at the meeting."

Putting down a glass of whiskey and not waiting for Frank's introduction, a well-dressed man walked toward John and handed him a full glass of whiskey. "I'm Jasper Sikes from Jackson and to answer that blank expression on your face, you might say I'm the head of the Democratic Party here in Miss'sippi. And young man I've been anxious to meet you."

Stunned, John took the glass and reached out to clasp his hand. "Sir, I don't know what you've heard and I surely don't even know why I'm here tonight. This isn't my normal kind of party. I think we could use more female companions."

With that, the group began to laugh, and even the solemn man with the scar smiled.

"Yes sir, Frank," Sikes laughed. "The man don't even know why we wanted to meet him. Mister Wilson, you do have a sense of humor, and I guess you can say, you might have wandered into your own destiny tonight. By the way, this here is Herschel Pierce. Ain't he one ugly son-of-a-bitch."

Herschel, rubbing his short scraggly beard, made no effort to shake John's hand. He just stood there with a face as cold as steel and glared straight at him.

Finally he said, "I could see you staring at me when you come in. The scar got yore attention, didn't it. Ugly ain't it. You know what caused it?"

John pushed his hair back revealing a large scar across the side of his head and replied, "Same place I got this one. Some blue bellied Yankee cut you?"

The man nodded and a slight smile came across his face. "You'll do, Mister Wilson. You'll do just fine. I rode with Forrest and up there at Brice's Cross Roads when we was trying to hack our way through them bastards, one of 'em took a chunk out of me with his saber. But I'll tell you this, he paid one hell of a price for it. I cut him from one end to the other and when he fell from that hoss, his guts was hanging from his saddle horn."

"Excuse me," Suzanne said, sickened by what Pierce had described so vividly. "I think I'll leave you gentlemen and see if I can be of help with the meal. You men do have a seat. I know you have much to talk over, and it will be a few minutes before dinner is served."

As Suzanne left the room and the men made way to their seats, John excused himself and followed her down the hall. Grabbing her arm, he pulled her to the side and whispered, "What's going on here tonight? What am I doing here?"

Suzanne quietly placed her index finger to her lips and said, "This is all about politics and those men are interested in you. You go on back in there and things will take care of themselves."

John shook his head and replied, "I don't like surprises and I don't especially care for politics."

Suzanne pointed to the parlor. "John, your future could be in there. Now you go on and we'll have dinner ready soon."

For the next half hour, all the attention was on John as Professor Hendon related to the group what John had accomplished under his supervision in school and how John's family was one of the first to move into the area. He stated that through the years, the Wilsons had been the foundation and strength of the community and those in need depended on John's family for help. The Professor stated that when the war began, John was too young to enlist, but as soon as he became of age, he was there.

While the professor was speaking, all eyes were focused on John. Frank, who had been John's closest friend as a youth, listened to every word spoken but said nothing.

Growing up, John took up for Frank and on several occasions intervened on his behalf in fights that Frank had started and had no chance of winning. John's intervention had protected Frank.

In contrast, Frank's attitude was that an Olliver could do no wrong and Olliver money could buy anyone out of anything. In fact, it was Olliver money that kept Frank out of the army when Frank and his friends enlisted.

Frank's jealousy of John kept him from speaking on John's behalf. He just sat there sipping on his drink and thinking, If it hadn't been for the war, it could be me sitting over there. My ideas are just as good as the next, and I've got all the time in the world to serve my state. I know good and well that John's folks can't run their place without him and with my money, things could get done quick. Damn his sorry soul, it should have been me sitting there.

As the professor was ending his talk, a Negro maid came to the doorway and announced, "Gentlemen, if you will please follow me, the table is ready."

Entering the dining area, the men were met by Suzanne and Mrs. Olliver who directed them to their seats. Even though Mrs. Olliver was well into her fifties, she was still a very attractive woman. Like Suzanne, she had piercing brown eyes and dark black hair that was streaked with gray and tucked in a tight bun behind her head. The years had been good to her.

When they were all seated, Mrs. Olliver smiled and said, "Gentlemen, it is a pleasure to have you in our home tonight. I know you have pressing business to take care of and I'm sure you will make the best of the evening. You may not know, but I was reared south of New Orleans in what some would say, Cajun country. So this evening we have prepared for you a special Creole dinner, and since the food is seasoned fairly well, there is plenty of water and other liquids available. I truly hope you enjoy the meal."

John was seated between Suzanne and her mother and during the dinner most of the conversation was directed toward him. John continuously answered questions about his family, their attitudes about politics, his experiences during the war and even his religious feelings. As time passed John became tired of the questioning and realized that for some unknown reason, this group was interrogating him. Frustrated, John wished there was some excuse he could give to leave. But the meal was soon over and after thanking Mrs. Olliver for a delicious dinner, the men returned to the front parlor where coffee would be served. Before John joined them, Suzanne whispered, "It might be late when you all finish. You can stay over, if you wish. I want to talk with you."

Looking down at her, he whispered back, "What have you got me into?"

Suzanne gently squeezed his hand and smiled up at him. "John, I have a feeling that it's about time for you to know why they're here and why they have been asking you so many questions."

John shook his head and muttered, "I don't know what they want from me and I really don't care. I think I've had my evening and it's been most uncomfortable, so if you will, I'll be excused now."

Suzanne stood speechless as John went to collect his hat and wrap. At that moment, Professor Hendon came out of the parlor.

Suzanne quickly took John by the hand while the Professor placed his arm around John's shoulder and led him into the library.

"John," Hendon said, "I can see that you are frustrated over the evening and perhaps we didn't conduct ourselves as we should have, but these men are interested in you. Let's just have a seat for a moment."

John eased down in a chair across from Suzanne and the professor and stared into the face of the man that had taught him practically everything he knew. Hendon had come to Little Rock when John was in the second grade and had served as his teacher and friend. John saw nothing but honesty and a love that years had bonded. Many times Hendon had come to their home to visit with the family or to check on one of them when things weren't going well. If there was anyone John could trust, it had to be the professor. "I don't know what's going on here tonight," John said, "but you and I are going in there so I can speak my mind. And if I don't get some quick answers, I will be leaving."

The professor nodded and got out of his chair. "I do think it's time. Suzanne, will you excuse us?"

Suzanne reached over and ran her hand softly down John's face. "I'll see you when you've finished," she whispered.

The men looked up as John and the professor entered the parlor and Frankie taking a long draw from his pipe, exclaimed, "We were wondering about you, John. Didn't know where you got off to."

John settled himself on the sofa next to Frankie and after a moment of silence said, "Men, I have no idea what you have in mind, but it's very obvious that you want something from me. If it hadn't been for the professor, I'd be on my way home at this moment."

Sikes cleared his throat. "Mister Wilson."

Before he could continue, John interrupted. "Please excuse me Mister Sikes, but let me finish. I was invited here tonight for what I thought was a social and when I got here I was introduced to strangers. That's fine, I have no problem with that, but instead of us enjoying each other's company, it became a John Wilson sideshow. I don't know what you'd call it where you live, but I call it downright rude. Now if you want something of me, it's time for you to lay it on the table or I'm calling it an evening."

Jasper Sikes nodded and raised his coffee cup that had been filled with whiskey and presented a toast. "This here's to John Wilson, the man who's seen through the plan, and for our rudeness, forgiveness if you can."

The other men raised their cups and McWorthan said, "Well said, Mister Sikes, well said."

Turning to John, McWorthan continued, "John, we feel that a new constitution is gonna be presented to the folks here in Miss'sippi later on this year, and if the voters approve it, it's gonna open political doors that have been shut since the military took over. Won't be no more of this here appointing Negroes and sorry white folks to office. Our source in Washington says this constitution is gonna happen and our job is to find men who are capable of carrying elections for the new Southern Democratic Party and willing to help us get control of the gov'ment here in Miss'sippi. We all feel that the damned Yankees ain't always gonna be down here watching things, and once they're gone, we've got to be ready to take charge. Your name was mentioned to us as a strong candidate for the state legislature. If elected, you would represent the folks here in Newton County."

Surprised, John sat silently in thought. He had knowledge of the legislative process and had spent hours studying the various law systems throughout history, but he had never envisioned himself as one of those who would actually be a part of the system.

John glanced over at Hendon and then back to McWorthan. "Gentlemen, I do appreciate your interest in me, and even though I do have some knowledge about how our gov'ment works, I don't think I have time for politicking. You see, my parents are getting old and we have a farm to run and like I said, I do thank you."

Hendon reached over and placed his hand on John's shoulder. "John, your brother-in-law, James, seems to enjoy working the place and with the Negroes living near by, I think they could get by without you for a spell. You know, most of the legislative work would be done during the first part of the year, during the late winter. Late winter's kind of slow ain't it?"

John nodded, then said, "Gentlemen, I'm not sure I'm qualified for this. Why do you think I could win an election? I'm —"

McWorthan interrupted. "Mister Wilson, we know more about you than you may know about yourself. When I look at you I see a young man that from all accounts is well educated and has a good reputation in the county. Your family is well known and since you fought for the South, undoubtly you have a sense of patriotism. Yes sir, we feel that you might just be our man."

John rose and walked over to the fireplace, stared into the leaping flames and replied, "I hear that men who served in the confed'rate gov'ment and those of us you took to the field ain't eligible."

Sikes got up, walked over to John, and while knocking the ashes out of his pipe onto the hearth said, "You joined up in January of sixty-three, part of a replacement bunch. A lot of things happened during the later part of the war. Lot of records got lost. I checked up on you, there ain't no records on no John Wilson in the confed'rate army, least none that we could find. As far as the gov'ment knows, you just didn't exist."

Surprised, John shook his head in disbelief. "That can't be, they sent me up to Pennsylvania. I fought with the Newton County Rifles. Almost got myself killed."

Sikes eased back to his seat and began repacking his pipe. "As I said, there ain't no records of you. And John, before you say no, I have one more question for you. Let's just say you decide to run for office, what's your idea about gov'ment? Just what do you stand for?"

Having warmed himself, John walked over, sat down and thought for a moment. "Gentlemen, I think gov'ment is really a simple matter. Basically, you've got to know right from wrong and I guess with me, reared in the Christian way, it begins with what the Bible has to say about how you treat folks. Then you've got to consider what the federal and state constitution dictates. Gentlemen, it boils down to knowing the rules and abiding by 'em."

"What do you feel about us wanting to take control of the gov'ment? That is, when the time comes," Sikes questioned.

John thought for a moment, then replied, "I feel, that there are men in Jackson who ain't knowledgeable about our law system and there are outsiders who have no business running Miss'sippi. I also think that the needs of the common citizens, not those outsiders who moved into Miss'sippi to take what they can from us, should be represented. Miss'sippi is a prostrated state under military law that needs to be fully restored both economically and politically. The taxes they are imposing on us are stripping us to the bone and gentlemen, this must be stopped."

At that, the men rose, applauded and stepped forward to shake John's hand in approval. The clock in the hallway chimed three times and McWorthan closed the meeting. Since it was late, John and Professor Hendon decided to stay over with the Ollivers while McWorthan, Sikes and Pierce had a carriage waiting to carry them to the Hickory Station. There was a train due at five a.m. that they had to catch.

᷍

As the men settled themselves in a coach near the back of the train, McWorthan, with a cigar extended from his lips, leaned over to Sikes. "Mind if I borrow your smoke for a minute? It won't take a second to light it."

Sikes handed his cigar to McWorthan. "What'd you think about the young man?"

McWorthan took several quick draws on his cigar and after seeing that his smoke was lit, replied, "Must admit, I was impressed with the man. Can't say that I've met any better. What do you think?"

Sikes took a long draw from his smoke and with the clankity clank sound in the background as the train gained speed, he said, "If that man can't win an election, we might as well forget the whole thing and let the Republicans have at it. After meeting with him, we might be setting our goals too low. We ought to run him for the senate."

Pierce, a man of few words, took off his hat and pushed his long greasy hair back as he reached inside his coat pocket and brought out a flask. Trying to be polite, he offered the group a sip of his spirits and seeing that the other two were not interested, took several swallows and after carefully replacing it, commented, "The man worries me."

Astonished, Sikes replied, "What do you mean, he worries you?"

Looking out of the window into the darkness, he answered, "Don't git me wrong, I like Wilson, but he might just be too honest for his own good. I don't think he is aware of how far we're willing to go to place our folks in office."

Sikes thought about what Pierce had said and then exclaimed, "He'll do just fine, but I did wonder why Frank Olliver didn't have more to say in Wilson's behalf. You know they're good friends and he stayed mighty quiet."

McWorthan shook his head and muttered, "Olliver probably didn't think he needed any help."

᷍

Back at the Ollivers, Hendon, wanting some fresh air, asked John to join him on the front porch. As they stood in the chill of the early morning, a rooster crowed down near the barnyard and several others could be heard in the distance. Looking east, the men could see the sky turning shades of gold and pastel blue as dawn was nearing.

Hendon pointed toward the glow and exclaimed, "John, Miss'sippi's been through some hard times but just like the dawning of a new day, there will be a new day in Miss'sippi. And John Wilson, you can become a part of it. Let's just say it is predestined for you."

John who had been thinking about all that had transpired that night, turned to his old friend and said, "Professor, you may see something in me that just ain't there."

Feeling the chill of the morning, the professor motioned John back into the house. "I've taught you all I know about history and gov'ment, and I guess I've been grooming you all your life for such an opportunity. You could represent us well."

But there were things about Hendon that John didn't know. As a young man he had graduated at the top of his class at the Harvard school of law and after studying hard for over a year, passed the Massachusetts bar exam and was employed by the firm of Solomon and Taylor located in Boston. With his sharp wit and persistence, he quickly gained the reputation as the most promising young lawyer in the state. With his success, came social demands and soon this promising young lawyer became engaged to Gloria Solomon, daughter of the founder of Solomon and Taylor. Like other men of wealth, Solomon felt like the government at times stood in the way of his financial success and if he could gain power in the state legislature, then laws could be adjusted to meet his needs.

As the family planned the wedding, Solomon already had plans to introduce Hendon to the Massachusetts elite and hopefully have him in office within the next two years. The only problem that Hendon faced was that Mrs. Solomon had become infatuated with the dashing young man who was engaged to her daughter and since she was a very attractive woman, he could not resist her advances.

An unexpected return by Mister Solomon one Sunday afternoon to an unlocked door brought Hendon's bright future to an end. Not wanting to be embarrassed by the scandal and afraid that a divorce would ruin his standing in Boston, Solomon, not a man of violence, paid Hendon a large sum of money to remain quiet and leave the state. In addition, Solomon, wanting to expose Hendon as a womanizer, arranged for his daughter to catch Hendon with one of the local whores in the city. Once again Hendon received compensation and as planned, the engagement was broken.

Hendon often wondered why he had not received harsher treatment but later discovered that Solomon had lost interest in his wife years earlier and also had made visits to the red section of Boston on a regular basis. Hendon lost no time in leaving the city and with it he could see his future in the courtroom and politics vanish. Resounding in his ears was Solomon's last statement, "You whoring son-of-a-bitch, if I ever hear your name called and if you say anything about my wife, I will deal with you permanently and I do have contacts all over this country. My family name will not be tarnished."

With that in mind, Hendon had fled to Georgia and finally found a place of employment deep in the Mississippi wilderness as a teacher at Little Rock.

Thinking back, Hendon saw how foolish he had been. In Boston he could have married into one of the wealthiest families in the east, had a political future that could possibly have placed him in Washington, and he could have had an attractive wife.

In John Wilson, he saw the man he could have become.

Meanwhile, as Frankie was sitting on the side of his bed struggling to remove his boots, there was a light tap on the door. Frankie, was surprised to see his sister enter.

Dressed in a full white cotton nightgown with a light pink woolen shawl wrapped around her shoulders, Suzanne tipped into the room. Seeing that Frankie was having a problem with his boots, she took one of his boots and pulled, easing it off his foot.

Frankie chuckled. "Well, I see you're good for something, but I thought you'd be asleep by now. You see 'Fessor and John to their room?"

Suzanne pushed Frankie aside, crawled up on the bed, crossed her legs and made herself comfortable. In an excited voice she whispered, "Tell me what happened? What did the men think of him?"

Frankie glanced over toward the mantle to see what time it was and answered, "Can't this wait?"

Defiantly, Suzanne crossed her arms. "I'm not leaving until you answer me."

Knowing how persistent his sister could be, Frankie got off the bed, walked over to get his housecoat and slumped himself into a chair across from the bed. "Suzanne, at times you can worry the living hell out of me. First thing, I really don't think John has a place in politics or in our family; our differences are too great. And if you do want him, you have got to take him like he is."

"I have no problem with the way he is," Suzanne said.

Reaching over for his pipe, he continued, "That's the problem with you Suzanne, you can't face reality. First, you wanted me to hire John to work for me, just to get him out of the field, and I knew damned well, feeling the way he does about me, that his pride wouldn't let him do it. Now you're hoping that a life in politics will give him the status and means that you want. You know what Suzanne, why don't you just leave him alone. Woman, if he wanted you, he'd take you. Lord knows, you've thrown yourself at him. You had him under the covers yet?"

Feeling an anger beginning to burn inside her, Suzanne unfolded her arms, raised her eyebrows and replied, "John has more of a future than working as a common field hand, and it may just take someone like me to show him just what he can accomplish if pointed in the right direction. He might find being wealthy is not so bad, and I don't plan to spend my life in no four-room shack. And as far as our sex life goes, that is none of your business."

Frankie began to laugh, "That means you ain't been too active in gloryland, doesn't it?"

Agitated by his remark, Suzanne got off the bed and walked toward the door. "Gloryland! You're crude and impossible, Frank Olliver, and I can describe every part of John's body, if'n I wanted to. We have been intimate."

Frankie laughed harder. "You may describe it, but that doesn't mean he's put anything to use, and I can see you right now out there in that hot sun digging them tators and sweating like a whore on Sat'day night. Just a pore ole country gal. You need to take him like he is, Suzanne. Nothing more, nothing less, and for intimate, you don't have the vaguest idea what that means. And to answer your question, I think the men were impressed."

Suzanne slammed the door so hard it rattled the windows through-out the house.

6

THE STORM ON THE HORIZON

A STEADY SNOWFALL WHICH HAD CONTINUED FOR FOUR days finally became single snowflakes freckling the skies. Soon the clouds separated and brilliant flashes of light layered the countryside as the falling snowflakes twinkled like millions of tiny stars.

The horse snorted and shook his head sending clumps of snow in all directions. A couple wrapped in layers of blankets cuddled close in their sleigh and shivered as icy particles gently fell on their faces.

"Didn't I tell you it would be spectacular," Robert said, edging closer to Lucretia who was wrapped so snuggly that only her sparkling eyes and frosty red cheeks were showing.

"Not a soul, man or beast has disturbed a single flake. God doesn't make it prettier than this, does He."

Lucretia, almost too cold to speak, nodded and gazed down the slope to the valley below.

Earlier that day as the storm began to break, Robert had borrowed a sleigh and horse from one of his friends, Bob Taylor, and had no trouble coaxing Lucretia out of the house that had held her captive for the past days. She loved the outdoors and a chance to get outside was welcomed. Being a protective mother, Mrs. Caulder at first discouraged the venture, but knowing that Lucretia was a grown, headstrong woman, she ladened them with quilts and told them that if they weren't back in a couple of hours, she would be coming after them.

Suddenly from down the way, Lucretia noticed a lone horseman making his way up the Emmitsburg road toward town and then for some strange reason, he reined his horse to a stop. Lucretia waved to the stranger, not expecting a response. The rider returned the gesture.

Robert shuffled uneasily and murmured, "He's disturbing everything. Why doesn't he just go on?"

Shivering, Lucretia replied, "What in the world are you talking about, Robert? The man is probably trying to get home before dark."

"He's tracking up the road, that's what he's doing. Everything was perfect," Robert said. "That is, before he came through."

A frown crossed Lucretia's face. She had no idea how he could rationalize such an absurd statement.

"Robert, when the man moves on, we won't even be able to tell that he was ever there."

"I'll know it. This was supposed to be our special encounter with nature. Snow is always the prettiest before anyone or anything disturbs it. I wanted at least a few moments before it's spoiled."

Lucretia didn't respond and once again stared out across the way. It was indeed beautiful. As far as she could see there were mounds of puffy snow, and even the branches of the evergreen trees, limbs bent downward, were completely covered. As enchanting as it was, at one time this hillside had been the very inferno of hell. Turning so that she could get a better view, she located the long winding pile of stones, a fence row, that had given the Union soldiers protection as the Army of the Northern Virginia broke the center of the line only to be thrown back in defeat. As a young girl hiding in her father's cellar, she could still hear the roar of cannon fire and its striking force that shook the very foundation of her house. She also remembered the constant rattle of muskets as men fired point blank at each other. Then through a lull of battle, she would hear the loud screams and cheers of men as they charged toward each other in mortal combat. But after the battle had ended, the most horrifying thing that she had ever experienced was the carnage of human destruction, so terrible that as a girl of thirteen she had all but blocked it out of her memory.

That day in July, this hillside was no white winter wonderland. The moan and shrieks of the wounded and dying returned vividly to her mind as did the recollection of the ground covered in blood, slimy and puddled. Not wanting to think about it, Lucretia shook her head as if that would clear her mind of what had happened.

Startled by her quick jerk and noticing a tear trickling down her cheek, Robert said, "Did I say something wrong?"

For a moment Lucretia couldn't bring herself to speak but gaining courage she murmured, "It's something from years back, something that I have tried to put past me, something—"

Robert took her hands in his and could see pain in her eyes. "You can share it with me."

Lucretia slowly pointed to the fields below. "Where you may see a wintery spectacle, I see a killing ground. I saw men laid out by the thousands killed and wounded. As a girl of thirteen, I had men die in my very arms. I saw things a child should never see."

Robert pulled her closer. "Why did you come out here with me? Why did your mother allow it?"

A few moments lapsed then Lucretia continued, "My father was a doctor and mother helped him, that is, when he asked her to. And after that terrible slaughter, every able-bodied man, woman and child came up here. We weren't asked; we knew we had to come."

"Haven't you been up here since then?" Robert asked.

"Maybe once and then I tried to shut it out," she answered.

Noticing that the sun was setting, Robert thought about what Lucretia's mother had said and with a slap of the reigns, the horse lunged forward through the deep snow.

This was supposed to be a special afternoon, one full of fun and fantasy, an afternoon when everything was to be perfect. He had been working under the supervision of Lucretia's father for the past two years and come October, he would be accepting a position in Baltimore in one of the finest hospitals in the East. When he left, he wanted Lucretia to go with him, but seeing how disturbed she had become, this was not the time to propose. Things were going well until that rider distracted them. If it hadn't been for him, I might have been engaged by now, he thought to himself.

As the sleigh made its way down the slippery trail, a lone cedar tree by an old barn that had been all but destroyed by cannon fire caught Lucretia's attention. Lucretia tugged on Robert's sleeve and said, "Can you pull up for a moment."

Sensing that no questions should be asked, he pulled the sleigh to a stop.

Being careful not to fall, she stepped down and made her way to the old cedar. As she approached, she could see the scars of battle where large chunks of bark had been torn off the tree and many of the limbs had been severed by musket fire. It was a wonder that it had survived. For a moment she could still see the masses of bodies lined up in long lines, many who would never see the light of morning. Straining, she tried to remember the young man, a Southerner, placed by himself down past the barn, wincing in pain. Reluctantly easing up to him, she had offered him water and gasping, he said, "Don't leave me. Don't let me die here." And for some strange reason, she promised to stay by his side, and told him she would never leave him.

A lone crow suddenly flew down and lit on one of the upper branches sending snow tumbling to the ground. Lucretia quickly stepped back to keep from getting covered and then made her way to the sleigh.

Robert extended his hand and helped her up. "You all right?"

Lucretia smiled at him and answered, "I'm fine, but I'm not sure I've been good company this afternoon."

Robert cracked the whip and as the two left the hillside, Lucretia wondered if she would ever see the young Southerner again. Then there was the evening in Philadelphia last Christmas. As she gazed out of the window she imagined him standing there by the lamppost smiling up at her and strangely enough, and beyond any reality, in the lone rider this afternoon that waved to her.

In a short time, they had made their way back to Lucretia's home. Mrs. Caulder hurried them inside and helped them remove their wraps.

"You two better get on into the kitchen and thaw up before the old frost bite gets to you. I've got some hot tea on the stove, and you can stick those toes right up to the oven," she said with a smile.

Settling in their seats, Lucretia glanced over to her father who was sitting with a book in his hand on the far side of the stove next to a window that overlooked the backyard and woodlands beyond.

"Papa, you haven't moved an inch since we left."

Doc Caulder placed a marker in his book, slowly closed and laid it on the lamp table and replied, "Don't see any need to go anywhere. I'm as warm as toast, got an interesting book to read, a good smoke, and I can still look outside and watch all that beautiful snow flutter down. Why in the world would I want to move?"

Adjusting his glasses, he peered over at the two sitting there with frosty cheeks and steaming shoes which he felt were too close to the heat. "Better get your feet back a piece. You know they're probably numb from the cold. You two must be fools to get out in this weather. You know when I was your age—"

Mrs. Caulder, pouring Robert another cup of tea, interrupted him, "When you were a youngster, your mother told me she couldn't get you in out of the snow. Said one time some of you boys even slept out in it. Now that sounds foolish to me."

Pointing to Robert and Lucretia, she continued. "All these two did was bundle up and take a short ride around the place."

Seeing the humor, Doc Caulder chuckled as he packed his pipe with fresh tobacco. "We didn't sleep out; we spent the night in Jamie Butler's father's barn. We made a bed of hay and had a mountain of cover to keep us warm. Yes, we had a fine time. We should try it some time, you know, just you and me? Could be a lot of fun," Doc Caulder said with a twinkle in his eye.

Blushing and trying not to smile, Mrs. Caulder said, "Mister Caulder, there are young people in our presence, so you'd better watch your tongue."

Seeing how humorous and youthful Doc Caulder could be at times, Robert and Lucretia smiled at each other.

Rising from his chair, Robert said, "Well, it's getting late and I've got to get the sleigh back, so if you will excuse me, I must be on my way. And, by the way, Doctor, if you two decide to visit the barn tonight, I'll be in the office in the morning to treat the both of you."

§§

Little Rock, Mississippi

In the days that followed John's meeting at the Olliver's, his parents saw a drastic change in him. Even though he was still dedicated to his work and to the supervision of the farm, he seemed to have a new approach to life. He became more social and optimistic, much more like the person his parents had known before the war: a young man full of dreams and ambition.

On his return from the Olliver's, John had told his parents the purpose of the meeting and his possible opportunity to represent the county in the state legislature. Even though the group had not officially offered him their support, John felt it would only be a matter of time until he would be asked to qualify.

John's father, Lott, was somewhat apprehensive about the whole ordeal and showed little enthusiasm about John's aspirations. Lott had heard talk of an organization that was meeting secretly and, from what he understood, the group was up to no good.

A few mornings later, Lott roused John a little earlier than usual, and after the two had finished their breakfast, he pointed to the jackets hanging on a set of pegs on the wall and said, "Son, we got most of the work done for a spell. I want you to take a walk with me. I want to go to the Big Woods."

When Lott and his brother, Jake, came into this country as surveyors in the 1830's they were able to acquire two sections of six hundred and forty acres. Later, Jake had married a Choctaw woman named Hatta and when the Choctaws were forced to leave, some were given land in return for giving up their tribal allegiance. In this way, Hatta's brother, Minsa, was also granted a section of land. When Jake was murdered, his land naturally went to Hatta, but when she and her brother Minsa decided to move to Oklahoma, they left the land in Lott's care. Since that time, Lott had not touched a tree or plant in the area and referred to it as the Big Woods.

As they headed down the steps and out onto the yard, John said, "Want me to saddle up the horses?"

Lott shook his head and walking with a slight limp, he headed toward a narrow lane that led to the woods and replied, "We'll walk this morning. Won't be too many years 'till I'll have to ride. We'll just walk."

John hurried to catch up with his father and before long they had crossed their farmland and entered a beautiful and somewhat sacred forest. The ancient long leaf pines seemed to reach their fingers to the sky. Observing the trees closely, John saw where fires and lighting had taken their toll on the giants, but they stood tall and commanding as if they were standing guard against anyone who threatened their existence. Enthralled by their size, John reasoned it would take at least five men, hand in hand, to reach around just one of the trunks.

After a while Lott and John left the hills and made their way down into the swamp bottoms which were covered with masses of hardwoods and, in the damp places near the creeks, ferns and canebrakes still grew in abundance. These trees with their summer canopy of leaves allowed little summer light to filter to the ground thus leaving little undergrowth and miles of openness.

Tiring, Lott motioned for John to help him down a steep bank that led to a trickling brook. Once down, Lott knelt and after cupping his hands together, brought a handful of cold water to his lips. John wasted no time in joining his father.

Then they settled down on a mound of soft moss to rest their backs against the trunk of an old beech tree.

Once entering the forest, John knew that his father seldom spoke. He was their gardener, their keeper. John also knew that he often came to these woods when something was bothering him.

John pulled out his pocketknife and began trimming a small reed of cane into a toothpick. Chewing on the cane produced an unforgettable sweet taste.

"This is something, ain't it, Son?" Lott said. "God don't make it any prettier than this. It ain't changed a lick since before the Choctaws were here."

Lott pointed to a thick canebrake down to their left. "Them sorry Yankees stole most of our livestock but I'll tell you one thing, that brake over there sure enough hid a few of our horses and cows. We got to telling them hoodlums about the rattlers down here in the swamp and they decided to leave well enough alone."

John chuckled, "You ought to have sent 'em on down here with a prayer the snakes would be out."

A few moments passed in silence and John sensed that his father had more on his mind than just a discussion of nature.

"Papa, I love to make these walks with you, but is there something on your mind we need to talk about?"

Lott stretched out his legs to relieve a cramp. "You mean it's that obvious."

John nodded. "You're concerned about me thinking about entering the race, ain't ya?"

"More than concerned, Son. I am somewhat troubled. John, you're the only son I've got left. James Earl died up in Virginia during the war and Thomas deserted when he thought you'd been killed. You remember. He came by here one evening with some more men who had decided to leave the army and said they was headed for Texas, Mexico or somewhere of the sorts. A few days later the army came looking for him and they told me that if they caught them, they was going to string 'em up. Never heard from him since. Don't know if he's dead or alive. Probably dead. So what I'm trying to tell you is that first, you're needed at home, and second, I have little respect for any politician. Them politicians in Washington and in Richmond started them a war that tore this country apart and took two of my sons from me. It would have been a different story if them bastards had been out there on the firing lines like you and the other boys. I have a feeling that war would have never been sparked."

John thought for a moment about what his father said, and then carefully replied, "The war cost me far more than you could ever imagine. There are details I haven't shared with you or mother. When I got home, I found that I had lost the thing I valued the most."

"You talking about Rebecca, ain't you, Son?"

John nodded. "The only reason I stayed here in Little Rock was because you needed help with the farm, and I guess I needed the healing power that only you and Mama and the good Lord could give me. I worked day and night for you, not because I loved working that much, but as long as I was busy, my mind tended not to wander."

John stood up and slowly rolled his neck around to relieve the stiffness. "Papa, the farm is in good shape. We got Andy to help us when we want him and James is chewing at the bits to get into the fields full time. He's tired of his soldiering, 'specially with the job he's got. What I'm saying is, you don't really need me."

For a moment Lott thought about what John said, then replied, "I guess I'll always need you, Son, but the problem is, I ain't never had much respect for no politician. If you want to do something else, I'd rather it be more of an honorable profession than that. Just look at that crowd in Jackson and what they're doing to us."

At that moment, a cold wind blew out of the northwest causing the leafless tree limbs to quiver. The groaning sounds as they twisted against each other sent a chill down John's back.

Shivering, John reached down for his father's hand and as he pulled him to his feet said, "We need to head for the house; it's gonna be a cold one tonight."

On their way home John said, "Papa, you know what you said about what was going on in Jackson? That's one of the reasons I want to try to help."

Hoping their talk about politics was over and that his son's mind had been changed, Lott became annoyed and said, "John, there ain't a tinker's damn you can do in Jackson."

"Papa, Mama told me that you was one of the smartest students in your class growing up in Savannah and that there weren't a math problem you couldn't work."

"So what if'n I was," grumbled Lott, ducking a limb that John had pushed aside as it swung backward toward him. "What does that have to do with politics?"

"Mama said she always felt that you could have done more with your life than farming. She feels that you always had dreams that for one reason or 'nother, you couldn't chase."

"John, Mama don't know everything that goes on in this here old mind of mine, and I'm doing just what I want. If I wanted to do something else, believe me, I would do it and nothing could stop me."

As they reached the path that would lead to the house, John replied, "And that's the way I feel too. Papa, I'm not bragging, but I learn easily, and you and Mama have taught me the difference between right and wrong. As you said, Miss'sippi is in one heck of a state and it needs good, honest, hardworking men to pull it through. I think I can make a difference, at least I think I want to try. Maybe this is a dream I need to chase."

Just then the hounds curled up on the porch began to bark and raced out to greet them. The cold wind had gained more strength now and the sight of smoke pouring from the chimney gave them a feeling of warmth. John reached down and stroked the back of one of the dogs while Lott bent down to pet the other.

Rising, Lott said, "John, you best check the livestock 'fore you come in; they might need some extra grain. I'll have us a hot cup of coffee ready when you get in."

John had a good feeling about the afternoon spent with his father and even though he felt he hadn't completely gained his father's favor, he knew he would consider all that he had told him.

Later that night after John had gone to bed, Lott and Sarah cuddled under a mountain of quilts and quietly watched the last embers of the fire dwindle away. An occasional gust of wind would rip through the open hallway whistling as it went. Sarah, her head on Lott's shoulder, listened as he told her all he and John had talked about that afternoon. When he finished, Sarah said, "You know, you've often said that John, as smart as he is, ought to do something besides farming. You've said it dozens of times. Why don't you give him some encouragement?"

Lott thought for a moment and sighed, "But I never said nothing 'bout politicking."

Sarah nestling closer to him replied, "Nobody's endorsed him, nobody's come by to pull his arm and he ain't even tried to qualify. Don't you think he might be just doing a little wishing? But one thing I do know, something good has come over that boy that I ain't seen in years and ever what it is, I hope it stays with him. He seems happy for a change."

Lott knew she was right and said, "I guess I've been a little selfish with the boy, and I have noticed the change. It's time for me to let go and let him chase his dreams, no matter where they carry him."

A few moments passed and he whispered, "You told John that you thought I had other dreams to chase when I was young, but I've always had one that I've been after and I've got her right here with me."

§§

Even though the military still held control of the state, the new constitution had been ratified guaranteeing that the Negroes were recognized as citizens and had voting rights. With many of the pre-war politicians and white citizens unable to hold office or vote, carpetbaggers, scalawags and Negroes dominated the majority of political offices.

The morning after John and his father had taken their walk, Professor Hendon rode over to the Wilson's and informed the family that his organization wanted John to represent the Democrats in the fall election and that he would be glad to help him with the qualifying papers. John was elated over his endorsement and even Lott showed some enthusiasm.

Hendon and his group knew that the whites were still in the minority and, to win the district, they would have to win some Negro votes. In John, they felt that they had a man who would definitely get the white votes and since the Wilsons were held in high regard in the Negro community, they felt that his election was assured. Newton County and the district would be in Democratic hands.

A short time after Hendon left the Wilsons, John, on his way to the barn to check a mare that was soon to fold, saw Andy approaching on his mule.

As he neared, John called out, "Andy, we got to do sump'n about how you're getting around. How 'bout letting me sell you one of our horses?"

Andy slid from the side of his mount and with a smile replied, "I don't need no better way to get about, and I'm sure I can't 'ford none of yore high-priced hosses."

John led Andy down to the barn where the horses were stabled and the two quietly crouched down outside the stall where the mare was laboring. The mixture of hay, corn and manure filled their nostrils

Andy nudged John. "Folks says you gonna politic. Anything to it?"

John easing into the stall to check the mare replied, "Been thinking about it. Think I can win?"

"You got my vote, that is, if'n I can vote. You knows I can't read."

John turned to Andy. "I told you that I'd help you get registered, and I'm sure there'll be someone to help you on election day."

"Mist' John, I'll tell you something else, the colored's gonna help you if'n you needs us."

John rising replied, "I'm gonna need all the help I can get."

The two then made their way down the open hall of the dark barn and into the bright sunlight. A brisk breeze blew in from the south, chasing the barnyard odors away.

They walked over to the fence of the corral that bordered the barn and peered out into an area that served as a breaking pen. John crawled up and straddled the top rail of the fence and Andy climbed up next to him. Sitting there together, Andy with a worried expression on his face said, "Mist' John, there's some things goin' on that I don't reckon I feel too good 'bout nor understands."

John, stretched upward in search of some cows that were supposed to be in the adjacent field.

"John, there's a colored man's house got burnt up the other night. Man called Matthews."

Finally spotting the cattle in the lower bottom, John settled himself back on the fence. "Sorry to hear about that; it happens to a lot of folks, you know."

Andy glanced down toward the ground and rubbing his nose, continued nervously, "When they went through the ash and pulled what was left of 'em out, somebody had cut his throat."

John grabbed Andy's hand. "You saying somebody murdered him?"

Andy nodded. "Killed 'em dead."

In disbelief, John replied, "That can't happen 'round here. You sure 'bout what you're saying?"

Andy slowly nodded.

"Anybody get the law to look into it? Could have been a case of a jealous husband looking for some justice. Happens you know," John said.

Andy shook his head "There was a lot of hoss tracks 'round the place. You see me ridin' that mule? Us colored don't have no hosses, and for the law, they sent some white folks out there. They just sat 'round for a spell, smoking, drinking and after a while they rode off laughing."

"Andy, tell me more about the man. Who was he?"

Andy muttered, "He was a northern colored who bought the Amos place when it went up for sale. Folks says that Mister Amos couldn't pay no taxes, and folks says that Matthews works for the Freemen's Bureau. The colored says that a crowd of white folks got 'em."

John bit his lip in disbelief. There was no way this could have happened in Newton County, he thought. There was some tension between the whites and Negroes down in the southern end of the county, especially in the Newton area, but murder, not a chance.

Climbing down, John said, "Come morning, I'm going down to Decatur and check on what happened. Gonna carry James with me. He still serves with the military. There's got to be some kind of explanation."

Mounting his mule, Andy looked down at his old friend. "Mist' John, you best stay out of that bus'ness. There's some things happ'ning that's got the colored skairt. You just set yore mind on politick'n and we'll see if'n we can take care of the rest."

Watching Andy ride off, the words, "We'll take care of the rest" stuck in John's mind. Was the colored man really murdered by whites, and was Andy telling him everything he knew?

Early the next morning John stopped by his sister's house and after speaking with James, the two rode the seven miles to Decatur to find the sheriff. As they inquired as to a burning of a house and a possible murder, the sheriff acknowledged the burning but blatantly dismissed the idea of a murder. He said that they found no evidence of rough play.

At the courthouse John ran into Professor Hendon who was trying to employ a surveyor to come out to check his property lines. While there the professor took John to the clerk's office where he could sign the necessary papers to be a qualified candidate for the upcoming election, and upon signing, the clerk assured him that he had the county's full support. John's opposition would be a republican named Jack Templeton, a transport from Ohio who had been appointed by the post-war government. Templeton was a drunk and had a streak of jackass stubbornness. No one in the county, black or white, cared for him.

Hendon, his business concluded, decided to accompany John and James back to Little Rock. While they were making their way home, Hendon looked over to James and said, "You ever get tired of wearing that uniform around here?"

"Sometimes, I get tired of the looks folks give me," James replied.

Following the war, James, interested in John's sister, asked to be assigned to the east central part of the state and even though he knew that resentment would be a part of his job, he wanted to pursue his relationship with her. He also felt that he could help the people in their struggle to regain their rights.

Looking over to Hendon, he continued, "Won't be long till I'll be taking off the blue and I'll just be a plain ole citizen."

"Folks around Little Rock kinda like you. Not like those Yankees posted down in the southern end of the county. They're going around looking for trouble, and the Negroes down there at Newton know they can get away with anything. There's lots of trouble down there," Hendon said.

"That's what I understand," James replied. "But if folks around Little Rock accept me, it's because I try to treat them with respect. I don't look at them as a conquered foe. I only see hardworking people trying to make a go with what they have."

As the three reached the Wilson property, James took the road that led to his house and Hendon invited John over to his place where they could talk about the fall election. Upon reaching Hendon's place, the professor found that his wife and children were down at neighbors, thus making for a quieter afternoon. Hendon added extra wood to the fire and reaching behind the woodbox, retrieved a bottle of whiskey. Pointing to a chair over near the fireplace, Hendon motioned for John to have a seat. With a loud pop, the cork flew up, hitting the ceiling and then bouncing over to where John was sitting.

"Kinda potent, isn't it," laughed Hendon filling a cup that always could be found at the end of the mantle. "Care for a shot?"

John shook his head.

After a deep swallow, Hendon licked his lips. "Best liquor in the county. Same recipe your Uncle Jake used. He shared it with me, and Timothy and I still turn it out."

The two then sat there quietly watching the fire burn. Putting the cup down, Hendon said, "I've known you since the day you were born and I've done all in my power to teach you all I can. You're by far the best student I've ever had the opportunity to teach."

John reached down and with a quick motion picked up a log that had rolled off the burning stack and lobbed it back to the fire. "You always made learning fun and you made me seek for answers not written in the books. You made me the student that I was."

Hendon reaching into his jacket pocket and pulled out a tobacco pouch and after packing his pipe, continued, "John, you have the making of a fine politician and knowing you the way I do, there is no limit to where you can go. Right now you will be representing us in the legislature, but, if I know you the way I think I do, you'll be in Washington one of these days. I can just see you sitting in the Senate."

John glanced over at Hendon whose eyes had become glassy from the corn whiskey. He knew the Professor respected and cared for him, but Hendon was always living in a dream world, always had plans to remake society.

"I think the bottle's talking for you, 'Fessor. I ain't won the local election yet."

Hendon smiled over at John. There's no way you're losing it. You got the popular support and if you shouldn't, I got the power to put you in. From here on out you'll speak at every engagement in the county. We're gonna have you at every church meeting, wedding, barn-raising and when the county fair rolls around this summer, we're gonna have you debating ever who the Republicans choose to run. Yes sir, Mister John Wilson, as you Mississippians say, 'We're gonna take names and kick asses.' And, by the way, when you get to Washington, I hope you'll carry me with you."

"What about your wife and family," laughed John.

Without stopping to think, he replied, "Why do you think I want to go with you? They're about to drive me crazy as a loon. They're staying here."

As John left Hendon's that afternoon, two things bothered him: first, the sheriff's nonchalant denial that a murder had been committed and then, the statement by Hendon about his power to control an election. John was becoming suspicious of Hendon's ethics, purpose, and source of power.

As he approached the house, John saw his mother hurrying out to meet him waving a piece of paper clasped tightly in her hand. John quickly dismounted and tied the horse. Never had he seen such pleasure on her face. Tears of joy streamed down her wrinkled and weathered cheeks. Without saying a word, she wrapped her arms around him, half crying and laughing with joy.

"What in the world's happened to you?" John muttered.

"I've finally heard from him; he's alive."

John took her hands in his and asked, "Who's alive?"

"Thomas is alive. He's somewhere out in Texas."

By that time, Lott had come out of the house to join them. "Y'all best come on in, yore Mama's not dressed for the cold."

Inside, John read the brief letter. Thomas hoped that all was well with the family and as for himself, he was making it all right. It was the most exciting news the family had received in years. Never had John seen such peace on his father's face, knowing that he now had two sons alive.

In the weeks that followed, Hendon scheduled John to be at every social function. Although women could not vote, Suzanne went with John and gave him her full support.

§§

Spring soon returned to the hill country with its usual array of flowers and budding trees. The buggy bounced and rattled as its driver carefully reined the horse down the rough road trying to stay out of the deep ruts made during the wet winter months. At mid-morning, the sun was shining brilliantly through the limbs of the trees that lined the roadway, sending flickers of light racing across their path. Even with the coming of spring, there was still a touch of chill in the air.

Suzanne snuggled closer to John and pretended to brush some lint from his trouser leg as she said, "It's mighty nice of you to escort me to church this morning. You know Easter Sunday has always been a special time."

John again noticed how beautiful Suzanne had become. She wore a heavy dark red ankle-length coat with a black hand-woven scarf wrapped around her neck. Her jet black hair, glistening in the morning light, was pulled back on each side and fell loosely down her back. With her brown eyes and dark complexion, she looked every bit the Creole of her mother's people.

"We'll see folks here that we don't see for the rest of the year. I guess one service a year takes care of their religious needs. Frankie'll be there, won't he?"

Easing away from him, Suzanne answered, "That's an ugly thing to say about your friend and my brother. Since when have you been in charge of the judgment seat. You know some of those men will be casting votes come election time and you might need their support."

John worked the horse down the road and when the animal balked at a deep washout, he took out his whip and with a sharp crack, sent the horse bolting forward, almost tipping the buggy over. Once through the eroded area, he replied, "I'm telling you the truth as I see it, and, that is, that some of those folks only come once a year and that's a fact."

Realizing that what John said was true, Suzanne said, "I guess you're right, but I don't think it's fair for you to place Frankie with them."

John glanced over at her. "I don't see why not. All you have to do is ask the preacher. He knows who's there at every meeting."

"John, you know Frankie's a busy man and with his investment in the railroad, he's hardly ever home any more. And what about you? I don't think you darken the doors too much either, do you?"

John didn't answer. Thinking back, there was a time when he didn't miss a service and even if he had wanted to, his parents gave him no choice. When he had been in the field all week from daylight to dark and the monthly service finally came around, it was a pleasure to clean up and spend the day worshiping and being with friends.

Thinking back, John could still see her as she awaited his arrival, always standing on the top step next to where the preacher was welcoming his congregation. As soon as he cleared the bend in the road, her hand would be up waving with that little white handkerchief she always carried. He could still feel the warmth of her body and the smell of her perfume as they sat together in his parents' family pew.

When Becca looked at me, I felt like I was standing there defenseless. She looked straight into my heart. She knew me better than I knew myself, John thought.

Suzanne suddenly eased closer to him and once again placed her hand on his leg. Trying to change the subject, she exclaimed, "You sure are handsome when you dress in your Sunday best."

John reached over and placed his hand on hers causing her to gasp. Even though she felt that he cared for her, he did not often show her the emotional love that she yearned for. They had kissed on several occasions and had become intimate once while swimming in the creek, but she wanted more.

John looked down at the suit he was wearing. What Suzanne didn't know was that John had never owned a suit of clothes at all and the one that he was wearing belonged to his brother.

Suzanne slid her hand from John's leg as they approached the church and straightened her coat as the buggy pulled into the churchyard. Throngs of people were making their way up the steps and into the hallway of the white frame building. Once inside, meeting friends on the way, they finally reached the aisle where John's parents were sitting. To John's surprise, Tim had settled himself on the family pew next to Sister and James. Tim glanced up at John. "Surprised to see an ole sinner like me here today?"

John shook his head in fun and winking at Suzanne whispered, "Not at all, Tim Johnson. Easter Sunday comes once a year. I just hope the preacher has a sermon that'll get yore attention."

Tim replied, "I'll be just fine long as he lays off the subject of adultery."

Pinching him as hard as she could, Sister mumbled, "Tim Johnson, you'd better watch your mouth or I might just pinch you so that you don't have to worry 'bout no adultery."

After a service of familiar hymns and a sermon on the resurrection of Jesus, the preacher closed his talk a little earlier than usual and to the surprise of the congregation, instead of giving an invitation, stepped down from the pulpit. As if contemplating the right words to speak, he took his hand and stroked his long mustache and finally said, "I know it is Easter Sunday and the Lord knows I have told His story to the best of my ability, but I have something more I want to talk to you about."

Surprised, people began to look around at each other wondering why he had ended his service in such an unusual way.

He continued, "I can see in your faces that you think I've probably lost my wits, but I've got something on my mind that I think the Lord won't mind me sharing with you. You all know what a perilous time we've all been through and every once in a while we get a glimpse of sunlight, better still, a magnificent rainbow after a storm."

He paused a moment and looked over to where John was sitting. "The other day when I was in Decatur, I heard that one of our own might be interested in throwing his hat into the political ring, might be running for the legislature. How 'bout it John? Anything to it?"

The congregation instantly applauded and one of the men in the back shouted out, "Let's hear from him, preacher."

The preacher motioned for John to come to the pulpit and after a nudge from his mother, John eased from his seat and made his way down the aisle to the platform.

Standing with his hands resting on each side of the pulpit, John thought for a moment and then began, "I'm not sure that this is the place to talk about politics, and I hope the Lord forgives me for using His time, but to get to the point, I have decided to run for office. As the preacher said, we are living in hard times and we all feel the oppression of a heavy yoke cast on our neck by a government bent on punishing us beyond what the constitution dictates. The war has ended, the issue of slavery has been settled, and it's time for this great country of ours to heal its wounds and return to the democracy that our forefathers had in mind when they sat there in Philadelphia. I believe there will be a time when the troops will be pulled out of the South and we once again will return to self-government. I see a time in Mississippi when we will once more prosper and will regain the status we held prior to the terrible conflict."

John paused for a moment and looked out into the congregation and the faces of friends and neighbors that he had known all of his life. He then humbly lowered his head and said, "I'm willing to do all I can to help you and all the people in Mississippi regain the freedom that has been ripped from our hands. I think you all know me and what I stand for, and as the Lord is my witness, I'll do my best."

For a moment the church was completely quiet and then, one by one, people began to stand in approval. Without hesitating, they came forward to clasp his hand and pressing around him, declared their support.

As John's parents saw the people crowd around him, a feeling of pride filled them and they felt that perhaps this was a sign from God as to what He intended to do with their son's life.

As the people finally dispersed to prepare for a lunch that would be spread outside, Suzanne eased down to where John was standing talking with Tim and held out her arms to him. Holding him tightly, she gave him a soft kiss on the cheek and said, "I'm so proud of you, John. You'll be in Jackson come this time next year."

Overcome by the reaction of the people and feeling a sense of warmth toward Suzanne that was unexplainable, he pulled her closer to him and whispered, "You know young lady, I might even carry you with me."

7

HAUNTING DREAMS

T̲HE GROUND BENEATH HIM SHOOK VIOLENTLY AND JOHN reached out to steady himself against the man next to him. The roar of cannon fire and the hiss of deadly missiles made speaking impossible. John struggled to get the attention of a nearby soldier but no words would form on his lips. Smoke boiled across the hillside in front of him engulfing all in its path. In the midst of turmoil a command was given, "Keep the ranks closed. If a man falls, stay tight and don't yell until we get close to 'em. Now move out, double quick!"

Men moved forward, rifles across their shoulders. Sun, filtering through breaks in the smoke, glistened off the fixed bayonets. Exploding shells crashed into the men as they moved forward, leaving large gaps in the line.

As hard as he tried, John could not keep up the pace. Smoke filled the air, burning his eyes and choking him. Visibility was limited to only a few feet. Straining to find the enemy, he tried to lift his legs but he was falling behind. Finally his muscles began to respond and he ran as fast as he could to the front line. A man turned and motioned for him to come close; it looked like his best friend Tim, but when he reached the line, the man vanished along with the other soldiers. Confusion overcame him.

As the smoke cleared, John could make out dismembered bodies strewn in grotesque positions. Most were lying on their backs with their eyes fixed toward the heavens as if God had collected their souls.

Across the field to his left, he saw men moving toward a clump of trees at the crest of the ridge. He recognized the stars and bars of the Confederacy. Once again, he saw Tim motioning to him. The sound of musketry became so loud it sent John to his knees. He threw his rifle aside and clamped his hands over his ears, but the roar continued. Fear engulfed him and sweat poured from his body as a violent pain shot through his head causing him to lose consciousness.

A strong wind out of the west rushed across the battlefield pushing the clouds of smoke away and John found himself standing alone. All around him lay the bodies of thousands of his comrades. There was no moaning from the wounded, no begging for mercy; they were dead. All was still and quiet; sound had simply evaporated from the earth.

Then he turned and saw one regimental flag fluttering in an unfelt breeze. John pried the staff from the fingers of the fallen soldier who had forced it into the soft ground and braced it next to his chest where it would not touch the ground.

John saw a field of stones forming a wall four feet high and the length of the hillside. Behind the wall were countless Union regimental flags and more soldiers than he had seen during the entire war. Grasping the flag, he stood at attention.

A Union officer standing on the wall called out, "Lay the flag down and come forward."

John looked around at his fallen comrades and heard the flag flap in the wind.

"Young man," the officer said, "The war is over. Put the flag down and come forward."

John slowly lowered the flag, returning it to the soldier who had carried it to his death. Gazing into the face caked with dirt, blood, and gunpowder, John recognized his friend. Tears streamed down his face and he again snapped to attention as he called out, "There will be no surrender here today, sir. I stand with the South."

The officer drew his sword and as thousands of Union soldiers crouching behind the wall stood with rifles in arms.

"Ready!"

John heard the hammers cock into position.

"Aim!"

Fear filled his inner soul.

"Fire!"

A gush of smoke rolled forward followed by a force so strong John's body fell backwards wrapped in the flag he had defended. He screamed, "No! Not like this! I will not die like this!"

Sarah, shocked by the scream from across the hall, nudged Lott and pushed the cover aside. She slipped on her house shoes and lit the lantern on the table beside her bed. As she made her way toward the door she said, "Lott, you'd better come with me. It's happening again."

Ignoring the early morning chill, she hurried across the open hall with Lott close behind. John was lying on his back with his covers pulled tightly around him. Sweat poured from his face and he shook violently. His eyes stared straight up at the ceiling and his breath was very rapid. Sarah gasped in fear.

Lott eased her aside. "Sarah he's done this before. Get a damp cloth and let me see what I can do."

Lott sat down on the bed beside him and gently pulled the covers from John's clinched hands. The bed was damp from perspiration and Lott could feel heat radiating from his body.

Soon Sarah returned with a damp, cool cloth and handed it to her husband. He wiped John's face and neck and then placed the folded cloth across his forehead.

In a few moments, John began to relax. Seconds later, he closed his eyes and his breathing returned to normal. Lott whispered, "It's all right, Son. Your mama and I are here with you. It's just a bad dream."

A trace of a smile crossed John's face and Lott could detect a slight nod of his head. Seeing the improvement, Sarah sighed in relief.

In the still of the night, Sarah broke the silence. "Lott what causes him to have spells like this? I don't understand it."

Lott thought for a few moments and answered, "Ain't nothing wrong with him physically. Something happened to him when he was in the war. Something terrible is causing him to have these nightmares. I've read that dreams are a way we face problems or fears that we can't deal with when we're awake."

As the early morning light filtered through the bedroom, John rolled over on his side and muttered, "My head is killing me. Please close the curtains. I can't stand the light."

Sarah closed the curtains and returned to his bed. " John, can you tell us what is happening to you? Can you share it with us?"

John passed his tongue over his dry parched lips, then replied, "Mama, I can't remember what happened."

A splitting pain shot through his head causing him to flinch. "My head feels like it's coming apart. If I could just sleep."

Lott eased from the bed and made his way to the kitchen. In a few moments he returned with a glass of yellowish liquid, and placing John's pillow under his neck to elevate his head, he put the glass in John's hand. "Drink it down, Son. It'll make you rest."

"Lott, why liquor?" Sarah said. "You know how I feel about it."

Lott helped him hold the glass and John slowly sipped the drink of whiskey mixed with honey. It wasn't long before he relaxed and fell asleep. Sarah and Lott then quietly left his room.

John slept throughout the day. As the sun was setting, casting long shadows across the barren front yard, the hounds alerted the family that riders were approaching. Tim and their son-in-law, James, were riding up and before Lott and Sarah could make their way to the front porch, the men had already tied their mounts and were walking down the hall toward them. James was dressed in his normal Union officer's uniform and Tim wore a dark gray homespun suit, not of the usual quality that he prided himself.

Seeing the couple, both men stopped and removed their hats. After handshakes had been made, James said, "John got in from work yet?"

Lott shook his head and pointed down the hall. "He had another bad night."

"One of those dreams?" Tim asked, shifting his weight off his good leg to the other.

Sarah nodded. "It seems to happen every so often."

Recognizing the voices, John called out, "You can come on in."

James and Tim pushed the door open and, in the dark bedroom, found John lying with a pillow rolled up under his neck, his eyes partly open. A damp cloth still covered his forehead. "You two sure do make an odd couple," he murmured.

The men chuckled and pulled two chairs up to the bed.

"You feel like talking," James asked, reaching over to adjust the cloth that had slipped down over one of John's eyes.

John reached up and removed the cloth. "I feel better now. Couldn't sleep last night."

"One of those damned ole nightmares," Tim said.

"I don't really know what I had," John replied.

Tim thought for a minute. "I can solve your problem. No doubt you got something on yore mind that's kickin' up yore dander and all we got to do is to substitute something good fer something bad."

James looked puzzled by Tim's reasoning. "Tim, what are you suggesting?"

Tim leaned back in his chair. "All John has got to do is to replace them bad dreams with dreams of women, naked women. Everywhere he looks in them dreams, he's gonna see 'em. They gonna be up in the barn swinging from the rafters, hanging from the tree limbs, running down the road and even plowing out in them fields. They gonna be everywhere, butt naked."

The men broke into such a howl of laughter, that Lott and Sarah came to check on John.

"That boy ain't feeling good. What do y'all mean by all that racket?" Lott said, with a stern expression on his face.

"Didn't mean to cause no ruckus," Tim said. "It's just ole Tim Johnson cuttin' the fool."

"Papa, I'm feeling better now," John said. " I think I needed that laugh."

But in the back of his mind all this talk about dreams bothered him. He didn't remember any dreams at all. He only knew that he had walked near death, a death that left a violent headache, severe cramps and a total weakness that came only with these difficult nights.

The men sat for a while sharing daily encounters and joking with each other. The conversation finally turned to politics.

James, lighting his pipe and blowing a large ring of smoke into the air, said, "John, you know you got the folks in the district excited about you running for office. I don't know a Democrat or Republican that can stand up to you and, in my business, I cover a lot of ground, and I'll tell you right now, you're one popular candidate. You're gonna take it. You're going to Jackson come next spring."

John was doing well in the eyes of the voters. Even in the bordering counties of the district, he was receiving nothing but positive support. His platform was simple: to get this district on its feet, taxes would be lowered, the extravagant and wasteful spending by the present administration would be stopped, low interest loans for struggling farmers would be made available and, most importantly, all state political positions would be filled by Mississippians, not outsiders. Not only were his ideas refreshing to the people longing for relief from a punishing reconstruction government, but he also found favor in the eyes of the Negroes in the district. They knew the reputation of the Wilsons and how in the past, they had befriended both them and the Choctaw Indians. They felt John would also stand up for them as they entered a new era of political freedom.

Even the republicans in the district felt that from what they could hear, this election was all but over for them; this district was going democrat.

§§

The door slammed open and with squeals of delight, children scampered out and down the steps of the church that served as a school for the community. The last day of school meant summer vacation had arrived and the youngsters lost no time in vacating the premises. In a matter of minutes, not a child could be seen.

Lucretia, chalk dust on her hands and smudges of ink streaked across her face, stood in the doorway, hands on hips, watching. They were all out of sight but she could still hear their shrieks of joy. In a sense, she was sad to see the school year end and she would miss every one of her students, but she also felt relief from the responsibility and long hours spent preparing for her first year as a teacher. She felt she had performed well and from comments made to her from her students and parents, she was encouraged.

Rethinking memorable events of the year, Lucretia didn't notice the buggy pulling up beside the building.

"You glad it's over?" a voice called out.

Turning quickly, she saw Robert sitting in the buggy dressed in his usual black suit, cleanly shaved and as neat as a button. His medical bag rested on the seat beside him.

"How long have you been here?" Lucretia asked, carefully walking down the steps.

Robert motioned for her to join him and holding out his hand to steady her, he answered, "Long enough to see those brats leaving like a wild herd of buffalo."

"I'll have you know, those are the sweetest children I've ever known," Lucretia replied.

"Well, I've heard your complaints of how bad those children were at times. You remember when the Wilkes boy put pine rosin in Cindy Taylor's hair. You assured me that one day he just might end up in jail. You remember that?"

Lucretia laughed. "Robert, you've been my sounding board this year. I really appreciate your letting me share my problems with you. But every job has its Jimmy Wilkes and when I think back over this year, the pleasant memories I've experienced make me forget the difficult times. Yes sir, I love every one of those children, even Jimmy."

Robert reached over and placed his hand on Lucretia's. "Enough talk about school. Your father is sending me out to the Lambough place. Appears the old man has up and cut himself and needs a little needle work. Since it's a pretty day and school is out, I thought you might like to ride out with me."

After about an hour, they found that Mister Lambough had cut himself while trying to sharpen his ax. In a matter of a few minutes, Robert had him neatly stitched. Mister Lambough thanked Robert and informed him he would pay Dr. Caulder as soon as he could market some of his hogs.

As Robert and Lucretia made their way down the dusty, beaten road, Lucretia said, "Watching you work was really impressive. Your hands are so steady. You know, Papa sure does think you're going to be a fine doctor."

Robert brought back his whip and with a crack that startled her, replied, "I'm not like your father. I'm going to the city to do my work. I couldn't make a living out here like him."

"What do you mean by not making a living out here?"

"What I'm saying is that Dr. Caulder will never see a penny from the work I just did and there are too many cases just like that. You know that's a fact."

Pushing her hair out of her face, Lucretia knew he was right. Times were hard in rural Pennsylvania and often people paid with what they had. Sometimes it might be a sack of freshly ground corn and another time it might be a cured ham, but usually compensation of some kind was made. With a smile on her face she said, "That's why I love him so much. He gives with no guarantee of return."

Robert suddenly reined his horse off the road and carefully eased the buggy through a grassy field that bordered a slow moving stream. Pulling up under a large oak, he suggested they take a walk. The sun was just beginning to set and a pleasant breeze rustled the leaves in the trees above. Walking hand in hand they followed the creek and found a couple of large rocks to serve as seats.

She has the purist beauty of any woman I've ever met, Robert thought as he gazed into Lucretia's emerald green eyes. She deserves a better place than this. She belongs with me.

Lucretia took a small twig and flipped it out into the water and it was soon lost in the current. Looking up, she noticed the strange look on Robert's face. "Did I do something wrong?" she asked.

Robert moved closer, placed his arm around her and gently pulled her to him. He first kissed her softly on the cheek and then their lips touched. It wasn't the first time he had kissed her, but it was one of passion. In a moment, Robert eased back and taking her by the hands said, "You do know how I feel about you and you know I'll be leaving at the end of the summer."

Lucretia knew that he cared for her and she was sure that he had already talked to her mother and father about their future together, but she wasn't ready for his proposal.

Robert kissed her again and whispered, "I want to marry you. I want you to go back east with me."

Lucretia didn't know what to say. She had learned to love him as her mother had predicted, but there was something, something she couldn't explain, that kept her silent.

"Robert, marriage is serious. I think I need a little time."

Robert reached into his coat pocket and unwrapping a handkerchief, brought out a small gold ring and placed it on her finger. "You take your time. This ring was my grandmother's. I want you to wear it."

ॐ

Tim, needing to see a man in Little Rock before dark who owed him some money, excused himself while John and James wanting some fresh air, ventured out to the front porch where they settled in a swing. It was dusk and there was a gentle breeze. The screeching sounds of tree locusts filled the evening.

"Peaceful country, isn't it?" James said, lighting his pipe.

John took a large swallow of water from a glass his mother had brought him and after placing it on the floor answered, "All these rolling hills, with tall stately trees and fields full of plush grass and wildflowers. It just has to be God's own paradise."

The two sat quietly for a while as the light slowly slipped away and the coolness of the evening came. James, a northerner and an officer in the United States Army, was John's brother-in-law. They were different in many ways, but the two had developed a mutual respect for each other, a respect that had gradually become a friendship.

Easing up from the swing, James said, "I need to be getting on home before your sister comes looking for me. You know how she is when night comes. Everybody is supposed to be home."

"How well I know it, James. I'm just glad it's you going home to her and not me," John teased.

James chuckled and in the dark, made his way down the steps to the hitching post where his horse was tied. After mounting, he said, "John, this election has got me a little worried. There are some things happening that could result in some serious action being taken against some folks."

John got out of the swing. "What are you talking about? I ain't heard of nothing."

James shifted in the saddle which caused a moaning sound of leather rubbing together.

"You ever heard of the Pale Faces or the Sons of Midnight?"

"Never heard of 'em. Why?"

"How about the Knights of the White Camelia?"

"Ain't heard of them neither," John said.

"Then how about the Ku Klux Klan?"

John was silent for a moment and then stammered, "I've heard of the Klan. What about 'em?"

"From my information, it's a group led by General Nathan Forrest that will go to any means to get what it wants and that does include murder. From what I hear this group plans to take control of politics here in the South by placing its handpicked men in office."

James, hoping that John was not involved with the Klan, carefully chose his words. "John, as I said earlier, I feel you can win this election but for God's sake, do it without any outside support. You are above what they intend to do."

After James had left, John returned to the swing and thought about what James had said. He recalled the meeting down at Hickory and how Forrest had called for Mississippians to band together in order to place their own people, Mississippians, in office. He also knew how corrupt the government in Jackson was and how the present laws were crushing the people as they tried to overcome the post war conditions. John remembered the group assembled there. They were his neighbors, men with whom he had suffered and fought, and, most importantly, many were his friends.

In the darkness, for the first time since James had become a part of the family, John questioned James' motives. In John's mind, Mississippi came first and as Forrest had stated, "It's time for us to take our state back." In a sense, this was going to be a political war. The outcome will be freedom.

Later that night, he recalled every statement made at the Hickory meeting and he thought of how Mississippians were being treated, especially those who had lost their farms. He knew that sooner or later, he would have to make a stand and when he did, he hoped that it would be in the best interest of all Southerners.

8

THE POLITICAL RALLY

NOT ONLY WAS THE SUMMER OF 1869 HOT AND HUMID LIKE most summers in the South, but the political arena in the post war southern states had become a boiling cauldron of excitement and fury. Those seeking office and their supporters found that "if they couldn't take the heat they had better get out of the fire." The southern plan was stewing and its aroma was evident to all. This plan included carefully selecting candidates to unseat the Republicans put in control by the reconstruction government. With a strong voter registration for those whites who were eligible to vote and with a little help from the so called Organization, things were moving on schedule. Come fall, Mississippi would be in Mississippian's hands.

When James had asked John about his knowledge of the Klan, John was only aware of what he had heard at the Hickory meeting and had little further knowledge of the group and its agenda. John supposed that the Klan was a flare of emotions of protest against a government that had been suppressing the people, but what John failed to realize was that the Klan was much more than a spark of emotion, that it was indeed a live fire that grew stronger each day. It was sweeping across the South like a scorching wave racing down a mountainside devouring all that was in its way.

James' questions about his possible involvement with the clan bothered John, especially when James made it clear that the Klan was a definite threat to the United States government and its citizens. John only knew that he was gaining support everywhere he went and that people appeared to approve of what he felt should be done.

§

June, 1869, Meridian, Mississippi

Tobacco smoke circled the group of men who waited for the dinner being prepared in the hotel kitchen below. As they talked with one another, a sense of confidence was obvious. Soon the door of the room opened and several Negro men carrying trays entered. As the plates were placed on tables, the men took their seats and began unrolling their napkins. Some placed the cloths in their laps while others tucked it in their shirt collars.

One man remained standing and after a short invocation, said, "I hope y'all like steak and sweet 'tators. You got a half a steer looking at ya."

The men laughed in agreement as they stared at their plates. The steaks hung over the sides of the plates, almost touching the table. The potatoes had to be placed on a smaller plate. A large roll of freshly baked bread was in the center of each table along with butter and cane syrup. One of the Negro men remained in the room, moving from person to person pouring steaming coffee.

When the meal was finished, Daniel McWorthan of Meridian rose to address the men. They represented the power structure of the tenth district which included a cluster of counties in east central Mississippi. This was the same group that had met earlier in the year to begin formulating a plan to place white democrats in office and to force non-Mississippians out. Among the fifteen there were Professor Hendon, Frank Olliver and one newcomer, Herschel Pierce.

McWorthan raised his glass and proposed a toast. "Gentlemen, to the new South."

"To the new South," they replied.

McWorthan glanced over to the door. "Jake, if you don't mind, would you stand watch outside the door. I don't want anyone interrupting us and you can go ahead and take your drink with you."

Jake nodded and left the room.

McWorthan then continued. "Men we're here to evaluate our progress and to see where we need to go from this point. The last time we met, we were talking about picking candidates to represent our party and what I want to know now is which one of those discussed earlier has what it takes to win."

A burly, bearded man in the back raised his hand.

"Okay, Baker, what you got up there in Kemper County?" McWorthan asked.

Baker rose to his feet. "We got a fellow named Sank Laster who has really got folks talking up there in Dekalb, and I must say he has done his work with the organization, if'n you know what I mean. When it comes to voter registration, them Negroes won't go near that courthouse, that is, those that's got good sense."

Laughter filled the room as Baker took his seat.

Another hand was in the air and McWorthan acknowledged Rosco Barrett from Clarke County.

Barrett remained seated and said, "Men, Jacob Thompson, a young lawyer down in our county has got some good ideas about where we need to go and being a good church man with a family, people sure have a tendency to like him. I think we need to give him some serious thought."

The group was quiet for a moment waiting for another announcement from one of its members when suddenly Professor Hendon raised his hand.

"Thought it was about time you said something, Hendon," McWorthan said. "We all know you got a hot 'tator on your hands there in Newton County. Everywhere I go, I hear about him. Care to share it with us?"

Hendon pushed his chair back, brushed some crumbs off the front of his jacket and stood. For a moment, his eyes moved from table to table gazing at the men awaiting his comments and finally he said, "Gentlemen, we've got a man in Newton County that will carry the election for us even if it were held tomorrow. As I told you earlier, he's smart, he's literate, he's a loyal southerner and he's a natural vote getter. Everywhere he's spoken, people flock to hear him. John Wilson can carry this district. I know he's our man."

The men followed every word Hendon said and nodded their heads in support.

Frank sat quietly peering down at the glass in his hand gently, swirling the whiskey around. In his mind, he knew John had the makings of a politician but he also knew that John didn't know the meaning of compromise. Frank also knew that John was ignorant of what this group would do to place its man in office, and John was too honest to accept the terms this organization would force upon him.

McWorthan once again addressed the men, "Well, we've said some good things about these men but on the other hand, what do you see in them that might cause a problem?"

A man blurted out, "I heard the gov'ment is on to Laster. I heard they's watching him like a hawk on a rat. I think you gonna see more of them Darkies show up at them polls up there in Kemper County than you can shake a stick at come election. They're sending more troops in there than I've seen in months. I'm not sure you can count on him being around for long. The way I see it, it's gonna get hot for them in Kemper."

"How about your man in Clarke? He got anything that's gonna hurt him?" questioned McWorthan.

"As I said, Thompson is a good man and I think he'll do what we tell him to do. Get him elected and we can run the show in this here district," replied the representative from Clarke County.

"How about Wilson, Hendon? Everywhere I go I hear his name spoken. Sounds like he can walk on water," McWorthan said. "How about it, Hendon?"

Hendon once again stood up. "I know him like the back of my hand. You can't beat him. As you said, everywhere you go you hear about him. I rest my case."

Everyone clapped in support of John, everyone except Frank. He sat there silently staring into his near empty glass, thinking back to a time when he would have been the first to stand in support of John Wilson.

Noticing this, Pierce called out, "What you got on your mind Mister Olliver?"

Frank looked over to Hendon and after a moment of thought said, "He might just be too good for us."

"Too good for us!" Pierce exclaimed. "What do you mean by that?"

"If elected, John may listen to us, but he's gonna speak his mind and vote his own convictions. I think he's too independent for us," Frank said. "I also think he's got too much support from the Negroes."

"Vote his convictions and Negro support! What you got to say about that, Hendon?" Pierce asked.

Angered by what Frank had said, Hendon rose to his feet. "Everything Frank said is true. John is a strong individual who has his convictions about how things should be done but his heart is with the South."

Glaring at Frank, he continued, "He stood there in the firing line placing his life at stake, more than I could say about some of you, and as far as the Negroes, I only know of one that he has helped register and I'll bet my life that come election time that Negro will vote for Wilson."

The group grew quiet as Hendon continued, "Men, what I'm getting at is the man can take the White and Negro vote in our district and that won't leave anybody else to vote against us."

For a short while the men then discussed state politics amongst themselves. Then McWorthan addressed the group. "Men, as I sat here thinking, my mind kinda got to wondering and I've got an idea to throw at you. We got some good candidates and before long folks got to decide which one of them they gonna get behind. Well, I say since Meridian is the so called social center of this here district and since I'd like to hear these here candidates do some talking, I say let's throw us a little political debate, a Democratic rally. We'll have us a big ole hog barbeque with stew galore and more beer and whiskey than Miss'sippi has seen in a month of Sundays."

At that, one of the men said, "Well, if them speakers drink as much as I have, they gonna make as much sense as them hogs we're gonna roast."

The men laughed.

Raising his hand, McWorthan continued. "Listen to me. We'll get the word out about this here shindig we gonna have and y'all know ain't nothing hotter right now on folk's mind than the hope of placing one of our own in office. I say, there's gonna be one hell of a crowd of folks here for the outing. They gonna come out of them hills and hollows like ants after syrup."

The men clapped in response to his proposal and Pierce muttered, "Free food and liquor will shore bring a crowd, and I also want to hear for myself what them politicians got to say for themselves. Especially 'bout Wilson and his Negro voters."

Plans were now in the process for the biggest cookout that this part of the state had ever experienced. Local farmers were contacted about donating hogs for the barbecue and the town's tavern keepers agreed to furnish the spirits. They knew that on an occasion such as this, people would arrive early and would have money to spend. They would simply raise the price of liquor during the rally at their own taverns and when it was all over, a nice profit would be realized. Since people normally felt a sense of patriotism for the Fourth of July, McWorthan decided to schedule the rally for that date and invitations were sent out to the candidates.

It was no surprise that word spread fast and as McWorthan predicted, people began to feel hope that a Democratic victory was possible.

〆

In the light of early dawn, John pulled up his suspenders and strolled out on the front porch. Even though June is usually a hot month in the South, the morning was cool and refreshing. Across the way roosters could be heard crowing their last calls of night, and the flapping of wings caught John's attention as the chickens began to fly down from their roost in the chinaberry tree growing out behind their outhouse. Stretching, John pulled his arms back over his head and took in as much air as his lungs could hold. Then from down at the other end of the porch, John heard a creaking sound that startled him for a moment.

"Gonna be a fine day, ain't it, Son?" his mother said.

Making his way to where she was sitting, John pulled up a chair and settled himself beside her.

"You been up long?" John asked.

"Long enough to read about half the book of Luke," she replied.

Being the daughter of a Methodist preacher and a devout Christian, she believed that one should start each day with Bible study and prayer. Those few moments before her family was up and stirring, were her special time with God. The rest of the day was spent satisfying the demands of the family.

John reached over to where his mother was holding her Bible in her lap and placed his hand over hers. "You know you're really sump'n, don't ya," John said, placing his other arm around her shoulders.

"Why'd you say that, Son?"

Nestling closer, he continued. "You always place our needs over yours to the point that you have to get up 'fore daybreak to find a little time for yourself."

Sarah smiled up at John. "It takes us all working together to make this farm go and only God knows how many hot tiring hours you and yore daddy spend out there in them fields. I've seen y'all so tired come quitting time you could hardly make it to the house. No sir, John Wilson, don't you go feeling sorry for me. As for me on this porch, I just figure this is the best time of the day to spend with my Savior."

John nodded in agreement and said, "One of these days I'm gonna sure 'nough take care of you two where you won't have to work so hard."

"I wanted you to go to college up at Oxford and keep on with your schooling, but that didn't work out."

"That was just a dream, Mama. There's other ways I can still make sump'n out of myself."

"You're already somebody, Son. You're a Wilson and a fine Christian man. Don't you go belittling yoreself."

"I know Mama, but I feel like there's more out there for me than on this farm."

"Don't you go knocking the farm. It's the way most folks 'round here make a living. It's that politickin' that's got yore dander up, and strange things happen when folks go to voting. I wouldn't depend on too much too soon, Son."

Finding it hard to get to her feet, Sarah took hold of John's arm. "Here, help me up out of this here chair. I hear yore daddy up and stirring. He'll want his breakfast soon."

Seeing her struggle to get on her feet bothered John. During the last few months, there had been too many times when John had noticed his mother needing help getting up. And she lacked the energy she once had. Old age must be courting with her, he thought. She's might near sixty-two years old, he reasoned.

With his Mother hanging on his arm, the two eased down the hall toward the kitchen. Before John opened the door, he said, "I'll tell you one thing, Mama. Everywhere I go, folks like what I have to say and most of 'em promise to vote for me. That's even in the counties outside of Newton. Your good Lord might just be getting me ready."

"That'll be left up to Him. Won't be no worry of mine. You need to do some praying 'bout it, that is if'n you hadn't."

In the weeks preceding the rally, Professor Hendon came almost daily to talk with John about what John was going to say and how he should present himself to the public. He wanted John to use correct grammar to show that he was educated but not to the extent of offending the average citizen. Hendon had studied speech while in college and had become versed in the art of addressing people. When working with John, he realized that the

young man was a natural orator. He also knew that John was committed to his beliefs and sometimes that worried him.

⅜

Suzanne lost no time preparing for her trip to Meridian. Without John's knowledge, she planned to have both her family and his leave several days prior to the rally by rail from Newton. Upon arrival, there would be a brass band and throngs of people there to welcome him to the city. During those days, she was planning meetings with people she and Mister Hendon considered the most influential in the district. There was no doubt in her mind that when they left Meridian, John would stand head and shoulders above the other candidates. The upcoming election would only be a formality.

On the Sunday before the rally John and his family, as usual, attended church services at the Little Rock Baptist Church. John met Suzanne and her mother outside the church and escorted them to the Wilson family pew. Suzanne was dressed in a long white dress with a full hoopskirt that touched the pews on both sides. Her clothing was the envy of every woman in the community, and she was overdressed for Little Rock.

During the service, John never moved a muscle as he took in every word that the minister spoke and often nodded in agreement.

As the meeting was ending, Suzanne reached over and took John by the hand, and whispered. "I've got a little surprise for you after the service."

As they left, they were greeted by many friends and neighbors pledging John their support come November. At the door, the preacher said, "It makes me proud to know that we've got a God fearing man running for office, and I want you to know that we all have you in our prayers."

John thanked him and edging their way down the steep steps, John noticed Tim under a large oak tree where several buggies were tied. Entertaining, as always, Tim had several young women with him.

Seeing John, Tim asked to be excused and hurried over. Tim couldn't take his eyes off Suzanne. Pretending to remove a hat, Tim swooped his arm forward and executed a bow. "My Lady, your beauty is more than an humble peasant such as I can stand." Reaching over, he took her hand and gently kissed it.

Suzanne laughed as John, amused by Tim's behavior, pushed his hand away. "Tim, you're about as full of foolishment as a person can be. I was kind of surprised to see you darken the church doors this morning, 'specially since I have a notion where you spent last night."

Tim laughed and suggested they move into the shade. "A man that sins as much as I do better go to church. He'll be hell bound if'n he don't."

Because of his crudeness and poor family background, Suzanne never really cared for Tim, but because he was John's friend, she tolerated him, especially since he could be amusing at times.

"Tim, you better enjoy your heaven on earth 'cause I have a feeling that your church going is not gonna help you a tinker's damn," Suzanne said.

Tim smiled as one of the women who had been waiting for him called out, "Timothy, we still have things to discuss."

"Suzanne, my Fair Lady, duty calls."

She's kind of young, ain't she," John said as Tim walked away.

"The younger, the better," he replied. "Plus some of the older women got better sense than to go out with me, 'specially the married ones."

"Tim, this is Sunday," Suzanne said.

"Right and I just went to church, didn't I, Young Lady. The cycle goes 'round and 'round. I'm starting anew."

As they reached the buggy where Suzanne's mother was waiting, Suzanne pulled a neatly wrapped package from under the seat and handed it to John. "This is just a little early Christmas present that we thought might come in handy."

Feeling somewhat embarrassed, John stared at the box wrapped in shiny red paper and tied with a silver ribbon. "I don't know what to say," he stammered.

"Open it up and see what you think," Suzanne said. " This is just a little something we'd like to do for you," Mrs. Olliver said. "It's a small way we can thank you for all that you have meant to our family through the years."

To John's surprise, he found a folded gray woolen suit, a new cotton shirt and a solid black silk tie. Looking up, he sighed, "This is just too much. I really can't accept this."

Suzanne placed her hand over his and said, " I had it especially made for you. Your mother even helped me with the sizing. It might just come in handy when you go to Meridian.

Admiring the texture of the material and feeling the smoothness of the weave, John said, "This didn't come from around here."

Mrs. Olliver smiled. "We had it made for you down in New Orleans. The tailor's been doing work for my family for years. The material came from Italy."

On the way home, Suzanne smiled with pride as she imagined John standing in front of all those people and her by his side. They would be the finest looking couple in the state.

§§

July the second soon arrived and John, his mother and father, Suzanne, Frank, and Mrs. Olliver all boarded the train at Newton. Sister, James, Professor Hendon and Tim would leave together the following morning after James took care of some government business.

Within an hour the group arrived in Meridian and as they stepped off the train, a brass band playing Dixie and an enthusiastic crowd shouting "Wilson! Wilson!" filled the air. As John and his family headed to the hotel that would be their home for the next few days, they noticed not only the busy street but also a city dressed for this special occasion. Each lamp post was wrapped in red, white and blue paper and on the windows of the stores, political slogans were printed. Everywhere John looked, he saw his name in large letters, but not one sign for the other candidates.

Nudging John as they neared their hotel, Suzanne exclaimed, "John, the city's yours, and so is the tenth district."

John, speechless, stood in awe as throngs of people crowded around him.

That evening the Ollivers had a large dining room reserved in the hotel, and over a hundred guests were invited to dine. The most prominent people in east central Mississippi were present. John and his family along with the Ollivers were placed at the head table, and after the meal, Mister McWorthan tapped on his glass to get everyone's attention.

"Ladies, Gentlemen, Democrats, I'm sure y'all enjoyed this here meal tonight and I know we're looking forward to a couple of days of some mighty fine politickin' and some of the best eating in this here state of Miss'sippi."

The crowd roared in applause and many stood and began shouting, "Democrats! Democrats! Democrats!"

Settling them down, McWorthan continued, "I know you've heard a lot about the man here with us tonight and without further-a-do, I introduce to you the next representative of the tenth district, Mister John Wilson."

The group once again shook the windows with their applause as John rose and made his way to the speaker's podium.

Suzanne noticed how strikingly handsome John was in his new gray suit. His beard was neatly trimmed and his thick black hair was combed back showing a trace of gray across his temples, which made him appear older than he was. Even though the suit was tailored to fit, his broad shoulders and muscular build were evident.

As John stood facing the group, a feeling of confidence came over him and as he relaxed, he began choosing his words carefully, "Ladies and Gentlemen, I first want to thank Mister McWorthan and the Ollivers for arranging this dinner tonight, and I thank you all for coming out in my support. You know, I'll be running against other candidates."

Before continuing, he pointed over to his right and said, "I'd like for y'all to meet my mother and father. Daddy was one of the first white men to set foot in this area, and Mother has always been the driving force in my life."

His parents stood as the group warmly welcomed them.

John then continued, "As you well know, Mississippi has seen some hard times and still has some major problems to overcome, but I feel that it won't be long before we'll be out from under this military rule and our destiny will be in our own hands."

Interrupting his speech, the people applauded and began to stomp their feet, shaking the floor.

"Thank you," John said, raising his hands to quieten his audience.

"Our task may be difficult, but our goal will be reached. And that goal is to rid our state of corrupt politicians, to lower our operating expenses and certainly to lower our taxes. Mississippi needs relief! If elected, I promise you that I will give every ounce of strength in my body to help clean up our fine state and return it to the days that we once knew. The military may be here today, but if we do our jobs at the polls, our laws under the Constitution will have to prevail and we will not remain a conquered province. We will be free!"

As the group vigorously applauded, McWorthan rose and walked over to John, placed his arm around his shoulder and exclaimed, "Ain't he sump'n, folks! I been telling you we got a dandy on our hands."

At that, the men left their seats and rushed forward to shake hands with John and give him their support.

Backing out of the crowd, McWorthan nudged Sam Dickens, a prominent Democrat from Jackson and said, "You ever seen anyone take hold of a crowd like this here boy's just done?"

"I'm might near sixty five and I've never seen nothing like this. Wilson's got 'em in the palm of his hand. I'm gonna keep my eye on this young man," he replied.

Suzanne pushed her way through the crowd and finally reached John's side where she stood, proudly taking in every compliment given to him.

Meanwhile, the ladies gathered in the back of the dining room and patiently waited for their husbands.

"They make a mighty fine looking couple," one of the women said.

Another one answered, "Couple, my eye, that's one handsome young man. If I could vote, I'd vote him right into my parlor."

All this time, Frank, not interested in the night's activity sat quietly playing the part of a supportive friend. He clapped when necessary and was among the first to give John his hand, but he was not interested in Mississippi politics and cared little for John's quest for election. He had more money than he could ever spend and if his sister wanted John to sire her offspring, that was her affair. She could shape him into anything she wanted. A seat in the legislature would get them to Jackson, the political center of the state.

Working his way to where his mother was standing, he said, "Things are going fine here, I'm gonna slip out now. I'll see y'all in the morning."

Mrs. Olliver caught him by the arm. "You can't leave now. It's impolite. Someone might notice."

Frank pulled away. "John made his point tonight. He don't need me around. Olliver money just bought him the city of Meridian and the election. It's what y'all wanted, weren't it?"

Walking away he mumbled, "Personally, I think it's a big waste."

As expected, people had flocked to Meridian from all parts of the district. The hotels were full, and since most people had traveled by buggies and wagons, camps were pitched outside Meridian in an open wooded area that had an excellent spring for watering. People slept in makeshift tents and out in the open on bedrolls and some even slept under their wagons. Most had brought their own food for the occasion and campfires brightened the dark night.

Inside the city, things weren't so peaceful. The streets were packed with people shopping and socializing. The merchants were thrilled over sales and their inflated prices did not seem to bother anyone. The excitement of the rally had caused a buying frenzy.

As the evening wore on, men lined the street and respectful women were nowhere to be seen. Liquor flowed freely in the saloons, and the gaming tables were full as people chanced their fortune. As it got later and later, drunks began staggering out into the streets and fights erupted. Loud shouting, cursing and an occasional gunshot filled the night air.

In the red light district, women in revealing dresses stood in their doorways beckoning anyone and everyone into their quarters. Many made their way into the bedrooms only to be beaten and robbed.

Military men were on every corner and were well prepared to keep order. A full company of infantry had been assigned to the city and was given orders to use their rifles if necessary to maintain order.

After the soldiers had arrested a large number of unruly men and it seemed that the city was almost out of control, a thunderstorm rolled in, sending heavy sheets of rain and torrents of water rushing through the streets. People scurried for cover and the town settled down.

9

A REVELATION

THE CURTAINS WHIPPED BACK AND FORTH AS RAIN POURED through the partially open window. Lightning flashed, thunder shook the windowpanes in the room where John was sleeping soundly, and a light mist dampened the cover John had pulled up around him. In his unconscious state, the sounds outside were not ones created by a thunderstorm; they were from a fallen angel from hell calling out to him.

A shell bursting over to his left sent branches and fragments sailing in all directions. Soldiers were crushed under a large fallen limb. One man's legs quivered for a moment and then all was still. Suddenly another shell exploded so loudly that for a moment there were only ringing sounds. John saw other soldiers lying face down, seeking protection and heard a voice echo, "Company, form ranks! It's time!" Then down the line somewhere in the distance another voice called out, "Sons of Virginia!" Men scurried to their feet, seized their muskets and fell into ranks.

As far as John could see were men dressed in gray and butternut, bayonets now glistening in the sun and rifles in a ready position. The order was made to advance and the puffs of smoke from a hillside across the way signaled that death was descending upon them. Then an exploding shell sent men and patches of earth in all directions. The devil's party had begun.

In the distance there was a persistent knock on the door. Rising on one elbow and shaking his head to clear his mind, John was confused. A voice yelled, "Let me in!"

He glanced about in the darkness.

"John Wilson, open up!"

Recognizing the voice, John hurried to unlock the door and found a collapsed figure outside.

Soaking wet, Tim looked up with glassy eyes. "'Bout time. Get me inside."

John reached down and pulled him to his feet. Reeking of tobacco, alcohol and cheap perfume, there was no doubt how Tim had spent the evening. John gently eased him down on the side of the bed, removed his wet clothes and covered him with a spread.

Light began to fill the room. Still trying to clear his mind, John quietly sat on the end of the bed.

Tim muttered, "Get the money bag outta my pocket. Made a killin' last night. Didn't do no whoring neither."

John fumbled around in Tim's coat pocket and brought out a bulging leather bag filled with coins. Holding it firmly in his hand, he sat down in a chair by the window and slung his feet up on the windowsill. All was quiet outside. John looked out on the empty streets below, then over at Tim. Although many might see a moral and social outcast, to John's eyes Tim was a special childhood friend with whom he had shared dreams and had stood shoulder to shoulder in battle not knowing what the next moment would bring. John saw a man he would risk his life for and one who would give his life for him. He couldn't ask for a finer friend.

John thought back on the dream Tim had interrupted and suddenly realized that this was the same dream that had been haunting him. In the past, he could never remember his dream and only felt the depression it left, but now it was as clear as the morning light streaking across the room. For the first time, he recalled every dream. Elated, John hurried over and shook Tim. "Wake up! Got to tell you sump'n."

Tim eased one eye open, smiled and murmured, "You gonna make some woman a fine wife."

John laughed quietly. "Go back to sleep, Tim. We can talk later."

John then washed himself, combed his hair and put on a clean shirt. Making his way downstairs to the hotel dining room, he found his parents having breakfast.

"Have a good night, Son?" his father asked as John approached.

John bent over and kissed his mother on the cheek and taking a seat, motioned for a waiter. "Papa, I had a great night."

"Storm really blew through here last night. I bet it's gonna be a fine day. You ready for it, Son?" his mother asked.

Spooning some sugar in his coffee, he answered, "Ready as I'll ever be."

Lott blew across his steaming coffee and looking over at John. "You'll do just fine. Just speak your heart and always be truthful."

Lott could see a lot of himself in John. His son was striving to find himself in a world shaped by other men, just as Lott had done when he first came to Mississippi. Lott also saw a young man seeking independence and preparing to face the pressures of the challenge, a man willing to give his all to help others.

Later that morning, Sister and James joined John who along with Suzanne and her mother had settled themselves in the hotel parlor to relax before the day's events began. Friends and strangers alike dropped by to wish John their best and to offer advise.

Around noon, people began streaming through the streets toward the western edge of town where the speeches would be given. Some were in buggies or on horseback, but most were on foot. Suzanne asked John and his family to join them in a carriage Frank had rented, but John declined, saying that he was nervous and a little exercise would be helpful. John's family also chose to walk even though Lott often grew tired because of back pains. Along the way John talked with some of the people; most didn't know he was one of the candidates.

As they approached the open field dotted with large oak trees, the smell of barbecue filled the air and the murmuring sounds of hundreds of people milling about made hearing difficult. Posted around the edge of the property was a full company of Federal troops with rifles at rest position. The way they laughed and talked with the people indicated that they expected no trouble.

At the northern end of the field, a large platform had been constructed and a podium along with several chairs were placed in order. Across the way several tents had been erected where barbecue and stew were being served, and under the shade of a tree next to the tents were kegs of beer. Long lines of people were waiting to be served. This was going to be a day east Mississippi would never forget.

Wiping sweat from his brow, John arrived with his coat slung over his shoulder and boots muddied. Never had he seen so many people gathered for a political meeting. At that moment, Suzanne rushed over. "Just look at you. You look like you been feedin' hogs. I even see some smudges on your pants legs."

Not waiting for a reply, she motioned for their Negro driver who they had brought from their farm to assist them in their needs. "Burt, get something and see if you can clean Mister Wilson up."

John waved him off. "Thank you, but I'm a grown man. I can take care of myself."

"Burt, you come on, now," Suzanne said.

John then turned and headed over to where his parents were waiting in line to be served, leaving Suzanne with a frown on her face.

"Kinda beat ya here, didn't we," Lott said. "The Graham's came by and invited us to ride in their wagon. We decided it beat walking in that mud. Came right by you, but you were too busy talking."

John glanced over to where Suzanne was standing with her hands on her hips and replied, "It was a mess on the road, but I did enjoy talking to folks."

"You ready to eat," Sarah asked.

"I'm really not hungry. I think I'll clean up a bit," John replied as he started back over to Suzanne. Burt still held a wet cloth, and taking it, John bent down and began cleaning his shoes.

"Why won't you let him clean your shoes? He is a Negro, you know," Suzanne said. "We have employed him."

John shrugged. "He's a man, and I bet he's never felt the touch of a coin in his hand."

Looking straight into Burt's eyes, John asked, "They ever pay you with real money?"

Burt stared at John for a few moments, then turned to Suzanne. "Has I ever got any coins, Misses Olliver? Can't recollect none."

Blushing, Suzanne replied, "Well, maybe not any money, but we do give you a place to live and food to eat. That's more than a lot of folks get."

John shook his head and handed the muddy cloth back to Burt. "Weren't long ago, you were nothing but a slave, and I bet you had a place to stay and food to eat then too, didn't ya?"

Burt thought for a moment. "I'm still living in the same place, but I ain't no slave no more."

John shook his head. "This man don't even know that he's still enslaved."

"Next time I'll not insist on someone helping you, and I'll have you know, Burt is a free man," Suzanne replied sharply.

At that moment McWorthan looked down at his watch, "Almost two o'clock. Time to get this show on the road," he said as he motioned for a Federal officer. "Sir, if you don't mind, it's time to get started."

The officer quickly stepped up on the platform, pulled out his revolver and fired a shot into the air.

People began to gather and since women were not eligible to vote, they moved aside and let the men through. Children, uninterested in what was about to happen and excited about being with other young people, continued playing in the outer fields.

"Folks gather 'round and you politicians can get on up here!" McWorthan shouted.

Taking a deep breath, John reached over and squeezed Suzanne's hand, straightened his shoulders and nudged his way through the crowd. As he reached the steps, a hand reached out and grabbed his arm.

"Solgier boy, you ready to stir this here crowd?" Herchel Pierce asked. Standing there with his usual greasy hair, scarred face and a rancid smell of filth, Pierce showed no emotion at all. "I suggest you say the right things up there. You hear me?"

John pulled free and made his way up the steps. Glancing back he replied, "I have no idea what you're talking about."

Reaching the stage, John shook hands with McWorthan and was introduced to Jacob Thompson, one of the candidates. Thompson was a small thin man with receding auburn hair and a well-trimmed mustache. He was dressed in a black suit and stood very erect. Mcworthan then asked John and Thompson to have a seat as he headed for the podium.

Holding his hands up, he said, "Ladies and Gentlemen, if you ain't finished your dinner, keep on eating, and if you go away hungry, it's yore own fault. The food's here a plenty and I can tell right now by looking over at them barrels, we got a thirsty bunch here. Right?"

"Right!" the crowd roared back.

Once again, McWorthan raised his hands to calm the group and then continued, "Miss'sippians, we are here today to introduce two democratic candidates who, if the Lord's willing, is gonna represent us in the state legislature come next year. We did have three of 'em, but the gentleman from up in Kemper has kinda dropped out of the race. We got to get another one from up there."

He paused for a moment, then continued, "You tired of them sorry Republicans, ain't ya?"

Shouts of agreement erupted so loudly that several horses that were tied nearby, bolted free and had to be calmed. To the concern of the soldiers, pistol shots rang out from somewhere in the midst of the crowd. Seeing that no one was hurt, the troopers kept their distance.

When everyone calmed down, McWorthan pointed over to Thompson and said, "We got a man from down in Clarke County who I want you to meet, and I think he has a few words for us. Mister Jacob Thompson, the floor is yours."

Slowing rising, Thompson walked over to the podium, grabbed the corners with all his might and in a soft shaky voice began. "Ladies and Gentlemen, it's a pleasure and honor to be up here to talk to you folks."

Suddenly a man out front shouted, "Can't hear you! You got to speak up."

Thompson cleared his throat and in a strained high-pitched voice began again.

Sitting there, John barely heard anything Thompson was saying. His eyes scanned the people in the crowd. Even in July, men wore coats when at public events, and the dark colored coats blended into a mass before John's eyes. In contrast, standing to the rear was a large cluster of umbrellas and more women wearing bonnets than he had ever seen in his life. They looked like a field of spring flowers. John chuckled to himself.

Then the speaker's words caught his attention. "If elected, I'll let you know right now, I'll do my best to serve your needs."

There was a warm round of applause and Thompson took his seat.

John then realized that he hadn't heard a word the man had said and knowing that he would be up behind that podium in a matter of seconds, his heart began to pound and sweat formed on his face and hands. John bowed his head and shut his eyes for a moment and prayed, Lord give me strength to say the right thing.

Noticing that John was in prayer, people up front nudged each other and the crowd became quiet.

"You ready?" McWorthan said.

John raised his head, smiled and rose to his feet.

McWorthan extended his hand and firmly holding it said, "Folks, this here is John Wilson from Newton County. Any of you men fight with the Newton Rifles?"

Yells pierced the air as fellow comrades gave him their support. Then the whole crowd began to shout and clap their hands. Hearing the Rebel yells sent chills down the backs of the Federal soldiers as they recalled the times when massed men in gray and butternut charged recklessly toward them at Manassas, Gettysburg, Chickamauga and what seemed like a million battles.

For a moment John gazed out at the people gathered before him, then looked up to the sky and realized for the first time that it was a cloudy day. The clouds were soft gray, puffy and clustered closely together. Standing there looking up, for a moment, he forgot all about the people waiting for him to speak and a sense of peace settled over him.

"Mister Wilson," a voice called out.

He smiled and slowly moved away from behind the podium. Standing tall and with a strong voice he said, "There was a time up there in Pennsylvania that I didn't know whether or not I'd see another day. A lot of my friends were left up there on those hills. Yes, everyday the good Lord gives us is a good day."

A hush fell over the crowd and some of the veterans' eyes filled with tears.

"Many of you have lost sons, fathers, husbands and friends to the cause. Then, some of you have even lost your farms, the very land you worked on so hard to provide for your living. Mississippi has been brought to its knees, and the pain and burden has been more than some can endure. But with this election we can begin to help ourselves. As I have said before, I believe that it won't be long until self-government will return to Mississippi and we will be free. It's guaranteed by our constitution."

Feeling a surge of joy, John shouted, "Mississippi will be free!"

A chorus of shouts rippled through the people who were pressing close to the speaker's platform.

"I don't have to tell you our problems," John continued. "You know them too good. High taxes, corrupt officials, wasteful spending and a government run by turncoat Southerners and outsiders. By placing good, honest, hardworking men in Jackson, the South can rise again!"

"Amen! Amen!" many of the men shouted.

One man shouted out, "I say let's get rid of them damned Yankee troops. I don't even like to see 'em around."

Feeling a breeze on his face and sensing bright sunlight, John looked up. The clouds were parting. Turning back to the people, he noticed a Negro man standing down near the steps to the platform. It was the same man who had helped him with his shoes earlier. The man stood there erect with his hands by his sides, a troubled expression on his face.

John turned back to his audience. "As I have said, there will be a time when we won't need Federal troops here in the South."

But concerned about the Negro man's face below, John glanced down again. The man hadn't moved an inch and his expression was more haunting than ever. "Please excuse me for a second," John said as he went over to the edge of the platform, bent down and motioned to the man. "What's wrong with ya? You look like sump'ns bothering you," he whispered.

The man shook his head. "Mistuh Wilson, I ain't got no problem. I was just a wondering what's gonna become of us colored folks. We ain't nothin' to nobody," he replied.

"Is the Nigguh giving you a problem?" a voice shouted out.

Turning, John saw McWorthan standing over him. "No problem, Sir. I was just asking the man to bring me a glass of water. My throat's a little dry."

The Negro smiled up at him and stammered, "I'll be right back, Mistuh Wilson."

John returned to the podium with the glass of water. "As I said a few minutes ago, there is no doubt that self government will return to Mississippi. Yes, we've been through a lot these past years. We've fought and endured a terrible war. As a conquered people, we have suffered from the loss of loved ones and many of you have lost everything you have worked for all your life, including the right to take part in our democratic process. But, I say to you, we still have the same soil that the good Lord has given us, we still have strong backs to work the fields, and, deep inside of us, we still have the Southern spirit to survive. The South ain't dead by no means!"

Excited, the people roared their approval.

In the midst of the noise, John's mind wandered back to years past and he remembered how the lives of the Negro, and Choctaws as well, had been affected by the white man's social and legal system. The Choctaws had been forced to give up their land, and those who chose to remain in Mississippi were reduced to wandering nomads, roaming a land that once was their own.

With the sun now beaming down on his tanned face, a sense of awe came over John and, as he spoke, it was as if the people standing there didn't exist. In John's mind, he was alone. Somehow, a power had come over him that was unexplainable.

"As we rebuild this country," John said. "We've got to find ways to take care of not just some of the people, but we have to provide for the needs of everyone and that includes the Negroes and the Choctaws as well. We may think we've got it bad, but they have nothing."

A hush came over the crowd and a voice called out, "You saying we need to place the Nigguh and Indian's rights above our'n? I say, we ain't worried 'bout no Choctaws and fer the Nigguhs, I heard tell the govn'ments thinking about sending 'em back to Africa. I say, to Hell with 'em all!"

Some began to clap their hands.

John raised his hand to calm the group. "Sir, I don't think you understood me. We got more than enough land for any man who wants to work and in regard to the Negro and Choctaw, just imagine this. Now follow me. Right now we're thinking about how to make the white man's life better, and like you, I'm concerned about my fate, but while we accomplish our goals, why not reach out and help the Negro and Choctaw as well. By bringing them up to where they can make a living, it would increase the productivity of our state and bring us more prosperity. Yes, I'm concerned about the plight of the white man, but there's room for all of us. Whether you know it or not, under the constitution, we're all nothing but Miss'sippians. It is up to us, all of us, to turn our state around and make it the productive and thriving state that it was before the war. If we unite together we can accomplish this very goal — a strong and invincible Mississippi."

Many in the crowd began to shake their heads in approval and a soft murmur rose over the assembly. Suddenly a man began to clap and then others joined in. Soon everyone was cheering and applauding.

John could see his parents proudly clapping along with the others while Suzanne waved her handkerchief above her head excited by how the people had responded to him. John glanced down and saw that the Negro man was still there, but now his face glowed and he had a big smile on his face. He slowly raised his arm and pointed upward. John knew that the man was thanking God for what had transpired.

Meanwhile, a well-dressed man standing at the outer edge of the crowd leaned over to one of the military officers nearby and exclaimed, "Sure don't sound much like a Democrat, does he?"

The officer shook his head and replied, "I think we have us a Republican at a Democrat's outing. Surprised me they accepted what he said about the Darkies. This don't sound like the South that I know."

"I'm going to keep my eye on this young man," the other man said. "He's somewhat idealistic, but there's something different about him. I just hope he believes what he preaches."

People were now crowding around the platform. For over two hours, John stood there greeting folks and sharing ideas with them. Jacob Thompson, impressed by what John said, worked his way through the people to speak with John and to congratulate him. McWorthan, Frank and several other influential politicians stood back away from the people and marveled at the response John had received.

Lighting his pipe, McWorthan said, "Damnist thing I ever seen. The man got up there, took control of the folks and even after he said what he did, they love him."

The other men shook their heads and one of them replied, "The man knows how to attract the people. You know, I didn't see but a few of 'em come up to Thompson. Wilson's the man, we just got to straighten out that nonsense 'bout the Nigguhs. As far as the Choctaws go, who cares about them."

McWorthan thought for a moment and said, "If anybody can get to 'em, Hendon can. I'll talk to him about it 'fore he leaves today. He'll stop the Nigguh talk."

Suzanne worked her way to the front and was finally was able to reach John. Nudging up to him, she took him by the arm and stood beside him as the people filed by. As soon as the last one left, he drew a breath of relief and, elated over the reaction of the people, took Suzanne in his arms and hugged her.

Softly he whispered, "I want to thank you and your family for making this possible. I hope I did all right."

Suzanne with her dark hair tossed by the wind eased up and gave him a kiss. Blushing, she said, "You'll have to excuse me. I couldn't help myself. I'm so happy for you. And to answer your question, you were simply wonderful, Mister Wilson."

As people began to disperse and go their separate ways, all the Wilsons gathered at the platform, overjoyed at the response John had received. Sarah gave him a big hug and even Lott became emotional as he shook his son's hand. James who was talking with one of the Federal officers was unable to get down front but finally excused himself and joined his wife who was there with the family.

As he approached John, James called out in his northern accent, "Didn't know you had that much politicking in you. One heck of a speech."

John reached out and clasping his hand, replied, "I hope I said the right things. Papa told me to speak my mind and that's what I tried to do."

"James, you know you're looking at our next district legislator, don't ya," Suzanne said.

Tim, shabbily dressed, with mussed hair and bloodshot eyes wandered up and reaching out to shake John's hand, said, "Kinda got a late start this afternoon, but I did get the last part of it. I do say I was proud of ya. But you got to tell me how in the world you gonna get yore Nigguh ideas across once you get to Jackson. It might be a problem. You know they're expecting a mule and forty acres."

At that moment, Professor Hendon rushed up. "John, hold up a second. Got to talk with ya."

10

CLOAKED

IN THE WEEKS THAT FOLLOWED THE POLITICAL RALLY there were mixed emotions and long discussions about John's words. Most people were convinced that he was genuinely interested in the welfare of all the people in the state, but did not take his remarks about the Negroes and Choctaws seriously.

The Meridian Times had endorsed him before the rally and continued to do so afterwards, applauding him for his spirited speech. Little comment was made in Meridian about John's feelings about the Negro.

But *The Jackson News*, owned by a local man indebted and loyal to the Republican Party, acclaimed John's speech as one made by none other than a staunch Republican. The paper stated that John's views on the welfare of the Negro had to be pleasing to the party and to those officials in Washington who were monitoring the political proceedings in Mississippi. *The paper* felt that if John, being a Democrat, should win the election against the Republican incumbent, the results would be the same because they would still have a Republican representing the tenth district.

As political tension grew, rumors began to circulate regarding John's concern about the status of the Negro. One story stated that John proposed to distribute land seized by the counties due to back taxes to the colored, while another rumor stated that John thought it feasible to break down the large land holdings and share that with the Negroes. Strangely enough, in all the rumors, nothing was mentioned about the Choctaws. As in any political arena, people heard what they wanted to hear, and in Mississippi, an undercurrent of falsified slander was circulating.

Worried about this turn of events, Professor Hendon lost no time in contacting John. A little before lunch as the July sun was burning down, Hendon rode up to the edge of the corn field where John was plowing, tied his mount and waited under the shade of a large beech tree until John made his return round.

Fighting his way through the long cutting blades of corn following a less than well trained mule, John finally made it to the end of the row. Stopping to wipe the sweat from his eyes he heard a familiar voice call out, "Think it's time to take a break?"

Startled, John pulled the mule to a halt and recognizing Hendon, wrapped the plow lines around the handles of the plow to secure the animal and walked over to where Hendon was waiting.

With dirt and sweat caked over his face and hands, John made no effort to extend his hand to Hendon. He simply took out his handkerchief, wiped his face and eased down in a sitting position with his back resting against the trunk of the tree. Taking in a big breath of air, he slowly exhaled and exclaimed, "I'll tell you Fessor, the good Lord has got to find me sump'n else to do. It's got to be hotter than ten hells out here today."

Hendon sat down next to him, crossed his legs and, pulling out his pipe and tobacco, thought how humorous it was. He could still see John standing up on the platform dressed to fit and appearing every bit the wealthy southern planter that most imagined, but, in reality, the man sitting there in front of him exhausted, dirty and reeking from perspiration was not far from penniless. Glancing back over to John, Hendon also knew that sitting there in front of him was a young man with a brilliant mind, his logic and understanding far ahead of their times.

For the next few minutes, they talked about the weather, how Hendon's unruly children were doing and a bit about the rally in Meridian.

Reaching over to a bucket of water, John took the handle of a gourd that had been shaped into a dipper, filled it to the brim and poured it over his head. With water running down his face and shoulders, John said, "Fessor, you don't usually get out in this kind of heat unless it's important. I feel like you got sump'n to say."

Hendon blew a large circle of smoke out and chuckled. "You know me too well, don't ya, John Wilson. That kinda bothers me sometimes. You know, I'm just glad my wife don't read my mind as well as you do."

John laughed and knowing that he would eventually get to his point, waited.

Twitching his right eye as he would often do when not knowing exactly how to say something, Hendon finally stammered, "Your talk about the Negroes has got some folks stirred up. People are making up all kind of stories about what you propose to do with 'em. That is, if you're elected."

John took a drink of water, showing no signs of concern. "I don't care what they're saying. We've got to take care of all our people. The war's over, the government freed 'em and we can't ignore their existence."

Leaning over to John, Hendon replied, "I know that and I realize that their best interest is in your heart, but the white voter doesn't want to hear it. John, it wasn't long ago those Negroes were owned property just like that mule of yours, worth millions. Can you imagine what it cost the planters to loose 'em?"

John nodded. "Our family made a living without 'em; cost us nothing."

Becoming agitated, Hendon blurted out, "No offense intended, but as far as wealth goes, you all don't have much either. Listen to me. Those planters lost a fortune and the way things are going, the Negroes are being brought back to the farm. The way the law states is that if they are homeless and without work, they can be assigned to labor."

Still showing no emotion, John replied, "Yes and most of 'em are going back to their old masters and unless sump'n is done, that's where they'll stay the rest of their lives."

"John, I know what's going through that mind of yours and, to be frank with you, I admire your ideals, but knowing politics like I do, you either give up those ideas about the Negroes or your campaign is in serious trouble. If you'll let me issue some clarifying statements to the newspapers, I think we'll do just fine. You know, once you are elected, then you can do what you can to help them. John, if you don't win, you will never be able to help them. And remember, even if you win, it will be difficult to help because you are just one vote, but you can begin things moving toward aid for the Negro and Choctaw people. But if you continue with this talk, you will never get a chance to help."

John slowly got up, stretched and then lumbered over to where his mule was waiting. Wrapping the plow lines around his neck, he looked over to where Hendon was now standing and said, "Fessor, you've known me all my life. If'n I did what you proposed, I'd be the worst liar in the county. I'll not sacrifice my character for votes. Folks are gonna have to take me like I am."

Hendon, shaking his head, replied, "John, politics aren't always pretty. You've got to give some."

As John headed down through the center of the row of corn, he called back, "But at whose expense."

While John disappeared into the mass of tasseled greenery, Hendon called out, "We got another rally to go to come Saturday night. Come by the house about dusk. You hear me!"

"I hear ya," came the reply.

§§

Finishing his work early, John made his way to the house where his mother had a tub of water drawn for him. After he had scrubbed himself and washed his hair, John put on a new pair of trousers his father had bought for him in Meridian and a shirt his mother had finished sewing for him that very morning. Standing before the mirror admiring his new outfit and carefully combing his hair, he thought, I haven't heard anything about any meeting around here. I wonder where the professor is carrying me. I guess there's no need to worry.

As he came out of the house, John met his father coming in from the barn. "It's quite obvious where you're going. A little Sat'day night courtin'."

John smiled and replied, "Not tonight. Fessor says we gonna do a little politickin'."

"Politickin'. I ain't heard nothing 'bout any meeting. You sure 'bout that?"

John nodded. "That's what he says."

"What time you gonna get in?" Lott asked.

"Don't rightly know," John replied mounting his horse. "I'll be fine. You all don't worry none."

As the sun was setting John approached the professor's house and for once, not one of Hendon's children could be seen. Usually, it was total bedlam. John often wondered how any of them would ever reach adulthood.

Hearing John approach, Hendon strolled out on the porch and, twisting his waxed mustache, said, "Quiet isn't it. They all went with Mrs. Hendon over to her sister's house for the night. Let me get my coat. I'll be right with you."

To John's surprise, Hendon didn't wear his coat. That was unusual because through the years, Hendon always wore a coat to public meetings. On the way, Hendon told John that the meeting was going to be near Chunky, a small village located on the western bank of the Chunky River. John was puzzled by Hendon's behavior. Usually he was a constant talker, but this evening he seldom spoke and only when John initiated the conversation.

With darkness approaching, Hendon kicked his horse in the flank. "We need to push it. We're a little late."

As they approached the village, Hendon directed them to a side road that led south, and, after riding a couple of miles, they came upon a farmhouse with a lantern hanging from one of its front porch beams. Several other horsemen were just arriving, and in the darkness, others could be heard approaching.

As John and Hendon rode up, a man standing at the edge of the house holding a firearm called out, "Are you Sons of Bitches!"

Startled, John heard Hendon reply, "We're Sons of Midnight."

The man then came out from the shadows and walked over to where John, Hendon and the other horsemen were waiting. He wore what appeared to be a long sleeved gray nightshirt that reached to his feet and a white hood with holes cut so he would be able to see.

John sat there stunned. He wanted to reach over and nudge Hendon for an explanation, but he sensed that it might be better if he remained silent. After all, the professor had never failed him.

The man then said, "It's dark out here. I can't see who you are, and I don't want to know you. Your password is your bond. Put on your cover. You can see the lights down behind the barn. Follow 'em and you'll do just fine."

As Hendon reached inside his saddlebag, John whispered, "What's going on here, Fessor?"

"Sh," Hendon replied."Put this on and be sure to cover your head. Don't say anything."

John did as he was told and to his amazement found that he was now dressed in the same long white night shirt and hood as the others. The group, not knowing one from another, then dismounted and leading their horses, followed the chain of lanterns down past the barn and through the woods. After about a half of a mile, the woods opened into a large field and, in the twilight, John could make out a mass of people milling about.

They were all told to secure their mounts and assemble up near the knoll of the hill. Everyone was dressed in cloaks and hoods. A strange feeling came over him as he stood in the July heat.

John nudged Hendon. "What is this?"

The usually polite man replied, "You need to keep quiet."

Then walking away, he said, "I'll see you after the meeting. Wait for me at the horses."

In the darkness, a man next to John whispered, "I know you, don't I."

Before John could reply, a ringing voice called out, "Reach over and grab the man's hand next to you and form a circle."

Lanterns had been placed in a circular fashion around the clearing and in a matter of moments, the men had done as told. The man then continued, "I want all of us to have a silent word of prayer, and during this time I want us to remember our friends and brothers lost to the Southern cause. Then I want you to pray for the children who'll never see their fathers again, and last and most important, I want you to pray for the state of Miss'sippi."

As John stood there praying, a peace came over him and he began to sense that with prayer, there must be something good transpiring. With his eyes shut, he then detected a crackle from what sounded like a fire and then a light. The light became brighter and opening his eyes, he saw a large blazing cross, some fifteen feet tall. The light was so intense that in a matter of seconds the entire hillside was illuminated. With sweat pouring from his body, he then saw to his amazement that there must be at least five or six hundred people there.

At that moment, a man with a solid white robe and a tall pointed hat walked over to where the cross was burning. He raised his hands and with the light of the fire flicking behind him, shouted, "In this circle, there is no beginning and no end. We are all one! In our strength and unity lies the future of Miss'sippi!"

The mass then began to chant, "Miss'sippi! Miss'sippi!"

The man raised his arms for silence. He then continued, "All over this great South groups are meeting just like we are here tonight. There's an army of us greater than the one that took the field in sixty-one. But unlike that army, we will prevail in victory, total victory. With our hands we are going to regain our state of Miss'sippi and the South. If we do our job, come election day, there won't be no turncoat Republicans or Nigguhs anywhere near them polls to cast their vote."

A sinking feeling began to come over John. He had a desperate urge to leave. What this man was proposing was against everything that he believed. John glanced around to see how the others were reacting and was surprised that the masses were totally entranced.

Turning back to the cross, John heard the man exclaim, "We will not be defeated! Ever what it takes to control the votes, will be done. Just like in war, there are no boundaries. Already, houses have been burned and lives have been lost. Right here in this county there is one Nigguh Republican who won't cast no vote come November."

A loud cheer ripped through the night.

John knew exactly who the man was talking about and hearing the men cheer turned his stomach and a sense of fear came over him as he stared at the masked group knowing that the murder of innocent people was advocated.

"Feel secure in what we have to do. As you look around, we are all covered. You don't know one man from the next. How can a deceiver turn you in to the authorities when he doesn't know who you are? He can't! The only people we have to be concerned about is the military and some of them can be bought. Throughout this great land we will become an invisible empire. The streets will run red with blood from those who stand in our way."

This kind of talk is insane. I want no part of it, John thought.

"I want you all to kneel and while continuing to grasp the person's hand next to you, make a solemn oath to God to support one another and our glorious cause."

As the men began to kneel, John could restrain himself no longer. John released the hands he was holding, turned and began running as fast as his legs would carry him. As a youth, no one in the Little Rock community could outrun him, and as he sprinted away, he ran harder than he had ever run before. He ripped the hood off and felt the cool night air brush across his face, and a sense of relief came over him as he distanced himself from the burning cross.

As he approached the barn where his horse was tied, he quickly brushed aside a man who was standing watch and with one leap, was mounted.

The man tried to grab John's horse's reins, but a quick kick sent him tumbling backwards. Quickly getting up, the man called out, "Where do you think you are going?"

As John galloped away, he shouted back to the man, "I'm sick!"

John was sick. Sick of all he had heard; the sight of the burning cross and the things that the man had advocated were a disgrace to the Christian faith.

In a matter of moments, John reached Chunky and still at a full gallop, turned his horse west toward Little Rock. Down the road they thundered as he tried to place distance between him and the hooded mass. Mile after mile he rode until he could hear the horse panting. Realizing what he was doing to his mount, he pulled his horse to a cantor and then to a slow walk. All was quiet with the exception of a few tree locusts, and in the stillness John thought back over what had happened. What he had seen and heard had disturbed him more than anything he had ever witnessed. Battle itself had not upset him as much. He had been proud to be a part of the Confederate army, but tonight he had a sense of shame.

As the sun rose the next morning Lott, pulling up his suspenders, strolled out on the front porch and glancing down toward the barn saw John's horse wandering around the barnyard, saddled and lathered in sweat. Making his way down the steps and out into the yard, Lott became distressed. You don't leave an animal like this, he thought. Something's not right. John's never left his horse in this condition.

As Lott approached, the horse threw up his head and slowly came to meet him. Lott took him by the reins and gently stroked his neck, causing some of the foamy matter to drop to the ground.

Lott didn't hear the footsteps approaching and began to lead the horse to the barn.

"Here, I'll take him," came a voice.

Startled, Lott turned to see John reaching out for the reins.

"What do you mean leaving a horse in this kind of shape," Lott scolded.

John lead the horse away and replied, "It's all my fault, Papa. It won't happen again."

Following him along, more frustrated about not understanding his behavior than angry, Lott continued, "John, this ain't like you. You're a grown man."

Leading the animal into the barn, John replied, "I had a hard night. I was so exhausted when I got home, I didn't make it to my bed. I slept on the porch."

"Hard night," Lott countered. "What do you mean?"

John turned to his father and said, "I don't feel like talking about it right now."

Later that day, Lott and Sarah went to have dinner with Sister and James, but John still exhausted from the lack of sleep, decided to stay home. With the heat inside the house, John took a quilt to the open hallway and, after making a soft pallet, was soon asleep.

Out of nowhere came a voice thundering, "Gonna sleep all day?"

Thinking he was dreaming, John paid no attention.

"Time to get up, John Boy."

Opening his eyes, John saw Tim sitting on the floor across the hallway and muttered, "I don't need no company right now."

Tim reached over and grabbed his pants leg. "You ain't gettin' rid of me that easy. I heard you outran the Klan last night. Folks said you tore through Chunky like a bat out of hell."

John suddenly recalled all that had happened to him and pulling himself to a sitting position, rubbed his eyes.

"You don't know what ya talking about."

Tim took a flask from his coat pocket and after taking a swallow, offered John a drink which John declined. Tucking it back into his coat, Tim said, "Word is you got sick or sump'n like that, but I know you too good. You didn't want no part of that bunch, did you?"

John twisted his neck about to relieve a stiffness and then replied, "You were there last night, weren't you?"

Tim pursed his lips and replied, "Don't rightly know. When you're hooded, you don't know one person from another. That's the way it works, ain't it, John?"

"You were there last night," John said. "And you know me too good.

I couldn't take what I was hearing. It's against everything I stand for. I can't believe you were one of 'em."

"One of 'em!" Tim said. "What in the hell do you think we were?"

Angered and rising to his feet, John replied, "A mob led by some insane fanatic. That's exactly what we were."

Knowing how John felt, Tim sat calmly and then said, "I'll tell you who that mob was. It was a lot of your neighbors, folks that go to church with us every Sunday. Then, I imagine that some of them fanatics were soldiers just like you and me that took up arms together. Fact is, a bunch of 'em were members of the Newton County Rifles. You want to hear more."

John walked out toward the front porch. "You're just a lying fool, Tim. You wouldn't know the truth if'n you ran head on into it."

By that time, Tim had gotten to his feet and walking over to John, placed his arm around his shoulder, "John, you're the best friend I've got. I know I got my faults but I ain't lying to ya. Them folks out there is part of us, and I don't want to see you get hurt. That's why I come by here. I picked up yore garb where you chunked it off, and I spread the word that you got sick, real sick. The man there at the barn got a good look at ya. They know who you are."

Without answering, John eased down and sat on the edge of the porch and said, "Didn't mean to call you a liar. I just don't want to talk about it no more. You understand?"

Tim nodded and after he had mounted his horse to leave, reached inside his saddlebag and brought out a bundle. "You want this?" he said, tossing it to John.

John caught the bundle and realizing what it was, immediately threw it back.

"Not in a million years will I wear that outfit."

Tim took the bundle, tucked it back into his saddlebag and replied, "I'll have it, when you need it. If you plan to make it to Jackson, you better think it over and I do mean seriously."

Later that evening after John's parents returned home, John told them that he needed to go over to see James about something and he should be home before too late.

Sister was on the front porch as John rode up; she invited him into the house and since they were about to have supper, invited him to share their meal. While they were eating, John was quieter than usual and both Sister and James could sense that this was not exactly a social meeting. As soon as they finished, Sister said, "James, I'll clear the table. Why don't you two go out front where it's cooler."

James walked over to the fireplace and reaching up to the mantle picked up his pipe and a small pouch of tobacco. They then wandered out to the front porch where some chairs were leaning against the wall. James took a seat while John decided to sit on the porch floor with his back resting against one of the columns.

After a few moments, John got up and began to walk nervously about. Finally, James said, "You might as well tell me what's bothering you. It's been on your face all night."

Taking a seat next to James, John hesitated for a moment, then said, "You once asked me about an organization. One the gov'ment was concerned about."

James, striking a match to light his pipe, replied, "You mean the Klan?"

Without speaking, John nodded.

"What can you tell me about it?" James asked.

In a soft voice, John answered, "It's here. Right here in Newton County."

James blew out a large puff of smoke and said, "That's right and they had a meeting down near Chunky last night and you were there with them."

Surprised, John blurted out, "But I didn't stay. I left 'em."

James reached over and placed his hand on John's shoulder. "I know you did, and I'm proud of you for it."

Suddenly realizing that James, a federal officer, knew the details of the meeting, John was astounded. "How do you know about this? Were you there?"

"I told you earlier, the government is most concerned over the activity of the group all throughout the South, and I can't tell you how I get my information," James said.

"James, there's more going on out there than you can imagine. You have no idea how strong they are."

In a few moments, James got out of his seat and walked over to the edge of the porch and knocking the used tobacco out of his pipe, said, "This stuff burns far too fast." Returning to his chair, he continued, "I know that there are literally thousands of people involved in the movement and I know that they plan to get rid of anyone who gets in their way. There's already been over forty deaths that we feel were committed by the Klan. They're a dangerous bunch. It's so serious that the government is sending hundreds of agents into the South to try to break up the organization."

John eased over to where James was standing. "You won't be able to tell who they are. They cover themselves and they are secretive."

James looked over to John. "We'll find out who they are and when we catch them, there'll be no mercy. They'll swing."

"You're talking about thousands upon thousands, James. I think not."

James, moving back to his seat, replied, "We'll get the leaders and the flock will scatter. I'm just glad you're not among them."

John, making his way down the steps to where his horse was tied, replied, "I don't think you know what you're dealing with. It ain't gonna be easy and you might be surprised who some of 'em are."

Stepping up in the stirrups, John said, "Tell Sister I enjoyed supper."

Watching John ride off, James thought about how much more he knew than he had shared with John. He was also aware that the Klan was working in every county in the state to place its handpicked men in office. The one thing that he could not understand was how John was fitting into their political scheme. No matter how hard he tried to justify John's popularity and community support, something was out of kilter.

⚡

The door opened and several well-dressed men made their way out of the parlor where they had been meeting for the past several hours. Suzanne hurried down the hallway to help them with their hats which had been left at the entrance. As the men left, they all thanked the Ollivers for their hospitality and then got into a coach that was awaiting them. As they were about to leave, one man called out, "Can we depend on you, Mister Olliver?"

Frank raised his hand to bid them goodbye and answered, "How can I refuse. It's unbelievable."

Seeing that the guest were finally leaving, Mrs. Olliver, who had not felt well that day and had been resting, walked out to where Frank and Suzanne were standing. Motioning, Mrs. Olliver shuffled back inside and called out to Lizzie, their housemaid, "Need something cool, Lizzie. Bring it to the study."

For some reason, the study located across the hall from the front parlor was always the coolest place in the house. Mrs. Olliver took her seat and after Frank and Suzanne had made themselves comfortable, said, "Tell me how the meeting went? It seems like you are pretty excited."

Suzanne, on the edge of her seat, could wait no longer. "Did you buy the stock? I know you did."

Frank, with a serious expression on his face, pursed his lips and looked first at Suzanne and then over to his mother. With suspense mounting and, unable to wait any longer, he blurted out, "They needed a little extra money, and I just bought me five thousand shares of Union Pacific. You won't believe the deal the gov'ment gave 'em to build that railroad through the territory. We're gonna have us a road running east to west, straight through this big ole country of ours, and I'm gonna make a killin' on it. I'll have more money than I know how to spend."

Elated, Suzanne and Mrs. Olliver rushed over to where Frank was sitting on the couch and placing their arms around him, almost smothered him. Frank, laughing hardily looked over to his mother and exclaimed, "Frank Senior would've been proud of me. He made his fortune farming and slaving, and I'll be damned if'n the gov'ment ain't gonna do the same for me."

Squeezing him tightly with a sense of satisfaction, Mrs. Olliver replied, "He often thought that you didn't always make good choices, but yes, he would be proud of you now."

Soon Lizzie returned bringing them tall glasses of lemonade, and after placing them on the table next to Mrs. Olliver, asked to be dismissed.

Frank shared everything that had transpired that afternoon and after thoroughly briefing them, looked over to Suzanne. "I'm gonna need someone to help me keep up with all our business. Between the farms, land dealings and this railroad, it's more than I can handle."

The women nodded in agreement.

"John Wilson could do a dandy job for us. He's smart, dependable and it's 'bout time you two got married."

Suzanne, laughing about what he had suggested, responded, "If we do get married, John and I will be spending our time in Jackson. We won't have time for that."

"Suzanne, your brother does have a point. We do need his help and a legislator won't make you rich," her mother said.

"He may end up more than a legislator, and I don't intend to spend my life here in Newton County," Suzanne replied.

Frank remained silent for a moment, then said, "Suzanne, John's campaign's in trouble. Folks are concerned over his feelings for the Nigguhs. A lot of tales are floating around. If sump'n don't happen, he might not be going to Jackson."

"I heard 'em. Don't mean a thing. People know he kinda wants to help all the people," snapped Suzanne.

"People 'round here may know him, but folks outside the county only know what they hear," Frank replied.

"That's right darling," Mrs. Olliver said. "People don't know him like we do and those stories are distressing."

Suzanne looked over to her mother and murmured, "Why did he have to say those stupid remarks about the Negroes? He probably didn't mean 'em anyway."

Frank, getting up reached over and brushed his hand lightly across Suzanne's cheek. "If he wins the election, you two go to Jackson, and if he looses, he can work for us. Either way, you win, providing you can get 'em to the alter, and I must say, you ain't been making much progress in that respect."

After Suzanne and Frank had left, Mrs. Olliver sat quietly thinking over what had been said and pondered how she could help her daughter with her relationship with John.

§§

School was out for the summer and Lucretia was enjoying a break from the busy schedule of preparing classes, grading papers and taking care of her students' every need. Even though she had little time for herself during the school year, she had thoroughly enjoyed her first year of teaching and had gained a feeling of confidence with her year of experience. Now that she had some extra time, she could be found down at her father's office, helping him with his patients.

After a busy day at the clinic, Doctor Caulder had finally seen his last patient. He and Lucretia were busily cleaning up his office and putting things away. Doctor Caulder removed the apron that he always wore and, hanging it on the peg next to the door, plopped down in a chair next to his operating table. In a moment, Lucretia brought him a cool glass of water to drink and began to wipe his face with a damp cloth.

"You enjoy this, don't you," Lucretia said, pulling a chair over next to her father.

Doctor Caulder thought for a moment, then answered, "It's been rewarding to me. I've become a part of the community. You might say, we, that is the folks and me, kinda depend on each other."

Seeing her father's exhaustion, Lucretia got up from where she was sitting and walked over and stood behind him. She then began to massage his aching shoulders. "I bet you sometimes wish you and mother had stayed in the east, don't you?"

Feeling Lucretia's strong fingers push against his tired muscles, he faintly heard her speak. It had been a long day and at his age, it didn't take much to tire him. Doctor Caulder shut his eyes and twisted his neck back and forth as the pains slowly subsided.

"Did you hear me?" came a voice.

Opening his eyes, he remembered what had been said and answered, "Yes, there were times I would have liked to been back east. It hasn't always been easy out here, but it's home now and I feel like I have made a difference. How about you? What do you want to do?"

Lucretia moved back to where she had been sitting and took a swallow of water from a glass that she had drawn for herself. Smiling over to her father she said, "I enjoy living with you and Mama, and I thoroughly enjoyed teaching this past year."

She thought for a moment, then continued, "You know Robert would like for me to marry him, but every time he starts talking about marriage, I change the subject."

"I know," chuckled her father. "He's talked to me about it on several occasions. I change the subject too."

Laughing, Lucretia threw a towel at her father deliberately missing him and exclaimed, "You don't think we'd make a charming couple?"

"Didn't say that. What I meant was, if I was in love with an attractive woman such as you, I would have already married you," he said slowly getting out of his chair.

"I truly think he loves me, Papa, and I really enjoy being with him."

Making his way to where his coat was hanging, Doctor Caulder mumbled, "You ought to get him to stay right here in town. I'm getting old, and I don't know how many more years I can practice. You see how I am at the close of a day. I think you two could make it just fine here."

Lucretia taking him by the arm as they prepared to leave the clinic said, "I just want to find someone as loving and caring as you. I'm not sure Robert is that man."

Using the handrails placed next to the steps that led from his office to the street below, Doctor Caulder steadied himself where he would not fall and upon reaching the ground below, replied, "I got my faults like all men. You just go out there and find someone who loves you as much as I love your mother. You do that and you'll be just fine."

After the two had boarded their buggy for the short trip home, Doctor Caulder glanced over to his daughter sitting beside him. Her curly blond hair sparkled in the afternoon sun, and her emerald green eyes twinkled.

She is indeed a beautiful young woman, he thought, and for a moment he remembered the first time he saw Lucretia's mother. Even after all these years, a warm feeling came over him as he thought back to the first time he kissed her.

Cracking his whip to get the horse on its way, he said, "Just remember, when you kiss him, expect something to happen."

"Papa, you're embarrassing me," Lucretia exclaimed, wondering why her father had brought up such an uncalled-for statement.

As they made their way out of town and down the dusty road that led to their home, Lucretia began to think about what her father had said. It wasn't the first time that he had mentioned how a man and woman should feel in an intimate relationship, and he always ended with a statement of his love for her mother.

As they approached home, Lucretia's mind turned to Robert and she began to fantasize. He would never practice here in this rural area, she thought. First, there's more money to be made back east and second, Robert loves the social life available in the city. He's at his best when he is sitting enjoying the sounds of an orchestra or having dinner at one of the finer restaurants.

Then thinking about the wonderful times she had enjoyed with him in Philadelphia and how his parents had graciously accepted her, she began to realize that life with Robert could be very fulfilling.

11

CAJUN COUNTRY

DAYS PASSED AND WITH NO FURTHER TALK ABOUT THE secret meeting in Chunky, John began to turn his mind and energy back to politics. Even though he knew the Klan was aggressively recruiting members and could be detrimental to his election, he felt that the people in the district were accepting him and his views. He also knew that to win the election, he would have to keep the support of the organization without personally becoming a part of it. He knew politically he could not alienate himself from them, but once elected, his conscious would be his guide.

During the last week in July, to John's surprise, he received word from Professor Hendon that Jacob Thompson, John's democratic opponent, had suddenly withdrawn from the race and, with no other candidate, John would only have to defeat the Republican incumbent to win the district. Knowing how unpopular Templeton was, John was assured by Hendon that the election was all but over. John would be going to Jackson come spring.

John knew that even though the Klan had dismissed some of the rumors circulating about his feelings toward the Negroes, the leaders did not share his compassion for the race. What John didn't know was that they felt that Negroes were inferior to Whites and should be kept in their place, which meant servitude. They also felt that a Democratic candidate must not advocate any type of Negro rights.

Hendon was concerned about the way John had left the meeting at Chunky and the effect it would have on the members of the Klan. He knew that more than sickness had made John run, and that John's chances of a victory without the support of the Klan would be close to impossible.

As the boat pulled into the dock, its large paddle wheels slowly churned to a stop flushing muddy river water toward its banks. Bracing themselves as the boat was secured, John, with his arm around Suzanne's waist, couldn't believe that he had consented to accompanying her to her Grandfather's home west of New Orleans. Holding an umbrella for protection against the sun, Suzanne looked over to John and exclaimed, "I told you it was a beautiful city, didn't I?"

John, watching the people as they scurried ashore, replied, "It's the hottest place I've ever been."

To a visitor, with the temperature soaring in the upper nineties and humidity so high that moisture clung to the skin, New Orleans was unbearable.

"See the steeple over there. That's St. Louis Cathedral," Suzanne said pointing ashore.

"The crowd's thinning out. Let's collect our baggage and go see the city. It's just a short distance to where we'll be staying. I think you'll enjoy the walk."

"May I help you?" asked a Negro man standing down below.

Suzanne pointed to several bags and a small chest being unloaded. "Can you can carry those for us? It's about four blocks."

"Yes Ma'am, I be right behind you," the elderly man replied as he went over to where the luggage was lying.

The streets were filled with people. Many were standing around talking while others were making their way to places unknown. Carts filled with produce, wagons loaded with covered goods, buggies and men on horses seemed to be flowing in all directions. Total chaos. Adding to the confusion was the constant hum of people talking. John recognized the English being spoken but also heard some men speaking in a strange French dialect that was confusing. Even the Negroes spoke differently from those in Mississippi.

Weaving their way down the streets through the masses, John couldn't help but feel the beauty of New Orleans. He saw trees with long draping Spanish moss, and along each side of the sidewalks were rows of two and three story buildings with small overhanging balconies extending from the second floors overlooking the streets. He noticed double glassed French doors leading from the porches and large doorways on the streets revealing fountain garden patios, utterly magnificent.

This is different from anything I have ever seen, he thought. This is not the America I know. It's like a foreign country, beautiful yet mystifying.

After a brief walk, John and Suzanne reached the Grand Hotel where rooms had been reserved. The Negro man carried their bags into the lobby where he was met by a well-dressed Negro. John pressed some change into his hand as he was leaving.

John stood in awe as he gazed at the marbled floors, massive columns, perhaps thirty feet high, reaching up to the ceiling and live plants growing in large earthen pots.

As they ascended the carpeted spiral stairway to their separate rooms, the man carried their luggage inside, and after he was assured that they were comfortably settled, Suzanne compensated him for his service.

As soon as the attendant left, John closed his door, removed his coat soaked with perspiration and rolled up his shirtsleeves. At that moment there was a light tapping at a door to his rear.

"Didn't know we had connecting rooms," he said as Suzanne reached out and took him by the hand.

"I want you to see the view down Bourbon Street from my balcony," she replied leading him to a large set of French doors that revealed a beautiful view of the city.

John was still spellbound by the elegance and decor of the room.

"Suzanne, these rooms must be costing you a fortune. I've never seen anything like this in my life," he said.

"It's nothing. My grandfather owns the hotel," she replied.

John shook his head in amazement.

"He comes to the city quite often. It gives him a place to stay," she explained nonchalantly.

Suzanne had already changed into a white cotton dress that was much cooler than the one she had been wearing and was cut much lower than John was used to seeing.

Noticing his embarrassment, Suzanne placed her arm around his waist, reached up and kissed him lightly on the lips. "This is New Orleans. Cajun country. Women don't mind showing their figure down here."

The late afternoon sun caused her dark black hair to glisten; John had never seen her more beautiful. With her dark hair and complexion, she looked more like the native Choctaws back in Mississippi than white.

John pulled her closely to him and kissed her passionately.

That evening Suzanne and John had dinner at one of the finer restaurants and, tired from the trip, retired for the evening.

Unaccustomed to the humid heat, John took off his shoes and shirt. Opening the windows leading out to the balcony, he carried a chair to the outside and settled himself with his feet resting on the railing. He could hear people talking down on the street and the sound of a banjo and some brass instruments. Off in the distance there were slight flashes of lightning. A row of dark thunderclouds hovered on the horizon. Occasionally a hint of a breeze caressed his face cooling him as he sat admiring the night.

John thought back to past days. When Suzanne had asked him to accompany her to Louisiana, he felt that he had too much farm work to do and with the upcoming election, he reasoned that it would be impossible to leave at this time. After talking with his father, he was assured that there was nothing pressing on the farm that couldn't wait for a couple of weeks, and with Hendon's statement about how he stood in the election, the Professor felt like a little rest would be rejuvenating.

Suddenly there was a clap of thunder as the dark clouds began to ease closer. Sensing someone's presence, he was surprised to find Suzanne standing behind him.

"How long have you been there?" he asked with a smile as he started to get up. "I need to get my shirt."

Suzanne placed her hand on his shoulder. "Keep your seat. I know you're tired from the trip."

Dressed in a long black silk gown with narrow shoulder straps and very little to cover her upper body, she eased into John's lap.

Feeling a sense of guilt but unable to resist her, John placed his arms around her waist and pulled her close. Under the soft folds of the gown he could feel every curve. Even with the cool breeze from the approaching storm, John felt a warm flushing surge through his body as his heart began to pound. Breathing became more difficult as his lips touched hers. John ran his hand down across the lower part of her back and thigh.

Flashes of lightning streaked across the sky, and Suzanne caressed his chest and arms that bulged with muscles developed from long hours of strenuous work. In her mind there was no way she was going to lose the man she had wanted from the first moment they had met. Even as a child, she had always cared for him.

A roll of thunder shook the window panes in the French doors behind them and it began to rain. She gently kissed John before they rushed inside.

"Why don't you stay with me tonight?" she whispered as soon as they were in his room.

Feeling her soft breath against his face and the smell of her perfume, John once again ran his hands down her back and murmured, "There's nothing I'd rather do, but..."

Suzanne taking him by the hand, replied. "We've known each other all our lives. I'm yours if you'll have me."

John gently brushed several strands of hair from her face and then slowly smoothed her hair that fell the length of her back.

"Not just yet," John said softly.

Kissing him lightly, she smiled. "I'm in the next room, if you need me."

John closed the French doors to the balcony and put on the pajamas that Suzanne had given him earlier. Falling on the bed, he was asleep in seconds.

With the storm raging outside and the constant roar of thunder, John began to turn and toss. As far as he could see large cannons had been moved into position across the hillside, their crews standing in a ready position. One by one they began to fire, first bolting backwards sending masses of smoke belching forward and then, as the firing became closer, the sound became deafening. At one moment he saw himself standing behind the guns. Suddenly he was there advancing with the army of the Northern Virginia as they faced the same pieces of destruction he had just stood behind. Approaching the cannons, he heard an order from across the way. "Load with double canister!" At the same time rows of Union soldiers, thousands in number, stood and with the order to fire cleared the field. Being blown backwards, an unbearable pain pierced his body. His head felt like it was between the jaws of a giant vice slowly crushing his skull. John screamed as loudly as he could, but no sound came. He struggled but could not free himself.

Wrenching in pain and sweating profusely, John faintly heard someone say, "It's gonna be just fine. You're having a bad dream."

A cooling sensation came over him as something damp was placed on his forehead.

"You're fine now. I'm with you."

John began to regain his senses and relaxed. The storm outside had ended. There was only the light tapping of water dripping off the roof onto the balcony to break the silence.

"Was it a bad one?"

"They're all bad," John replied.

Suzanne placed the damp cloth over on the bath table next to the pitcher of water and said, "You want me to stay with you?"

With the light of day, John feeling better, quietly eased out of bed so as not to awake Suzanne. Dressed in only the bottoms of his pajamas, he tipped out onto the balcony for a breath of fresh air, closing the French doors behind him. Seeing a Negro man on the deserted street below him, John said in a soft voice, "Know where I can get a good cup of coffee this early?"

Surprised to see someone stirring, the man looked up and replied, "I'll get ya one for two bits."

"Go get it then," John said as he slipped back into his room for some coins.

In a few minutes the man returned with a fruit jar of steaming coffee and handed it up to John. John paid the man and then eased down on a damp wrought iron chair. It was the strongest coffee he had ever tasted but the flavor was delicious and he savored every swallow.

"You usually dress like this," came a voice from across the way.

Surprised, John noticed a middle-aged woman sitting on the balcony next to his. Only a few feet away, she was dressed in a dark red gown and was smoking a rolled cigarette. She was slightly plump and had traces of gray streaked through her dark hair, but was attractive never the less.

Noticing John's embarrassment at the way he was dressed, she began to laugh. "Just have a seat. At my age I've seen more naked men than you can shake a stick at."

She then blew a long puff of smoke. "I will give you credit for being a fine looking young man."

John bashfully eased back into the chair, not knowing how to respond. He finally said, "You live down here?"

The woman smiled. "You want some breakfast?"

"Coffee filled me up, thank you," John stammered.

At that moment Suzanne eased out on the balcony holding John's pajama top. Unaware of the woman on the adjoining balcony, she said, "You look like you feel better. People will be stirring 'fore long. We'd best get dressed."

"Dressed! You want to ruin an old woman's fantasy?"

Startled, Suzanne quickly tried to cover her almost bare breast and eased behind John.

The woman laughed even harder. "I should have known this dandy was with you. I didn't expect you until tomorrow."

Peeking around, Suzanne recognized the woman and began to laugh. "Miss Elizabeth, I didn't know anyone was out here this early," she said, making her way to the edge of the balcony.

Reaching out, the women embraced. Suzanne remarked, "It's not quite as it seems."

Elizabeth winked at John and replied, "All I see is a half-dressed man and a woman that might as well be stark naked. What am I 'spose to think?"

Later after John and Suzanne had packed their suitcases and were on their way down to a carriage that would be taking them to her grandfather's plantation, John asked, "Who was the woman upstairs?"

"Just a friend of the family," Suzanne murmured.

As the carriage pulled out from the hotel, John glanced back. He had never seen such an eloquent establishment.

It took a while for the carriage to wind its way through the narrow streets choked with masses of people, but by noon, they were out of the city traveling west. Soon they were on a narrow desolate road bordered by large oaks draped with moss so dense and heavy that the lower limbs almost touched the ground. Around noon they stopped and had a light lunch Suzanne had brought along. John was not surprised that Suzanne had thought of everything.

Around mid afternoon lakes called bayous, filled with dark murky water appeared on each side of the road. Beyond that John could see swamps that continued as far as the eye could see.

"Won't be long 'till we reach the bridge," Suzanne said.

"What bridge?" John asked.

The Negro driver began to chuckle. "Lord knows, Mister Wilson. You is about to enter the Kingdom."

Suzanne reached over and squeezed John's hand. "This is Papa's Kingdom. Not even the Yankees put foot on it."

At that moment they rounded a bend in the road and before them was the longest bridge John had ever seen. John judged that it must be at least three to four hundred feet long. When they got across, it was like a different country. The land rose gently from the bridge and in the distance, John thought he could make out the shapes of low lying hills.

"Like I said. When the war came and Papa heard that the Yankees were burning and looting the plantations 'round about here. He burnt the bridge. That left his whole place surrounded by swamps. Since the water was too shallow for the big gunboats, the soldiers figured it wasn't worth the trouble. What fools they were. Papa had more than forty thousand tons of sugar stored in his warehouses, a fortune for most folks."

"Forty thousand tons!" John exclaimed. "How much land does he have out here to make that kind of a crop?"

"I think it's between four and five thousand acres," Suzanne replied. "That's just on this place. He's got two other farms."

Speechless, John wondered what kind of man could accumulate such wealth. From all that he had been told, her grandfather was a hardworking, honest person, but if he were anything like Suzanne's father, his gains might be at someone else's expense.

"You've been mighty quiet, John," Suzanne said.

"Just enjoying the scenery," John replied, not wanting to show how astonished he was.

On the other side of the bridge, sugarcane, head high, was growing along each side of the road. The rows were so long and the sugarcane so tall there appeared to be no end. With their long branches, they quickly blended into a waving mass of greenery as far as the eye could see.

Mile after mile they traveled with nothing but sugarcane about them.

"How many hands does it take to work this place?" John asked the driver.

The man scratched his head. "Mist' Wilson, I don't rightly know for sure but, I expects maybe a thousand."

"A thousand!" John exclaimed, looking over at Suzanne.

Suzanne laughed. "No Abram. There's only about two or three hundred on this place. Not a thousand."

"Where are they?" John asked.

"It's laid by, Mister Wilson," Abram answered. "Lord's got to do the rest of the work. People's doing other jobs just now."

Soon the land rose again and they entered a large stand of live oaks, massive in size. The road began to widen. Suzanne quickly placed her hands over John's eyes. "I've got a surprise for you."

In a moment, the carriage came to a stop and Suzanne removed her hands. John was astounded. Among a massive stand of virgin oaks stood a mansion larger and more stately than anything he had ever imagined, so large that it towered over the oaks that surrounded it. At first glance, it appeared to contain three stories and had steps leading up to the entrance. Columns supported the roof on all sides and each floor had a balcony that wrapped around the building giving it even a more magnificent appearance. John was speechless.

"What do you think?" Suzanne asked amused by the expression on John's face.

John shook his head and muttered, "I ain't never seen anything like it."

The buggy moved forward and pulled up in front of the mansion. Several Negro women bustled down the stairway to meet them.

Opening the door of the buggy, a slender middle-aged woman with a smile across her face said, "Welcome to the Oaks, Miss Suzanne. We's been a waitin' for you most of the mawning."

Pushing the woman aside, an elderly Negro dressed in a dark suit said, "You will excuse Tibby. I do the welcoming 'round here. Welcome to the Oaks. Let me take you bags."

As Suzanne and John stepped from the buggy, the front door opened and Suzanne's mother, who had arrived several weeks earlier, rushed down to greet them.

"Well, I see you two made it fine," Mrs. Olliver said, reaching out to hug Suzanne. Then turning to John, she exclaimed, "I feel comforted that you were able to escort her."

John still mystified replied, "It was indeed my pleasure, Mrs. Olliver."

"It's too warm to stand out here in this sun. Let's retire into the house," Mrs. Olliver said, leading the way up the steps.

Inside, John continued to marvel at the beauty of the house. The receiving room, as Mrs. Olliver called it, was floored with a grayish tile; the ceilings were at least sixteen feet high. The plastered walls were as white as any he had ever seen, and in the adjoining rooms, the tile floors gave way to exported Philippine mahogany. Every window was bordered with blending shades of pastel curtains that reached to the floor, and outside there were heavy shudders that could be closed in case of violent storms that often swept through without warning.

While Mrs. Olliver went to find her father, Suzanne took John on a tour. The mansion had a lower floor where buggies and carriages were kept along with rooms for the servants. The first floor that they entered from the staircase contained a parlor, library, an office for her grandfather to conduct his business, her grandparents' bedroom and several other rooms that were used for entertaining guests. To John's surprise, the second floor was divided into eight bedrooms, each containing two large glassed double French doors that led to the outside balcony. On the balcony, John could see for miles across the bayou country, and everywhere he looked there were oceans of sugarcane branches waving in the afternoon breeze.

Taking John by the hand and leading him up another winding set of stairs, Suzanne exclaimed, "You've got to see what's up here."

With the excitement of a youngster at Christmas, Suzanne pulled John along until they reached a set of heavy oak doors at the head of the stairway. Suzanne pushed the doors open, revealing an enormous ballroom with polished oak floors so smooth one could literally slide across the surface when dancing. The walls were lined with glassed French doors identical to the ones below to allow the evening breeze to flow through, making it comfortable for guest. Even more impressive, was a large glassed cupola overhead that on a clear night allowed one to marvel at the wonders of the heavens.

Suzanne then took John out onto the balcony. There above the trees, John said, "Suzanne, you could have described this place to me, but in all of my imagination, I could have never envisioned it. It's breath-taking."

Suzanne placed her arms around his waist. "Breathtaking. John, it's more than that. It's an empire."

Faintly, the sound of hoof beats caught their attention as a rider approached. Recognizing the horseman, Suzanne threw up her arm and waving a handkerchief called out, "Papa! Papa Bordeaux!"

Covering his eyes from the glare of the late afternoon sun, he looked up for the familiar voice. "I see you're at ya favorite place, Young Lady. Better get on down here and give yore pappy a hug."

Suzanne bounded down the two sets of stairs and in a matter of seconds, was standing, open-armed before her grandfather who was still on his horse. Sitting in front of him on the saddle was a beautiful two year old girl with curly red hair and dark green eyes.

"Suzanne, help me with Amanda, then I'll take that hug."

John, who had followed Suzanne down, stepped forward. "Here, let me take her, Sir."

"You're John Wilson, aren't you?" he asked as he handed the child down.

"Yes sir," John answered, extending his hand

"John," Suzanne said, "I'd like for you to meet my grandfather."

"Very nice to meet you," John said.

Suzanne's grandfather and John were about equal height, well over six feet tall, and by the way Mister Bordeaux carried himself, John could sense a certain air of confidence. His thick course hair was snowy white, and he was much thinner than John with a face lined with wrinkles earned by too many hours in the sun.

"These are two fine women here, aren't they Mister Wilson?" Mister Bordeaux said.

John nodded and smiled. But in his mind he thought, she looks so much like her. The child is the perfect image of her mother.

"About time you two got back. You should tell someone when you go off riding," Suzanne's mother said as she made her way down to where they were standing.

"Papa, you know you're not in the best of health."

Reaching over to John, she said. "I'll take this sweet child now, and you folks better get cleaned up for dinner. Won't be long."

That evening they were served pompano en papillote (pompano fish baked with shellfish sauce in a paper bag), a popular dish in southern Louisiana. When dinner was finished and wine was served, Mister Bordeaux, impressed by John's manners and how easily he conversed, raised his glass and said, "Welcome to my home, Mister Wilson. Welcome to the Oaks."

"I appreciate you having me. It is indeed my pleasure."

"I understand you run a plantation of your own."

John glanced over at Suzanne. Clearing his throat, he replied, "Where did you hear that, Sir?"

"Why Suzanne told me. She's told me a lot about you," Mister Bordeaux replied with a smile.

"Sir, I think she made more of our place than is really there. It's only —"

"A large farm, Papa, is what he's trying to say," Mrs. Olliver said seeing that Suzanne had embarrassed John with her exaggeration. "A very large farm."

Later John and Suzanne returned to the ballroom. Pushing the glassed doors back, they went over to a large couch made of small interwoven vines and covered with thick cushions. A half moon was hovering over the treetops, and the sky was covered with stars. In the distance owls screeched to one another, and over in the swamps, the cry of a panther sent chills down their backs.

John sat quietly with his arm around Suzanne.

In a few minutes John got up and walked over to the railing that surrounded the balcony. "Why'd you make that remark about our place. You know it's not true," he said softly.

Suzanne eased over to John and placed her arm around his. "I don't know. I guess I just got carried away. Can you forgive me?"

"I am what I am. No more, no less. From now on, just tell the truth."

Suzanne squeezed his arm. "I promise I won't do it again. Let's sit down."

John sat quietly thinking about all he had seen and experienced that day and how practically nothing had been said about Mrs. Bordeaux. Turning to Suzanne, he said, "Tell me about your grandmother. You say she's here. If it's something that I don't need to know about, please excuse my questioning."

Suzanne dropped her head and sighed.

"Grandmother was the most beautiful, charming person I have ever known, and Papa worshiped the ground she walked on. Even though he spent long hours running this place, when he came home, they were always together."

Suzanne paused for a moment then continued, "They traveled abroad, gave numerous parties in New Orleans and I can't tell you the times the ballroom upstairs rang with the sound of music and dancing. She was the toast of Louisiana. We've entertained governors, foreign dignitaries — then we lost her."

Seeing the pain on her face, John pulled her to him and whispered, "You don't have to tell me any more."

Clearing her voice, she murmured, "Something happened to her. Over time, Meme, that's what I call her, began to forget things and finally she didn't recognize us any more. She would wander out of the house, and Papa had no idea of where she was. She went missing one night and, with the help of Papa's hounds, he found her down in the swamp, waist deep in water, just standing there glaring up at the moon."

Suzanne paused for a moment. "She has her own room. Papa keeps her there. He can't bear to see her that way. He still loves her more than life itself. He loves her too much."

"I'm sorry, I shouldn't have asked."

12

LOUISIANA BALL

Meridian, Mississippi:

THE TRAIN SAT IDLY ON THE TRACKS, STEAM STREAMING from the sides of the great engine while smoke swirled upward from the blackened smokestack. Since no arrivals or departures were expected for the next two hours, there were few people around the station. At that moment two men came out of the side door of the station and made their way to the train and then up the steps to what appeared to be a new coach. Once inside, the two stood there admiring the craftsmanship.

"What ya think about it, Tim?"

Tim scratched his head in awe as he glanced around at the plush carpets, solid oak gaming tables with chairs to match and gas lamps with elaborate decorative covers. Down each side of the coach were large couches. At the far end was a bar that stretched the width of the car with six softly padded stools fastened securely to the floor. Behind the bar were numerous shelves of liquor.

"Never seen nothin' like it. It's got to be yours, ain't it, Frankie?"

Frank having a seat at one of the gaming tables, leaned back, crossed his legs and began to roll a smoke.

"It's mine," he replied, nonchalantly, "and I want you to run it for me."

"Run it for ya!" Tim exclaimed easing into the chair next to Frank. "What do you mean?"

Frank put his smoke down and reached behind him for two glasses and a bottle of bourbon.

"Tim, we've been friends all our lives, and I think it's time we made you a little money," he said as he poured them both a glass of whiskey.

True, he had known Frank all of his life, but thinking back, Tim could not recall anything Frank had ever done for him. In fact, it was general knowledge that Frank's parents had never approved of him or his family. As the late Frank Olliver had stated, "That Johnson boy ain't our kind of stock."

Finally Tim said, "You mean I'm to run a gaming house on a train?"

Frank smiled and replied, "You're one of the best gamblers I've ever run into in this part of the state, and it's about time you used your talents. Folks ain't traveling by horse and buggy no more to make long trips; they're going by train."

"That's shore the truth," Tim said, taking a swallow of bourbon.

"Well, the way I got it figured," Frank said, "is that it won't take long for the news to get out that we're running games with big money. I'll have some girls here, and I mean some good looking ones, and the drinks will be on the house. I ain't never seen many men that with a little whisky and a fancy whore, can't be sidetracked. You get my meaning?"

"I got it, but I'm still gonna run a good table," Tim said pushing his glass over for a refill.

"I know you will, and if you run into any trouble, I'll have someone here to handle things. If you have to, you can just throw 'em out the back," Frank laughed. "A few bumps and bruises probably won't kill 'em. You can leave here on a Monday and go to the likes of Memphis, St. Louis then down to New Orleans or you could go east to Birmingham, Atlanta or up the east coast. Tim, you can go where you wanna go. We should make a killin'."

Tim sat thinking about the proposal and knowing that there must be something in it for Frank, said, "What's the split, and what if'n I take a loss?"

Frank looked down into his near empty glass. "I own the coach and pay the girls. I'll take sixty percent. Knowing you, there won't be many losses, and if there is one that we can't handle, there's ways to get it back."

A worried look came across Tim's face. "Frank, I ain't never been in trouble with the law, and I'm not planning on it in the future. You know, I got an elderly mother to take care of."

Frank assured Tim that he wouldn't allow anything to happen to him and that this endeavor could make him a rich man. As far as the law went, Frank's experience through the years found that Olliver money had a way of persuasion.

As the two sat enjoying the afternoon, talk eventually turned to politics. Tim feeling light headed from too much liquor exclaimed, "He's gonna win it, ain't he, Frank? John is gonna win."

Frank, lying on one of the couches, also feeling the effect of the liquor, blurted back, "Like I told ya, Olliver money can put 'em anywhere I want 'em. I could send 'em to Washington, if it hit me just right. But I'll tell you one thing, he needs to quit that Nigguh talk and I mean right now, or else there might be someone else running against 'em."

Suddenly, the door opened and an attractive woman entered.

"You need something, Mister Olliver? I thought I heard you call."

Frank raised up on his elbow and motioned over to Tim. "You bring us another woman in here. Me and Mister Tim is in bus'ness."

Still stunned by Frank's offer, Tim was apprehensive that, after all of these years, Frank was making this offer now. He had never done anything for him before, and as youngsters, they certainly had not been close. Tim also knew that with the wealth Frank's father had accumulated, Frank didn't need the money they could make together. The earnings would be pocket change for Frank.

⚜

In the days following their arrival, John had been given several tours of the plantation, had been dined in the finest fashion and had on one occasion accompanied Suzanne back to New Orleans for a shopping trip. After a long discussion, Suzanne finally persuaded John to be fitted for a new suit. After viewing bundles of fabric, they decided on black velvet. As usual, John felt that he would be over dressed and did not want her to pay for the clothing. Suzanne's argument was that he had taken time away from his work to escort her to her grandparents' home, and this was a way she could compensate him for helping her.

The visit gave John time to get to know Frank's young daughter, Amanda. He had always been concerned about the way Frank sheltered her from anyone who would display any affection toward her.

John found that Amanda loved to join them on their walks near the crystal springs. The springs was a place where clear cold water gushed from under the roots of a giant cypress tree and formed a pool of crystal clear water that fed into a stream that eventually flowed into the Mississippi. He also discovered that she had a fascination for horses, and she was elated when allowed to ride along with him. He had never met a more lovable child. He couldn't understand why Frank treated her the way he did.

The next morning there was gray dawn outside and waking early, John tipped down the stairs with his boots in his hands so as not to awaken anyone. Sitting down on the bottom step, he put on his boots and quietly walked past the study. He thought he saw a glint of light coming from the room. Looking inside, he found Mister Bordeaux slumped over his desk. An empty whiskey bottle was lying on the floor by his feet, and an oil lamp was burning dimly on a shelf over his desk. Mister Bordeaux's eyes were partially open, and he was as still as death. Fear came over John as he eased over to where the man was sitting. Reaching down, John gently shook Mister Bordeaux's shoulder.

Bordeaux blinked his eyes and looked up at John. "Uh, who are you?" he grunted.

"It's me, Mister Bordeaux, John."

Mister Bordeaux ran his hands across the desk in search of his glasses, knocking an empty glass off the table.

"Damn!" he exclaimed, barely catching the falling object before it struck the floor. "Can't see worth nothing!"

"You might have stuck 'em in a pocket, sir," John said.

Mister Bordeaux quickly searched his pockets and found them exactly where he had placed them the night before. He put on his glasses and straightened himself.

"You been here all night?" John asked.

The old man motioned for John to take a seat and looking over at an open ledger, replied, "I'm off thirty-two thousand, four hundred and seventy dollars, and I don't know where in the hell it is."

"Have you been off this much before, sir?"

The old man frowned as he pushed his long grey unkempt hair out of his face. "More than I'd like to talk about."

"You mind if'n I take a look. I keep my family's records. I'll keep it confidential," John said.

Getting out of his seat, Mister Bordeaux muttered, "Don't mind at all. You find the error, and I'll make it worth your while. In the meantime, I'll go get us some coffee. I feel a little under the weather."

Mister Bordeaux soon returned with two steaming cups of coffee. The large clock standing over by the window ticked away as John flipped through the pages.

Finally, John turned to his host. "It's all here."

John then pointed out where the mistake had been made, and knowing that all was well, a calm came over the elderly gentleman. He explained to John that he had been troubled with his eyes for the past few years, and often when he was frustrated over not being able to balance his books, he would turn to the bottle. He knew this only made calculating more difficult and that he really should use better judgment.

Now content that all was well, he offered to pay John for his services, but John shook his head saying that no compensation was necessary and that he was glad he could help.

As Mister Bordeaux was closing his book and placing it away, a voice was heard from up the hall. "Breakfast is ready, Mast' Bo'deaux."

Bordeaux chuckled. "Dan never could say my name right, but he's a dandy of a cook."

As the men were finishing breakfast, the sun was just tipping the horizon and a light fog rested over the low places in the fields below the house.

Mister Bordeaux had enjoyed the past few days having John there with them and seeing how he generously gave of himself to help around the place; a friendship had developed between the two. In John, he could see a lot of himself as a young man.

Mister Bordeaux pushed away from the table and with a glint in his eyes, exclaimed, "I think it's time for us to take ride. I'm feeling a lot better now. I got some horses that need working. You do ride, don't ya? "

John grinned. "Most Southerners do. Seems like I was born in the saddle."

Dan, stirring a large pot of grits, stopped what he was doing and looked over toward Mister Bordeaux. "S'cuse me Mast' Bo'deaux, but if'n you is thinkin' 'bout them fast 'ens, the Misses ain't gonna like it narry a bit."

Mister Bordeaux looked over to John. "That's why I don't like for my daughter to come down here for too long. She thinks I got one foot in the grave. I may be gettin' older, but I ain't old, yet.

Changing the subject, he continued, "Suzanne says y'all raise some fine horses. That so?"

John nodded. "Yes Sir, some of the best. Yankees stole a bunch of 'em though."

"Heard about it. Them Bastards tried to get to my place, but I burnt the bridge, and them devils didn't want to take on the gators," he said as he led John down to the barn. "I wish them Yanks had tried to cross. Them gators would've taken a chunk outta their hides quicker than a bee makes honey."

The building was a typical two story structure that contained a loft where hay and grain were stored, and on the bottom floor ten stalls lined each wall. Smelling the aroma of horse manure and grain, John felt at home. Pushing the door open, Mister Bordeaux called out, "Henry! You here?"

A door in the back squeaked open and a large Negro man wearing only his longhandle underwear and barefooted, wandered out.

"Yes Sir, I'se heah, Mastuh," Henry replied rubbing his eyes. "What can I do fer ya?"

Mister Bordeaux pointed to the end stalls. Saddle up my horse and give Mister Wilson the big Bay."

"The big Bay," Henry stammered with a concerned look on his face. "You shore 'bout that?"

"Do what I say," Mister Bordeaux said softly.

It didn't take Henry long to saddle Mister Bordeaux's mount, but when he entered the Bay's stall all hell broke loose. Between the horse's whinnying, Henry's cursing and the sounds of objects being knocked around in the stall, John felt it would be luck if Henry came out alive. Finally the stall door opened, and Henry emerged covered with dirt and manure, leading one of the largest horses John had seen in quite some time.

Once in the open hallway, the Bay reared up and kicked. Henry, meeting the challenge, held the bridle tightly. After the horse almost broke free, Henry exclaimed, "Mastuh, I'se not shore you needs to put Mister Wilson on this 'un!"

John stepped forward and took the reigns.

The horse tried to pull free, but John pulled its head close to him and with his right hand began to stroke the side of his massive neck. As the horse calmed down, John began to whisper to him. In a few moments, the Bay relaxed and John mounted.

Astounded, Bordeaux and Henry looked at each other and then back to John.

"How'd you do that, John." Mister Bordeaux asked with a puzzled look on his face.

"He was just a little nervous, that's all," John replied.

Henry readied another horse for Bordeaux, and he and John galloped out of the barnyard and across the fields. They rode all the way to the bridge some four miles from the house, and then took side roads on their way back. Seeing a large stand of live oaks ahead with a cluster of houses beneath, John asked, "Who lives over there?"

They reigned their horses to a stop and Bordeaux said, "That's my quarters. Used to call 'em slave quarters. Just call 'em quarters now. Want to see 'em?"

"I'd like to," John replied turning his horse in that direction.

Since it was still early, there were only a few people stirring about. As they entered the quarters, John was amazed at the number of cabins. On each side of the road for at least a half mile were one- or two-roomed log dwellings well kept and neatly spaced with enough room between them for a small garden. The roofs were covered with cypress shingles, and each contained a stoned chimney. By normal standards, this was a better than average Negro quarter.

As they rode through, dogs ran out from under some of the front porches to meet the riders, alerting residents that someone was invading their territory. Bordeaux scolded them back with his long whip, and the two continued down the road. On several occasions John would hear someone call out, "Good to see ya, Mastuh Bordeaux or Mawning Mastuh."

As they were leaving, John thought it was like walking back in time to slavery. Nothings changed here. He's still their master, and they're still in bondage.

Seeing the concerned expression on John's face, Bordeaux asked, "That place bothering you?"

Slowing his horse to a walk, John paused a moment, pursed his lips and replied, "Seeing those Negroes back there made me think." Then he shook his head and continued, "It ain't nothing."

Sensing his feelings, Bordeaux said, "You haven't been around me for long, but I know a thinker when I see one. What ya saying is that nothing appears to have changed here in regards to my plantation and my Nigguhs. It's just like the old days before the war."

John smiled. "That's about it, Sir."

Bordeaux reached over and grabbing John's horse's reigns, pulled them to a stop.

Staring out over the fields up ahead, the elderly gentleman said, "John, this farmland is the only place these people have ever known. Most of 'em were born here, and in most cases they've never even crossed the waterway. I feed and cloth 'em and take care of 'em when they're sick. In a sense, this is the only world they know. They have no idea what exists outside of the plantation."

"Are they free, Mister Bordeaux?"

Mister Bordeaux looked over at John. "When the war ended."

Then he corrected himself. "When the Federals took control of this part of the state, I called all my hands in and told 'em that if they wanted to go, they had my blessing."

"Did any of 'em go?" John asked.

Bordeaux nodded. "Out of over four hundred, seven left. The rest went back home, and they're still here and I'm still taking care of 'em."

Then looking at the long stretch of road ahead, Bordeaux said, "Enough of this talk. See that stretch up front. Fifty dollar gold piece says that Bay can't outrun this Tennessee Walker!"

"Heaaaah!" Mister Bordeuax shouted kicking his horse in the flank. The animal bolted forward throwing dirt all over John.

Taking the challenge, John responded and in seconds they were thundering down the road. Bordeaux, was over ten lengths ahead, but John leaning near the horses neck and high in the saddle soon began to gain ground. Nearing an open field, Bordeaux suddenly turned off the road and in one leap, cleared a rail fence and was racing across a grassy meadow. Not knowing whether or not his Bay could follow suit, John pushed the horse forward. With one giant leap, the horse easily cleared the timbers and the chase was on. Bordeaux glanced back to see if John was following and smiled when he saw them not ten lengths behind. At the far end of the field, the men could now see the roof of the barn. John pushed the Bay harder as they crossed the field, and soon he was only a half-length behind. At that time he relaxed, and the race was over.

As they cantered into the barnyard, Bordeaux reigned his horse to a stop and sitting there, exclaimed, "You didn't want the fifty, did you Son?"

John, pulling his horse to a stop next to Bordeaux replied, "You beat me, Sir."

Bordeaux stepping down from the stirrups, reached into his front coat pocket, pulled out a fifty dollar gold piece and flipped it over to John. "You're too much of a gentleman, Young Man. You let me win. First I got a head start on ya, and you closed to a half-length and could have took me. That horse'll outrun anything in the parish."

John tucked the coin in his pants pocket and replied, "Was it that obvious?"

"Downright clear. You know most folks can't even mount that devil, much less ride 'em," Bordeaux said.

Henry, now dressed, came out to meet them. "See y'all made it back. Can't believe Mist' Wilson stayed on that hoss."

"He did just fine. You know, I think I'll try 'em next time," Bordeaux said, handing his reigns to Henry.

Taking the reigns of both horses, Henry shook his head. "Lawd have mercy Mast' Bordeaux, please wait 'till Miss Judith leaves here 'fore you tries it."

Walking up the path toward the house, Bordeaux placed his arm over John's shoulder and said, "I'm really enjoying your visit. You've made life interesting around here. You and Suzanne need to come down here more often. How 'bout us going to get some coffee?"

With coffee in their hands, Bordeaux and John made their way out of the steamy kitchen to a bench outside where they made themselves comfortable. A gentle breeze swayed the long strands of moss hanging from the trees growing about the place. John had never felt more relaxed.

Taking a sip of coffee, Bordeaux said, "What ya think about the place?"

John, blowing his coffee to cool it, replied, "I've never seen anything like it. Suzanne tried to describe it to me, but she didn't do it justice."

Bordeaux chuckled. "Well, she's always liked the place. It'll be hers one day."

"What do ya mean?" John asked, easing his cup down.

"When I'm gone, this place will go to my daughter, Judith, and from her to Suzanne."

"How about Frank? He is your grandson."

Bordeaux took another swallow of coffee. "He's got enough to keep him busy, plus I got two more farms that'll be his one day. Hell, I don't know whether I trust him to run it."

He then reached over and placed his hand on John's arm. "You care for my granddaughter, don't ya?"

Startled by the question, John hesitated for a moment and then replied, "She's a fine woman. I'm very fond of her."

"She talks about you all the time. You know the girl loves you."

Feeling a cramp developing in his legs, Bordeaux stood up to stretch. After a moment of twisting and rubbing his calves, he eased back down.

"I'm getting too old to run the place, and from what I've learned about you, you could take over the whole operation. You'd be one of the richest men in Louisiana. What do you think about that, John?"

John blushed, and looking over to Bordeaux said, "I've got something I've got to see through back home before I commit to anything like this."

"You talking about that damned ole election. You won't make no money at that. You marry Suzanne and come on down here with me, and I'll see to it that the two of you will do just fine," Bordeaux said, hoping to coax John into considering the offer.

Meridian, Mississippi:

The men sat quietly around the table chatting, while outside it was business as usual in the town. Wagons were squeaking and rattling as they made their way down the rough street, and up the way, the high-pitched voices of women laughing and talking made the men chuckle as they unintentionally eavesdropped on their conversations. A light tap at the door was heard.

"That you, Hendon?"

"It's me," came a voice as the door opened.

"Come on in. We've been waiting on ya."

Entering, Hendon found six men seated around a large round table with a haze of smoke skirting the entire ceiling of the room.

"Have a seat, Fessor. Time's short. You know everybody here, don't ya?"

Hendon nodded and then went about shaking each of their hands, "Sorry I'm late. There was a delay down at Hickory Station."

"I understand," McWorthan said taking charge of the meeting. "Now let me get to the point. "Fessor, we got a hot boy in that Wilson. Folks listen to 'em, and they can't help but like 'em. Is he electable? Damned right he is. Is he gonna be elected? I'm not so sure. He's beginning to worry me."

"What do you mean by that?" Hendon asked. "The boy's a winner."

Looking over the top of his glasses resting low on his nose, McWorthan explained. "There's a Nigguh problem. There's Nigguhs in the legislature and senate. There's Nigguhs roaming the streets down there in Newton throwing insults at every white that dares to cross paths with 'em. There's Nigguhs gettin' white folk's land, and you know what the Nigguhs did to Mister Frank Olliver a while back. They killed 'em! Shot 'em to pieces."

"I know that. What are you getting at?" Hendon said.

McWorthan suddenly brought his clinched fist down against the table sending glasses rolling about. "Listen, Hendon! That boy of yores wants to give 'em land. He even feels we ought to educate the bastards. 'Fore long, I guess they'll be the masters and we'll be the Nigguhs."

"Over my dead body!" scowled one of the men. "Democrats ain't gonna stand fer that."

Hendon stood, shaking with anger. "Let me tell you something. There's not a man running in the state that has the qualifications of Wilson. Yes, he made some remarks about seeing to the needs of the Negroes, but he's not about to forget our needs either. He's a man of vision. Like most politicians, he's a dreamer."

"Vision, Dreamer, my ass!" McWorthan interrupted. "He wants to help the Nigguhs, and the party ain't gonna stand for it one bit, Fessor."

"What do you plan to do, take 'em off the ballot," Hendon muttered.

"Sit down, Fessor. No sense gettin' upset. What I'm saying is that there is a lot of people outside of Newton County that ain't so sure about what he's got in mind," McWorthan said.

"I'm not sure he's our kind of Democrat. His talk has scared some folks."

"Then what are you saying?"

McWorthan glared over at Hendon. "We can't afford to lose this election. If Wilson should falter, then our district would still be in Republican hands. It'll be a cold day in hell when that happens."

The room became quiet, and in a moment McWorthan sighed. "But you know, there is more than one way to skin a cat. What if'n we placed one of our own men on the Republican ticket. That'd be interesting, wouldn't it?"

Louisiana:

With their visit nearing its end, Bordeaux and Judith decided to host a Louisiana Low Country cookout and ball in honor of Suzanne. Invitations were sent throughout the neighboring parishes and plans were made to transform the grounds into a tropical garden. Scores of Negro women were brought from the field to prepare the house for the guests who would be attending the ball, and outside, men worked with grass blades manicuring the grounds. Wagons loaded with a variety of potted plants arrived from New Orleans. Mister Bordeaux employed a Mister Sylvester Hubert, one of New Orleans most renowned chefs to supervise the food preparation. As custom, dinner would be served at seven o'clock, and from around nine to ten o'clock the bar would be open for the men to relax and socialize while the women changed into their evening attire.

On the day of the ball, people began to arrive at mid-afternoon. Most came in buggies and carriages and all were well dressed. Even in afternoon attire, the women were dressed as fine as John had ever seen back in Mississippi. Even though it was hot outside, the men were dressed in suits, ruffled shirts and ties.

Suzanne was radiant. All eyes were directed at her. Her looks plus the flowing light gray dress with white silk blouse made it difficult for any man to ignore her beauty. Her jet black hair was pulled back and away from her face and softly traced the curve of her back.

John, dressed in a dark gray suit, escorted Suzanne throughout the afternoon, and he caught the eye of the ladies who were anxiously waiting to meet him. Tall, sturdy and extremely handsome, John portrayed a southern gentleman in every aspect.

As in New Orleans, a flow of French or Creole dialect could be heard, and to John's pleasure, everyone was exceptionally friendly and courteous.

At seven o'clock, Bordeaux stepped up on a platform that had been constructed for the occasion and lightly tapped on a glass to get the crowd's attention. "Ladies, Gentlemen, Friends, welcome to the Oaks."

A warm round of applause was heard as the guests began to gather about him.

"If you haven't met my daughter, Judith, she's that gorgeous woman there in the lavender dress," Bordeaux stated, pointing down to a blushing but smiling Judith. "And I'd like for you all to meet my granddaughter, Suzanne. Come on up here, Sugar. I'm not going to hide you."

As Suzanne made her way up the steps, the men could not restrain themselves. They clapped and whistled their approval.

Taking her by the hand, he said, "She's sump'n, isn't she?"

Once again the crowd applauded.

"Won't do you no good to get your hopes up, She's got an escort. Mister Wilson, you better get on up here and claim this fair lady 'fore some of these Louisiana boys get some ideas."

Suzanne blushed as John worked his way through the crowd to the platform. As he stepped next to Suzanne, it was the women this time who began to cheer and nod their heads at the striking young man standing there.

Bordeaux held his hand up and then continued, "This is John Wilson from Little Rock, Miss'sippi, and from what I've heard, he's headed for the state legislature next year."

"Is he a Republican?"

Bordeaux laughed and shouted back, "No Sir! He's a damned ole Democrat!"

The guest roared with laughter.

After a moment, Bordeaux raised his hand again and said, "Folks, we're here to show these young folks how we party down here in the Bayou, and I hope you all have the time of your life. If you go away hungry, it'll be your fault. We've got barbecued pork, beef, and goat with all the trimmings. We've got boiled shrimp and crawfish for those who have the taste, and fresh boiled corn on the cob and every treat you can imagine. Also, you must try our huitres en coquille a' la Rockefeller. We say the bar opens at nine, but that's just a figure of speech. It was open the time you set foot on my property."

Never had John enjoyed a meal like the one the Bordeaux's had prepared, and as he thoroughly enjoyed talking with the native Louisianans, the evening quickly was coming to an end. Around nine, John went to his room to freshen up and get dressed for the ball. Standing in front of the body-sized mirror, he put on his new black suit, combed his hair and paused to reflect on all he had experienced there in the Bayou. Thinking to what Bordeaux had proposed, John became excited over the possibilities that could await him here in Louisiana. Never had he seen such a display of wealth.

The melodic sound of music coming from above caught John's attention, and knowing that it was time for the ball to begin, he quickly adjusted his tie and made his way to Suzanne's room. As he tapped on the door, droves of couples were passing by on their way to the ballroom. Some women's dresses were so full they completely filled the hallway. The door opened and Suzanne, dressed in black velvet, stood waiting. Unlike the other women, her dress was more form fitting and was not as full at the skirts. The top of her dress was tight and revealing, causing John to blush.

"Is something wrong, John," smiled Suzanne, well aware of how easily he could be embarrassed. "Do I look all right for you?"

John stammered, "You look stunning."

John could feel a tingling sensation as he looked at how beautiful Suzanne appeared. Never had he seen her more sensuous.

Suzanne whirled around so John could get the full view of her dress and exclaimed, "It's from Paris. I'm wearing it just for you."

Unable to control his emotions, John reached out and gently took her hand and said, "You're really something," and closing the door behind them, embraced her.

By the time John and Suzanne reached the ballroom, most of the guests were already dancing and enjoying the music of a string ensemble from New Orleans. All the French doors around the massive room had been opened to allow fresh air to circulate.

As they were about to enter the ballroom, Suzanne eased her arm under John's and nudging up to him whispered, "You know you're the most handsome man here tonight. I'm glad you decided to come down with me."

Again John blushed.

Seeing Suzanne and John enter, Bordeaux pushed his way through the crowd to where they were standing. He gently hugged Suzanne and gave her a quick kiss on the cheek and then turned to John. "This ball is for both of you. Your visit has meant a lot to me."

Then squeezing John's hand, he continued, "You remember what I told ya, John."

The sound of music and laughter filled the night as couples floated around the floor waltzing the hours away. Suzanne and John tried to be together as much as possible, but by custom, it was rude for the women not to dance with others when approached.

Later in the evening as he and Suzanne were dancing, John noticed that Bordeaux had finally made it to the floor, and to his surprise, he saw him with a woman who looked familiar. Dancing closer to where they were, John suddenly remembered.

"Suzanne, you see who your grandfather's dancing with? That's the woman I met at the hotel."

Suzanne glanced over his shoulder and then leaning up whispered, "They're old friends. Papa still enjoys a little feminine companionship."

Trying not to stare, John replied, "I'm not sure what you mean. What about your grandmother?"

"She is really not here anymore. The grandmother I once knew really doesn't exist," Suzanne said softly.

At that moment, Suzanne and John turned to find Judith motioning them over to where a table of refreshments was waiting. Extending glasses to them, she said, "You like a Louisiana Ball, John."

"Yes Ma'am, I've never seen anything like it."

Judith laughed and reached out and took each by the hand. "Suzanne, folks can't believe you're the same little skinny girl that was so shy she wouldn't dare step from behind my skirt tail. And for you, Mister John Wilson, to the ladies here, you are a handsome sight to behold. It seems like I've spent the whole night answering questions about you."

As dawn approached, many of the guests retired for the evening, and only a few were still dancing. The sound of people talking and laughing had given way to a slight murmur.

John took Suzanne by the hand and led her to the outside porch that extended entirely around the ballroom. A cool morning breeze brushed against them. A glow in the east gave notice that a new day was dawning, and off in the distance birds were singing. Patches of fog covered the countryside.

"It's beautiful at this time of day, isn't it?" Suzanne asked, placing her arm around his waist.

John smiled down at her and looking into her eyes, felt as if she could see to the depths of his soul. Strangely, he was opening the barrier, allowing her to enter where only one other had ever been before.

An unusual warm feeling of elation filled John as he stood holding Suzanne, one that he had seldom experienced. Pushing a strand of hair from her face, he pulled her to him and said, "It's an enchanting country."

Feeling the warm touch of her breath and the soft touch of her bare shoulders, he murmured, "We've known each other a long time. Maybe we should be together. Maybe it is time for us."

13

FALL ELECTION

As THE MASSIVE WHEEL CHURNED AWAY AT THE MIGHTY Mississippi, sending waves of muddy water rolling toward the shore, John, standing next to the guard railing on the second floor, watched as the boat struggled against the current. To him it seemed as if his visit to the low country of Louisiana was a dream. It was a strange land, a land where Negroes were free to leave the plantation but chose to stay and remain in servitude. They had no concept of what life held for them on the outside, but only knew that their basic needs were being met.

Immersed in his thoughts, John was startled as an arm slipped under his.

Flinching, he said, "You surprised me."

Pointing toward a large stand of cypress trees growing at the edge of the water, Mrs. Olliver exclaimed, "Beautiful, isn't it?"

John nodded. "I've enjoyed every moment."

She smiled up at him and squeezing his arm replied, "This place is enchanting, a place you never forget. Yes, the bayou country can surely cast a spell on you."

The two stood quietly, enjoying the cool breeze brushing against their faces as the boat slowly moved upstream. The sun was now setting, and the trees along the banks were casting long shadows across the water.

Mrs. Olliver finally broke the silence. "You'll never know how happy you've made me. I couldn't have picked anyone more pleasing than you. You know you've always been special to us."

John, in reflection, felt elated about his engagement to Suzanne. She was fun, exciting and beautiful beyond imagination, but John was aware of barriers between them that must be overcome.

Looking out across the way and in a soft voice he replied, "I'll try to do my best."

Mrs. Olliver reached over to where John's hand was resting on the rail and placed her hand over his. "You two will do just fine. When Frank proposed to me, I wasn't sure I wanted to spend my lifetime with him, and I certainly didn't want to move to Miss'sippi, but we survived."

Survived, thought John. I don't want a marriage that just survives. I want a marriage that flourishes, one that grows stronger as the years pass, one strong enough to endure the trials that life will certainly bring, one like my mother and father's.

"It's almost seven. We're supposed to meet Suzanne for dinner," Mrs. Olliver said.

"It would be a pleasure for you to escort me," she teased, reaching for John's arm.

Even in her early fifties, Mrs. Olliver didn't look a day over forty and was still capable of turning a man's head. Taking his arm, they made their way down the walkway to the steps that led to the first floor where dinner was being served.

§§

When the party finally reached the Olliver's home, John stayed and rested for several hours then said his goodbyes. Since the minute he had proposed, Suzanne was energized by thoughts of their wedding and had already begun making the necessary plans. Never had he seen her more talkative.

Cantering down the rough red clay road leading to Little Rock, he slowed his mount to a trot. Leaving the Ollivers and with thoughts of home, a different feeling crept over him. Gone was the excitement of visiting the Queen City, and no longer could he remember the smell of the bayou as the wind swept through the fields of sugar cane causing an eerie whistling sound. As hard as he tried, he couldn't recall even the melody of a single song the orchestra had played the night before they left. No longer did he see the stately homes that dotted the landscape along the Mississippi nor the well-dressed people displaying their wealth openly. Thinking of his neighbors and their hard times made the extravagance in Louisiana embarrassing to him.

As he passed small farms with log cabins and barns out back and a small garden site within walking distance, John felt he was truly home. As John stopped to water his horse, a few people could be seen, most dressed in common homespun clothing and many were barefoot. He suddenly realized that he was reluctant to hurry home, and the reason had to do with his engagement.

Nearing the house, John spotted his mother sweeping the front yard. Custom dictated that no grass was allowed to grow in front of a house and any that was found was quickly pulled up by the roots. Hearing hoof beats, Mrs. Wilson stopped her sweeping, turned and holding her hand over her eyes to shut out the mid-morning sun, squinted to see the rider.

Reigning the horse to a stop, John quickly dismounted and hurried over to his mother who was waiting with open arms.

"'Bout time you got yoreself home, boy. Thought you'd be here yesterday."

John squeezed her gently. "Been a long trip, Mama."

"Hey, Son," called Lott from the tool shed where he had been repairing some mule harnesses. "I'll be right there."

After a long embrace and a handshake, Lott told John how they had missed him and that Andy had even brought along one of his Negro friends and some Choctaws to help them with their work. Lott also told John that they had received several hard rains and the corn and cotton could not look better. Wanting to show John how well the crops were doing, Lott saddled two horses and with little coaxing, persuaded John to ride out with him.

What was supposed to be an hour ride turned into an afternoon as Lott and John rode for hours looking, talking and enjoying each other's company. Although Lott never asked about John's trip to Louisiana, John knew that he had to share his experiences with him. At one point when they stopped to water their horses, John started to tell Lott about his engagement to Suzanne, but held back.

With the sun setting, the two finally made it back home. As they unsaddled their horses and were brushing them down, John said, "Mama ain't doing too good, is she Papa? She looks a might sickly."

Lott reached up with his handkerchief, wiped his forward and with an expression of concern that John had rarely seen, replied, "Can't hold out no more. Doc's not sure what's wrong with 'er. He said it might be consumption. Might even be her heart or just like me, she might be just gettin' old."

John placed his arm around his Father's shoulder and said, "Papa, she's gonna be just fine. You don't need to be worrying none."

Tired from the long trip with little rest, John retired early that evening. Gone was the soft bedding of silk-like sheets. No longer could he hear the lonely sounds of boat horns bellowing in the night on their arrival at the docks in New Orleans. Only the familiar sounds of locust and tree frogs could be heard, and sleep came easy.

The next morning John opened his eyes to the creaking of a chair and a sense of light. At first, he thought he was in New Orleans, but immediately warmly remembered where he was. Sitting on the far side of his room next to a window with a lap of yarn was his mother mending a pair of his father's socks. This was her favorite spot to work. Here she had an excellent view of the front yard, the barn and the road that led to Little Rock. This spot allowed her to notice company coming and hurriedly get out to greet them.

His mother glanced over at John and stopped what she was doing to exclaim, "'Bout time you woke up. It's might near half past seven."

Seven-thirty was a late hour for the Wilson's since they were usually up before daylight and in the field by first light.

John rubbed his eyes. "Can't believe I slept so long. Must've been worn out. If'n you'll excuse me, I'll dress and be gone 'fore you can count to ten."

His mother shook her head and replied, "No need to hurry. Your pa says you need yore rest. By the way, Tim come by here 'bout daylight."

"Tim? What'd he want?"

She began to chuckle. "He was dressed to the kilt. I ain't ever seen nobody with them kind of clothes. He had a fancy suit with a vest and tie and a pair of new shoes with something that he called spats 'bout his ankles. Yore Papa had to fight to keep from laughing. He was sump'n to behold."

Rolling his pillow up under his head, John repeated, "Mama, what'd he want?"

"Wanted to see you and when we wouldn't let him wake you, he settled in for breakfast with us. That's might near all of it," she replied.

Feeling that certainly some details had been omitted since Tim never visited at this time of the day, John exclaimed, "He wanted sump'n. What's he up to, Mama?"

His mother dropped her head and fumbling through her yarn in search of the needle that had fallen beside her chair, she murmured, "I think you need to tell us something, don't ya, Son."

John knew exactly what Tim had told them. He always knew the secrets of the town before anyone.

John drew a deep breath, thought a moment, then replied, "I should've told you yesterday." Almost too soft to hear, John continued, "Suzanne and me is marrying."

Mrs. Wilson eased out of her chair and edged her way over to the foot of his bed where she settled herself. With a sweet expression she said. "I think that's wonderful, Son. I've worried about you through the years. The way you lost Rebecca and what the war seemed to do to ya. You deserve some happiness. If you two love each other, I think you'll do just fine."

Hearing her comforting words, John felt better, but in his mind he questioned why he hadn't mentioned his engagement to them earlier. Reaching out and clasping one of his mother's hands, he said, "You sure it's all right?"

"Suzanne'll make you a good wife. She's always cared for ya."

"What'd Papa say?" John asked.

She thought a moment, then answered, "He didn't say nothin'. He finished his coffee, excused himself and went on outside; didn't say a word."

John knew what his father's silence meant. He knew that his father had nothing against Suzanne, but the Olliver family had always been a thorn in his side. Even though Frank Sr. was dead, he could not dismiss all that Frank had done. He had used people, destroying their lives to gain his fortune. Even from his grave, the hatred was still there. As hard as he tried, he could not forgive Frank Olliver, especially for his part in the murder of his brother.

Never had such a stir of excitement rustled a community as the one caused by word of the engagement of Suzanne to John. Seeing them together over the years, people were not at all surprised, and when word got out as to the elaborate wedding plans, the community became ecstatic. In fact, a rumor was circulating that since Suzanne's mother was Catholic, they had already made arrangements to have the wedding in the St. Louis Cathedral in New

Orleans. Since money was no factor, it was further rumored that anyone who wanted to attend would have free transportation and lodging, compliments of the Ollivers.

Several days later, an unusual shift of weather dropped the temperature down into the forties. Since it was late summer in southeastern Mississippi, this temperature drop was a phenomenon. With a light rain falling, little work could be done so John and his parents sat in front of a crackling fire enjoying its warmth and a much needed day of rest. Even the hounds under the house didn't venture out to greet an approaching lone rider. Hearing footsteps in the hall and a tap on the door, Lott called out, "Come on in. We're here by the fire."

Taking off his wet oilcloth, the man hung it on a peg in the hallway and entered. With his dripping hat in his hand, he said, "Can't believe this weather."

"Fessor, what in tarnations are you doing out on a day like this? You'll catch yore death for sure," Mrs. Wilson exclaimed motioning him in. "Seems more like early winter, don't it?"

John and Lott got up to greet Hendon and then pushed their chairs about to make a space for him.

Shivering from the cold, Hendon settled himself and reaching out his hands toward the flames, said, "Miss Sarah, any chance to get one of your hot cups of coffee. I'm might near frozen."

Sarah chuckled as she got up and headed toward the kitchen. "Fessor, you never could rough it out here, could ya? I'll be back shortly. Y'all must have some politickin' to do."

Hendon smiled over at her and nodded.

Shortly Sarah returned with steaming cups of coffee for all the men and then excused herself.

As Hendon sat sipping his drink, his damp clothes began to produce steam from the heat of the fire. After some talk about the weather and how the crops were doing, Hendon took out his pipe and began packing it for a smoke. He then reached over and took a small piece of flaming bark from the fire and held it to the end of his pipe. After a few deep draws, he stared at the flames flickering about in the hubble of logs stacked in the fireplace and said, "There's been a turn in the political scene."

John leaning back, straight legged with his feet to the fire, straightened himself, sat his coffee cup down on the floor and looking over at Hendon, asked, "What do ya mean by a turn?"

Hendon glanced down at the floor and then slightly back toward John. "Your talk about the Negroes has upset more folks in the district than we figured."

"I know that," replied John, rising and turning to warm his back. "We've all known that."

Lott, not overly concerned about the conversation but wanting to know what Hendon meant, muttered, "So what's going on?"

Hendon took another deep draw and blowing smoke from his nose, continued, "Gossips going around. You might even say there's a lot of exaggeration and downright lies."

"That's not unusual in politics," John said easing back to his chair.

"It may not be unusual, but with all the talk and discontent, the head of our party feels that we have a chance of losing this district if we don't do something, and they don't want to lose," Hendon replied, twisting his neck about as if to relieve a crick.

Lott then got up to warm himself and looking down at Hendon, said, "Fessor, seems like I've known you all my life and every time you start that neck twisting, sump'n ain't right. So what have y'all up and done?"

Hendon reached up rubbed his nose and then working his fingers about as if to increase circulation, said, "They're not sure you can carry the district. So what they've done is to put one of our men on the Republican ticket just in case you don't win it. They feel that one of our own white Mississippians can easily beat Templeton and if you do win, that'll be good and if you don't, well. "

"But as you say, if Templeton can be so easily beaten, why bother with running someone else on the Republican ticket? I believe I can take him," John said, becoming uneasy over the turn of events.

Hendon again rubbed his nose and gave a faint cough. "John, there's a lot of negative talk out there, and yes, I think you can win the district but what if you don't."

The men sat there silent for a moment and then Hendon said, "With our dual plan, we feel that no matter what happens, we can carry this election."

John got up and walked over to the window and with the rain steadily dripping off the eaves of the house, said, "Who's gonna run on the other ticket?"

All was quiet and finally with another nervous cough, Hendon replied, "The committee thinks that maybe Frankie is the man for it. He didn't want to, but reluctantly he agreed to help us if we needed him."

"Frankie!" Lott said, rising from his seat. "What in the devil do y'all mean doing sump'n like that. The boy ain't got a bit of common sense. Hadn't been for his daddy's stealing ways, he'd be as poor as a church mouse."

Shaking his finger in Hendon's face, he continued, "You better go talk to that so-called committee and straighten them out. My boy is gonna win this here election, come hell or high water!"

Hendon shook his head. "I think he will win, Lott, but with this plan, we can't loose. We feel that if Frankie can take enough votes away from Templeton then John will get the majority. He's only trying to help John, you understand?"

John, with his back to the group and still watching the rain fall replied, "I guess what's important is for us to get control of our gov'ment, and if it takes this, then maybe it might just work."

John knew in his heart that even though he and Frankie had been close friends growing up, Frankie never did much to help anyone unless there was some ulterior motive behind his action.

After Hendon left and John had time to reflect on what had transpired, he wondered why Suzanne or Mrs. Olliver hadn't said anything about this earlier. He had spent at least half the morning with them and Frankie at the house when they had returned and not a word was spoken about this new plan.

In the months that followed, John spent most of his time making trips with Professor Hendon to various social events in the district. Hendon felt that John needed as much exposure to the public as time would permit. It didn't matter whether it was a barn raising, church revival or an organized political rally, they would be there.

During this time, Frankie kept a low profile around Little Rock. John received word that he was out circulating around the district talking to the people and apparently was gaining some attention.

Fall had finally arrived bringing a cool crisp breeze out of the north.

The smell of cotton in the field and frosted golden leaves fluttering to the ground was invigorating after the long hot summer. A full late October moon was cresting the tree line to the east as the sound of an organ began to play. Inside a large tent well lit by lanterns, a group of over one hundred people swayed and sang as the revival preacher led them in a hymn. As they sang many bowed their heads in prayer while others raised their hands upward in praise.

Professor Hendon, sitting on the front bench leaned over, nudged John and whispered, "He'll give you some time after the closing prayer. Be ready and it's gotta be brief. It's kinda late."

Sitting there, John remembered how nervous he was when he first started speaking in public. He would worry about questions that might be asked and if he would have the knowledge to answer them. Then he would remember what the Professor had told him. If you don't have an answer, change the subject. He recalled that even on some of the more challenging questions that had been presented to him, he had handled them well.

As the preacher closed his prayer, John was completely relaxed and confident.

"Folks, I know it's a little late, but I have a young man who'd like to say a word. Mister Wilson, you can come on up now."

John quickly stood and made his way to the podium. After shaking the preacher's hand, John looked out at the congregation.

Clearing his throat, John said, "As brother Baker said, I'm John Wilson from Little Rock up in Newton County, and I first want to say that I enjoyed the service here tonight. Sitting here with you, I felt the spirit of the Lord moving amongst you, and at a time like this, I don't feel it's appropriate to mix church and politics. I would like to say that I was born and raised a Baptist, and I'm out trying to represent you in the state legislature. When y'all go out to the polls next month, I'd appreciate you remembering me, and if any of you want to talk with me, I'm here for ya if'n you got a little time."

Several of the men shook their heads in acknowledgment of his comment as they rose from their seats. Then as the people began to make their way to the inner aisle, a man in the back called out, "Heard tell you gonna shore 'nough take care of the Nigguhs. Anything to it?"

Since John's earlier comments about how he planned to help the Negroes, John had avoided the subject. Hendon had advised him not to bring it up now, but when elected, he could push his program as far as possible.

I need to change the subject if I can, but as he looked in the faces of the people seeking an answer, he knew he must respond.

John dropped his head in thought for a moment and ran his fingers across the side of his face as he contemplated what to say. Then raising his face to the crowd said, "If you've noticed, the Negroes have no place to go. Some of 'em have returned to the farm and a lot of 'em are simply roaming about looking for some way to make a living. Without some direction, I feel that they could end up in trouble with the law and could be a burden to society. I feel that for your benefit and theirs, someone has to take control of their welfare and give 'em some direction."

John hesitated a moment then closed by saying, "That's my stand on the issue, Sir."

The man in the back nodded his head, and the people began to filter out of the back of the tent to where their horses and wagons were waiting. No one came forward to meet John and talk with him, and in a matter of minutes everyone including the pastor was gone.

Standing there alone in the dark with John, Hendon exclaimed, "This has not been a good night. They ask one question, then don't respond to what you had to say, and then walk out on us. I don't know what to make of it."

"I guess what folks has been saying 'bout me is true, but you know I just have to be honest. I know the way I feel is not helping. Who knows, maybe some of them agreed with me. I'll know come election day, won't I."

John had made it clear to Suzanne that he was in no hurry to marry and when the election was over, he would then turn his thoughts to matrimony. Suzanne had already begun plans for a Christmas wedding, and since John's mother was not well enough to travel, the ceremony would be held in the Olliver's home. They needed more space than the local church afforded. For a wedding present, Mrs. Olliver had arranged for Suzanne and John to spend some time touring the Mediterranean coastline, and upon their return, Mrs. Olliver would arrange to purchase a house in Jackson, if the election went in his favor. In addition, she would build them another house in the Little Rock community with cost being no factor.

The officials expected a larger than normal turnout on election day.

Knowing the Negroes would turn out in mass, every white male eligible to vote was making plans to visit their local precinct. The white South knew that if it was to regain power and cast off the chains of reconstruction, it would have to be done at the polls. They also knew that to be successful, the Negro vote would have to be controlled.

In rural Mississippi, communication and protection was limited, especially at night, and it was in the dark that hooded men with torches traveled the countryside terrorizing and threatening any Negro who was a voter. For years, the Klan had been organizing and planning for such a time when they could release their force on anyone who stood in the way of the re-emergence of white supremacy. In the nights preceding the election, Negroes along with those whites who were supportive of the reconstruction government were warned to stay at home and away from the polls. They were threatened that those who made their way down the desolate country roads to cast their vote needed to keep in mind that the return home could be costly. Even though the military tried, they were unable to stop the raids, because they did not have enough troops to cover such large remote areas. The Negroes, mostly unarmed and extremely superstitious, were at the mercy of ghostly raiders or "haunts" who they believed came from the pits of hell. The nights prior to the election were filled with terror, burnings and in some isolated cases, murder. The South was again in a state of uncontrolled turmoil.

As the sun was setting, James, dressed in his Union uniform, rode up to the Wilson's home and dismounted. Mister and Mrs. Wilson and John had just finished supper and were sitting on the front porch enjoying a warm November evening.

"Where you been lately, James," Mister Wilson asked. "Missed you and Sister last Sunday."

James took off his hat, beat it against his leg to remove the dust, and answered, "Military has had us busy. A lot of devilment going on."

"What do you mean by devilment?" John asked.

James hesitated for a moment then replied, "Well, you're family, and what I say has got to stay right here."

Mrs. Wilson stopped her rocking, shook her head and said, "You don't have to tell us, not if'n you don't want to. Don't want to get ya in no trouble."

"No trouble," assured James. "You know that election day is day after tomorrow, and to be plain with you, the Klan is doing everything they can to stop the Negro voters."

"I ain't heard nothin' like that 'round here," Mister Wilson said. "That's news to me."

"Is that why you've been gone so much lately?" John asked.

James, reaching inside his coat pocket for his tobacco pouch replied, "Been doing a lot of riding. I don't have to tell you about the Klan. You know they're here, and you know there's an army of 'em out there; probably some of our own neighbors. They're riding around in the night scaring the Negroes to death. In fact, they've also burned some barns and homes and have actually murdered some folks. Washington is most concerned about what's happening down here. If they catch any of 'em, they're gonna string 'em up. The government's gonna stop this killing."

"Killing!" shuddered Mrs. Wilson. "That can't be, and it certainly ain't none of our neighbors. That's ungodly."

"It's happening all over Mississippi, and if the Klan has its way, there won't be a single Negro show up at the polls."

James suddenly stopped, scratched his head and then continued, "But thinking about what you had to say, Lott, it is strange that not much is happening around here. In fact, I've heard of very few instances of trouble in this district; maybe a little down below Newton."

Puzzled, James thought for a moment. "You know, I haven't thought about that before tonight, but there really isn't much activity at all around here."

After they had talked for a while, James got up from where he had been sitting, put on his hat and, looking over to John, said, "Been all over this district; looks like you're doing well with the voters."

He then began to chuckle. "In fact, I think you're even going to get some Negro votes, that is if they can make it to the polls. They like how you seem genuinely interested in helping them."

John, getting up to shake James's hand and to see him off, replied, "You never can tell. I understand I've upset some of the white folks with my Negro talk."

Lott got up slowly and twisting his back to relieve a cramp, muttered, "If he wins, I'll be proud of 'em but if'n he don't, we Wilsons will keep on doing just fine."

As James was mounting, John called out, "You hear much from Frankie? You run into him anywhere?"

Adjusting himself in the saddle, James replied, "He's out there talking the Republican talk. He's telling the Negroes he's gonna give 'em their forty acres and a mule just like some of 'em think Lincoln would have done. He's telling them whatever they want to hear."

James began to laugh as he rode off and shouted back, "He's lying through his teeth! I guess you of all people know that."

With a light frost on the ground and a beautiful clear sky, election day arrived. John and his family all went together down to Walker's store in Little Rock, the site of their local precinct, to cast their votes. Since James was away, they invited Sister to go along with them. Arriving at midmorning, they found the small village flooded with people excited about the election. Though only men could vote, Little Rock was full of women and children who had accompanied their husbands to town for a day of socializing. As they were getting out of the wagon, John spied Suzanne and her mother riding up in one of their buggies.

Waving, John called out, "Didn't know you were coming."

Suzanne waved back. "Didn't want to miss seeing you cast your vote."

John helped Suzanne down and then walking over to assist her mother, exclaimed, "I'm glad you made it. I appreciate you coming."

Mrs. Olliver smiled down to him. "We wouldn't have missed it for anything."

Later that afternoon, Hendon came over to visit the Wilsons, and as they talked together, he told John that it would take a couple of days for all the returns to come in and as soon as he knew something, he would let him know.

As the sun sank below the horizon, John knew that the votes had been cast and there was nothing he could do. It would only be a matter of time until he would know the results. He felt like he had done his best, and it was now left up to the people of his district, his fellow Mississippians, to decide who they wanted to represent them.

Anxious about the election, John found sleep impossible. Tossing and turning, all he could think of was, had the people found faith in him and, if elected, could he fulfill his promises. With day breaking and still wide awake, John got out of bed, dressed and went to the kitchen to make a pot of coffee.

Lott got up when he heard sounds from the back of the house.

Easing the door open, Lott saw John sitting in front of the wood stove, legs crossed, relaxed and trying to cool his coffee.

"I thought I could smell some coffee brewing. How 'bout pouring yore Daddy a cup," Lott said, pulling a chair up to enjoy the warmth of the stove on a nippy wintry morning.

"Bet you didn't sleep none last night, did ya?" Lott asked.

John shook his head. "Not a wink."

Taking a sip of coffee, Lot said, "I wouldn't have neither, but to make things better, you'd better stay busy today. You know, keep yore mind off it. As soon as it gets light, I want ya to go down to the mill and get some corn ground. Yore Mama says we're gettin short. That'll take most of the morning."

As soon as he had finished breakfast, he loaded the wagon with corn and headed for Little Rock. The village was quieter than normal that morning. Most people who had ventured out for the election the previous day were now at home trying to catch up on their farm chores. By a little past ten, John had the corn ground, bagged and ready to make his return trip home when he saw Tim riding up the street at the far end of town. John waved to him.

Tim kicked his horse in the flank and galloped to where John was waiting. Pulling his horse to a stop, Tim looked down and with a smile said, "What's going on, John?"

John reached up and extended his hand to Tim and answered, "Hadn't seen ya lately. What's going on in Tim Johnson's world?"

Tim dressed in what appeared to be a new woolen suit, white dress shirt, a black tie and mounted on what John judged to be a Tennessee thoroughbred, had obviously come into some money.

Sensing that John was scrutinizing him, Tim threw back his shoulders, tilted his head up and said, "Handsome devil, ain't I. I don't mind if'n you call me Mister Johnson."

Then glancing down to where his pants stopped and his shoes were stationed in the stirrups, John began to laugh and blurted out, "Well, Mister Johnson, yore suit looks fine but them spats has got to go. Mama told me you was wearing 'em."

Tim took his feet from the stirrups, stretched out his legs in a V position and admiring them, replied, "That one on the left decorates my peg leg, and most of all, the women love 'em. Other night I was under the cover with a nice lady of the night, and she wouldn't let me take 'em off. So I think I'll change my name to Spats Johnson, the King of the Night."

Both men broke out in laughter.

"You're the King of Fools, Tim Johnson, that's what you are. Now tell me how you got all that money you told Mama about. Sounds like you're one rich man."

Becoming more serious, Tim replied, "Frankie and me has a bus'ness deal going."

"Bus'ness deal! What's Frankie got you into? Trouble, I bet," John said, shaking his head.

"Ain't no trouble, John," Tim replied. "Frankie and me is running a gambling establishment on the rails. You've always said I was a wizard at the cards; well, that's where my talents fall, and I have made a ton of money at it."

"Tim, as much wealth as Frankie's family's got, he don't need to fool with any gambling on the side. He's setting you up for sump'n. You best get out of it as fast as you can," John said uneasily.

Upset, Tim blurted back, "You know what's wrong with you! You're too self-righteous, and you don't think Frankie ever does nothin' to help nobody but himself. That's what you think."

"You said it, my friend," John replied. "I just don't want to see you get in trouble, that's all. I apologize, if'n I upset you."

Tim relaxed and reaching down to shake John's hand, said, "Didn't take no offense. We go back too far for that. Got to go now. Got to check on my maw. By the way, it's 'bout time you put that Olliver woman to bed. Congratulations."

As he rode off, Tim called back, "You gonna win that election, and when you do, there's gonna be one more self-righteous, Bible-toting Democrat in the legislature. As for ole Tim Johnson, he's gonna keep on rolling them dice and shuffling them cards and wearing these love spats. Who knows, I might even buy me a governorship."

When he was almost out of hearing range, John heard him exclaim, "That'd be a hell of a note, Governor Tim "Spats" Johnson ruling the State of Miss'sippi. The King is here."

"You gonna be my best man, ain't ya?" John shouted.

"You can count me in! I ain't missing that party for nothin', John."

John arrived home in time for his family's midday meal, and after finishing and being excused from the table, he wandered outside. That morning a new colt had been born and, loving horses the way he did, John could not resist another visit to where the wobbly-legged beauty was corralled. Upon reaching the barnyard, John crawled up to the top of the railed fence and looked down where the colt was nursing. The mare nervously nudged the little one away to protect him and then eased over to the opposite side of the encirclement.

Warming his shoulders in the midday sun with a slight wind bristling his hair, John thought about all he had experienced over the past year. His family was doing well and with the help of Andy and a few migrant Choctaw laborers, the farm had never looked better. He then wondered how he had ever become interested in running for a political office and how had he found time to get so deeply involved with campaigning.

Another thought crossed his mind, why hadn't Suzanne come over to be with me? We are to be married next month and here I sit alone, anxiously waiting the outcome of the race. She should be here to help me through this frustrating time.

The wind ceased to blow and everything became still. For no understandable reason, a feeling of loneliness crept over John as he stood there alone.

Captured by his thoughts, John did not notice the rider approaching from the direction of Little Rock nor did he hear the dogs barking.

Then from behind he heard a familiar voice call out, "Mighty fine animal you got there."

Startled, John turned to find his father and Hendon standing below him. The looks on their faces were not encouraging. John felt a sense of distress in their eyes.

John slowly climbed down from the fence and feeling short of breath, held on to one of the rails for support. The three stood there momentarily and then John said, "It's not good news, is it?"

Hendon dropped his head, then straightening himself, answered, "The election's over."

Leaning forward in anticipation, John said, "I didn't win."

Hendon once again dropped his head and digging at the ground with the toe of his boot, replied, "We came up short."

John turned from Hendon and looked over to his father. Lott's face showed his disappointment.

"You ran one heck of a race, John," Hendon said, easing over to the railing where John was now leaning.

John swallowed and replied, "I guess we'll have to put up with Templeton for another term."

He paused for a moment, then continued, "We'll make it though. Won't be long 'till we'll get one of our own in there."

Lott cleared his throat. "Tell 'em Hendon. Tell 'em all of it."

Hendon rubbed over his mustache, twisted his neck and stammered, "Frank took it. He won."

All was quiet until finally John asked, "Was it a close race?"

"We carried Newton County, but lost the other counties," Hendon replied. "There was a lot of talk about your Negro proposal while you were away in Louisiana. Someone sure distorted your views. It's a shame."

Seeing the sorrow on John's face, Lott placed his arm around him. "You did fine boy. I'm proud of ya. You are honest, Son, and just too good for politics."

John was speechless. He turned back to where the young colt was nestled up to his mother and said, "Mama know about it?"

"She knows," Lott answered, walking up to the corral fence.

"How's she taking it?" John asked.

"She didn't feel like coming down with us," Lott replied.

John turned and, extending his hand to Hendon, said, "Want to thank you for all the support you gave me. I've always been able to depend on you."

Then turning back to his father, stammered, "I think I need to check on Mama. She may need me. Y'all excuse me."

14

CHRISTMAS FOLLY

News about the fall election spread like a wild fire swept by strong winds as the South saw young white Democrats voted into office. Everywhere people assembled, and excitement filled the air as the hope of a return to self government was felt to be near. But the military was still in control, supervising every aspect of government, even down to the most minor offices such as the county justices of the peace. One did not have to look far to see Federal soldiers walking the streets, a constant reminder that the South was still in a state of submission.

In the tenth district, when Frank was declared the winner, many were shocked, but after discovering that he was a native born Mississippian with a Democratic background, he was readily accepted to the dismay of the Republicans.

In the days following the election, John tried not to think about what had transpired. He knew he had done his best, and if the majority chose not to elect him, so be it. He was proud of the democratic process that allowed citizens to choose their representatives, this process that made the United States government unique among nations.

Even so, a great sense of disappointment overwhelmed John as he struggled with his loss, and he tried to allow his mother's words, "You've got to place your trust in God that He'll lead you where He wants you to go," to penetrate his heart as he began to realize that politics were not God's will for his life at the moment.

Another great disappointment for John was the lack of support he had received from Suzanne. He had just received a note asking him to meet her before the monthly church service. The note indicated that she had been ill, but was now better and would like for him to come a little early so they could talk. All this was strange, John thought, after all, this is the woman I plan to marry.

John took the note, folded it and placed it in his coat pocket. It's a little late for talking, he thought to himself.

Sunday arrived with a gray sky and a cold wind blowing out of the north, a prelude to a dreary December day. John, dressed earlier than usual, left the house without saying a word to his parents except that he was going to church.

Riding up to the church grounds, John found the place deserted. The trees that had been covered with red and gold leaves only a few weeks earlier were now bare. Their naked limbs swayed back and forth in the strong wind, whistling and moaning with each bend. The eerie sound made John shiver and a feeling of loneliness crept over him. Chilled, he pulled his collar up about his neck and then reached and rubbed his hand down the long, muscular neck of his mount. A quiver rippled through the muscles of the horse's neck and shoulder and it shook its head and snorted.

Enjoying the warmth of the horse's body on his legs, memories flooded John's mind. He remembered that in times past when he approached the church grounds there would be a young girl waving for him, her auburn hair, almost red, glistening in the morning sun. His heart had pounded as he ran to meet her, and in her smile and warm embrace, he knew that she loved him deeply and he loved her more that life itself.

Sitting lost in his thoughts, John didn't hear the carriage approaching and, as his mount bolted forward a few steps, he regained his thought. Turning in the saddle, he heard a familiar voice. "Mawnin' Mister John. Hopes you ain't been a waitin' too long."

John recognized Sammy, one of the Olliver's Negro drivers sitting high in the front of a covered carriage that was pulled by a well-trained team of horses. Like John, he was bundled up for a cold morning ride and looked like a stuffed cigar with his layers of clothing.

With a smile, John dismounted and leading his horse over to the carriage, replied, "Morning to you, Sammy. You bring the cold weather with ya?"

Sammy laughed. "Naw Suh, but it's a slight warmer inside the rig. You best get on in there 'fore you freeze."

"Thought I never would get to see you," Suzanne said as she motioned John inside.

The carriage was warm and welcoming. Sammy had wrapped heated stones in old quilts and placed them under the seats in the carriage.

Stepping inside, John was surprised to see Frankie sitting opposite Suzanne. As Suzanne slid over to give John room, Frankie reached over with an extended hand and said, "Wanted to see you 'fore now. Thought gettin' here early would give us some time to talk."

Reaching out to clasp his hand, John remembered how as children they had been inseparable. It often appeared that Frankie had rather stay at the Wilsons' home more than his own. John thought about the times they had roamed the woods in search of the lost clan of Choctaws that mysteriously disappeared one cold winter night never to be seen again. It was during these imaginary ventures that Frankie would become so frightened he would stay so close that he would step on the back of John's heels as they trudged through the woods. This closeness was gone. Too much had happened; too many hurts and disappointments.

John no longer saw the skinny lanky insecure boy always searching for manhood, but saw instead a well-dressed man filled with an air of confidence and pride. Frankie had grown into a self-assured man with many ambitious goals, and now he would be representing the district.

Shaking his hand, John replied, "Good to see you, Frankie."

Frankie smiled. "Most folks call me Frank now."

Suzanne nestled closer to John. "Now you boys be cordial."

Frank reached up and stroking his short cropped beard began to chuckle. "Yes Ma'am, we'll do just that. Remember the time when yore mama caught us out behind the smokehouse seeing who could out cuss the other'n. I mean we was doing some bad name calling. She came around the side of that house with a switch in her hand and tore into both of us. Remember that?"

John smiled, "How can I forget it. She was a switching and we was high stepping with every swing she made."

The three laughed and then talked briefly for the a few moments reminiscing over old times and for the first time in years John began to see the Frankie he had once known.

Finally, Frankie dropped his head and then glanced out the partially open window. "I wanted to come over the day I found out about it, but I didn't know what to say."

Frankie paused a moment then continued, "The election should've been yours. I had no idea I'd win. We just wanted to be sure that that sorry Republican didn't stay in office."

John glanced over at Suzanne and then back to Frankie. "Don't matter," he muttered. "I guess it just weren't meant to be. I wish you the best, and you have my support."

Suzanne reached over and placed both of her hands on John's. "I didn't know what to say to you either, but I just want you to forget about this all this. We've got plenty to keep us busy and a lifetime to build our dreams. You're a good man, John Wilson, and I know you can accomplish all of your dreams. Together, we can be anything you want to be."

Frankie straightened himself and opening the door, stepped out. With a brisk wind to his back, he quickly buttoned his coat and looking up at John said, "The Democrats put a whooping on 'em, John. We all done right good."

John, taking Suzanne's hand to help her out of the carriage replied, "That's kinda funny coming from a Republican."

Frankie laughed. "You and everybody else in the district know damned well, I ain't no Republican."

As people began arriving for church, Frankie lowered his voice. "We shore hoodwinked 'em, didn't we?"

John didn't answer, but seeing Frankie walking to the rear of the carriage where a horse was tied, said, "You ain't going to church today?"

Untying the horse and mounting, Frankie answered, "You two go get some religion. I've got some things to do today . . . some folks to see. Tell the parson I'm sending him a little sump'n to help out."

Rubbing his fingers together he continued, "You know, a little jingle."

As he rode off, he called back, "We're giving you two one hell of a party next Sat'day night. Got to get ready for that wedding. Grandpaw Bordeaux is even gonna be there, and I'm turning over the party plans to Tim."

Laughing harder he shouted out, "He ought to have things right in place, if you know what I mean!"

Church was almost beginning and John didn't have a chance to talk to Suzanne about her lack of support, the one thing that deeply troubled him.

The week rushed by and Saturday afternoon found John and James out harnessing a team of horses to one of their wagons. Since the whole family was attending the dinner with him, two extra benches were placed in the wagon to accommodate the party.

As they were finishing up, John looked over at James. "You ain't been wearing your uniform lately. Is the army gettin' slack on ya?"

James, stepping up to the driver's seat and grabbing the reigns replied, "It brings too much attention to me."

Motioning for John to climb up, he continued. "Lot of things are going on around here that I've been assigned to look into."

John settling himself next to James said, "What kind of things you talking about?"

"The Klan activity hasn't been as strong in this district as other places in the state, but there's a feeling that the tenth district is the headquarters for the whole state. You might say the Klan's governing body is right here, right under our noses."

"That's hard to believe," John replied. "I know there's been a few meetings, but I've been all over the district talking to folks and I ain't heard nothing like that.

With a slap of the reigns, James headed the team toward the house where the family was waiting and muttered, "John, I'm not at liberty to tell you everything and I don't know a lot about Southern politics, but from what my men have observed, there was a lot of liquor and five dollar gold pieces being handed out around the polls. Looks like somebody bought 'em an election. One that should have been yours."

Reaching out and grabbing the reigns from James' hands, John pulled the wagon to a stop and said, "Hopefully that's not true. You know how tales circulate after an election."

James reached over and took the reigns. "I've got proof. Some of my own men dressed in plain clothes took bribes. Tell you one thing, somebody spent a lot of money to place Olliver in the legislature, and it's not hard to trace it. Who do you think benefited the most from it?"

The two men sat there in silence as John, shocked over what he had heard, knew who James was talking about. Finally he said, "It's hard to believe he'd do this, expecially since I'm marrying into his family."

As the wagon neared the house, James said, "Didn't say that he did it, but either he pulled it off or the Klan did it. Best thing for you to do is to forget for now. It's over. Remember, politics can get mighty dirty and can attract strange bedfellows."

Pulling up to the house, James stepped down to help the women up on the wagon while Lott climbed in from the back.

"You all bring some quilts. It's gonna get a little chilly coming home tonight," James said, helping Mrs. Wilson up.

"It slipped my mind," Mrs. Wilson replied, "Sister, would you please run in and get 'em for us. They're folded up on my bed."

Mrs. Wilson had not been feeling well for the past few months, but she was not going to miss this special time for John. The excitement about the social seemed to revitalize both her health and spirit.

Sister bound up the steps and soon returned with her arms full. "Mama, they said we'd be welcome to spend the night. You know it's gonna be late and mighty cold. They do have lots of room."

Lott, pulling his wife closer to him to keep her warm, blurted out without thinking, "It'll be a cold day in hell before I sleep under Frank Olliver's roof."

With squinted eyes and a frown that accented the wrinkles on her face, Mrs. Wilson said, "Lott Wilson, you don't use them harsh words around the family. You hear me. Frank is dead and gone."

"You're absolutely right, Sarah. The old days are gone. I'm trying the best I can to put it behind me," Lott replied.

James, looking over at Sister with her blond curly hair pulled back neatly in a bun and a twinkle in her eyes, smiled down at her as he pulled her scarf closer around her neck.

"Why are you looking at me like that?" Sister whispered

James pulled her closer and, placing a quilt over their laps, whispered back, "You're one beautiful Southern belle I can hardly keep my hands off."

Flushed with embarrassment, Sister nudged him away only to grab his hand and smilingly pull him back. "Shh," she whispered. "Mama might hear ya."

Lott and Sarah, sitting behind them, tried not to laugh. Lott placed his arm around Sarah, and whispered, "Love is sump'n, ain't it. Can't wait 'till I get you home tonight. It's gonna be a good night to cuddle."

Sarah squeezed his hand and quietly said, "You watch yore talk, Lott

Wilson, and if'n you behave yoreself, I might be just in the right mood."

With the sun setting, the sound of music could be heard even before they reached the Ollivers. As they rode up the drive leading to the house, they were astounded by the number of people who had already arrived; there was hardly space to secure the wagon. The horses, buggies, and carriages were all placed in orderly rows by the directions of the Olliver's Negroes who were dressed in black suits.

As it grew darker, the two-story mansion with its massive columns looked enormous with the opulent lamps illuminating the long floor length windows. James edged the horses forward searching for an open place to stop. A steady stream of people lined up at the front entrance waiting to be admitted, and as the door opened, music flowed out into the evening. The sound of the banjo, fiddle, and the quaint sound of an accordion brought a smile to John's face.

"You hear it? That's Louisiana music," John exclaimed. "Those folks down there'll drink and dance 'till the sun comes up. That's some lively sounds, ain't it?"

Suddenly a voice called out. "Been a wait'n for ya. Let me take the rig. Folks been a wantin' to see y'all."

Holding a lantern up near his face, the man continued," You didn't know it was ole Sammy, did ya?"

James, stepping down from the wagon replied, "I'd know that smile anywhere. Here, take the reigns, and I'll get everybody down. Good to see ya."

As soon as Suzanne heard that the Wilsons had arrived, she hurried out to greet them. To avoid the crowd at the front door, she took them to a side door, gathered their wraps and led them toward the front parlor.

Walking down the wide hall, Mrs. Wilson was facinated by the decor and spellbound by the mansion's beauty. Never had she seen rooms as large as these, or seen such elegant chandeliers. Almost tripping, she felt a soft cushion under her feet and noticed that the glassy polished hardwood floor was covered in a lavish carpet embroidered with strange looking birds in a dense forest.

Seeing the look in her mother's eyes, Sister whispered, "I think that they're flamingos."

"What?"

"Flamingos. Birds from somewhere in South America, I think," Sister explained.

"They look more like peacocks to me," mumbled Lott.

As they entered the wide center hall that ran the length of the lower story, the sound of people talking and laughing almost drowned out their own voices. A haze of tobacco smoke clung to the ceiling, and the smell of tobacco and alcohol mixed with strong perfumes caused Sister to sneeze. Everywhere people were clustered together in conversation. Never had John seen so many people crammed so densely into one house. Politely nudging herself through, Suzanne led the family to the parlor where Judith and Mister Bordeaux were waiting.

Bordeaux, dressed in a smart gray pin-striped suit and with a bright smile on his face, reached out his hand to John. Over the noise of the crowd he shouted, "Good to see ya, Young Man," and looking over to John's parents, continued, "Been lookin' forward to meeting you all."

Judith gave each family member a traditional hug and welcomed them to her home. As she was clasping Mrs. Wilson, she whispered, "It's a pleasure to have you here. It's been a long awaited visit."

Mrs. Wilson smiled. She personally liked Judith, but since Lott had always been at odds with her husband, it had been difficult to pursue a relationship with her.

After shaking Bordeaux's hand and speaking to Mrs. Olliver, Lott looked over the crowd expecting to see some of his friends and neighbors, but only recognized Professor Hendon. Looking closer, he found the men and women to be extremely well-dressed and definitely wealthy. Glancing down at his well-worn suit, he suddenly felt uncomfortable.

James, observing his father-in-law, sensed his feeling and edging next to him softly said, "I know a few of them. Most come from up North, and all that they own is on their backs. They can't even pay their debts. They're poorer than a house cat. I think you Southerners call most of these folk carpetbaggers. I call 'em white scum. By the way, where are our neighbors?"

Feeling better, Lott chuckled. "Don't see none," he said.

James pointed toward a refreshment table in the back hallway. "Well, let's make the best of it. Come with me and we'll find the punch bowl. We might not be dressed as well, but we can drink with the best."

Overhearing James, Mrs. Wilson caught Lott by the sleeve and pulling him close whispered, "You better stay away from that bowl. You know my father was a preacher, and he said that liquor was nothing but the Devil's tonic. You just settle for some coffee or tea."

No sooner had James and Mister Wilson left, than a shrill cry was heard to their right, and out of the mass struggled Tim with a well-inebriated woman. Slightly taller than Tim and with a dark complexion and crinkly black hair, she staggered toward John and Suzanne.

Seeing Sister, Tim, also intoxicated, pulled the woman along until he reached Sister and then loudly exclaimed, "Well if'n it ain't Miss Sister Wilson, The Queen of the Little Rock Baptist Women's Corner."

Embarrassed by his drunkenness, Sister turned her back to him and moved toward John and Suzanne. As she was about to speak to Suzanne, she felt a light tap on the shoulder. Turning, she found herself face to face with Tim. The smell of liquor on his breath, and his bloodshot eyes and unkempt hair nauseated her. She tried to ignore him but finally muttered, "Tim Johnson, you are a drunken disgrace. If you care anything about John and our family, you'll go sober up and take that women out with ya."

Tim replied, "What? No kindly church manners for me?"

Tim always enjoyed teasing Sister, and she had never been able to abide it.

John knew Tim's condition would only get worse with time, so he took him by the arm and led him and the woman to the front door.

"Let's get some fresh air. You need to leave Sister alone."

"You trying to get rid of me or sump'n," Tim exclaimed, jerking loose from John's hold. "I can talk to Sister anytime I want to. It's a free country, you know."

As the people around began to take notice, John pointed toward the door and said, "We need to talk."

Once outside, John walked them to the kitchen located a distance from the main house. John prodded the two, stumbling, cursing and laughing with each step, down the walkway. As they entered, the woman collapsed. John carried her to a room at the back of the kitchen and placed her on a bed. He then returned to the kitchen to the pot of coffee brewing over the fire. Helping Tim to a chair, he poured him a cup.

Sitting slumped over in his chair, Tim looked at John, "You know, I ain't drunk. I can hold my liquor as good as any."

"I know Tim, but the woman is. How come you brought her out here anyway?"

Tim chuckled. "You know, John, I might just be that drunk."

For a while the two men sat quietly, sipping coffee and watching the fire burning in the large fireplace. Finally, John said, "You part of the Klan, ain't you?"

Tim ignored the question.

"I know you've been to some meetings," John said, looking directly at him.

Irritated, Tim turned away from the fire and replied, "Don't you think that's my own damned business. What gives you the right to pry into my personal life? Hell, if'n you'd been more of a part, the Klan would've made sure you won."

"What right do I have to pry? 'Cause we been friends as long as I can remember, and I don't want to see you get yourself into trouble. What do you mean about the Klan would've made me win?"

Tim shifted in his chair trying to change his statement. "I've been to a few meetings, but that's about it. I've been on the tracks most of the time, and the Klan would have helped put you in office, I think. But this whisky's probably got my words tangled."

"How are you doing on the tracks?"

A big smile crept across Tim's face as he reached into his coat pocket and brought out a roll of banknotes. Slapping the roll into John's hand, he said, "I've made more money than I could ever dream of. If'n I don't make five hun'erd to a thousand a week, I ain't working."

Shocked at the sight of so much money, John quickly shoved the rolls into Tim's hands. "You cheated anybody to get this kind of money?"

"Hell no, I ain't cheatin'! I'm that good."

"What kind of cut does Frankie get?"

Tim hesitated, then answered, "Frank gets his share. Maybe thirty percent or so."

John shook his head. "Can't believe that Tim. That don't make business sense. Gotta be more than that."

Tim shook his head. "You got 'em all wrong. He makes a little money on the deal but for Frank, it's just spending money. You know, we all growed up together. Out of the goodness of his heart, he's put me in business."

John got out of his chair, placed his cup on the table and turning said, "I've gotta get on inside. This is mine and Suzanne's night, and as far as Frankie helping you, I say you need to be careful and watch your back."

Tim tried to stand but falling back into his chair he blurted out, "You just don't have no faith in 'em, do ya? You just can't forget what he done to ya. But I tell ya, John Wilson, Frank Olliver might just be one of the best friends I got."

"As soon as you get straight, come on back to the house."

As John neared the house, a man was hurrying toward him. He stopped and called out, "That you, John?"

"It's me," John replied, glaring out at the figure.

"Where in the world have you been? I been looking all over for ya."

John pointed toward the kitchen, "Taking care of Tim."

In disgust, Frankie put his hands on his hips. "That son of a bitch is drunk again, ain't he! I bet he's got that whore with 'em too. Half-breed ain't she?"

John didn't answer as they walked toward the house.

"I told him to leave her in Meridian. He's gonna be the ruin of me yet."

"He's been making money for you, ain't he?"

"I ain't concerned 'bout Tim's business."

Seeing them enter, Suzanne hurried to meet them. More guests had arrived and by the loud sound of laughter, it was obvious that the liquor was taking hold.

Brushing up to him, Suzanne stammered, "Where have you been? It's time for our announcement."

Ignoring her remark, John looked around for his family. They pushed their way down the hall to the large dining room where a small platform had been placed. Stepping up, Frank raised his hands to get the crowd's attention, but unable to be heard over the noise, he pulled a double-barreled derringer from inside his coat pocket and fired toward the ceiling.

Silence filled the house. "Son, was that necessary?" his mother said.

Frank with a smile across his face, followed the voice and finding his mother blushing, replied, "Had to find a way to get their attention, Dear."

Bits of wood and dust floated down from the place the bullet had shattered a board in the ceiling. Frank blew the smoke from the barrel and looked back to his mother and then up toward the ceiling, "You want me to fix the ceiling or build you a new house?"

Everyone burst into laughter.

Frank then motioned to Suzanne and John.

John took Suzanne by the hand, as they joined Frank on the platform. With a glass of wine in one hand, Frank placed his other hand around his sister's waist and said, "I wish my father, the late Frank Olliver, could have been here tonight to bless this union, but with his absence, it is indeed my pleasure to introduce this couple to you. Before I go any further, I want my mother and Grandpaw Bordeaux from down in the Low Country to come up here with us, and if the Wilson clan will come on up, I'd appreciate it."

The families assembled on the platform. Although Mrs. Wilson was uncomfortable with the amount of drinking and profane language that had been loosened during the evening, she was determined to overlook the behavior and give John his night. In contrast, even though Mister Wilson did not often touch the spirits, he was more tolerant than his wife and to his surprise, was enjoying the evening.

"As some of you know," Frank said, "The Ollivers and Wilsons were some of the first whites to enter this country, and if it hadn't been for my father and Mister Lott here, it wouldn't be what it is today."

"Amen," shouted several men over a round of applause.

Extending his hand to John, Frank said, "This here is Mister John Wilson. We've known each other since we were teething children, and even though we've had our points of differences, like most folks, I still feel that John is one of the best friends I've ever had."

Once again, there was a round of applause.

"Let me tell you sump'n else. If'n I ever got in a tight and I have been in a few," Frank chuckled, "this here man is the one I'd call for. He's never let me down."

Then in a more serious tone, he continued. "You know, we just went through one hectic political battle here in this district, and sometimes you just don't know how to rectify the results, but I'll tell you one thing, John fought one heck of a battle. I wish we both could've won."

Lott looked over at John and catching his eyes, winked at him with a slight nod.

Then turning to Suzanne, Frank drew her close and kissing her on the cheek sighed, "Thought I'd never get 'er married off. Feel sorry for the man she marries."

Suzanne playfully punched him in the side and looking over to John said, "I promise you all, John Wilson is gonna be well cared for; the best any man can be."

Frank then looked over to his mother. "Miss Judith, you got any words?"

She eased up to where John and Suzanne were standing and, after giving each a hug and a kiss, looked at her guests and with a Cajun accent said, "I think they'll do fine together," and with a laugh stammered, "and I think we have all said enough."

Frank then beckoned to his grandfather. "I know Master Bordeaux has something to say. How 'bout it, Grandpaw?"

Easing up to John and careful not to fall from the crowded platform, he placed his arm around John's shoulder and looked out over the people. Overemphasizing his Cajun accent he said, "When Mister John, here, and Suzanne come down to da bayou for a visit, I got to know da young man, and it didn't take me long to see dat this is one fine gentleman. Yes, in just a few days he was just like a son to me."

John, extending his hand, replied, "I'm honored, Sir."

Stirred by the emotion of the moment, people made their way up to congratulate the couple and their families and to wish John and Suzanne their best. After what seemed to be an hour of greetings, some of the guests began to make it to the door.

Shortly, Bordeaux, tugging on John's sleeve, led him to the hallway next to the study. Leading him inside, he quietly shut the door. Turning to John he said, "When I got something on my mind, I got to get it off 'fore it worries me to death. You know what I mean?"

Pointing over to a desk where Frank's father had always kept his books, Bordeaux, taking a seat said, "My books ain't in balance, and I can't get no sleep 'till I knows their where 'bouts. Can I call on you again?"

John smiled. "I'd be glad to."

The old gentleman, slinking down into a chair, took a big swallow of bourbon from a flask he had taken out of his pocket and replied, "I'd be much obliged."

Motioning for John, Bordeaux held out his hand and murmured,

"Here. Take this key. I locked it."

John unlocked the desk and found a ledger in the top right drawer. Placing it on the desktop and lighting a lantern where he could see, John opened it and turning back to Bordeaux said, "You know, all you need is a good pair of eye glasses."

The old man pointed back to the ledger. "I can't even see good with glasses. I trust you, Boy."

"I'm sure it's all here. It shouldn't take me long to put your mind at ease," John said.

Skimming through the figures page by page, John only looked at the entries and didn't pay any attention to those involved in the transactions. No errors were to be found. In fact, he had rarely seen a better-kept set of books. As he continued to search, he became aware that the names and businesses listed in the ledger were not the same as those he had seen while checking Bordeaux's books in Louisiana. Instead, these entries were from businesses located in Jackson, Meridian and even some local towns such as Union, Decatur and Hickory - all Mississippi towns. Shocked at what he had discovered, John looked closer and found a listing from Atwell's Brewery of Birmingham, Alabama, for a little over five thousand dollars. Scratched beside the sum was a brief note — fifty kegs of light liquor.

John thought to himself, fifty kegs of cheap whiskey! Why would anyone buy that?

Realizing that this could not be Bordeaux's book, John closed the ledger and looked over at the old man who had dropped off to sleep. As he placed the book back into the drawer, a loose piece of paper from one of the back pages caught his attention. His first impulse was to leave the book alone, but he reopened the ledger to the loose page. The top entry on the page showed a withdrawal of twenty thousand dollars from the First Bank of Meridian.

Baffled, John then unfolded the slip of paper that had been crumpled between the pages.

After a few moments, stunned and with a deep sense of anger, he pondered over what he had found.

Finally, he clinched his fist together and regaining his composure, he turned to the front of the ledger where names were normally listed.

All he read began to make sense, and as he placed the book back in the drawer, he heard the door screech open. Straightening himself with the ledger still clasped in his hand, he turned to find Frankie standing in the doorway.

Frankie, with a drink in one hand and his arm around a woman who appeared to be well on her way, stammered, "You need to come on back to the party."

John stood silent, staring directly at him.

Frank, seeing the anger on John's face and recognizing the book in his hand, clinched his teeth and pushed the woman aside.

Slamming the book down on the desk, John took a step toward Frankie and pointing into his face exclaimed, "You take one more step, and I'm gonna beat you to death with my bare fists!"

Drunk and enraged, Frankie shoved John's hand away and shouted, "What in the hell are you doing with my books! Where'd you get a key?"

Aroused by the commotion, Bordeaux exclaimed, "What in the world are you two shouting about?"

Stepping back from Frank, John said, "I came in here to check your grandfather's books. That's all. He gave me the key. I was just trying to help him."

Shaking with anger, Frankie stalked over to his grandfather who was trying to stand and grabbing him by the coat collar shouted, "You old bastard! You ain't got any sense. Why don't you go on back to yore Cajun country, you senile old fool!"

As Frankie was about to push his grandfather down, he felt a hand grab him by the shoulder and turning, felt a sharp pain as he flew backward into the wall.

Enraged and with a bloodied fist, John turned to find Suzanne, Judith and his family clustered in the doorway.

Frankie eyes were fixed on the ceiling as he slid slowly down the side of the wall and collapsed unconscious on the floor. Bordeaux was slumped speechless in his chair.

"It's gonna be alright, Son, " his father said as he entered the room. "I'm right here with you."

John looked over at Suzanne and Judith, and pointing to Mister Bordeaux stuttered, "You best check on him." Then motioning to his family, he said, "I think we'd better go."

Suzanne rushed over to her grandfather as he began to regain his senses. Frankie was still slumped over by the wall as Judith kneeled beside him.

Suzanne then ran after John and his family and caught up with them as they were making their way down the front steps.

She reached out and caught John by the arm. "I don't know what happened in there between you and Frankie, but please don't let this ruin our evening."

John turned, pulled away, and shook his head. All he could see now was the anger in Frankie's eyes as he came toward him with clinched fists, and as his fist tore into Frankie's face, it was like years of anguish found release, and he felt no remorse.

"Everything is gonna be just fine," Suzanne pleaded. "Frankie is drunk and is a downright fool. You know that."

John took a deep breath, "It will never be the same, Suzanne. I don't talk to my dogs the way Frankie did to yore Grandfather; it's just not gonna work."

"I had nothing to do with whatever happened in there tonight," Suzanne pleaded.

"Even if that is the truth and I'm not sure it is, when you marry someone, you also marry their family, and I think the breach is just too wide. Some things can never be mended. I'm sorry for you. No, I'm sorry for both of us."

John jumped up into the wagon and motioned to James to get the horses moving. Glancing back to Suzanne, he called out, "Ask Frankie about the ledger, if you don't already know."

In the early morning mist, the words vanished into the darkness.

Somewhere a clock struck four. In the study there was only a light glow of coals twinkling in the dying fireplace. The lantern flickered, it's light casting shadows across the room. On the desk, the ledger lay where it had been placed. Inside the drawer under a set of papers was another book, the one belonging to Bordeaux.

Crumpled on the floor was a note and Suzanne found scribbled across it, "Had to see several banks to get it broken into five dollar pieces, but with this and the whiskey, you'll be in Jackson come spring. And by the way, damn good idea to get Wilson out of the state for a while. I knew she could do it for us. H. Pierce."

15

CHASING THE DREAM

A BRISK BREEZE OUT OF THE NORTHWEST BLEW LEAVES AND snowflakes about on the cobbled streets. At this time of evening the streets were usually vacant, but this was Christmas Eve and Philadelphia was alive with the holiday spirit. Throngs of people cluttered the sidewalks for last minute shopping while familiar Christmas melodies were heard from carolers crowding corner street lamps that were adorned in green ivy for the season.

Frank and Tim carefully made their way up the street so as not to bump into shoppers laden with Christmas presents. Easing between two women, Tim politely asked to be excused, as he led the way.

"How much further to the restaurant?" Tim called out as he motioned back to Frankie.

"It's right around the corner to your left," came the reply.

Frank had been invited to attend a stockholders meeting in Philadelphia called to seek financial support for a new rail line emerging across the western frontier that would one day connect the east and west coast. The project was an enormous enterprise that would produce profits beyond Frank's imagination.

Removing their overcoats and shaking the snow from their matted hair, the two made their way into the lobby of the Dutchman's Delight, the fanciest restaurant in Philadelphia. Frankie pointed to a large room on their right where drinks were being served. Seeing no table available, they managed to find two stools at the far end of the bar that stretched the length of the room. The tobacco smoke was dense, but it was warm inside and the food was known to be tasty.

Settling themselves at the bar, Frankie got the bartender's attention.

He slowly worked his way down to where the men were sitting.

Removing two glasses someone had left on the bar, the bartender smiled down and in an Irish brogue said, "Merry Christmas to ya, Gents. Can I serve you some spirits?"

Startled by his accent, Tim almost laughed but catching himself answered, "What ya got?"

The bartender placed his hands on his hips and announcing to all in the bar, exclaimed, "What ya got! Well, if we don't have some Southern Gents here with us tonight."

Turning back to Tim and Frank, he said, "I got anything your heart desires, sir, and may the spirit of Christmas be with ya."

Tim couldn't help thinking how much this man resembled ole Santa. He was short and very plump with rosy cheeks and his hair was as white as cotton. He was bald, but who knows, under his cap, Santa may not have had much hair up top either.

At that moment the other men at the bar lifted their glasses and turning to Frank and Tim, toasted, "May the spirit of Christmas be with ya."

Setting two large mugs of ale down on the bar, the bartender said, "I'm Oscar O'Rally, and gentlemen the first round is on the house. I know you laddies must be a long way from home, and I want to welcome you; so drink up."

Suddenly noticing an open table in the back of the room where a fire was burning in a large fireplace, Tim and Frank thanked O'Rally for his hospitality and headed toward the warmth of the fire and a chance for a little privacy.

"How'd ya like the orchestra, Tim."

" I liked the fiddles, 'specially the big ones. Never heard noth'n like it."

Frankie howled in laughter. "They weren't fiddles! Them were violas, and your so called fiddles are really called violins."

Lowering his voice, Tim asked, "If'n them ain't fiddles then what do ya call them bugles that made so much racket?"

Frank laughed again. "Tim Johnson, them so called bugles are called trumpets. You can tell you ain't ever been out in society."

Embarrassed, Tim twisted in his seat for a moment and seeing that no one was really paying any attention to them, murmured, "I don't know what you call all them instruments, but I ain't never heard no better sound than that bunch made, and I'm glad you find me entertaining. You know, you can be a first class ass at times."

Frank reached over and patted Tim on the shoulder. "I was just joshing with ya."

Tim took another swallow and, hearing the carolers outside, began thinking about what a special night this was. Looking over at Frank he said, "You know, you ought to be back home with yore folks. That little girl of yours is gonna be up and stirring in the morning to see what ole Santa's brought 'er, and if'n I was you, I'd be there sharing that time with her."

Tim motioning for the bartender to bring some fresh drinks replied, "Mama and Suzanne will be there with her. They'll take care of it."

Tim shook his head. "If'n that was my little girl, I'd be there. She's a real little lady."

Pushing a mug over to Tim, Frankie said, "You don't know a damned thing about Christmas, and since you don't have no children, that is legitimate ones, you don't know nothing about them either."

Tim stuttered, "Well, I guess you're right. We never had Christmas around our place. Never had no money for presents. Paw always said Christmas was for rich folks. So I guess you're right. I don't know what it's all about."

As Frankie was about to comment, a couple entered the lobby and caught his attention. The man helped the woman as she removed her wrap and, as he handed their coats to the doorkeeper, Frank, mesmerized, noticed how strikingly beautiful the woman in the dark maroon dress with a white furry collar was. In his travels about the country he had seen his share of beautiful women but never one of such pure beauty. Standing a little over five feet tall, she had thick ringlets of blond hair neatly pulled back behind her ears and sparkling emerald eyes that twinkled as she smiled. Erect and dignified, she stood out from all the other women waiting to be seated.

Noticing Frank's stare, Tim exclaimed, "She's a looker, ain't she!"

With his mind on the woman now being ushered into the dining room, Frank never heard a word Tim said.

Tim reached over and nudged Frank. "She's probably married. You might as well get 'er off your mind."

"She ain't dead, is she?" Frank replied.

Then getting up, Frank motioned toward the lobby. "Come on, it's time we had some supper."

The dining room was almost full. Approaching the maitre d', Frank called him to the side and with the passing of a few bills was given a table adjacent to the woman and her escort.

Placing his napkin on his seat, the man said, "Please excuse me. There's a gentleman motioning for me out front. It appears to be Dr. Jack Walker. I'll be right back. "

As he left, the napkin fell to the floor.

Reaching down, Frank said, "Pardon me Ma'am. The gent seemed to have dropped this."

She smiled. "Thank you. You have a very pleasant accent."

Tim said, "We're from the South. It does raise some eyebrows up here."

Looking first at Tim and then back to Frank, she said, "I find the accent interesting. Where are you from?"

Turning in his chair, Frank replied, "We're from Miss'sippi. South Miss'sippi, that is."

She took a deep breath and murmured, "What part of Mississippi?"

Before Frank could reply her escort returned and seating himself, said, "I've got an interview in the morning. Looks like we'll be coming to Philadelphia come spring."

All during the evening the woman couldn't help but listen to the men dining next to her. Their voices were so familiar.

Maybe fate brought them here. What if they were from the same county, she thought. What if they knew him? Maybe he might be here too, somewhere.

When they finished their meal, the man helped the woman from her chair and extended his arm. "Darling, an Easter wedding sounds good to me, and I think you'll learn to love city life. We'll be the toast of Philadelphia."

Leaving the room, the woman glanced back. How she longed to know more about them.

After the couple left, Tim looked over to Frank, "Told ya she was taken. A woman that looks like that ain't gonna stay single long."

Frank reached over and, lifting his glass to his lips, replied, "She couldn't keep her eyes off me. You give me one hour with that woman, and she'd be coming home with me. I saw it in her eyes."

"One hour." Tim said. "Our southern talk got 'er, that's all. She don't give a tinker's damn 'bout neither one of us. You just dreaming."

"Dream or not, that woman wanted sump'n. You can take that to the bank with ya."

Frank reached up and lightly touched the bruise on his face. Feeling a dull throbbing pain, he shook his head in anger. "That son of a bitch is gonna pay dearly for this."

Tim, reaching inside his vest pocket to retrieve his tobacco pouch, replied, "You were drunk. You didn't know what you was doing. You would've done the same to him."

"I'll tell you sump'n. Ain't nobody coming in my house and embarrassing me 'fore company, and with God as my witness, I'm gonna kill John Wilson one of these days," Frank shouted.

Tim caught him by the coat sleeve and whispered, "Shh. I hear you, and you don't mean that. You ain't killing nobody. That ole liquors talking for ya again."

⁄⁄

John now knew that the election had been bought and also knew who had furnished the money, but what he didn't know was who else was involved and why. The fact that Frank was part of the scheme didn't surprise him, but feeling that Suzanne, in luring him out of the state, must have also been part of the plan, was crushing.

After Christmas, John followed his normal way of dealing with controversy. Working incessantly from daylight to dark until exhaustion drove him home limited his thoughts. His family knew, with time, he would sort out his feelings and would be fine.

Suzanne tried to talk with him several times, but John would not see her.

One day as John was returning from the woods with a wagonload of split white oak for burning, Lott put on his jacket and hat and went out to meet him. By the time he had reached the barnyard, John had unhitched the mule and was brushing him down before turning him out to pasture.

John hung the mule's collar up on a peg on the inside wall of the barn as Lott came down the open hallway.

"Got in a little early. Cold drive you in?"

"No sir, Papa, just got a little tired," John said, rubbing his upper arm. "That ax gets heavy sometimes."

Lott trudged down the hall and opened a door where saddles were kept and slinging one over his shoulder, he walked back to where John was standing and dropped it by his feet, "That bay out there needs riding. There's a gent from Port Gibson coming up sometime next week to buy 'er. We need to have her manageable."

Forgetting his pains, John picked up the saddle and grabbed a blanket and bridle. Swinging under the weight, he made his way to the corral. Looking back, he said, "She's a pretty one, ain't she. It's good to see our herd on the come back."

Lott walked out to the corral and, leaning up against the fencing, thought how right John was. When General Sherman came through, the Union soldiers took all the livestock on the place and had it not been for Andy hiding a mule and several of the horses deep in the swamp, their breeding and training of thoroughbreds would have ended.

John mounted, and Lott opened the gate. "Get 'em on out and work 'em good."

The mare tried to buck a couple of times and swirled about kicking mud in all directions before John could steady her, but in a matter of moments they galloped out of the barnyard and down the road.

Even as a young boy John had a way with horses and by the time he had reached manhood, he was considered one of the best riders in the county. There was something about being mounted high in the saddle and the challenge of man over beast that had always intrigued him. He also felt strongly that an animal should never be abused, but always treated with kindness. To him, the horse was a friend.

For the next hour John pushed the horse as hard as he could and feeling her tiring, he brought the Bay to a slow trot. In a short while the mare was completely under his control. Stopping at a stream to let the horse rest and water, John dismounted and sat down on the creek bank. The water rippling and gurgling as it rushed over the stones gave John a sense of peace. The sun was low in the west, and with all the trees stripped of leaves, the forest could be a lonely place; but the stream was alive and singing. Suddenly a gray squirrel in an oak tree to his right began shaking his furry tail and barking at the two because his domain was now invaded.

Laughing to himself, John murmured, "I know, we need to get on our way, Mister Bushy Tail," and, grabbing his horse's reign to mount and kicking the bay in the flanks, he sent her galloping once more.

Slowing to a trot, John began to think over all that had occurred in the preceding months. There were so many unanswered questions, questions that haunted his every thought. Why had the Democratic Party turned against him when he had tried to be honest in his pursuit of office, always considering the needs of the people? And why had Suzanne disappointed him in this way? Why had she not been honest? And exactly how involved was she in all that occurred.

Stopping to let the mare rest again, John stroked her neck several times and patted the bulging shoulder muscles. The Bay shook her head and snorted her approval while pawing the ground. Then as if someone had opened a door of knowledge, John knew who could answer his questions. It was so obvious. How had he overlooked it?

Who loved politics more than life itself and would go to any lengths to become involved in the process? Who pushed me into the race and directed me through the election?

Since there was still time before dark, John turned the horse and galloped back down the road toward Little Rock.

Noting the dogs barking, Mrs. Hendon eased up from her chair and went to the window. As John dismounted and headed toward the house, she went out to greet him. "Kick them mangy mutts out of the way and come on in out of the cold."

John, fastening his reigns around one of the porch beams and reaching down to pet one of the hounds, looked up at Mrs. Hendon who was standing there with a woolen shawl wrapped around her shoulders and asked, "'Fessor in?"

Opening the door for him, she replied, "He's in, but he's a bit ailing."

Even though the Hendon's house contained several bedrooms and a kitchen, it was the Professor's bedroom where they spent most of their time during the cold winter months. A huge fire was blazing in the fireplace, and the smell of burnt hickory and oak filled the room.

Recognizing the voice, the Professor called out, "That you John? Come on in."

Mrs. Hendon took his coat and scarf and showed him to a rocking chair directly across from Hendon. Hendon was snuggly wrapped in a thick quilt with two pair of woolen socks on each foot. His hair was mussed and he had bloodshot eyes and a red nose.

"Woman, go fetch John some hot tea," Hendon said as he reached for a cup on the table next to him.

John settling himself said, "I'll just take what he's drinking. Don't bother with fixin' nothing."

"I think you need to reconsider that. I'm sipping hot liquor and peppermint. Unless you're sick, you don't need any of this."

The three of them laughed and Mrs. Hendon excused herself so she could check on the children. They had left after dinner to play in the woods, and it was time for them to be coming in. Most of the farmers in the South had bells positioned in their yards for ringing to let the men in the field know dinner was ready, but for the Hendons, it was a way of communicating with their children.

When the bell was rung, the children knew that they had better get home fast or face the wrath of the leather. Hendon kept a razor strap on a nail in the hallway, and it was well worn.

Taking a sip of tonic and bracing himself to keep from coughing, Hendon looked over to John. "What are you doing out on a day like this?"

John pushed his feet up near the edge of the fire and held his hands out to the flames. "Ain't that cold outside. You just have to bundle up, and to answer your question, I'm working one of our horses. Got a buyer coming in next week."

Hendon sneezed a couple of times, blew his nose and taking another sip, answered, "You all are doing pretty well, aren't you."

"We're getting by. Bout as good as most."

For the next few moments, Hendon's mind seemed to wander. When John asked him something, he would simply respond, then silence filled the room.

John knew he must be on his way, but he also knew that he did not want to leave until his questions were answered. The minutes ticked away on the old clock over the mantle.

Getting up and turning his back to the fire, John looked down at Hendon. "'Fessor, I've known you all my life. In a way, you've been part of our family, and you know you've taught me most that I know. You're more than a teacher to me. You've always been a friend."

Hendon nudged the quilts closer around his shoulders and nodded his head.

"I'm gonna ask you some questions, and I want you to tell me the truth."

"What's on your mind, Son?"

"Why wasn't I elected to office and how did Frankie get involved in this? I know you know what went on, and I pray you weren't part of it."

Hendon stared at the floor. Standing before him was a young man he admired more than any of his own sons. Even as a young boy, he recognized that there was something special about John. In the classroom he was smart, inquisitive and always had a sense of honor. He felt that in John Wilson there was the making of a great man.

Ashamed to look up at him but feeling that John deserved a response, Hendon slowly lifted his head until their eyes met. With watered eyes, he said, "I don't know where to really start."

"Just tell me what happened."

Hendon stared into the crackling flames, shook his head and took a deep wheezing breath. "John, these aren't normal times here in Mississippi. We came through a war on the short end and lost might near every political right we ever had. With the ratification of our new State Constitution, we have begun to find favor with the folks in Washington and have a chance to regain some of our power."

"'Fessor, it's getting kinda late. Maybe I need to be gettin' on home. We can talk later."

"Just hold on a minute. You want to know the truth, now let me finish. As I stated, these aren't normal times. The White South got a chance to place some of its folks into positions and time was of essence. Ever what it took to kick them Republicans out was done, and as you know, we did quite well. The thing that caused your problem was your stand on helping the Negro."

John pulled his chair closer to Hendon. "'Fessor, I feel we have to take care of all our people, and heaven knows the Negro needs it. You and I have often talked about the vast resources that Miss'sippi has and what could be done if the Negro was ever freed."

Hendon reached over and placed his hand on John's arm. "All we were doing was philosophizing, just dreaming. Didn't mean it would work."

John thought for a moment, then replied, "What you're saying is my attempt to help the Negro cost me the election."

"It cost you," mumbled Hendon. "White folks were afraid of what would happen to them if the Negro was elevated in status."

"'Fessor, what is gonna happen to 'em?"

Hendon thought for a moment, then answered, "Some of them have left the state. I hear they're headed west, and lots have gone north to the cities to find work."

"What about the ones that stay, 'Fessor?"

"Only God knows. A few have been lucky to acquire land, but most of them are floundering hopelessly just trying to stay alive. If something isn't done, they'll be back on the farm working for the whites. That's what I believe. They won't be much better off than before."

Seeing darkness setting in, John got out of his chair and reaching over to get his jacket, said, "I mean, we could have come up with a plan to help all of 'em, even the Choctaws."

"Choctaws!" coughed Hendon. "There's not a soul in Mississippi who gives a damn about the Choctaw. To most, they're just animals."

John reached over and tucked the quilt snuggly around the old man's neck and patted him on the shoulder. "'Fessor, the people should have given me the chance. There's room for all of us."

Hendon looked up and nodded his approval and in a raspy voice said, "John, you're an idealist, a man far beyond our time. You were born too soon, Boy."

Seeing the sincerity in his eyes, John knew that Hendon had told him the truth. As he was about to leave, John turned and said, "What part did Frankie and the Klan play in the election?"

Without hesitating, Hendon answered, "Money buys votes, and Frankie's got more than any man can ever spend. Like I told you, the organization was determined to win and at all cost. As far as the Klan goes, you really don't need to know any more about it because it doesn't concern you. You can do without the Klan."

Leaving there at dusk, John felt that some of his questions had been answered, but still there were things going on that he didn't understand and perhaps never would. One thing he knew for sure was that life for the Negro and Choctaw would not be good in Mississippi in the coming years.

§

It was good to be back home in Gettysburg after a visit to the city, and in a matter of hours, Lucretia would be with her students in the classroom once more. The sun was setting, and after heating some water and making a cup of tea, Lucretia settled herself in her father's chair and pulled a blanket over her lap. Enjoying the flavor of the tea and the warmth it brought, she gazed out the window toward the back yard. A light snow covered the ground and occasionally a few late flakes floated down from the tree branches out back. Sipping the tea and feeling the security that only home can bring, Lucretia began to think. The visit to Philadelphia was fun and entertaining and the thought of living there permanently was exciting. As a wife of a talented young physician, all the social doors of the city would be opened to them. How could life be better?

Finding Lucretia curled up asleep, Mrs. Caulder nudged her. "You best get on to bed young lady. Those children will be waiting on you in the morning."

Lucretia slowly opened her eyes and pushing the quilt off her lap stretched and reached for her mother's hand. "I'll be ready for them, and you and I have a lot of planning to do before my Easter wedding."

Placing her arms around Lucretia, Mrs. Caulder gave her a hug. "I think you've made a good choice. We'll miss you, but Robert will make you a fine husband. You wait and see. He'll give you the best that Philadelphia can offer."

16

RETURN TO GETTYSBURG

THE MARCH WINDS WHISTLED AND WAILED AS THEY RUSHED down the open hall at the Wilson's house. Spring had come early this year in Mississippi, and even though the nights were still cold, the dogwood trees were in bud, and the fields were dotted with early blossoms of wildflowers.

With a squeak of an opening door then a crash as the wind slammed it shut, Dr. McLauren stepped into the Wilson's kitchen.

"Sorry," he said apologizing to startled Lott and Sarah. "The wind kinda caught it."

Smelling the coffee brewing on the wood stove, he shuffled over to enjoy the warmth of the fire and after receiving a cup from Sarah, settled himself in a chair next to Lott.

Moving his chair to make room for the doctor, Lott asked, "How's my boy doing?"

McLaurin took a sip of coffee and shook his head. "Just like always. Physically, can't find nothing wrong with 'em. He has these dreams or spells, and after the headaches wear off, he seems fine for a while."

Sarah, having made a pan of biscuits and frying up several slices of smoked ham, brought the doctor a plate. Easing down next to Lott, she replied, "They may be just dreams, but every time it happens, it just gets worse. I've seen him shaking and sweating and when it's all over, he can't hardly breathe for the pain in his head. Sump'ns wrong with 'em, and someday it's gonna kill 'em shore as we is sitting here."

"The boy can't keep going like this, and neither can I watch him suffer the way he does. There's got to be an answer, Doc," Lott murmured.

McLauren thought for a moment, took a big swallow of coffee then replied, "I'll be seventy-three come July, and in my years I've treated many a person with many a problem. I have seen one case kinda like this back in fifty-three. Excuse me, Sarah, but what I'm gonna tell you is the truth. As I recall, the woman had been raped by a bunch of drunk Choctaws who were on their way to the territory, and for years, she told no one. She just held it in. Didn't even tell her husband who was away when it happened. Then one night she started having nightmares, kinda like John's, and like his, she had shakes and headaches. They got worse with each spell. I never could find nothing wrong with her, physically."

"What happened to her?" Lott asked.

McLauren paused for a moment. "Her husband came home one evening and found her."

"Found her!" Sarah exclaimed.

"She hung herself and left him a note telling about what had happened to 'er," McLauren replied.

Lott cleared his throat. "What kind of story is that? You saying that John is gonna kill himself. That's a fine way to console us."

McLauren, shook his head. "Didn't mean it quiet like that. What I meant was that after that happened, I did a lot of reading, and what I found out is that sometimes when something terrible happens to someone, they try to shut it out of their mind, but no matter how hard they try, it's still there. Some folks can't shake it, but some come to terms with what happened to 'em and then go on with their life."

Lott thought for a moment. "You know, there was a time when John didn't know what was causing the spells, but with time the dream emerged, and he told us what happened up there. I'd say he's trying to face it. He is talking about it. I hear a lot of soldiers have these kind of problems when they come back."

The fire crackled inside the stove, and the winds outside shook the windowpanes prompting McLauren to ease his chair closer to the stove.

"Lott, sump'n happened to that boy up there in Pennsylvania, and he may recall it now; but instead of getting better, he's getting worse. I've done all I can for 'em. I think it's time we ask the good Lord to give us some help."

Sarah nodded, and then remembering the time the report was given that John had been killed up north in that terrible battle, a voice had come to her when she was on the porch rocking. The voice had told her John was alive and would be coming home. It was a voice clear and unlike any she had ever heard.

That evening when Lott and John were asleep, Sarah eased out from under the covers, and kneeling by the fireplace with only the glow of a few faint embers, she prayed through the night.

In the days that followed, John did seem to feel better, but he was unusually quiet. He still entered into the normal family conversation, but it was obvious that something was on his mind.

Sunday morning dawned clear and brisk. Since it was time for the monthly church service, Sarah and Lott dressed and tapping on John's door, told him they would be pleased if he would go with them. John thanked his mother for waking him but said he had rather stay home. He had some things to do.

When the Wilson's returned, they found a note on their bed. It stated, "Don't worry about me. You can pick my horse up down at the stables at Newton Station. I will be back home when I've finished with what I've got to do. I took a little money with me to get me by. Love, John."

Bewildered, Lott stood there and scratched his head.

Sarah took the note and, folding it neatly, replied, "I know exactly where he's going."

§§

With his jacket rolled up for a pillow, John leaned his head against the window barely able to keep his eyes open. With the rocking motion of the train and the constant clacking sound of the wheels against the rails, he soon fell asleep.

The cold northern wind sent shivers down his back as sleet peppered the soldiers clustered together trying to warm themselves the best they could on the open flatcar. Some of the luckier ones had found shelter in boxcars, but even with a roof over their heads, the cold was unbearable. When John joined the army, he had no idea of the trials and suffering that lay ahead. To the boys down in Little Rock, war was all glory and love of country. How wrong they had been.

With a sudden jolt, John awoke as the train came to a stop. John saw a large man making his way down the aisle, and seeing the seat beside John empty, he plopped down next to him. Easing over to give him more room, John asked, "Where are we now?"

The man reached out his hand to John. "I'm Amos Truitt from Nashville. I don't know the name of the stop but we're 'bout to get into West Virginia. Where you going?"

Where am I going, John thought. I don't rightly know. I should have stayed at home. It seems like I have been on this God-forsaken rattletrap for an eternity, and with every passing mile I'm placing distance between me and my family and what little security that exists in my life. I wonder if I'll ever get back home again?

Noticing the young man's dazed look, the gentleman asked, "Son, are you feeling all right?"

John shook his head and clearing his mind apologized, "Yes, Sir. I've been on this train for over two days, and I'm rightly tired."

Extending his hand he continued, "I'm John Wilson from Little Rock, Miss'sippi, and I'm going up north."

"Where up north?"

Finding it uncomfortable to answer, John finally announced. "I'm headed for New York."

With the words barely out of his mouth, John couldn't believe he had made such a statement. Why couldn't he just tell the man the truth.

"It's a fine city. You can find anything you want up there," smiled the man, nudging John.

Then catching a smile from a woman across the way, the man whispered to John, "Sir, I hope you find New York delightful, but I think that young lady is beckoning."

Once more he extended his hand, "It has been a brief pleasure, Mister Wilson. Remember what I said, New York can be invigorating."

As time passed, John tried not to get involved in any other conversations and with the light of day, found enjoyment in scanning the countryside dotted with picturesque farmhouses and pasturelands. Instead of going into West Virginia, the train had swung south and was now traveling northeast directly up the Shenandoah Valley. With the sun hovering on the horizon, the train finally came to a stop at Winchester, a small town on the northern border of Virginia. Here John would have to change trains and then resume his travel the following morning. He also knew that it would only be a matter of hours until he was there.

Staying in a hotel overnight gave John a chance to get a good night's sleep, and to his pleasure, a hot bath was available. Rested, he was up early the next morning for his coffee and breakfast. Making his way to the station with the sun topping the mountains to the east, he couldn't help but stop to admire its grandeur. Stretches of purple and orange clouds feathered the horizon, but John knew that it wouldn't be long until the sun with its brilliant rays would push them aside. John had always felt Mississippi was God's country, but the beauty of this valley was astounding.

"All aboard! Leaving in five minutes," shouted a conductor up the tracks.

Many new passengers had arrived crowding the train more than ever. Since it was impossible to find a seat, John saw a wooden box resting in a corner next to the rear doorway and putting his travel bag down, made himself comfortable. It wasn't long before the train crossed the large bridge that spanned the Potomac River and entered the state of Maryland. John knew that in a matter of hours they would skirt the western edge of the state and would be in Pennsylvania.

John thought he recognized some of the places they passed, but that had been years ago. He was then a member of Lee's Grand Army of the Northern Virginia on its march into destiny. The July heat and the dust created from thousands of men marching in tight ranks was the devil's delight. As uncomfortable as it was, this was Lee's Army, the invincible Army of the Northern Virginia. With visions of Bullrun, Fredericksburg and Chancellorsville, nothing could stop this army. It was like a giant avalanche sweeping aside anything and anyone who attempted to stand in its way. This Army would not be denied victory. This was Lee's Army.

Time passed and deep in thought, John didn't hear the whistle as the train screeched to a slowing stop. As it chugged to a stop, a loud voice called out, "Gettysburg! All out for Gettysburg!"

John's first impulse was to stay right there on that box and continue on, but somewhere he found the strength and, reaching down, retrieved his bag and made his way up the aisle.

As the train clattered away sending billows of smoke floating across the walkway, John stood silently watching it move down the tracks. If he ran he could still catch it. With a faint whistle, it rounded a bend, and soon all John could see was a swirl of smoke rising over the treetops in the distance.

Feeling the silence, John found that he was alone. All the other passengers had hurried to their destinations while he tangled with his dreams.

"May I help you?" came a voice down the walkway.

Turning, John found an elderly man with both hands full of luggage and a chest sitting on the boarded walkway beside him.

John smiled. "I'm fine. Looks like you could use some help."

The man shook his head. "If you'll grab that chest and follow me, I'd be much obliged."

Shouldering the chest, John carried it inside the station and placed it on a shelf where bundles of other luggage and boxes were stacked. The old man took several deep breaths and stretching his back said, "That chest would have been more than I could have handled."

"Weren't no trouble, Sir."

The man extended his hand to John and replied, "You looked like you were lost out there. The train leave you?"

"No, I'm where I'm supposed to be."

With bag in hand, John left the station. The town appeared larger than he had remembered, and the buildings and homes showed no signs of the destruction caused by the horrendous battle fought here. The buildings had been repaired and people seemed to be stirring about as if nothing had ever happened. The trees were still bare from the winter months, but in front of some of the businesses small beds of yellow daffodils were beginning to bloom. Glancing over his shoulder toward the west, he could make out the grounds and buildings of the Lutheran Seminary. He had always wanted to tour the college and meet some of its professors and maybe even talk with the students, but as a prisoner, his freedom was limited.

In no hurry, John made his way down the main street toward the center of town occasionally speaking or nodding to a bystander. Soon he reached Elm Street where he took a right, and staring down the way and to his delight, it was still hanging there. Picking up his pace, he could now see the shingle hanging over the door of a white-planked building that still read, "Doctor Caulder, MD."

Entering the building, John placed his bag down and went over to a desk that contained a small bell that when rung, would alert the doctor that a patient was waiting. Nothing at all had changed in the office. The small front room, a waiting room, contained the same row of six chairs neatly lined against the back wall, and across the room two windows were placed where patients could enjoy looking outside while they waited. John rang the bell and took a seat and, after a few moments with no response, got up and rang the bell again.

A familiar voice called out, "I heard you. I'm busy right now. If you're dying, come on in. Otherwise I'll get to you in a minute."

"I ain't dying," John called back.

Puzzled, Doc Caulder, a plump short man in his sixties, hearing a familiarity in the voice stopped what he was doing and rubbing his chin thought, I've heard that voice before, and it's certainly not from anyone around here.

Then, looking down at the man on the table in front of him, said, "Sam, I've sewed you up for the last time. You get drunk on Saturday night, get into a fight with your wife and end up here again, and I am just going to leave you. Understand? One day she's going to kill you and you probably will deserve it. So straighten up."

The patient, carefully pulling his shirt on so as not to disturb the bandage on his stomach, shrugged his shoulders and muttered, "If you were married to my woman, you'd drink too."

"Well, I'm not married to your woman, and if you'd quit drinking you two might just get along."

The man made his way out of the office, and Doc Caulder washed the blood from his hands, removed the apron that he wore when operating on someone and made his way into the waiting room.

As the doctor entered the room, John stood nervously twitching his fingers by habit.

Doc Caulder stopped in the doorway, stared at the young man standing as if at attention in front of him, and thought that he looked perfectly healthy.

Still drying his hands on a towel Doc said, "How can I help you, Young Man?"

John smiled and drawled, "You don't know me, do you?"

Doc Caulder quickly adjusted the glasses that normally rested near the tip of his nose and squinting for a moment suddenly gasped, "Are you who I think you are?"

"I'm John Wilson, Sir."

"John Wilson! My goodness, Boy. Where in the world did you come from?" Doc Caulder exclaimed, reaching out for John.

Embracing, the two men patted each other on the back and even though trying to restrain themselves, both men's eyes watered.

Standing before Doc Caulder was not the thin shallow-cheeked beardless boy that was half dead when he had taken him into his home after the battle. This John Wilson, who now stood well over six feet tall with broad shoulders and a short cropped beard, had grown into a healthy and striking young man.

For a moment the doctor just stood there looking at John and shaking his head. Finally he said, "Son, I thought I'd never see you again."

"I told you I'd come back, didn't I?"

"That you did," the doctor replied.

Doc Caulder took a seat and motioned for John to join him. He was so surprised to see John that for a while he didn't even wonder about the circumstances that brought John to Gettysburg. He only knew that the boy who had come into their home as a wounded Confederate soldier, an enemy, one who had become more than a son to him, had returned. He could still see the train as it pulled away from Gettysburg carrying the prisoners to Camp Douglas. Knowing the condition of the camp, he was afraid he would never see John alive again.

For the next few moments, Doc Caulder asked about John's family and the South under the reconstruction government. Through the media and from people returning from the South, stories had circulated as to the harsh treatment the Southerners were receiving under military rule, and to the delight of many Northerners, it was said that many Southern planters had lost everything.

Finally, Doc Caulder asked, "Now tell me what you're doing here?"

John thought for a second. He didn't really know why he had come except that deep inside he felt impelled to return to the place that had haunted him like a demon seeking its prey, and on the other hand, he yearned to see the family that had shown him compassion and had given him hope that he could survive no matter what he had to face in the Northern prison.

John's first impulse was to say that he was just passing through and he must catch the next train out, but he caught his breath and muttered, "You all saved my life. I'm here in gratitude."

Excited, Doc Caulder reached over and clasped John's hand. "I'm glad you're here. How long can you stay?"

John glanced down and replied, "I thought I'd stay a couple of days. Is the hotel still open down the way?"

"Hotel! Heavens no, Boy. You're staying with us."

John said, "I know the Misses is fine or you would have told me but what about Cretia. I guess she's grown and married by now."

Doc Caulder chuckled. "She's still with us. In fact, Lucretia's down at the church. She's a school teacher now. Would you believe that?"

John shook his head. "I can't believe she's old enough to be a teacher."

"Old enough? John, it's been eight years since you left here. In fact, I'm supposed to meet her in about thirty minutes to carry her home, but I've got a patient coming in. I tell you what, you take the buggy out back and pick her up. The Misses is sure going to be pleased to see you."

"You sure it's gonna be all right for me to stay with y'all?"

Doctor Caulder grinned. "Best thing that's happened to me in an upteen-dozen years. You get on down there. Lucretia's gonna be proud to see you. No, she's going to be shocked."

"Which church is she at?"

"You still remember how to get to the house, don't you?"

"Yes Sir, I remember," John replied.

"Well, you'll go right by it. It's the Baptist Church on the outskirts of town. They're building a new school on the south side of town. The old one burned down. Right now they're holding school in several of the local churches to get by."

John shook the doctor's hand and making his way out the back door found the horse and buggy under a bare elm tree. Carefully reigning the horse down the street, John soon was through the center of town. Glancing down the road, he saw a tall white steeple rising above the last row of buildings. This has to be the church, he thought.

Pulling the horse to a stop, John became nervous. Like Doc Caulder had said, it had been eight years. Even though he had been a soldier in arms, he and Lucretia were just youngsters. Perhaps she had changed; certainly times had changed, but he wasn't sure he should accept the invitation to stay with the Caulders. Getting down from the buggy, John secured the horse to a hitching post and, after brushing the dust from his trousers and running his hands over his hair, climbed the row of steps that led to the entrance. As he neared the door, he could hear a voice inside, a woman's voice. Knowing she was busy teaching, John felt that he should wait until the class was dismissed but impulse told him otherwise.

Slowly pushing the door open so as not to disturb the class, John eased into the sanctuary and finding an empty pew in the back, quietly sat down. The pews had been moved to the sides of the room and desks had been placed in neat rows facing the pulpit. A portable blackboard had been brought in and a larger desk, a teacher's desk, was placed next to the pulpit. Several children who appeared to be nine or ten years old were sitting in the back of the room. They turned sheepishly and looked at John as he entered the room. The remainder of the class sat silently listening to the teacher.

Shades of green, red and purple light streaked across the room as the afternoon sun's rays illuminated the stained glass windows. The woman with her back to the students fervently scratched a set of numbers on the board, and as she moved about, the bright sunlight streaming through the windows sparkled across her blond curly hair creating a halo effect.

"Now children, what do you get when you multiply nine times seven and then add three?" she asked turning to the class.

All was quiet for a moment, then a boy up front raised his hand and answered, "Sixty-six, Miss Caulder."

Not noticing the man in the back of the room, she replied, "That's right, Samuel. It is sixty-six."

John suddenly twisted in his seat creating a screeching sound and immediately the children in the back once again turned and stared at him.

Seeing the children distracted, the teacher called out, "All right children, what do you think you're doing back there? We still have thirty minutes left and I do expect you to pay attention."

A freckled-faced girl with platted red hair and a shy smile across her face raised her hand and pointed toward John. All the students then stared at the stranger and started to murmur to one another.

The students became quiet as their teacher called out, "May I help you?"

Rising, John replied, "Ma'am, I certainly am sorry that I caused this distraction."

Hearing the man's Southern drawl, the children began to giggle as they whispered to one another.

This can't be happening, Lucretia thought. This can't be.

"Sir, would you please step where I can see you."

John stepped out into the aisle. The bright light crossed his face causing his deep blue eyes to twinkle.

Taking a deep breath, Lucretia asked, "Do I know you?"

"Yes Ma'am. I think you do."

With all eyes on him, John walked slowly down the aisle.

With a big smile, he said, "Been a long time, Cretia."

Studying the man in front of her, nothing appeared the same as she had remembered. This man was tall and strong and now was fully bearded with a trace of gray across his temples. Only his blue eyes and smile appeared the same.

As he stood facing her, she carefully reached up and pushed the hair back from his upper forehead revealing a long thin scar.

"It is you," she said quietly.

"Yes Ma'am," John replied with a smile.

Looking up at the large clock at the front of the room, she said, "It's almost three o'clock. You can go early today, Children."

Grabbing their books and lunchboxes, the students squealed in joy as they bounded down the aisle and out of the building.

In moments, all was quiet.

Looking down at the woman in front of him, John couldn't believe how she had blossomed. Her emerald green eyes and unmanageable curly blond hair had not changed, but her body was not that of the girl he had known and her face was that of a mature woman, a beautiful woman. Reaching out to her he said, "Do I get a hug?"

For a few moments, the two embraced and then realizing that she had responded beyond a hug, Lucretia pulled away. "It is so good to see you, but what are you doing here?"

Reaching out and pushing a curl out of her eyes, John replied, "Your father asked me to come down and see you home."

As the two reached the buggy, John extended his hand and helped

Lucretia up unto the seat. With the warm spring sun bearing down, John removed his jacket and rolled up his sleeves revealing bulging muscles developed from hard strenuous work.

Turning, John found Lucretia with her hand to her mouth, face flushed. A little self-conscious, John looked down at himself and then back to her and said, "Did I do something wrong?"

"No! I'm just amazed to see you. I guess I really never expected to see you again."

As the two approached a crossroad at the edge of town, they met a young couple in a buggy. Recognizing them, Lucretia asked John to stop.

"That's Sally Edwards. She's a friend of mine," Lucretia said, waving. "The boy with her is Amos Parks, her beau."

As soon as the rigs had stopped, Lucretia called out, "How're you coming with the Easter music? You know it's not two weeks away."

Looking past Lucretia and at the man next to her, Sally paused for a moment and with a squinted expression on her faced, muttered, "We'll do fine."

Amos then leaned over the side of the buggy and spat out a plug of wasted tobacco. Looking over to John, he said, "I'm Amos Parker. Who might you be?"

Then realizing how it must appear with her escort a strange man, Lucretia cleared her throat and said, "This is John Wilson, a friend of the family."

John tipped his head. "Nice to meet ya."

Wiping the juice from his lip, Amos tilted his head, eyeing John. "You're a Southerner, aren't you?"

Sensing a slight hostility in his voice, John replied, "I'm from Miss'sippi."

Then reaching inside his coat pocket he brought out a twist of tobacco and tossed it over to Amos, "Try this if'n you will. Picked it up down in Virginia."

Amos bit off the end of the twist and working it around in his mouth for a moment, smiled and flipping it back over to John exclaimed, "Mister John Wilson, you'll do just fine."

Sally noticed John's good looks, blushed and quickly adjusted her bonnet tucking some loose strands of hair neatly away. Impressed by the stranger's appearance and manners, Sally was eager to know more about

John Wilson. After a short while, Lucretia stated that she needed to be on the way and as they parted, Sally called out, "I'm going to try to come see you Saturday, if convenient."

Lucretia waved back to her. "I'll be home."

As the buggy pulled up, everything was exactly as John remembered. A white picket fence bordered the small yard that surrounded the place, and neatly tucked beneath several large oaks was an elegant one story white clapboard house with a wide front porch.

John quickly got down and hurried to help Lucretia. She placed her hands on John's shoulders as he grabbed her around the waist and eased her down. Looking him in the face and feeling the touch of his breath, she blushed.

"I'll go put up the rig and stable the horse," John said climbing back into the buggy.

Gathering the bag that contained her schoolwork, Lucretia called out to John as he was leading the rig to the barn located at the back of the house, "Where are you staying?"

John glanced back over his shoulder and replied, "Your Daddy wants me to stay with you all."

At first Lucretia was startled, but then a warmth grew in her heart and the thought of John and her family together again caused a feeling of joy. Lucretia, picking up the front of her skirt and quickly following John as he led the horse into the stables, said, "Can I help you with something?"

"No. It won't take long."

When Mrs. Caulder heard voices, she came to the back porch and with her hands resting on her waist, called out, "That you Lucretia?"

"Yes Mother! And I've got a surprise for you."

Talking and laughing, the couple made their way across the back yard toward the house. When they reached the porch, the two stopped and Lucretia, with a sheepish smile, stepped away from John and holding her hand out toward him, said, "Who do you think this man is, Mama?"

Mrs. Caulder tilted her head to the side for a moment as she eyed the young man standing below and then rubbing the side of her face and nodding her head replied, "You're a lot bigger and stronger than I remember, but I'd know those blue eyes anywhere. Mister John Wilson, you better come up here and give an old lady a hug."

For the remainder of the afternoon, Lucretia and John sat in the parlor talking over what had happened in their lives, but there were some things neither was willing to share, not at this time.

Following dinner, Doc Caulder asked John to come out front for some men's talk. As they were leaving, the Doctor pulled a bottle out of a cabinet and then going to a lower shelf, collected two glasses.

Mrs. Caulder, still sitting at the table, looked up at the two and adjusting her glasses, said, "You know I don't like you drinking."

John and Doc Caulder put on their coats and then headed to the front porch where a swing and a couple of rocking chairs were waiting. Once settled, Doc poured himself a glass of bourbon and then offered John a glass. Not much of a drinker but not wanting to offend Doc Caulder, John took the glass. Swirling the brownish liquor around, John occasionally took a sip as the two talked. At times all would be silent as they rocked, but with time, the bourbon took hold and Doc Caulder became loud and humorous. There were jokes he had heard in the office and outlandish tales about his practice that he freely shared with John.

At one point, Mrs. Caulder, who had her bedroom window open and was only a short distance from where the men were sitting, called out to them that she could hear every word they were saying, and if they got any louder, Lucretia would hear them too.

As it neared midnight and with the bottle almost empty, Doc Caulder finally began to wind down and knowing his limits put his arm around John's shoulder and said, "I'm really glad you came to see us. I want you to go on some calls with me next week, and we've got to go fishing."

With the cool spring breeze rustling through her bedroom window ruffling the curtains about, Lucretia pulled her covers snuggly under her chin. She could not believe John had returned to Gettysburg. She remembered the terrible battle; she could still recall curling up in her mother's arms in their underground cellar listening to the rolling thunder of muskets and roar of cannons. But the worse of all was that when all became still, she, her mother and father loaded up in the buggy and with her father's medical bag made their way through the shambles of what was Gettysburg and to the fields south of town. Bodies were strewn about in every position, sometimes clustered in neat rows as they had been slain in their long lines of formation. Lucretia shuddered as she saw bodies torn to pieces, an arm here, the top of a man's head there. She could still visualize the long rows of wounded solders placed on the ground near an old barn, waiting for help, help that in many cases came too late. The cry of pain and the chorus of moaning men begging for water still haunted her.

And then as she walked about with her water bucket, she saw a soldier, no a boy, lying there pawing his heels in the dirt in agony begging for someone to help him. Leaning beside him, she had lifted his bloodied head and gently trickled some water across his lips. The boy had opened his eyes and asked if she were an angel. Later that night he had begged her not to leave him. Lucretia had assured him that she would not. She never expected him to see the break of day.

He did live and that boy, a Confederate soldier, an enemy of the United States Government, was now sleeping across the hall from her, only a few feet away.

17

REKINDLED SPIRITS

Before leaving for school, Lucretia quietly opened the door and looked in on John who, exhausted from the long trip, was sleeping soundly. His covers were nearly to his waist. This was certainly not the thin beardless boy she had nursed back to health many years ago. His muscular body spoke of the man he had become, one who was healthy and knew hard work.

She then made her way to the kitchen for a quick cup of tea and a buttered biscuit. Lora with her floured apron secured firmly around her waist, had been up for more than two hours and was taking a break before continuing her household duties.

Pouring herself a cup of tea, she settled in a chair across the table from her daughter and pulling up her skirt tail, wiped a smudge from her eyeglasses. She looked up the hall and sighed," I guess your father will be sleeping in this morning. I thought they never would get to bed."

Then after taking a sip of tea she continued, "I don't like to see him drinking like that."

Lucretia glanced up the hall and replied, "He doesn't drink often and when he does, it's always at home. It could be worse."

Lora nodded in agreement and after thinking for a moment said, "He sure does like that young man. He's been nothing but a chatterbox since John arrived. You know, he wasn't sure he would ever see him again. You two seemed to enjoy yourselves yesterday."

Lucretia smiled. "He is an unusual man. I find him fascinating."

Fascinating, Lora thought. When you two walked up from the barn yesterday, your face was all aglow and you would not leave his presence. I'm not sure I understand or approve of your feelings for this young man.

Then all of a sudden, she remembered. "Lucretia, in all the excitement I forgot to tell you there is a letter from Robert. I put it on the parlor table next to the Bible."

Lucretia hurriedly gathered her school bag and on the way out picked up the letter. As she left the house, she called back to her mother, "Tell John he can pick me up after school."

Later that morning, Lora heard faint groans coming from her bedroom. From past experience she knew that a strong cup of coffee and a few more hours of rest would normally bring her husband around, and like a child, he always wanted her there with him. With a steaming cup of coffee, strong enough to keep a grown man awake for days, Lora eased into their bedroom. Lifting his head and fluffing the pillow under his head so he would be elevated enough to drink, she whispered, "Now don't let it burn you."

The doctor slowly took a few swallows, leaned his head back on the pillow and moaned, "I think I'm dying."

"You're not dying," she said. "The Lord's just punishing you for being such an ole fool."

He then eased off back to sleep and later awoke feeling somewhat better. Lora, sitting in a rocker next to him reading, wiped his face with a damp cloth, straightened his hair and said, "See, you're still alive, aren't you?"

Doc Caulder gazed about the room for a moment, then his eyes brightened and he threw back the covers, almost falling in the process.

Startled, Lora caught him by the arm. "I think you need to get back in bed."

"Bed? I don't have time for that. Is John up yet?"

"I think so," Lora replied.

Going to the kitchen, they found John dressed and pouring himself a cup of coffee. Dressed in dark trousers with black leather suspenders and with an off-white pullover puffed sleeve cotton shirt, John looked ready for the day.

Lora helped her husband into his chair by the table, then said, "John, are you sure you stayed out there with the doctor last night?"

John pulled Lora's chair back, helped her take a seat, and replied, "Yes Ma'am, I was there. I just didn't indulge as much."

At midday a rider galloped up to get the doctor because his wife had just begun labor. Even though mid-wives were used frequently in rural Pennsylvania, the rider's wife had had problems delivering in the past. If it hadn't been for Doctor Caulder a few years back, the man felt for sure he would have lost his wife and baby.

Still feeling sick, Doc Caulder hesitated, but John volunteered to go with him.

Meanwhile, Lucretia thought the day would never end. As hard as she tried not to, her mind was on spending time with John. Even her students noticed her cheerful mood. When one of the boys misbehaved, she handled the situation with a stern, but jovial attitude, not with the strict disapproving discipline she normally used.

The church bell finally rang dismissing the students. Lucretia hurried the children out and, closing the door for the weekend, glanced across the grounds. At first she thought she recognized a buggy coming toward the church, but as it reached Elm Street, it turned. No one was in sight. For the next half hour, Lucretia waited and finally realizing that he was not coming, headed for home.

She thought as she walked, Perhaps, Mother didn't give John the message. Sometimes she does seem to forget things.

And then a disturbing thought entered her mind. What if John decided to return home? But certainly he wouldn't leave without saying goodbye.

Lucretia was relieved when her mother told her that John had gone with her father and would both be home as soon as the baby came. While her mother prepared supper, Lucretia waited impatiently on the front porch. As the sun was setting, she made out a buggy in the distance churning up dust. Pulling up the front of her dress, she hurried down the steps to meet them.

Recognizing Lucretia, John pulled the buggy to a stop.

That evening, the four of them sat in the parlor talking until Doc Caulder, finally exhausted from the long day's work and the preceding night's binge, asked to be excused. As Lora followed, she turned to her daughter and said, "When will Robert be arriving?"

Lucretia gasped, "I can't believe I didn't read it!"

Lora shook her head as she left the room.

Lucretia went to the front hall where her coat was hanging and going through the pockets, found the letter and returned to the parlor.

Sitting there with Lucretia, John couldn't help but think that every part of her was perfection. Her once thin girlish face was now full, and her emerald green eyes twinkled as she smiled up at him.

Feeling a little uncomfortable, Lucretia took a deep breath and said, "I guess you wonder who Robert is."

"Is he a friend of yours?"

Lucretia paused a moment and then said, "Yes. He's been studying under my father for a couple of years."

"That's good. If he'll pay attention to your father, he should make one fine doctor."

Then following an implulse, John pulled Lucretia to him and gently held her in his arms. He whispered, "I just want to thank you for all you've done for me. You know you're special. You were my angel."

Lucretia smiled up at him and clasping him tightly replied, "I'm glad you're here. I've never seen Papa so excited."

Their eyes met and as they gazed at each other, John wished he could have met her earlier.

Later, with the moon sending a haze of light filtering through the bedroom window, Lora nudged her husband. "I'm not sure I like the way Lucretia is acting around John. What do you think?"

Doc Caulder grumbled, "Number one, it's none of our business how she feels about him and secondly, I am sleepy, so just hush. I'm sure that they are just friends."

"I say friendships can lead to other things. I don't like it a bit," Lora replied.

In the morning John and the Caulders pulled out of the front yard in the family buggy headed for the First Methodist Church of Gettysburg. John and Doc sat on the front bench with John at the reigns while Lucretia and Lora huddled behind them to stay warm. The doctor enjoying a little male companionship, talked incessantly. John listened to every word and nodded his head in acknowledgement.

Pulling up to the church grounds reminded John of his church back home in Little Rock. Resting on the crest of an oak clustered hill, the white clapboard building sat on large pillows of stone and a tall steeple with a cross spiraled upwards. As they entered, John was taken by the beauty of the sanctuary and especially the pastel light glimmering through the stained glass windows. Making their way down the aisle to the family pew, Doc Caulder introduced John to as many as he could. Like any small community, everyone wanted to get to know the handsome young stranger.

Edging her way around her father, Lucretia eased next to John and quickly took a seat before her parents could come between them.

Lora whispered, "I think it's best that John sit next to your father, don't you?"

Ignoring her comment, Lucretia replied, "We're fine."

Lucretia heard a rustling sound down the pew and turned to see her friend Sally Edwards easing in toward John.

The choir then began taking their seats next to the pulpit as the preacher settled in his large padded chair in front of a massive stained glass picture of Jesus holding a newborn lamb. Sally nudged up to John and murmured, "I'm sure glad you all made it to church this morning. You sure are nicely dressed."

Lucretia leaned over to Sally and whispered, "You don't think you'll hurt your family's feelings by not sitting with them this morning?"

Ignoring her comment, Sally smiled up at John and said, "Could you help me with my wrap."

John glanced over at Lucretia, hesitated, then reached back and lifted the woolen shawl from Sally's shoulders and tucked it behind her. Glancing down, John noticed Sally's shapely figure. Sally smiled and turning to John, whispered, "Thank you, Sir."

When the congregation was asked to stand in prayer, John seemed to stand a full head taller than those around him. There was something about John, Lucretia thought looking up at him. He seems so confident, so self-assured, but also shy and polite.

John barely heard the minister as he enjoyed the beauty of the church and the two women at his side. One was small and dainty with bundles of curls, and the other one tall with auburn hair plaited down to her waist. John almost laughed as he thought how Tim would love to be here with him to enjoy the ladies.

After the service had ended, Lucretia slipped her hand under John's arm and introduced him to all those eager to meet him.

While John and Doc Caulder were fetching the buggy, Lucretia and her mother waited out front talking with the other women of the church. Suddenly feeling someone tugging at her sleeve, Lucretia turned and found Sally standing behind her. Leading Lucretia away from the cluster of women, Sally exclaimed, "You have got to invite me over for a visit. I want to get to know more about this gentleman that's just dropped into our lives. You know, I can hardly keep my eyes off him."

"Can't keep your eyes off him? I thought you were interested in Amos."

Sally tilted her head and with a sly expression exclaimed, "I see Amos on occasion, but at least I'm not engaged to him. Can you say the same?"

"If you like, come by the house this afternoon and we'll have tea," Lucretia quickly replied.

On the way home Lucretia thought how ludicrous it was for her to think about John the way she did. It's only infatuation, she reasoned. As a young girl of thirteen, he was my first love, and after he left, he then became a dream and in dreams reality seldom exists. John Wilson had been Lucretia's imaginary standard of excellence as she grew up, but at best, a figment of her imagination.

That afternoon, Sally's father brought her over to the Caulder's home and while he and the doctor spent the afternoon discussing everything from politics to fishing, Sally, Lucretia and John whiled away the time in the front parlor. It was difficult for Lucretia to handle the advances Sally made, but she knew that he was not hers. Every time she left the room, she would return to find Sally huddled next to John with her hands in places inappropriate for a lady. Even worse it appeared John enjoyed Sally's flirtatious behavior and was even encouraging her.

Just as Lucretia's patience was at an end, Sally's father came up the hall. "Time to get on home, Sugar. Getting late."

Sally leaned over and gave John a hug. "I'll be glad to show you around the community. Lucretia can tell you where we live."

"I think that would be fun. Perhaps tomorrow," he said as the young people walked out to the porch.

With the sun setting, Sally and her father were soon only a whirl of dust down the road. Turning to go back inside Lucretia was stunned to find John slumped in one of the porch chairs with his hands clasped about his head. She noticed his hands were trembling. He suddenly toppled out of the chair and lay motionless on the floor.

Lucretia called for her father and knelt over John's lifeless body. Horrified, Doc Caulder rushed up and loosened John's tie and the top button of his shirt. "Go get me a cold wet cloth," he said to his daughter.

John tried as hard as he could to free himself. Then a hand clutched him around his throat and suddenly released him and with a loud cry pushed him backwards through a curtain.

In the distance, John could barely hear the voice of a woman crying, "You're not going to do this to me again. You're not going to leave me."

Slowly opening his eyes, John could make out the late afternoon sun sparkling through a woman's hair and feebly reaching up, he caressed her cheek

"What happened to you, Son?" Doc Caulder asked.

John stared over at him and then back to Lucretia. Taking a deep breath he eased up on an elbow. "Dreams, terrible dreams," he muttered.

Then trying to get up, he said, "Can you help me to my bed, please?"

At that moment Lora rushed out as Lucretia and Doc Caulder were helping John to his feet. Hurrying over she exclaimed, "What in the world has happened out here?"

Doc Caulder motioned for her to open the door, and John was soon resting on his bed. Later, once he had regained his strength, and with the family sitting around him, John reluctantly told them about his spells and nightmares. Then he dozed off to sleep.

Still sitting beside him, Lucretia asked her father, "Is he going to be all right?"

Doc Caulder shook his head. "Don't know, Daughter."

Then reaching over, he gently touched the scar on John's head and sighed, "The boy had a terrible wound. It's God's miracle that he ever came off that battle field alive."

When her father had left the room, Lucretia, without thinking, reached over and placed her hand on one of John's.

It is much larger than mine, she thought.

Glancing over to her mother, she said, "Have you ever seen anything like this?"

Lora nodded. "It's a working man's hand." She straightened her wrinkled skirt, and then continued, "You know, you have never been one to hide your emotions, and for the last few days I've watched your behavior around John and I'm not sure I approve."

Lucretia quickly removed her hand from John's and replied, "We're just friends, that's all. I don't see how you could see anything differently."

Lora reached over and placed her hand on Lucretia's, "Darling, you appear to be more than friends, and you know you're to be married in a couple of weeks."

Lucretia smiled over at her mother and said, "I know. I guess I've acted a fool, haven't I?"

"You remember when you brought in that little puppy that had been trampled by the horse. You set his broken leg, bandaged his cuts and would not let the little fellow out of your sight. Once he was well, you two were inseparable."

"What has that got to do with John and me?"

"Lucretia, you've always had a big heart. If any creature is down and out, your heart goes out to it. What I'm saying is that what you have always felt for John beginning with finding him on the battlefield, is compassion. He's always been your special puppy dog, someone to worry over. You need to put your relationship with him in perspective."

Lucretia eased her hand away from her mother's and looking over to John replied, "I don't mean to be disrespectful, but he's not my puppy dog, never has been. He's a fine young man who has had a hard time, and I do feel close to him because I was with him when he almost died. If it hadn't been for me and dad, I don't believe he would be alive today."

For the next few moments, the two sat quietly, Lora thinking over what she had said and worrying that she may have over-reacted to Lucretia's behavior. Before she could apologize, Lucretia reached back over and began pulling her mother's shawl up around her shoulders.

"You know, you're right. I guess I have some feelings for John, but I do plan to marry Robert come Easter."

"Have you told John about him?"

Lucretia shook her head. "No, I haven't."

18

TRUTH REVEALED

A STRONG MARCH WIND WHISTLED AROUND THE CORNER OF the house and the constant rhythm of a screeching rocking chair aroused John. Slowly opening his eyes, then blinking to clear his blurred vision, John noticed Doc Caulder sitting next to his bed. Doc, wrapped tightly in his housecoat with his glasses low on his nose, was flipping through a large leather bound book, completely engrossed. John lay watching him for a while, then said, "What ya looking for?"

Startled, the doctor almost dropped the book he was holding and sliding his glasses further up his nose replied, "Just looking for answers."

John smiled over at the old man. "Medical book, huh. They got my problem in there?"

Doc shook his head, reached over to the lamp table next to him, and handed John a glass of water. "Can't find anything. I don't have a clue. Drink all you can."

"March is going out like a lion, ain't it?"

Doc Caulder peered out the window and seeing the bare limbs of the trees outside pushed to and fro, said, "These winds will be gone 'fore long. Things will be budding out before you know it."

Feeling better, John eased up in a sitting position and reached up and rubbed the back of his neck. Often after a spell, John's whole body seemed strained to the limit. This time was no different.

Stretching his arms over his head, he glanced toward Doc Caulder who was staring at him and said, "I appreciate your hospitality, but I think it's about time I get on home. I think I'll be leaving tomorrow."

"It took you years to get back up here to see us. You don't need to go just now," the doctor replied.

"Don't want to wear out my welcome," John said, reaching for his trousers.

"Feel like eating?"

On their way down the hall to the kitchen Doc Caulder said, "You've been a lot of help these last few days. Why don't you just stay up here with us? You and I work good together."

John placed his arm around Doc's shoulder, patted him on the back and laughed, "I'd just get in your way. You don't need me."

This past week has been the most enjoyable one in years, Doc Caulder thought. The boy seem to enjoy spending time with me, and we've never lacked for conversation. That's more than I can say for most folks around here. People claim that I just don't talk very much, which is nonsense. And John has been most helpful to me on house calls. Robert never wants to go out on calls in the country. I know that there is not a thing John wouldn't do for me, if I asked him.

Having lost a child, Andrew, years ago to typhoid fever, John felt like the nearest thing to a son Doc Caulder had ever had. Doc needed him to stay.

Reaching the kitchen, the two saw Lora out in the back yard hanging out some clothes to dry. Lucretia had already left for school. After the two enjoyed a light breakfast, John asked Doc Caulder if he had any house calls scheduled for the day. Doc Caulder told John that he should probably stay in the house and rest for the day and perhaps he could help him tomorrow.

As John watched the wind whip the clothes and heard the cracking sound as the sheets were thrashed about, he began to think of home. He could vision his mother out back, just like Lora, hanging out the family wash, singing some hymn and daring the chickens to come near. Home seemed like a million miles away.

The door suddenly swung open as Lora bristled in with her hands clasped around the bottom of her skirt as the wind whipped it about.

Surprised to see John, Lora quickly closed the door, straightened her skirt and exclaimed, "The wind's about to beat me to death. Won't take those clothes long to dry."

John got up, took her clothesbasket and returned it to its usual place in the corner of the kitchen.

Later, as John sat around the house, he found Lora to be less talkative than normal and any conversation that did occur, he had to initiate. John knew something was wrong.

Perhaps, he had stayed too long, he reasoned. For the past couple of days, she had acted somewhat differently toward him.

John joined Lora in the kitchen as she was preparing lunch, and went over to the window. He peered outside and said, "They ought to be dry by now."

He then picked up the clothesbasket and as he started outside, turned and said, "I'll be leaving come morning. You all have sure been good to me."

Surprised, Lora, who had been cutting up some potatoes, put her cutting knife down and rubbing her hand across her cheek, replied, "John, come on back in, I think we need to talk. Those clothes can wait."

Before she could continue, a loud rapping was heard at the front door. She glanced over to John. "If you don't mind, please answer the door. I'm just not presentable."

John hurried to the foyer and turning the latch on the door, called out, "I'm coming."

A neatly dressed young man with a dark leather satchel in hand stood at the door. The stranger was quite a bit shorter than John and was handsomely dressed. The man's long brown hair was oiled and combed straight back, every hair was in place, and his face was closely shaven.

John thought he must be some kind of salesman. Extending his hand, he said, "Sir, can I help ya?"

With an astonished look, the man stood motionless.

John, tanned faced and needing a shave, dressed in long-sleeved underwear stuffed into his trousers looked like a lumber jack prepared for work.

"And who might you be?" the frowning stranger asked as he slowly reached for John's hand.

"My name is Wilson, John Wilson. You need to see the Misses?"

"What are you doing here?" the man asked releasing John's hand.

Confused by John's appearance and his Southern accent, the man called out, "Anybody home?"

He then tried to push John aside, but John grabbed him by his coat and pushed him back.

Closing the front door behind him John sternly warned the man, "I don't know who you are or what your intentions may be, but you're not going to get past me. So just tell me what you want."

At that moment the door swung open and Lora appeared in the doorway. John, with fist up, glanced back at her. "He won't tell me who he is, and he tried to break on into your house."

Lora eased past John and reached out to the man. "We've been waiting for you. Thought you might have gotten here earlier. "

After a long hug, Lora then turned and said, "John, this is Robert Townsend. Lucretia has told you about him. Robert, this is John Wilson, a friend of the family."

"Mister Townsend, I'm sorry. Cretia has told me about ya. Please forgive me."

They all went into the house and while John was out back taking the clothes off the line, Lora explained. After learning about John, Robert felt a little better, but he was still resentful of the rough treatment he had received out front and didn't like the idea of John staying in the house with Lucretia. He was glad that Lucretia had not been there to see him get pushed around.

After a short visit, Robert left to find Doctor Caulder. He found him preparing his satchel for a visit to the country and without any greetings, exclaimed, "Why's that man staying with you?"

Doc, continuing to pack his bag, just glanced over his glasses and mumbled, "Good to see you, Robert. Everything go well for you at the conference?"

"What is that man doing staying in your house?" Robert repeated bristling.

Doc stopped what he was doing and turned to face Robert. "First thing, Young Man, you could have at least had the manners to give me a greeting of some kind, and as for Mister Wilson, he's a friend of mine."

Then thinking for a moment, he continued, "And as far as who stays at my house, that is entirely my business."

Embarrassed by the scolding, Robert apologized and went over to the desk to check their daily appointments. Glancing at the list, Robert asked, "You want me to stay in the office or take the buggy?"

Doc, now in the back room replied, "Makes no difference with me."

Everything was quiet for a moment then Robert said, "I would like to see Lucretia as soon as possible. Just for today, I'd like to stay, if I may."

Doc, pulling on his heavy coat, came trudging out of the back room with his medical bag in hand. "I figured as much. Lock up when you leave."

"Yes sir, I will."

"By the way, I guess you'll be coming over for supper tonight. Hope you have a profitable day."

Feeling that Doc had forgiven him for his rudeness, Robert followed him out to the street and, as Doc was settling himself in the buggy, said, "If you keep on taking chickens for your service, you are going to have one huge flock."

Slapping the reigns on his horses' flanks, Doc called back, "Least we won't go hungry."

Watching Doc ride away, Robert was puzzled at the old man's philosophy on life. Here in the back country of Pennsylvania was one of the most renown surgeons in the country. Doctors from all over the United States had come to Gettysburg to talk with him and observe him at work. He was constantly being asked to speak at medical conferences and, thinking back, Robert recalled several colleges back east that had begged Doc Caulder to join their staff as an instructor. But, no, here this man stays out in the wilderness and works for chickens, hams, turnip greens and occasionally a few coins. Outside of an occasional operation, he's nothing but a country doctor.

"Unbelievable," murmured Robert. "Not me. I'm going east and get paid for my work. No chickens or hams. With what I've learned from Doc, I'm going to put it to good use."

Lucretia, expecting John, was surprised to find Robert waiting for her out front. With time to spare, the two decided to take a ride in the country before going home. As they rode, Robert related all that had happened to him during the past several weeks but took little time getting to the subject of John Wilson.

Lucretia told him how she had met John and assured Robert that at the time, she was just a young girl and they were no more than friends.

As they approached Lucretia's house, Robert's thoughts of John came to surface. As the buggy came to a stop, Robert climbed down and with a smirk he looked up at Lucretia, "As far as John goes, I don't think it's proper for him to stay under the same roof as you. He needs to be at the hotel. You know he's nothing but a murdering Rebel. I can't see you all taking the traitor in."

Surprised by his remark Lucretia exclaimed, "That's hardly a way to speak. The war is over. He's no traitor! He was fighting for his country."

"Country," Robert scowled. "Our country is the United States of America."

Anger was beginning to show on Lucretia's face, and Robert decided to change his approach. "Maybe I was too hasty with my words, but it really doesn't make any difference. He's leaving tomorrow."

"Leaving tomorrow. How do you know that?"

Taking her hand, Robert replied, "That's what he said this morning."

Upon entering the house, the two found John in the dining room helping Lora set the table. John smiled. "'Bout time y'all got in. We were beginning to worry about you. Your Papa's ready to eat."

"No need to worry," Robert replied as he went into the kitchen to wash his hands.

Lucretia helping her mother finish setting the silverware and nudging up to John whispered, "What is this about you leaving tomorrow?"

Neatly folding a linen napkin and placing it next to one of the plates, John replied, "I think it's best I get on home. My folks are probably needing me."

Lucretia, placing silverware on the napkin John had just arranged, placed her hand on his and replied, "Shouldn't you have discussed it with me first?"

Seeing her father enter the room, Lucretia quickly removed her hand from John's and blushing, eased away from him.

Doc Caulder dropped his head, coughed and smilingly said, "You got a problem, Daughter?"

Lucretia hurried down to the end of the table next to her mother and replied, "No Papa, I'm fine."

Doc Caulder sat at the head of the table, and Lora sat on the opposite end facing him. Lora then placed Robert and Lucretia on one side, and John across from them.

John, clean shaven with his dark curly hair brushed back, unfolded his napkin and placed it on his lap and sat waiting.

Doc Caulder looked over at him. "You care to say the blessing, John?"

"It would be my pleasure, Sir."

Robert looked to Lora and then glared across at John and thought, Doctor Caulder always blesses the table. What kind of a hold does this man have on the old man? Have I missed something?

With head bowed, John began. "Lord, thank you for this wonderful day you've blessed us with, and thank you for this family and the love they share with others. And Lord, please heal this nation torn by war and last but not least, bless this food and the hands that prepared it. Amen."

While John was praying, Lucretia looked up and was startled to see John staring straight at her. She smiled at him and blushed.

As soon as John finished the blessing, Lora began passing the food around the table starting with John on her right.

Taking a serving of roast beef, John handed it over to Doc Caulder.

"Roast beef with tators, green beans and freshly baked rolls," John said. "It's just like southern cooking."

Robert glanced at Lucretia and imitating a Southern accent laughed, "I thought y'all lived on collard greens and fat back down in Miss'sippi."

John looked over at Robert, offended by the remark, but before he could respond, Doc Caulder muttered, "I've eaten collard greens plenty of times. Nothing wrong with them."

Seeing that the doctor had sided with John, Robert quickly added, "I was just kidding with him. I've eaten them too."

During the meal, conversation was mostly centered around Robert and all he had accomplished while at the conference. Lora sat quietly, listening but made no comments.

Suddenly, Robert reached over and placed his hand on Lucretia's. "How are the plans progressing for the wedding?"

"Who's gettin' married?" John asked as he put down his glass.

"Who's getting married?" Robert then reached into his coat pocket and taking Lucretia's hand slid a diamond ring on her finger. Then looking over to John, Robert continued, "She didn't tell you about us?"

Unable to look John in the face, Lucretia blushed and gazed down at the ring on her finger.

John was dumbfounded as Lora got up and went around to her daughter.

"Let me see," she said lifting Lucretia's hand. The diamond sparkled in the light. Lora then leaned over to Robert and hugging him said, "I think you two will do just fine."

Doc Caulder put his fork down, looked over to Lora, and mumbled, "I hope the two of you don't have to learn to love each other."

Surprised at such a statement, Lora exclaimed, "What a foolish remark. What do you mean by that?"

Doc Caulder looked directly at Lucretia. "It doesn't really matter. It just an old man's senility."

Knowing what he meant, Lucretia reached over and patted her father on the hand. John, recovering from his shock, said, "I'd like to congratulate you both and wish you the best."

After dinner while coffee was being served the conversation turned to John who had been unusually quiet during the meal.

Pushing his chair away from the table and crossing a leg, Robert said, "Tell me about the South. Word is most folks down there can't even read or write. Anything to it?"

John glanced over to Doc Caulder and with a frown answered, "I think our literacy rate is about the same as the rest of the country. When you get out in any rural area, people, that is farmers, are more concerned about simply putting food on the table. Sometimes the children are needed in the field. They don't have no time for books."

"Of course, they don't have no time for books." mimicked Robert. "What about you? You go to school?"

"Of course he did," Lucretia said, coming to John's defense.

"Let him answer, Lucretia," Robert said, enjoying the moment.

John smiled over at Lucretia and then looked across to Robert and began, "So live, when the summons comes to join the innumerable caravan, which moves to the mysterious realm, where each shall take his chamber in the silent halls of death, thou go not, like the quarry-slave at night, scourged to his dungeon, but, sustained and soothed by an unfaltering trust, approach thy grave, like one who wraps the drapery of his couch about him, and lies down to pleasant dreams. Thanatopsis. William Cullen Bryant."

Robert nodded. "Bravo! Well done!"

"Good job, John," Doc Caulder said. "I don't see how you can remember those lines."

Not a bad response, Robert thought, but I'm not through with you yet.

He then continued, "Talking about farming, I understand that's how your family makes a living. Did you keep any slaves down there?"

"Slaves!" John shook his head. "We don't believe in holding slaves. Mama always said it was ungodly. Fact is, most of our neighbors didn't hold 'em neither."

Robert laughed, "Then why in blazes did you fight against the government?"

John thought for a moment, pursed his lips and replied, "You know I've wondered the same thing. I guess it's the politicians who start the wars, and it's ignorant folks like me that get involved."

"You're not ignorant," Lucretia said, becoming uncomfortable about the turn of the conversation.

"I must be, to go through what I did, and look at the South now. Our economy is in shambles, and Federal troops are in control of our gov'ment."

"By the way, talking about troops, did you ever kill anybody? Doc said you are a pretty good shot," Robert asked, glancing over at Lora.

Lora dropped her head and began folding her napkin neatly on her lap.

"We don't need to talk about that here at the table," Doc said, seeing how uneasy John was becoming. "That's all over now."

With sweat beginning to form on his brow and a slight dizziness, John hesitated, then muttered, "I am a good shot and perhaps I did. I'll never know. When we were standing on the firing line all we could see was smoke in our eyes and a haze of blue across the field where the Union troops were massed. The roar of muskets was so loud, you couldn't even hear your own rifle fire. One moment the man next to you was standing and firing and the next moment, he was gone. We just stood there — like fools — killin' each other."

Lucretia, looked over at Robert who was sitting nonchalantly sipping coffee and stammered, "That's enough of this talk."

With sweat running down his face and a tremble in his hands, John glared over at Robert, "That's all right, Cretia, I guess your next question

Robert is, do I consider myself a murderer and my answer is, I might be just that. You see, we were all murderers, Yanks and Rebs."

Suddenly a pain shot through his head. He shut his eyes as tightly as possible and clasped the table with both hands to steady himself.

Doc Caulder pushed his chair back and rushed over to where John was now swaying in his chair. With his arm around John, Doc Caulder whispered, "Is it that spell again?"

Turning to Lucretia, he pointed to the washbasin on the table. "Go get a cold damp cloth! Quick now!"

Shocked, Lora and Robert sat silently, not knowing what to do.

As John wrenched his hands together in pain, Robert thought, pays you back for what you did to me.

As suddenly as the pain had come upon him, it strangely vanished, leaving John normal but weak. As Lucretia wiped his face, John opened his eyes, smiled up at her and mumbled, "I'm all right. I don't know what happened to me."

Brushing the hair out of his face, she smiled. "You sure you're fine?"

John nodded and took a deep breath.

Feeling better, John looked over to Lora, "Please excuse me, I think I'll go out front for some fresh air."

Doc Caulder put his arm around John's waist and as they were leaving the room said, "I think I'll go out with you for a while."

John eased the doctor's arm away and replied, "I think I need a little time to myself."

With the cool evening breeze pushing against his face, John felt much better as he settled himself in the swing and began to rock back and forth. Hearing the door squeak open, John turned to see Doc Caulder coming toward him with a couple of cups of steaming coffee.

"Kinda cold out here, Son. I know you wanted to be alone but I thought you might need warmth."

John pointed over to the chair next to the swing, "Care to have a seat?"

Putting his cup down on the porch floor, Doc Caulder muttered, "It was rude of him to ask you those questions."

"I probably had it coming," John said as he explained the earlier encounter at the door.

"Son, can you tell me what bothers you and brings on these spells?"

John took a sip of coffee and thought for a moment. "It's always the same. It's the war and that battle. Always that battle."

"Maybe you should go down there. It might clear up some things."

John shook his head. "I've thought about it, but, no Sir, I don't think I can do that."

It wasn't too long before Robert asked to be excused for the evening. Lucretia saw him to the door.

As he came out onto the porch he extended his hand to John. "I didn't mean to upset you. I hope you'll accept my apology."

"No offense taken," John replied clasping his hand.

After Robert left, Lucretia turned to the men.

"You all need anything?"

"No, but I think I've had enough for one night," her father replied as he slowly pulled himself out of the chair. Giving her a kiss on the cheek, he turned to John, "You think about what I just said. It might do you some good."

"What's he talking about?" Lucretia asked edging over to John after her father had gone in.

"It's nothing. Care to sit a spell?" John said, motioning to her.

Lucretia straightened her skirt and eased into the swing next to John. For a while they sat quietly, swinging as the breeze swirled Lucretia's curls.

Finally she said, "I'm sorry about this evening. I know it must have been uncomfortable for you."

"It's really all right."

Feeling Lucretia shudder in the brisk evening cold, John placed his arm around her and snuggled her closer to him. "Why didn't you tell me about Robert?"

Lucretia thought for a moment then replied, "To tell you the truth. I don't really know."

"I would have understood. He seems to be a fine young man. From all accounts, he'll be more than a good provider. I'm happy for you. When's the wedding?"

She whispered, "Easter Sunday. About two weeks from now."

"I want you to know I've enjoyed spending this time with you, I'll be leaving tomorrow," John said after a few minutes of silence.

"Why tomorrow?" she asked, looking over at him.

"I've been here long enough. Maybe too long," John replied, reaching down to push some unruly curls from Lucretia's face.

"You could wait a few more days, couldn't you? You know Sally really wants to get to know you better."

"She and I don't have a lot in common, and I feel I need to be gettin' on home."

"One thing that's been puzzling me, John. Why'd you really come all the way up here?"

John thought for a moment. "I owe you all for saving my life. You didn't have to do what you did. And I did tell your father I'd be back someday."

Lucretia sat quietly taking in every word, but felt there was something he wasn't sharing with her.

Then John reaching over and placing his hand over hers said, "I wanted to see you one more time. Wanted to be sure you were all right."

"Don't leave tomorrow. Just stay one more day."

Glancing away in deep thought, John whispered, "You know, I've thought about what your daddy just said. I've got one more thing I need to do, and if'n it ever is gonna happen, it's got to be tomorrow."

"What's that John?"

"It's something I've got to do by myself. That is, if I've got the nerve."

Later that night Lucretia unable to sleep, kept trying to get her relationship with John in perspective. She had been infatuated with the Rebel solder who had been sheltered in their house until he recovered from a wound that should have taken his life, and now that he was back, she was more confused than ever. John was always considerate, intelligent, humorous and, most of all, she felt comfortable with him. These past few days when she would think of her future with Robert, her mind would always return to John.

19

BREAKING THE SPELL

WITH A HAZY SKY AND A BRISK BREEZE BLOWING OUT OF THE West, darkness still shadowed the grounds as Doctor Caulder pulled up his suspenders and shuffled down the hall to the kitchen. Peering outside, he thought to himself, don't like the looks of those clouds tumbling about. We got some bad weather brewing up there.

In a few moments, Lora joined him to fix breakfast, and it wasn't long before Lucretia and John appeared. Lora soon had breakfast prepared, and then they all settled around a table of hot pancakes with syrup, scrambled eggs and ham, and steaming coffee.

Normally conversation flowed freely, but this morning everything was different. Lora busied herself tending the table and keeping the coffee cups filled while Doctor Caulder occasionally made some remark about the weather or what he had planned for the day.

As she had her breakfast, Lucretia never uttered a word but would glance over at John from time to time. If their eyes met, she would drop her head and continue with her breakfast. John was also quiet.

As hard as he had tried, he had been unable to sleep. Lying in bed, with the chiming of the clock down the hall, he had heard each hour pass. Being reared by the Word, John tried to pray but could not find words for consolation. Nothing seemed to be going right in his life. Where was his future? He had thoroughly enjoyed his visit with the Caulders but was bothered by the unexpected feeling he had toward Lucretia. Unlike Suzanne, she took him as he was and was willing to openly share her feelings with him. John realized that even though they hadn't seen each other in years, she had become the closest friend he had ever had. Just to think about being with her excited him.

John shook his head as he thought how ridiculous it all sounded.

Finally, Lora spoke out, "John, I'd like to be sure all your shirts are clean and ironed before you leave."

John eased his cup down and nodded. "That won't be necessary. They'll just get wrinkled up in my satchel."

Lucretia looked over at him. "When will you be leaving?"

"The train is s'pose to leave about seven tonight."

"You'll be traveling at night?" Doctor Caulder asked.

"Won't make any difference. I'll catch me a nap or so. It'll make the trip a little shorter."

At that moment Lucretia pushed her chair back and said, "You'll have to excuse me."

John started to get up then eased back down into his chair and turning to Lora said, "Is Lucretia well?"

Lora looked over to her husband for a moment then replied, "She'll be fine."

John nodded and turning to Doctor Caulder said, "If'n I might, I'd like to borrow a horse this afternoon."

A short time later Robert came by in his buggy to take Lucretia to school. Normally talkative, she was quiet and when questioned, was evasive. The wind was blowing in gusts and twisting the treetops sending young leaves and small limbs swirling on the road in front of them almost spooking the horse. Glancing up, a chill came over Lucretia as she saw the darkened clouds above tumbling and rolling as if pushed by an evil force. Then off in the distance, there was a roll of thunder.

"I don't like it," she murmured.

"What's that?"

Still looking upward, she replied, "Papa thinks we might have bad weather today."

"Bad weather! So that's what's bothering you," Robert said. "Didn't know what the problem was."

They soon pulled up to the church and as Lucretia was stepping down from the buggy, Robert leaned down and stole a kiss. Then handing down her books exclaimed, "Mrs. Tucker wants to meet with us as soon as you get out of school today. Your mother says she will be directing the wedding. You know we only have thirteen days."

The morning crept by as Lucretia tried to concentrate on her children and the studies at hand, but as hard as she tried, she couldn't forget the look on John's face as she sat across from him that morning. The twinkle of his eyes and the hint of a smile crossed his face each time she looked at him. The realization that after today, she would probably never see him again caused her to shudder. She remembered that he had asked her father about borrowing a horse. Where would he want to go? He hadn't met a lot of people. He had spent most of his time right with the family and, as for Sally, he appeared to care nothing for her.

Unable to concentrate on her teaching and with the weather outside becoming more unstable, Lucretia called the children in early from their morning recess and told them that since a storm might be in the making, she was dismissing school for the day.

Meanwhile, as John rode through Gettysburg, few people were out. No doubt, the anticipation of bad weather was keeping them close to home, he reasoned. Kicking the big gray in the flanks, John rode past the Seminary and headed west down the Chambersburg Pike. When he passed the college, several of the students waved to him as they scurried toward the safety of the buildings.

Even with the threat of a storm, the landscape seemed peaceful now with its lush green carpeted grass and massive oaks, but it wasn't peaceful that terrible day, he remembered. John visioned shells screaming across the sky, the constant thunder of musketry and shouts of men massed in long lines heaving to and fro, testing their inner courage as they slaughtered one another. He shuddered at the scene implanted in his mind.

Deciding to go no further, John tried to turn his mount, but the animal ignored John and stubbornly continued down the road. Reaching a stately barn, John reined his horse southward and after riding a short distance, crossed the Hagerstown Road. Then, as if by instinct, the big gray galloped up a gentle wooded slope and then trotted down a path that ran the length of Seminary Ridge. It was here that thousands of soldiers waited for their call to duty. Glancing about, John could see some napping while others were praying and those who did have the Word with them, tried to find comfort in the reading. Occasionally exploding shells would send limbs and bark sailing in all directions as they sought the lives of men scurrying for safety. Meanwhile some of the veterans simply turned their heads and cursed as missiles tore into the Southern ranks.

Riding down the lane and seeing the different regimental flags, John immediately recognized the units waiting the order. They were all here: Virginia, North Carolina, Georgia and there down the path was Barksdale and his Mississippians. That's strange, thought John. Barksdale was killed yesterday. This can't be. Looking at all the men assembled there, a sense of pride came over him and seeing them patiently waiting, a warm feeling of belonging filled him as he saw familiar faces, men he had learned to respect and love. But as he rode past them, no one acknowledged his presence. It was as if he didn't exist. No one waved nor did any officer beckon a salute. The horse meticulously tipped its way through the men crouched low to the ground. No one was touched. The force of the wind twisted the tops of the trees as thunder rumbled above. Hearing horses up the way, John recognized General Picket and several of his staff as they approached. Then as clear as any voice he had ever heard, Picket called out, "Men, form your brigades! Get them on their feet. Tell the Virginians it's time to go forward. Today may be our last battle."

Back in town with leaves thrashing her in the face and dust swirling so thick she could hardly see, Lucretia fought her way down the street to her father's office as droplets of rain began to fall.

Surprised to see her, Doctor Caulder rushed into the front waiting room where Lucretia stood nervously staring out the window. Seeing how distressed she was, he asked, "What's wrong, Girl?"

She quickly turned and stammered, "Where'd he go!"

"Who go?"

"John. Where is he?"

"He went to the battle field. South of town."

"I'm taking your buggy. I'm going to find him."

Doctor Caulder caught her by the arm as she tried to leave. "You can't go out in weather like this. It's not safe."

Pulling away, she replied, "He's out there by himself. He needs me!"

"This is something he's got to do by himself, Lucretia."

Starting for the door, Lucretia stammered, "I'm going to either walk or take the buggy."

"If you've got to go, then I'm going with you," he said as he handed Lucretia an oil cloth and reached for his coat.

"No, I have to do this on my own," she said as she rushed out the door and jumped up into the buggy.

With the roll of thunder and the almost constant clash of lightning, Lucretia pushed the horse as hard as she could and quickly made it out of town and toward the site of the battle. She soon reached the Codori house and pulled her horse to a stop. Peering out to the far slopes of Seminary Ridge she scanned the countryside. For a moment she thought she saw someone out in the field to her left, but it was only a cow moving toward safety. Seeing a side road that ran westward toward the crest of the ridge, she pushed the horse forward up a grassy path. Suddenly she spotted something moving out to her right and wiping the rain from her eyes, saw that someone was out there. Dropping the reigns and climbing down from the buggy, she shouted, "John! John Wilson!"

He stopped for a moment and turned toward her, then continued walking down the slope toward the road.

"Wait for me!" she called but he only quickened his step.

With the wind blowing fiercely and rain stinging her face, Lucretia struggled forward.

Long lines of soldiers stepping shoulder to shoulder had now cleared the front where the cannons had been dueling for the past two hours. As they passed the cannoneers, the soldiers attending the big guns waved to their comrades and cheered them forward. Knowing that these men had to cross a mile of open land before they could engage the enemy filled their hearts with anxiety as they realized many would not survive the hour.

Feeling a nudge, John glanced over and was relieved to find Tim next to him but his comfort soon vanished when he realized that he had no musket of his own. Looking down at his empty hands, John asked, "Where's my rifle?"

Tim never turned his face nor opened his mouth but John heard him say. "You can pick one up in a minute. There'll be plenty to spare."

This can't be happening, John thought. I heard him speak but he doesn't seem to know I'm here.

"You gonna be all right," a voice muttered to his left.

Quickly turning to the sound of a familiar voice, John recognized

Robert, another one of his boyhood friends. Plump and rosy cheeked, Robert smiled at John but as he was about to speak, a large explosion erupted sending dirt, grass and men in all directions. Wiping the mud from his face, John turned back to Robert.

"He's gone," a voice whispered.

Terrified and seeing that he had now fallen behind, John tried to catch up. Up front, Tim turned and waved him forward but John could not move his legs. No matter how hard he tried, he kept falling further behind. Seeing men falling in front of him, John rushed up to grab a rifle but each time it fell apart.

As they crossed Emmitsburg Road, solid shot, explosive shells and canister were now ripping the Southern Army apart. Soldiers were falling at every step. With only a few hundred yards to go before they would clash with the Union soldiers, John finally caught up with his unit. As he reached them, a mass of blue appeared over a stone wall to his front, and John could see the American and Regimental flags fluttering above. An order was given to fire and a volley erupted in their faces. Men fell like wheat before the sickle. John tried to fire his rifle, but only smoke curled from its barrel. With the deafening sounds of musket and cannon fire, John's ears rang so loud he could hardly hear. Men continued to fall in scores as shot ripped into them. The hiss of mini balls buzzed past his ears and nipped at his clothing. Seeing the men fall all around him, he knew it would only be a matter of time. Standing there, he could see the Southern Army wilting away. Every second brought death.

Then in the turmoil and confusion, he heard a voice behind him. "John! Wait for me!"

Hearing a woman's voice startled him and he turned but saw no one, only clouds of smoke hovering over the ground.

Seeing the crazed look on his face, one she had never seen before, Lucretia stopped in fear. The cold rain mustered her strength and she called out again.

The smoke lifted temporarily and recognizing Lucretia through the haze, John called out, "What are you doing here? You'll be killed!"

Lucretia lunged forward and fell into John's arms.

John held her closely and turned his back to the Union line to protect her. "Why did you come down here? They're gonna kill the both of us!"

"No one is going to kill us, John. It's just a dream!"

"That's cannon shot! This is no dream!" John shouted.

"It's lightning! This is only a thunderstorm! There's no battle here!" she replied.

Ignoring her, John glanced around. Bodies cluttered the ground around him so thick he could hardly move. Then he heard a voice call out, "There's one left! Take him out!"

Seeing thousands of rifles pointed at him, he knew death was imminent. As he heard the order to fire, he pushed Lucretia to the ground shielding her from the onslaught. Lying there the rumble and flash of muskets was so loud his head felt as if it were going to split.

Over and over, Lucretia murmured, "It's only a storm, John."

As the moments passed, the rumble and roar slowly faded away until it could barely be heard in the distance.

John looked down at Lucretia and slowly turned his head toward the stone wall. To his dismay, no one was there. The clouds above began to break allowing streams of sunlight to streak across the field. All was peaceful. Unable to believe what was happening, John jerked around expecting to see masses of bodies but only saw shining blades of wet grass sparkling in the sun.

"Where are they?" he whispered.

Lucretia pulled herself up and wiping the rain from his face said, "Your war is over, John It was just a storm."

Taking a deep breath, John smiled over at her, "This has haunted me since July of sixty-three."

For a few moments they lay there in each other's arms watching the clouds vanish away while sunlight warmed their drenched bodies. With their faces touching, they could feel each other's warm breath and without thinking their lips touched. Then with no guilt or embarrassment they passionately kissed. Wrapped in each other's arms, one kiss followed another as the moments crept by.

"Lucretia! John! Where are you?" came a voice in the distance.

Clasping John by the hand, she pulled him up and waved.

"We're down here, Papa!" she called out as she and John hand in hand worked their way up the muddied slope.

Doctor Caulder, with a quilt in his arms, stepped down from his buggy and hobbled to meet them. "We've been worried sick over you. That was a terrible storm. The horse came back to the house, then the buggy and mare. We thought the both of you might be dead."

He then wrapped the quilt around Lucretia and turned to John. "You all right, Boy?"

John patted him on the back. "Yes Sir. Thank you, Sir."

Making their way back up the hill, Doctor Caulder pointed to the buggy and his horse. "You two take the buggy, I'll ride on home and let everyone know you are all right."

As they approached the house, Lora and Robert rushed out to meet them.

"What in the world came over you to get out in a storm like that? " Lora said, scolding Lucretia.

"Only a fool would do something like that, " Robert said, staring directly at John. Then turning to Lucretia, he continued, "We are to be at Mrs. Tucker's within the hour. You need to dry yourself and change clothes. We can't be late. "

Lora, taking the quilt from Lucretia looked up at John. "The train should be leaving in less than two hours. You need to be on it. My husband is down at the barn. If you will, please take care of the buggy."

As John headed the buggy to the barn he realized that he should not have returned to Gettysburg. His relationship with Lucretia, whatever that might be, had complicated her life. With her marriage approaching, this should be a time of joy and happiness. He should not have kissed her.

Entering the barn, John found Doctor Caulder waiting for him. "Doctor Caulder, if you'll take care of the rig, I'm gonna go change clothes and get on down to the station."

The doctor rubbed his nose and knocked some mud from his shoes. "We never did get to go fishing."

John climbed down out of the buggy as Doctor Caulder muttered, "I'll keep him harnessed. I'll take you to the station."

John thanked him and trudged on up to the house and entered through the back door to change his clothing and collect his belongings. He wanted to thank Lora for her hospitality and speak to Lucretia once more, but he felt it was best that he leave well enough alone.

Doctor Caulder was sitting quietly in the buggy when John returned to the barn. "Dry clothes must feel better," he said.

Before John could answer, Lucretia, flushed face, rushed through the doorway. "If it's all right, I'd like to take John to the train."

"You are more than welcome, Young Lady," Doctor Caulder replied, easing out of the seat and stepping down. "You take him on down there and take your time."

The sun was now setting and water still puddled the road as the buggy splashed its way toward town.

Suddenly John reached over and took the reigns and pulled the buggy to a stop. He gazed out across the countryside and stuttered, "I want to apologize for my behavior today. It was completely uncalled for."

Lucretia gently placed her hand on John's face. "Do you love me?" she said quietly.

John thought deeply, took a breath and replied, "Yes I do. I do love you."

"Like a friend or sister?"

"No, not like that."

John took her hands in his. "Do you care for me?" he asked.

With a trickle of tears running down her face she whispered, "For the last several days, I've realized that I've always loved you. I've never stopped loving you. Since the first time I saw you on the battle field, you've always been with me."

The two embraced and holding her tightly, John said, "If it hadn't been for Rebecca, I'd been back long 'fore now."

"I'm sorry things didn't work out for you," Lucretia said. "What do we do now?"

John dropped his head and replied, "I think you need to drop me off at the station and never look back. Robert is a good man and can give you things I could never imagine or afford."

"Is marriage out of the question for us? Is that what you're saying."

John, eyes watering, looked into her eyes and replied, "The South's in a mess, total chaos. I live with my folks and don't have a dollar to my name. What kind of future do you think you'd have with me?"

"Money's not everything."

John stared into her face for a moment wanting to embrace her but instead, he handed the reigns to Lucretia and stepped down out of the buggy. "I have nothing to offer you. I can walk from here."

20

HOMECOMING AT NEWTON STATION

STRONG WINDS, FOLLOWED BY AN APRIL THUNDERSTORM, swept through the Little Rock community bringing waters which flooded the streams and powerful gusts that stripped the trees of their young leaves. In the freshly plowed fields water puddled in the neatly cultivated rows where small green tips of corn would soon be emerging from the damp soil.

Amanda, afraid of the lighting and thunder, quickly wrapped herself in her most coveted blanket and ran as fast as her short legs would carry her to her aunt's room which was adjacent to hers. Knowing Amanda's fears, Suzanne smiled as she hurried toward her. Suzanne picked her up and tucked her securely under the covers next to her. Cuddling close to Suzanne, Amanda whispered that she was not really afraid. Suzanne smiled, and soon the two were deep in sleep.

Hours later, Suzanne, listening to the song of birds and enjoying the stream of light streaking across the room from the morning sun after the storm had passed, gently nudged Amanda. "You ready to get up, Sweetie-pie? Breakfast time."

Amanda took a deep breath, opened her eyes, then blinked hard trying to remember where she was. Then remembering the storm, she smiled and cuddled close to Suzanne. "Where'd the storm go?" she asked.

"Far, far away," Suzanne replied, giving her a hug and a kiss on the cheek. "It's a beautiful day."

"Then let's go see MeMe," Amanda exclaimed as she threw back the covers and slid off the bed onto the hard floor below.

Suzanne handed her down her blanket, and Amanda scurried down the hall toward the stairs that led to the lower floor of the house. As she passed her father's room there was a loud crash. Amanda reached up on her tiptoes, turned the knob, and eased the door open.

In a few moments Suzanne heard the patter of little feet coming up the hall toward her and with a bang, the door swung open as Amanda rushed in. Running over to the bedside she whispered, "There's people in there!"

"What do you mean people in there?" Suzanne asked.

"Somebody's in Papa's bed."

Puzzled, Suzanne reached for her shawl and easing out of bed took Amanda's hand. "Let's go surprise your father," she whispered with a smile.

Trying to be as quiet as possible, the two tipped down the hallway and reaching the door, Suzanne whispered, "When I count to three, I'll push the door open and we'll surprise your father."

Amanda, with a wide smile nodded.

"One, Two, Three," Suzanne said as she pushed the door open. With loud squeals, the two bounded into the room and over to the bed.

At that moment, an empty whisky bottle rolled from under the covers and crashed to the floor as a startled Frankie jerked himself up. With mussed hair, red eyes and shirtless, he stared at Amanda and then to Suzanne. Then with a scowl on his face, he blurted out, "Get her out of here! What in the hell are you two doing in here anyway?"

Before the two could respond, the covers next to Frankie rustled and a mass of matted red hair appeared.

Surprised at her audience, an obviously naked woman tried to muster a smile as she looked over at Frankie and asked, "Part of yore family?"

Ignoring her, Frankie shouted, "I said get her out, Suzanne! Can't you see I got company!"

Frightened by the loud shouts and the stranger in her father's bed, Amanda huddled behind Suzanne and hid her face in her aunt's nightgown. Then Suzanne turned and hurried Amanda out of the room and back into her bedroom. "Wait for me, Honey, I'll be right back," Suzanne whispered to the frightened child.

Filled with rage, Suzanne returned to her brother's room. Seeing his sister standing over him, he glared up at her and muttered, "This ain't none of your business, Suzanne."

Standing her ground, Suzanne said firmly, "You get dressed and get that whore out of our house. You've got a precious little girl that you apparently don't give a damn about. Thank God she's too young to know what you're doing. If you ever do this again, I'll make sure you're never allowed in this house again."

"Whiskey got me last night, Suzanne. The weather was bad and as God is my witness, I thought I was at my own house. You got to believe me."

Suzanne shook her head and as she left the room replied, "As I said before, don't ever do this again or it will be the last time you are welcomed here. Now get her out of here."

Returning to her bedroom, Suzanne took Amanda on her lap and tried to explain that what had occurred was not important, just a mistake and that Amanda must keep it all a secret.

Later, as they went to the kitchen, Suzanne and Amanda found Belle, the family cook, preparing breakfast and to Suzanne's relief, her mother had gone down to check on one of the hands that had become ill during the night. Breakfast was ready at almost the same time as Mrs. Olliver came bustling through the back door.

Smiling, she took off her bonnet and looking over at the two waiting, exclaimed, "My you two are up and stirring early. That storm was really something."

Mrs. Olliver then sat down at the table and as she unfolded her napkin and placed it on her lap, in walked Frankie. With his hair combed and still damp, he went over to his mother and kissing her on the cheek said, "Morning, Dear."

Mrs. Olliver leaned back, wrinkled her nose and replied, "You smell terrible. What have you been up to?"

Suzanne glared over to him. "Yes Brother, what have you gotten into?"

Frankie blushed and sniffling his nose replied, "I was a little sick last night. Stomach problems, you know."

As the family had breakfast, Frankie had little to eat and less to say.

After they had finished, Mrs. Olliver took Amanda down to the back pasture to see a newborn colt, leaving Suzanne and Frankie alone in the kitchen.

Trying to get a little coffee down, Frankie glanced over at Suzanne and said, "I'm glad you didn't tell "er."

"I was more concerned over your daughter than mother."

"It won't happen no more," Frankie promised. "You have got to forgive me."

Feeling that he was sincere, she replied, "You know you drink too much."

With Suzanne's warming toward him, Frankie began to feel better. Suddenly remembering, he blurted out, "Yore man's coming home today."

"What do you mean?" Suzanne asked.

"John's coming in today."

"How do you know?"

"Saw Tim last night. He said the Wilsons got a telegram yesterday and said he would be on the four o'clock train at Newton. 'Bout time you two make amends."

Pursing her lips, Suzanne said, "You know that you're part of the problem. If it hadn't been for the way you cheated him out of the election, we'd be married right now."

Thinking back over the past months, Frankie didn't know when he had so much fun. Sitting in the State Legislature, he had finally received his due recognition. He was now Mister Frankie Olliver and immensely enjoyed the benefits of the job.

Before the rail line, running west to east, crossed the county, Newton was only a small village located in the southern part of Newton County. Its few stores with their limited array of goods catered to the local farmers, but with the arrival of the railroad, the town's growth exploded. Stores of every kind sprung up overnight and with the town's growth came a new bank and a large hotel that could accommodate almost a hundred people. Due to the railroad, locals could now acquire goods quickly that once took weeks. Because the population had increased, the need for entertainment came in the form of taverns and gambling rooms. With people flocking in droves from all parts of the county on Saturdays to purchase goods, meet the train and to simply socialize, Newton became the toast of the county. As one old gent exclaimed, "Sat'day in Newton looks like a giant ant hill after somebody's kicked the top off. People are scurrying everywhere."

It was such a day when Mister and Mrs. Wilson and Sister pulled their wagon to a stop in the oak grove behind the blacksmith shop on Main Street and only a few hundred feet from the train station. Lott, stepping down on the muddy spokes of his wagon, carefully eased to the ground and looking up at Sarah said, "You ain't been feeling too chipper lately. Don't see how this trip will do you any good."

"We'll see," Sarah replied, easing out of the wagon.

Sister followed and straightening her skirt, brushed at a mud smudge on the lower fringe.

"Well, y'all follow me," Lott said after he had secured the horses and wagon. "Got to hurry. If the trains on time, it'll be here in about fifteen minutes."

Avoiding the chaos of Main Street, Lot led them down a path that ran behind the row of buildings located on the eastern side of town, and in a matter of minutes, they reached the depot. There was barely standing room on the boardwalk that bordered the railroad. Concerned about Sarah's health, Lott looked up and down the walkway for an unoccupied bench and seeing one down the way, escorted Sarah and Sister to the seat.

Fifteen minutes passed and then another thirty before off to the east, there was the faint sound of a whistle. Stretching up, Sarah eased to the edge of the bench as Sister got up and with her father headed down the walkway through the crowd. With a billow of smoke rising over the trees in the distance and a shrill blast from the whistle, people, chattering incessantly, crowded the tracks. Slowing to almost a creep, the massive locomotive screeching its wheels eased into Newton Station. As it rolled a hissing wall of steam was released from underneath its engine like a giant tidal wave, and people began to scurry for safety. With a jerk and another screech of metal against metal, the train finally came to a stop.

Conductors waiting inside the doorways of the passenger cars then stepped down on the walkway and began asking those blocking the way to step back.

As people began to step down from the cars, family and friends waiting pushed forward to greet them. With handshakes, hugs and laughter the sidewalk became a mass of joyous reunions. To see over the crowd, Lott stepped up on one of the benches next to the depot. With many of the passengers already leaving the depot, Lot began to feel uneasy.

Becoming frustrated, Sister decided to join her father.

Minutes passed and now with only a few people milling about, Lott shook his head as he started to get down. "I guess something' must have happened," he said. "I'll see when the next train might be coming through."

Then suddenly, Sister pointed and shouted, "There he is!"

Lott wheeled around and there was John in the doorway of the last car waving to them. He indicated that he would be back shortly and then went back inside. Sarah struggled to her feet and began to hurry down the sidewalk.

As John's family hurried down to greet him, he reappeared and stepping down, waved. Reaching up, he took the hand of a young woman.

Lifting her skirt to come down the steps, she took John's arm and said, "So this is Newton Station."

Puzzled, Lott and Sister stopped for a moment as Sarah caught up with them.

"I bet you thought I wasn't gonna make it," John said. He then cleared his throat. "Mama, Papa, Sister, I want you to meet Mrs. John Wilson. Cretia, these here are my folks."

Lott scratched his head for a second, nodded, then smiling said. "Well, if'n that ain't a surprise."

With a wide grin, he reached out to his son's bride. "Down here in the South we hug our daughters and loved ones. Welcome to Dixie, darling."

Sister then gave her sister-in-law a warm embrace and whispered to her, "You got to tell me how this happened."

Stepping aside, Sister made room for her mother. The two women stood for a moment eyes locked and tears forming. "I knew you was coming home with 'em. Lord told me so."

They hugged each other and Cretia whispered, "I only hope I can be a good wife to him."

Sarah squeezed her gently. "You're God's answer to my prayer. Welcome to the Wilson family."

"There's a lot of luggage," John said. Y'all bring the wagon?"

Moments later, Lott pulled in with the wagon and soon all was loaded. Since James was meeting some military officials in a government office at the north end of town and would be riding home with them, Lott headed the wagon toward Main Street to pick him up.

Sister was sitting on the bench with her parents in front of Cretia and John. With a smile she turned and blurted out, "I can't wait no longer. You got to tell me how you two got hitched."

John laughed. "I knew you couldn't take it."

Pretending to be in deep thought, he scratched his head and said, "Well, you see it was like this, I was in this poker game and came up with a pretty good hand."

Shaking her head Lucretia said, "Don't believe a word he said. It wasn't anything like that at all."

"Sister, don't be so anxious," Mrs. Wilson said. "They'll tell us soon 'nough."

As the wagon creaked along the street, Lucretia was amazed at the crowd and the unusual mix of people. Lucretia noticed Union soldiers standing nonchalantly on the sidewalks high above the muddy quagmire of a street with rifles by their sides and rolled tobacco dangling in their mouths. Although stationed to keep order, they seemed unconcerned. Droves of citizens were busy buying goods and enjoying their visits with one another.

As they eased forward, Cretia also noticed many Negroes in the crowd. This wasn't new to her, because of her visits to the eastern cities, but here it was definitely different. In the eastern cities, the Negroes dressed formally in coats and ties, but here, alarmingly, most were barefoot and in rags.

"You don't have many of 'em where you live, do you?," replied John as he saw the concerned look on her face.

"No. I mean yes. Its just different."

Suddenly a loud, shrill voice called out, "Weelson!" and from nowhere, a dark bare-chested man with long black hair ran and leaped on the back of one of the horses pulling the wagon. Straddling the horse backwards, he faced them and began waving an empty whisky bottle in the air.

Startled, Cretia grabbed John as the man called out to them in words Cretia could not understand. Then sliding off the horse, he staggered down to where Cretia and John were sitting and grabbed the sideboards to steady himself.

Seeing the terrified look on his wife's face, John got up and gently pushed the man away. "Shoemake, my ole friend, the whiskeys got you."

Pointing to the sidewalk, John continued, "You need to get on out of the street 'fore somebody runs you over."

Laughing hysterically, the man staggered backward and fell to the ground uttering strange words.

To Cretia's surprise, John answered him in a language she had never heard, and as the man lay there in the mud babbling, John and Lott started laughing.

Cretia looked down at the man and then back to John and his family. Sarah and Sister were ignoring the man and were apparently not concerned.

"I don't see anything amusing about this. He could have hurt someone," Cretia said, confused over the reaction to the man's attack. "Who is he?"

John and Lott laughed even harder. Finally Lott said, "Shoemake said he thought you was a good lookin' woman and he'd trade what was left in the bottle for you, and as for who he is, he's a Choctaw."

"What is that?" Cretia asked, looking down at Shoemake again.

"He's Indian," John answered with a wide smile.

"He's a wild one, isn't he?" Cretia said, clinging closely to John.

Cracking the reigns across the backs of the horse to get them moving, Lott turned back to Cretia, "He may be a little wild right now, but I guess you could say he's kin to us."

"You mean I'm related to an Indian?" Cretia said with a gasp.

Sarah began to chuckle. "Don't listen to them men. Shoemake in a way is kin but not blood kin."

"Woaaaaaa!" Lott called out as he brought the wagon to a stop in front of a building that had been used as a land office before the war. There was a group of federal soldiers on the porch that bordered the street. The flag of the United States hung from a long pole in front.

Nudging Lucretia, John said, "This here is the military headquarters for the county. James is suppose to meet us here."

At that the front door opened and James emerged through the crowd of soldiers. They quickly moved out of the way, came to attention and saluted. James dressed in an officer's uniform with the markings of a captain returned the salute and with a wide smile turned to the wagon waiting out front. James walked with a slight limp across the porch and carefully grasped the handrail to steady himself. Reaching the wagon and looking up at the family, he exclaimed, "It's about time you folks got here. I'm ready to get home."

A wide smile crossed his face when he noticed the pretty woman sitting beside John.

John helped James up into the wagon and when he was settled he looked over at the newlyweds.

"James, I'd like for you to meet my wife," John said with a grin. "This is Lucretia Caulder Wilson."

James smiled and exclaimed, "You do know how to surprise folks and what a beautiful surprise."

He then reached out his hand to Lucretia. "You've got a good man here. Take good care of him."

Taking his hand, Lucretia replied, "I've heard a lot of good things about you. I'm looking forward to getting to know you all."

John then turned to James and muttered, "You hurt? You're getting 'round kinda slow."

"I'll tell you later," James replied. "It's a long story."

As the wagon rolled out of town, Lucretia and John told them about all that had happened. The Wilsons sat amazed, listening to every word.

As the wagon creaked and rattled down the rough and muddy road, Lucretia was fascinated by the countryside. She saw virgin forests with massive trees reaching to heaven that had never been touched by the axe. They crossed trickling brooks and streams where the water rose almost up to the wagonbed as the horses struggled to gain their footing. Out of nowhere a neat row of split rail fencing would appear holding rows upon rows of young corn and cotton laid out in perfect order. As they passed the fields and pastures, houses were snuggly tucked underneath large oak trees. There were still the typical log cabins which had been constructed when the land was open for settlement, but some were framed clapboard houses like those in Pennsylvania.

The thing that impressed Lucretia the most was that each time they passed a home where people were outside, they always waved and spoke to them. Even though Gettysburg was considered a rural community, it was nothing like this. To Lucretia, this country was like a step back in time. This was indeed a strange place. Then with a smile, she looked over at her husband and thought to herself, this is a beautiful and enchanting land. These are my people. This is now my home.

It was almost dusk when Lott dropped off Sister and James at their house and by the time they reached their place, it was dark. In the dim light of the evening Lucretia could tell that the house was large and she was astonished by the size of the logs that had been carefully hewn to precision.

After Sarah prepared a quick meal, the family, exhausted, retired for the evening.

Lying in John's arms, Lucretia felt the gentle touch of a spring breeze as it softly ruffled the curtains. She realized how very happy she was and fell asleep with thoughts of this enchanting land and the future it would bring her.

21

STRANGE GUEST

As THE STILLNESS OF THE EARLY SPRING MORNING DAWN evaporated into a constant chorus of birds singing and chickens clucking as they searched for food, Lucretia awakened. For a while, she lay warmly snuggled next to her husband, listening to all the pleasant sounds outside their window. Then she eased out of bed, grabbed a shawl to protect her from the morning chill and quietly opened the door.

To her surprise, she found two black and tan hounds curled up on the floor in the open hallway and afraid that they would not welcome a stranger, she eased back into the bedroom. But the hounds, dew soaked and exhausted from a night's run through the hills, never acknowledged her. Regaining her confidence, Lucretia tipped past the dogs and down the hall toward the porch.

As the sun began to ease up over the eastern horizon, Lucretia shielded the bright rays from her eyes with her hand and then moved to a shadowed section near the edge of the porch. The cranky chickens that had awakened her were scouting the yard for any insect or lost kernel of grain and when finding a prize, all the other birds noisily rushed in to share the meal. Laughing to herself at their behavior, she went slowly down the steps to the front yard, which was completely bare. She gazed across the countryside. A large shingle roofed barn made from massive hand hewed logs stood like a bastion on a hill surrounded by a corral of horses. Across from the barn lay acres upon acres of freshly plowed fields with rows stretching down to the woods in the far distance.

Hearing an owl off to her right, Lucretia turned and was surprised by massive trees and a forest of immaculate beauty. Spellbound, she walked toward the edge of the yard.

"It's something, ain't it?"

Startled, Lucretia turned to find Sarah standing beside her. With the sun illuminating her face and causing her grey hair to sparkle as she moved, she seemed almost angelic. Only the deepened lines across her face from hard years and toil made her seem real.

Lucretia smiled and replied, "I couldn't imagine such beauty."

Sarah placed her arm around Lucretia's waist and together they stared at the woodlands. Sarah said, "Them woods, six hundred and forty acres of 'em, is Jake's."

"Jake's?" Lucretia replied.

"Well, not Jake's no more. He got himself killed. Jake is Lott's brother. You might say the land will be Homer's. That was Jake's boy," Sarah explained.

"Where is Homer now?"

"Last I heard, he and his mama, was in the Territory."

"Territory? Where's that?" Lucretia asked.

"Oklahoma, Indian land," Sarah replied.

Sarah then squeezed her hand. "Let's get you on in the house 'fore the morning chill gets you. I left the coffee brewing. Want to help me with breakfast?"

Placing her arm around Sarah, she was beginning to feel at home in this beautiful land. "I'll be glad to help you, Mrs. Wilson."

"You don't have to call me Mrs. Wilson," Sarah said.

"What do you want me to call you?"

"If you don't mind, you can just call me Mama."

Walking back to the house, Lucretia felt fortunate to have become a part of such a loving family. Thinking back over what Sarah had just told her, it all became clear. Uncle Jake's wife was a Choctaw. That's what they meant by being kin to that Choctaw down at Newton.

Reaching the kitchen, Lucretia found John and Lott sitting at the table talking. John reached out and pulled her into his lap. "How's my beautiful wife this morning?"

Embarrassed, Lucretia quickly moved over and settled herself on the bench next to him. Reddened, she quickly glanced at Lott and Sarah.

"Darling, the man loves you. It don't bother us none," Sarah said with a smile.

After Sarah and Lucretia had cleared the table and washed the dishes, Sarah spent the morning showing Lucretia around the house and barnyard while Lott and John rode over the farm inspecting the fields and livestock. Around the middle of the morning, John rode up to the house on the tallest horse Lucretia had ever seen. Pulling to a stop, John called out, "Cretia, crawl on up. You and me is in for a ride."

Seeing how spirited the large red stallion was as it stomped its large hoofs, Lucretia was apprehensive.

Reaching his hand down to her, John smiled. "Get on up here with me. You'll be just fine."

Lucretia had ridden horses before, but nothing like this. The dark red stallion with its long legs and bulging muscles was the essence of intimidation.

Feeling her warm body next to his and sensing her fear, John held the horse to a cantor as they rode away. With the reigns in one hand, John reached back and placed his other arm around Lucretia's waist. Taking their time, the two rode past fields of corn and cotton where tender green shoots were pushing their way through the loosely plowed soil, and upon reaching a large pasture secured with an endless split rail fencing, they stopped to admire a herd of horses grazing.

"John, they're beautiful. They're all magnificent," Lucretia said.

"You should have seen 'em 'fore the war."

"What do you mean?"

"We had more of 'em and I think a better breed," John said. "I imagine there was many a Yankee officer rode off this place with a better mount than he come in by."

"There's more than thirty head down there! They all look like thoroughbreds to me," Lucretia said.

"These are just the mares and colts," John replied. "The stallions are kept separately until time to breed. We're raising horses that are a mixture of western quarter horse and Kentucky thoroughbreds. They've always been in high demand throughout Mississippi."

Then kicking the horse in the flank, John galloped down the trail past the fencing and toward the forest Lucretia had marveled at that morning. As they entered the woods, John said, "I'm going to carry you through over a thousand acres of woods that ain't ever been touched by human hands. It's just like the Indians left it. The trees you'll be seeing got to be hundreds of years old at best."

Even after all his years, John entered the forest with a sense of awe. Slowing the horse to a walk, John gave him his reign. For the next hour they wandered up and down the leaf matted hills, crossed streams, skirted thick mud filled cane breaks, always under the canopy of massive long leafed pines and hardwoods. On occasion, deer resting in nearby thickets would leap up and bound away flashing their white tails and snorting, alerting the other animals. Then while wading down a creek, several turkeys feeding on the tender grass on the upper bank flew directly over John and Lucretia, almost spooking the horse.

To Lucretia's amazement, there were hundreds of squirrels about. Most were scampering about digging for acorns that had been hidden during the fall.

Working their way through the forest, John directed the horse down paths once used by the Choctaws as they traveled through the swamp bottom.

Pushing the horse across the shallow Chunky River and up a steep riverbank matted with plush green ferns, Lucretia noticed a clearing up ahead and what appeared to be an old road. Clearing the woods, she noticed that the road was actually some kind of old oval race track. Back to her left was a dilapidated platform rotting and overgrown with vines.

"What is this place?" she asked.

John reined the horse to a stop and pointed to the clearing. "At one time this here was the best race track in the county. Uncle Jake and Dad built it. Folks from all over the state would come to see the horses run. Many a fortune was lost and won right here."

"What happened to it?" Lucretia said.

John pushed the horse forward and as they cleared the far bend of the track, he turned in the saddle for one last glimpse and replied, "I don't know. When Uncle Jake got killed, nothing was the same. You know, he's the one that really loved the racing, or maybe the war ended it. Cretia, I really don't know."

Taking a road that led away from the racetrack, they soon were out of the woods and were once again edging their way down the side of a newly planted field of corn. At the far end of the field, surrounded by oak trees,

Lucretia noticed a log cabin with a swirl of smoke rising from its chimney.

As they approached, an old gray haired Negro rose from where he had been sitting on his porch and recognizing John, waved.

Reining the horse to a stop just short of the front porch, John reached out his hand. "How's it going, Toby?"

The old gent struggled out of his chair and looking inquisitively at Lucretia, took John's hand and replied, "I guess I'se fitt'n Mas John."

He was a large man, well over two hundred pounds and even with age, looked strong. His lined face held several scars. Time had taken its toll.

"Lucretia, this here is Toby. Toby, this is my wife," John said, releasing Toby's hand.

Toby glared for a moment, then a smile widened across his face. "Lawd have mercy, Mas John. You has up and married you a pretty 'en."

Then turning toward the house as John and Lucretia dismounted, he called out, "Sadie, you best get on out here. I'se got somp'n to show you."

Wiping her flowered hands on her apron, a small Negro woman appeared in the doorway. A bit timid, she hesitated for a moment then eased out behind Toby.

Toby took her by the hand and pulling her from behind him, said, "Sadie, Mas John has up and married. That there is Mrs. Wilson."

Seeing how uneasy the woman appeared, Lucretia reached her hand out to her. Standing there with her hands at her side, Sadie first looked at Toby and then back to John.

"You can shake her hand, Sadie. It's all right," John said.

Sadie eased her hand forward and softly clasp Lucretia's but no sooner than they had touched, Sadie quickly jerked her hand back and dropped her head.

Lucretia gently reached out and placing her fingers under Sadie's chin raised her head until their eyes met and then tenderly said, "You can call me Cretia, if you'd like."

Sadie dropped her head again, then looking up until their eyes met, smiled.

John and Toby talked for a few moments and then John asked, "Where about is Andy?"

Toby pointed down to the fields. "He and d' boys down yonder are working. You shore needs to show 'em the misses."

Sadie suddenly turned and went inside, coming back out with a freshly baked slice of cornbread wrapped in a cloth for Lucretia. Lucretia smiled. "Thank you for your kind welcome."

Sadie drew her shoulders back and softly replied, "You mighty welcome, Mrs. Wilson."

John then took Lucretia down to meet Andy and the boys before they left for home. Later, stopping at a spring, they enjoyed the cornbread as the morning slipped away. Resting in John's arms, Lucretia looked up into her husband's face and said, "What did he mean by calling you Mas John?"

"He used to be a slave and slaves all call their owner, Mas, for master."

"Were you his master?"

John laughed. "Heavens no. He belonged to the Ollivers. My paw and me bought 'em and then set 'em free, but he still calls me that."

"I assume Andy and Sadie are husband and wife," Lucretia said.

John reached down and pushing some curls from her face replied, "The black folks don't get legally married like we do. They kinda come together. Actually, she was Caleb's woman. That is 'fore he got killed. Then Andy kinda took her in."

Lucretia thought for a moment then said, "This is really a strange country you brought me into."

"Are you glad you're here?"

"Are you glad you married me?"

John pulled her to him and kissing her, whispered, "I couldn't be happier."

John's marriage to Lucretia, a Northerner, spread like a wild fire pushed by a March wind. Knowing that John had been engaged to Suzanne Olliver, the local gossips couldn't wait to see how the Olliver family would respond.

In the days that followed Lucretia's arrival, the Wilsons had more visitors than they could ever remember. Many came to welcome the new bride to the community while others simply came to see the woman that took Suzanne Olliver's would-be husband.

Suzanne had taken the news as might be expected. She had gone and locked the door. Hearing her crying, Judith tried to coax her into unlocking the door, but after hours with no results, Judith sent for Frankie.

Storming up the stairway, Frankie red faced and with drops of sweat dripping from his forhead and reeking with the smell of liquor, approached his mother. "I've been away for the past two weeks and I got things to do. This better be good."

Grabbing him by the arm, Judith pointed to the door. "Suzanne won't come out."

Frankie took a deep breath, glared up to the ceiling and with a look of disgust exclaimed, "I rode most near two miles over here thinking something's wrong and you tell me Suzanne won't open the door. WHat's wrong with you folks?"

Pushing his mother out of the way, he brought his foot up and with a hard kick splintered the door sending what was left of it banging against the inner wall as it swung open. For a moment he glared in at Suzanne curled up on her bed and then turning to his mother said, "You can see her now."

As Frankie staggered down the stairs, Judith called out, "Don't you want to know what's troubling your sister!"

"Don't give a damn! She always got problems of some kind!" he shouted.

Having a change of heart, Frankie went back to Suzanne's bedroom to find Judith wiping the tears from Suzanne's face.

"What's wrong with 'er anyhows?" he asked.

"John got married," she said, not looking at her son.

Stunned at first, Frankie blurted out, "Well, it's prob'ly for the best. You deserve better than him."

Then he started to laugh. "I guess you ain't woman enough for 'em, are you, darling."

"That's a terrible thing to say to your sister," Judith stammered.

Through her sobs, Suzanne muttered, "You hate him."

"Why should I hate him?" Frankie replied. "He's got nothing I want."

Even though it was early summer, a steady rain fell on the hill country sending all the farmers to the shelter of their homes. Using all the available time, John and Lott worked repairing the barn and farming equipment until there was nothing left to do except wait for a change in weather.

They were on the front porch sitting and watching the rain make deeper puddles when Sarah and Lucretia joined them.

"Papa, you ever see anything like this before?" John asked.

Lott took a draw from his pipe and blowing a ring of smoke into the air replied, "Saw it back in thirty-eight. Rained for might near ten days."

Reaching up and pushing a loose lock of John's hair out of his face, Lucretia asked, "Will it hurt the crops?"

Sarah smiled over to her. "No child. We'll do just fine. Come August, this land could be as dry as an old gourd."

Seeing the forlorn look form on Lucretia's face, Sarah said, "Ole Saul, that's what I call the sun, will come out one of these here days and chase this ole rain away."

John reached over and placed his arm around Lucretia and snuggled her to him. "Rainy days can be a little depressing. Just wait 'till the sun comes out. It sure changes things."

Getting up from her chair, Sarah chuckled, "Another thing that helps is to stay busy. Cretia, if you will, let's go make us up a batch of chick'n and dumplings for supper."

The steady rain dripping from the roof and an occasional rumble of thunder gave Lucretia one of the best night's sleep she could remember. With the coolness that accompanied the showers, Lucretia and John cuddled under the covers as the hours slipped away.

Always an early riser, Lucretia awoke as the dim morning light filtered into their bedroom. Only a few sporatic drops of rain dripping from the edge of the roof broke the silence of the morning. Thinking back, Lucretia recalled that several times during the night, she had been aroused by what sounded like hounds moving about in the hallway. Why not, she thought, with all the rain, they were probably seeking refuge from the weather.

Knowing that Sarah usually was up by daylight and might need help with breakfast, Lucretia eased out of bed, wrapped a shawl about her shoulders and opening the door, entered the open hallway.

I'm not afraid of those hounds anymore, she thought. If they bother me, I'll just give them a little kick. Just like John told me to do.

But it wasn't the hounds in the hallway this morning. Terrified, she rushed back into the bedroom slamming the door behind her.

Startled, John woke up. "What in tarnations is wrong with you Cretia?"

Shaking with fear, she replied, "There are Indians out there."

John thought for a moment and then began to laugh.

"They're there," she whispered pointing to the hall. "A lot of them."

The door swung open and Lott with a lighted lantern waddled in. "You all right, Cretia?" he asked.

"She's fine Paw," John answered, holding his hand up to shield his eyes from the light.

"That's good," Lott replied. "Cretia gave'em a scare."

"What are they doing in the hall?" Lucretia asked.

"Well it's like this," Lott drawled. "They don't really have no place to live. They move about settling for what work they can find. Work for us sometimes, but they know when they need a place to stay, they can always stay with us. Sometimes they sleep up in the loft of the barn and like last night, they found the hallway to their liking."

Dressing as quickly as possible, John and Lucretia went across to the kitchen and found the room filled with Choctaws. Some were sitting on the long benches beside the table and others were settled on the floor. To her best count, Lucretia found that the group consisted of three men, four women and five children. Glancing over, Lucretia saw Sarah preparing their breakfast. The smell of freshly brewed coffee and ham in the frying pan filled the room.

Sarah smiled at Lucretia and said, "If'n you will, get the flour bowl off the shelf and fill it 'bout half full. We got a lot of biscuits to make."

Before long breakfast was on the table and after Lott had offered a blessing, he invited the Choctaws to eat.

Looking at the men, Lucretia noticed that they were much alike. None were as tall as Lott and John and most appeared fairly thin. Their hair was long and braided down their backs. In contrast, the women were somewhat plump and wore dresses made of calico cotton that flowed from beneath their breast to the ground. The upper part of the dress that covered them up to the neck was so tight they almost appeared to have flat chests.

Glancing over at the children, Ludretia thought how handsome they were. Their shiny black hair worn shorter than the adults and their full, bronzed, pleasant faces hinting at a smile caught her attention.

There was very little conversation during breakfast, but they soon began to talk with Lott and John in a language Lucretia had never heard. Suddenly Lucretia felt a stroke on her hair and turning found one of the girls touching her curls. The child then ran back to one of the women and whispered to her. All the Choctaws began to laugh.

Embarrassed, Lucretia blushed and looking over to John whispered, "Did I do something wrong?"

John began to chuckle. "Cretia, the little girl has never seen hair such as yours. She thinks you're an angel or maybe the Virgin Mary."

"You mean they're religious?" Lucretia said.

The older man sitting next to Lott raised his hand to the ceiling. "We believe in Catholic."

The longer the Choctaws stayed, the more friendly they became. Later, with the rain ending, they collected their bedrolls and other belongings as they prepared to leave.

The men walked first followed by the women. The children ran about playing but always stayed near their parents.

As they reached the outer edge of the yard, suddenly one of the boys turned back and running to Lucretia held out his hand to her. "Mary, you take," he said.

In her hand was a beautifully beaded necklace.

Sarah placed her arm around Lucretia's waist and said, "I think they took a likin' to you."

"They always leave something when they leave," Lott said. "They think you're special."

Lucretia looked up at John and then to Lott. "Where are they going?"

"Who knows," Lott sighed.

John explained, "All this country was theirs 'fore Papa and Uncle Jake came in here, but I'm not sure any of 'em own an acre of it now."

22

THE MYSTERY WOMAN

With the coming of summer and need for more laborers in the fields, John went out into the county and returned with several Choctaw families who had worked for them before.

To Lucretia's disappointment, none of the group that had visited them were to be seen. As she looked at the beaded necklace, she wondered what had become of the Indian boy who had given it to her. It seemed there was little concern over the welfare of either the Choctaw or the Negro. As far as she could tell, there was no indication that a Choctaw owned property, and to the best of her knowledge, only a small percentage of Negroes had a place of their own.

Of all the people she had met in Little Rock, Lucretia found Professor Hendon to be the most interesting. She found him to be articulate, well educated and obviously partial to the Wilsons. She couldn't help but be impressed with the man but quickly became aware of how eccentric he was. Still, Lucretia couldn't count all the times John had expressed his fondness for the professor.

It was through her conversations with Hendon that she learned that a few of the Choctaws were being schooled by Catholic missionaries. But to his knowledge, the Negroes were practically all illiterate.

"In fact, under the laws of slavery," Hendon stated, "Negroes were not allowed to learn to read or write. Being laborers, it was not practical for their well being and would simply be a waste of time."

"Have you ever considered teaching them now that they are free?" Lucretia asked.

Hendon laughed and said, "They would string me up."

Sunday beamed bright and sultry as late July finally arrived. Lucretia, standing before the full mirror John recently purchased for her down at Walker's store, and holding two dresses, turned to John and said, "Should I wear the beige or blue?"

Sitting on the edge of the bed pulling on his boots, John glanced over and replied, "I like you in blue. Just don't wear those hoop skirts. Women don't wear those here in the country. Too dressy."

Lucretia blew a kiss over to him. "You know, I must please my man."

"You definitely do that," John replied as he sat there admiring Lucretia. Aroused by her appearance, he got up and taking her in his arms, kissed her passionately.

You deserve someone a lot better than me, he thought as he held her closely.

Lott, John, and Lucretia enjoyed the morning as they sat on the porch waiting for Sarah to finish dressing.

Looking over at John, Lucretia said, "You know, I've met a lot of your friends and neighbors. Do I get to meet some of your boyhood friends this morning?"

John shook his head. "Don't imagine there'll be none of 'em there."

"I've heard your mama talk about Robert, Timothy and some Clearman boys. Will any of them be there?"

All was silent for a moment then John mumbled, "Robert and three of the Clearman boys got killed during the war and I doubt if'n Tim will be there."

Then chuckling to himself, he muttered, "He prob'ly needs to be though."

"What about Frank? Your mother said you used to be friends. He didn't get killed."

John took a deep breath and throwing a frown toward his father replied, "You're right about Frank. He was a long way from the shooting line. What all do you know 'bout him?"

Aware of John's change in mood, she hesitated then replied, "I'm sorry, I shouldn't have brought it up."

John got up and looking down the hall called out, "Mama, you 'bout ready."

Adjusting her bonnet, his mother slowly came down the hall toward the porch only to suddenly stagger. She reached for the wall to steady herself and moaned, "I feel one of them dizzy weak spells coming on."

John rushed to her and taking her in his arms helped her to one of the chairs on the porch. With perspiration forming on her brow, Sarah struggled to get her breath.

"You know, I best stay here today and rest."

Lott told John and Lucretia to go on without them, but to be sure to check on Sister and James if they were not at the service.

"Papa, is something wrong with James? He ain't gettin 'round too good. Horse throw 'em?"

Lott took his index finger and rubbing under his nose thought for a moment then replied, "You know nothing about it?"

"No sir," John replied.

"You don't need to say nothin' about it, but somebody shot 'em a while back," Lott said.

"My gracious, why?" Lucretia asked.

Lott shook his head. "Nobody knows. It was about dark and James was making his way from the depot down at Newton up to the Federal office up the street when somebody opened fire on 'em. Hit 'em in the leg."

"Why would somebody want to shoot him?" John asked.

Lott shook his head again. "From what I know, he's working on something for the gov'ment and can't tell us nothing about it. That's all I know. Now you two better get on if'n you gonna make it on time, and for heaven's sake don't say nothin' about no shooting."

On the way to the service, Lucretia said, "John, I worry about your mother. She's had several of those spells lately."

"She's just gett'n a little old," John replied, coaxing the horse over a rough spot in the muddy road.

"I fear it's more serious than that, Dear."

"Well, what do you think it might be?" John asked, whistling out to the horse.

"I think she has a heart problem," Lucretia replied.

John shook his head. "I hope not. I get dizzy myself sometimes. These days do get hot down here."

Lucretia enjoyed the church service that morning and recognized many of the people in attendance. After the preacher had given his closing prayer, several of the congregation came over to her and welcomed her to the church and community. For the first time, she began to feel that she was becoming a part of Little Rock. Because she was a Northerner, especially the way the locals felt about the outcome of the war and Yankee occupation, she wondered if she would ever be accepted.

In contrast, John seemed distracted and could hardly listen to the service. He was nervously working his fingers back and forth and looking over his shoulder as if expecting someone.

On the way home, John was about to turn down the lane that led to Sister's place when the sound of a galloping horse caught his attention.

John reined his horse to a stop. "He's running that animal mighty hard," John said, focused on the mystery rider.

Then over the rise in the road fifty yards away appeared first the head and shoulders of a man leaning low in the saddle with his hair whipping at his face. It was as if he was racing for his life. In a brief moment the entire horse and rider became visible. The muscles of the large bay carrying the rider bulged with every step and it threw dirt in all directions when its hooves dug into the damp dirt that lined the roadway.

John turned around on the bench and as the rider sped by yelled, "Ride 'em hard, Man!"

"Who is it?" Lucretia asked, glaring out at the rider.

Struggling to slow the animal, the rider finally got his horse under control and cantered back to John and Lucretia.

"You running that animal mighty fast, ain't ya?" John said, smiling.

The man straightened himself in the saddle as he trotted up and pushing his windswept hair back, replied, "Fact is, I was a looking for you. Your daddy said you was at the preaching."

"That I was," John said, reaching out his hand.

The rider reached out to clasp John's hand, but his full attention was on the beautiful but bewildered woman in the buggy.

Staring at Lucretia, he said, "This is her, ain't it?"

Lucretia dropped her head and blushed.

John swelling with pride turned to Lucretia. "Tim, this here is my wife, Lucretia."

Tim scratched his head and then reined his horse around to the side of the wagon where Lucretia was seated. "Darling, may I take a look at ya? Not every day that I get to meet John Wilson's wife."

Lucretia slowly raised her head and extending her hand. "It is my pleasure to meet you. I've have heard some stories about you."

Tim took her hand and carefully studied the woman for a moment. Her blushing cheeks had now disappeared and she smiled up at him.

There's something about this woman, Tim thought. She seems familiar but I can't tell where 'bouts.

Tim returned the smile and glanced over to John. "You shore got yoreself a looker, Big Boy. I heard you got married. Didn't believe a word of it. That's why I went to your house. Had to find out for shore."

Lucretia also felt she had seen this young man somewhere before but couldn't remember where.

John and Tim talked for a while and hearing the men talk and laugh gave Lucretia a warm feeling. She often wondered why John seldom spoke of his boyhood friends, but seeing the two enjoy each other's company made her forget her concern.

As they pulled away, Lucretia glanced back at Tim. To her surprise, he was still sitting there in his saddle watching them. She waved to him and he responded with a polite bow and called out, "I hope you believe everything you hear. Folks say I'm a rascal, but the ladies do love me."

John laughed. "That is one crazy man. You see why you can't help but like him."

As he rode away, Tim wondered if Suzanne had been in church that morning which would surely make for an interesting service. He could just see John sitting squirming in his seat not knowing what to expect from her. How would he introduce her to Lucretia? That would be a scene to behold.

Tim could not get his mind off the woman John had married. Over and over he recalled every feature of her face knowing that somewhere or somehow, he had seen her before. Thinking about her curly blond hair and pleasant smile, he suddenly gasped and murmured, "Golly, it can't be her!"

Turning up the lane to Sister's house, Lucretia caught the smell of fried chicken and freshly baked bread. As usual, the hounds resting under the front porch of the house burst out to greet them. The door screeched open and James hobbled out the front door.

With a cane in his hand he called out, "Get on back under the house before I beat you all to a frazzle!"

Hearing the tone of his voice, the dogs dropped their heads, tucked their tails and scurried back under the house.

"If I could train your sister to mind that well I'd be most proud," laughed James.

"I heard that remark," Sister replied, making her way through the door wiping loose flour from her hands. "'Bout time y'all got here for dinner. You are staying, ain't you?"

Sister was noted for being an excellent cook, but her kitchen was usually complete chaos. She had no specific place for any of her utensils; one drawer was just as good as another.

Lucretia offered to help Sister on getting the dinner on the table, but for the most part Lucretia just washed some of the cooking utensils and wiped the table before setting the plates and silverware.

While they were eating, Sister wasted no time inquiring as to who was at the church service and if anything unusual had occurred in the community since the last meeting. In other words, what was the local gossip?

Knowing how to irritate his sister, John vaguely answered that as far as he knew, it looked like the normal group. Then winking over to James he said, "One thing did happen that shocked all of us. When the preacher gave the invitation, Tim walked the aisle."

"Tim walked the aisle?" Sister said, her mouth open.

"Yeah, not only that. He's going into preaching," John continued, looking over to Sister to get her reaction.

"He'll come nearer walking on water. I don't believe a word of it," Sister said.

Then glancing over to Lucretia she said. "Any truth to it?"

Lucretia looked to John who was as straight faced as could be then over to James who was doing all he could not to laugh. Shaking her head, she smiled over to Sister and said, "Tim wasn't even there today. We did meet up with him on the road though."

"I knew you was lying to me, John. You ought to be ashamed and for you James, you shouldn't let him go on with that kind of mischief."

At that the men burst into laughter.

Later, when Sister calmed down, the conversation turned to education. Lucretia was surprised to hear that James had graduated from West Point at the top of his class and as soon as his military obligations were over, he would like to become a college professor.

Remembering her conversation with Hendon, Lucretia said, "I've heard what a good school you have here in Little Rock, but it saddens me to see how illiterate the others are."

"Who you talking about?" Sister asked.

"I'm talking about the Negroes and Choctaws," Lucretia replied.

"Negroes! Choctaws! What good will readin' and writin' do 'em?" Sister said, becoming uneasy.

John and James raised their eyebrows knowing that Lucretia had just entered a sensitive area that most Southerners did not like to discuss.

Sensing that she had offended Sister, Lucretia took a deep breath and continued, "The way I see it is, you've got plenty of land and resources to develop down here and educating these people to be self supporting citizens could do nothing but enhance the standard of living for the whole South. I see no need for any people to be vagrants and wanderers."

Sister rubbed her brow as she thought about what Lucretia said and finally, nodding her head in agreement, said, "You may have a point, but it won't work down here."

John said, "Cretia, I preached the same thing and it cost me a seat in the State Legislature."

Surprised, Lucretia said, "You never told me about that."

"There's probably a lot of things he ain't told you about," Sister said with a smile.

"Hush your mouth," laughed James. "They haven't been married that long you know."

Lucretia knew there was more truth in the statement than she had realized.

After dinner as James, John and Lucretia were walking up the hall to sit a spell on the porch while Sister was clearing the table, James settled himself in one of the chairs and looked over to Lucretia, "The government is trying to find folks to teach the Negroes. Not having much luck, though. Locals don't want to get involved."

Pleasantly surprised, Lucretia replied, "I can't believe that. There's got to be somebody out there that would do it."

John quickly replied, "I don't think you'll find anybody around here that'll do it."

"I'd teach them if someone would ask me," Lucretia said.

James, packing his pipe, glanced over to her and then to John. "There's a need for it and John, you've been preaching about it."

"I don't reckon so," John muttered. Then looking to Lucretia, continued, "I don't want nothing to happen to you."

"Somebody's got to do it, Darling. I don't think anybody would harm me for just teaching a few Negroes to read and write."

"Cretia," Sister said as she came out into the hall. "Come with me out back. I want to show you my new batch of kittens."

Feeling a cramp developing in his leg, James shifted in his chair and groaned as a pain shot through his thigh.

John reached out to help him. "You all right?"

With the pain subsiding, James took several light breaths and mumbled, "I'll be just fine in a few minutes."

"Papa said somebody shot you."

"Don't mention this to anybody. Not even Cretia."

"What do you mean?" John asked.

James turned to his brother-in-law and softly replied, "What I'm going to tell you, I'm not telling you. You understand?"

John nodded.

"Have you noticed how the Democrats are slipping back into power," James said, taking a deep draw from his pipe.

"They're winning the vote," John replied. "That is the Democratic procedure, ain't it?"

"Not so!" James replied. "You ever hear of the Pale Faces, the Sons of Midnight or Knights of the White Camellia?"

"No I haven't."

"Then how about the Ku Klux Klan, John? How about them?"

"What about the Klan?" John said.

"The so called Klan, a movement to restore white power to the South is a widely and well organized movement that from all accounts is sweeping the South like a storm and there are no limits to what they will do to gain control of the government. They burn homes, threaten voters, spread terror and won't hesitate to kill when necessary. That, my friend, is the Klan. Now, do you know about them?"

John dropped his head. "Just what we talked about before, during the election. I've heard of 'em but I ain't part of it."

"I know you're not," James said. "Neither is your father."

"How do you know that, James?"

James blew another circle of smoke into the air. "Because it's my job to know. I've been out and around asking questions. I guess I've asked too many questions. That's why somebody shot me."

"They could have killed you," John said.

"They could have killed me, but no, they just intended to scare me a bit. That shot was just telling me to back off," James said.

"Why the interest in the Klan around here? I ain't heard much about it in Little Rock," John said.

"From what I've learned, the Klan movement in Meridian controls all the East Central part of this state, and a lot of the leadership is coming right out of the southern region of the county. There's more activity here in Little Rock than you'd think," James said, rubbing his leg. "Could be even some of our neighbors."

John shook his head. "I can't believe that James. I would have heard of it."

"You've heard of them. Been to a couple of meetings a while back, right?"

"That was a long time ago," John replied. "I didn't want no part of 'em."

The two sat quietly for a few moments then John said quietly, "You talk like they're right around here. No sir, I don't believe that."

James reached over and patted John on the shoulder. "Beware my friend. I've got a hole in my leg that says differently."

Meanwhile, driving his horse as fast as possible, Tim reached the Olliver house and pulled the animal to a stop. Before he could dismount, the front door swung opened and Judith came out to greet him. Winded, Tim stammered, "Top of the day to ya, Mrs. Olliver. Could you tell me the where 'bouts of Frankie. Word is, he was headed home."

Still upset over the recent incident and not feeling like talking, Judith pointed down the road. "He's gone over to his house."

Noticing how flushed she was and not acting her normal self, Tim asked, "You all right, Mrs. Olliver?"

"You might want to go check on 'em. He's been drinking again," she said, ignoring his question.

Tim enjoyed a drink on occasion, but it seemed like Frankie was forever with a drink in his hand. Since Frankie's place was only a half of a mile down the road, Tim quickly reached his house and, trotting up the lane, spotted Frankie sitting alone on his front porch in a rocking chair and clasping a glass of liquor.

Frankie tried to get up but lost his balance and tumbled to the bricked floor. His glass fell, sending shattered glass and whiskey across the front steps.

"Damn!" he growled as he lay there with blood oozing from his right hand.   Rolling over to get on all fours, he slowly stood up and motioned to Tim as he struggled to get back in his chair.

"You hurt?" Tim asked, securing his mount to the hitching post. "Looks like you shore cut yoreself."

Making his way up the steps, he took out his handkerchief and wrapped Frankie's hand to stop the bleeding, "You gonna be fine. It ain't that deep."

Frankie looked down at the blood stained handkerchief on his hand then to the shattered glass on the front steps. With a thick tongue he stammered, "I guess you better go get us another bottle. You know where I keep it."

Tim pulled up a chair next to him. "I've got some news for ya. The drinking can wait."

Frankie slumped backwards and almost lost his seating. "Something's wrong with this here chair. Can't seem to stay in it. I think another drink might steady me a bit."

"You won't believe it but John has up and got married on us," Tim said, ignoring Frankie's request.

Frankie began to laugh. "I know all about it. Just came from Mama's house. Suzanne is shore tore up by it. You know what I told 'er? I said, if'n she'd gotten him to bed, he would have probably married her right off. You know what a noble cuss he is. He'd feel obligated to marry her. Now that's a hell of a note, ain't it. I don't feel sorry for her one bit; she's better off without him, but I really just don't care."

"That's not really true," Tim said. "You care more about yore family than you let on. But what you don't know is who John up and married."

"Tim, like I said, I don't give a tinker's damn who he married. I try to stay out of his life, and he better stay out of mine."

Tim then helped Frankie sit upright in his chair. "You remember when you took me to that meeting up in Philadelphia."

"Christmas time," Frankie stammered.

Tim cleared his throat. "You remember that woman at the restaurant that got our fancy?"

A smile crossed Frankie's face as he recalled the meeting, "Damn right I remember that little blond. I looked at her and she looked at me and I could tell she wanted me. You give me ten minutes alone with her, and I'd have her under the covers."

"Well, Mister Olliver, that woman you talking about is none other than Mrs. John Wilson. What do you think about that?"

"That's a lie and you're the biggest liar in Mississippi!" Frankie shouted. "Everybody 'round here knows they can't believe a word you say."

Then he began to laugh. "I give you credit, Tim Johnson, that's the best one you ever made up."

Angered, Tim replied, "You just go over there and see for yoreself. That is if'n you can get sober long enough. You know, I'm getting tired of taking care of of your sorry ass every time you go on a binge."

Frankie motioned for Tim to help him up. "You better watch yore mouth. I put you in a good business and I can shore take you out of it. You wasn't nothin' 'fore I set you up. Now get me to my bed."

Sitting on the side of his bed while Tim struggled to remove his boots, Frankie looked down at the man who had been his friend since childhood. Tim had come from a poor family that never seemed to care whether Tim lived or died. When Tim's father died, Tim nor his mother shed a tear. Times became hard for them, but they survived. As time passed no situation, no matter how difficult, bothered him. He was a survivor and, as undisciplined as he could be at times, Frankie knew that there was no question to his loyalty. Yes, Frankie knew Tim was telling the truth.

23

ANGEL OF MERCY

JOHN WAS UNUSUALLY QUIET ON THE WAY HOME. Approaching a stream, he reined the horse to a stop and without offering Lucretia an explanation, stepped down from the buggy. At the water's edge, he knelt down, and filling his cupped hands with water, he splashed his face. He then took out his handkerchief and drying himself, crawled up on a mossy rise overlooking the creek and sat down. Confused, Lucretia sat silently watching him throw twigs out into the stream for a few moments then eased down from the carriage and walked over to where he was sitting.

Settling herself behind him, she placed her arms around his waist. "Care to tell me about it?"

Placing his hands on hers, he muttered, "I'm sorry. I can't talk about it."

Lucretia nestled closer to him and holding him, watched the small twigs float lazily down the stream.

Later, as they were turning into the lane that led to their house, they saw a horse and buggy in front of the porch steps. "That's Doc Mc Lauren's rig! What's he doing here?" John said, recognizing the one seater.

John pulled the buggy to a stop and quickly helped Lucretia down.

As they reached the hallway, the door to his parent's room eased open and Doctor McLauren motioned them in. Adjusting his glasses, the tall elderly man took John's hand and said, "Your Mama's kinda ill. Y'all best come on in. She's resting for now."

Sarah was on her bed with a pillow under her head and only a slight rise from her chest could be seen as she quietly breathed. Lott in his chair next to the bed held one of her hands.

With a tired drawn expression, he looked up to John and then over to Lucretia. "I'm afraid," he murmured. "I ain't ever seen her like this."

His eyes began to water as he motioned them closer.

Lucretia walked to him and placing her hands on his broad shoulders, bent down and kissed his cheek. "She's going to be okay, Papa."

Lott took a deep breath, placed one of his hands on Lucretia's and looking up to her, smiled and said, "That's the first time you've called me that."

Doctor Mc Lauren then motioned to John to join him in the hall. He led him to the porch and making himself comfortable on the steps, reached inside his coat for his tobacco pouch and quietly said, "She's a very sick woman."

John sat down beside him, afraid of what he was going to say next.

"John, I've done a heap of doctoring in my years and it don't get no easier. I was here when you and your brothers and sister come into this world. I love your mama and daddy like they's kin."

The two sat quietly for a few moments. "I gave her something to make her rest," the doctor said. "When she wakes up, you best spend some time with her."

A lump formed in John's throat and he muttered, "I can't lose her, Doc. God can't take 'er from me."

After the doctor left John, Lucretia and Lott sat silently, hardly speaking, as they watched over Sarah. A cool evening breeze finally rippled the curtains giving them a break from the heat.

With dark approaching, Lucretia lit the lantern on the mantle and upon returning found Lott slumped over the edge of the bed, asleep. She whispered to John, "Why don't you and your father go on to bed. I'll stay up with her."

"Can't leave her just now," John replied recalling what Doc McLauren had said.

Lucretia leaned down and, pushing the hair out of his eyes, said, "You two go. If anything changes, I'll come get you."

The hours slowly passed. A night could not be quieter. Only the steady ticking of the clock on the mantle broke the silence. Lucretia sat silently watching each breath that Sarah took.

Lucretia finally drifted off to sleep and sometime in the early hours of the morning a warm sensation on her hand awakened her. She woke to find Sarah holding her hand. With a smile, she mumbled, "I'm glad you let the men sleep."

"You best not talk. You need your rest," Lucretia replied.

Sarah pulled herself up as Lucretia adjusted her pillow and continued, "I'll be fine. I've got some things to share with you."

Sarah reached over and feebly clasped her daughter-in-law's hand. "I don't think I'll be here much longer," she said.

"Don't talk like that. There's a lot of things we've still got to do together."

Pointing to the fireplace, Sarah faintly said, "You know, there's an angel over there by the hearth."

Lucretia glanced over but saw nothing.

"Now listen to me," Sarah said. "I knew you were coming. The Lord told me He was sending you to us."

She hesitated a moment then continued. "You know the Lord. I mean from time to time, His angels do visit with me."

A cold chill came over Lucretia as she listened to Sarah's words. She looked into Sarah's kind face. A warm feeling spread throughout her body as she realized that her mother-in-law was at peace and was making perfect sense.

Clasping her hand, Lucretia said, "John has told me that you sometimes have revelations."

"I've raised four young'ns and have cared for a husband I love deeply. I've had a good life, more than I deserve, but the Lord wants me to come on home. You know, when John left here troubled, I knew where he was going and I knew what he was gonna do. I saw the two of you up on that rain soaked battlefield holding one another, and I saw you pull at them reigns to stop that horse on the way to the depot when John was about to leave without you. I said to the angel, you bring them two on home and he done just that."

At that moment, a breeze rippled the curtains again, and Lucretia looked over at the hearth half expecting to see the angel.

"He's gone now," Sarah said, her eyes on Lucretia. "No need to be afraid. They're wonderful creatures."

Sarah then eased off to sleep and awoke feeling better. She even asked for her morning coffee.

Sister and James came over to spend the morning with her and stayed for lunch.

After they left, with chores to do and knowing that Sarah was in good hands, Lott and John headed out to get their tasks finished before dark.

Lucretia, needing some fresh air, took a book out to the front porch. Pulling her chair next to the window of Sarah's bedroom allowed her to keep a watchful eye out.

Around mid-afternoon, a movement caught Lucretia's eye and looking up she recognized Sadie and her two sons approaching. When they reached the porch, the boys shyly hid behind their mother's skirt, peeking a glimpse at the new Wilson woman.

"Heard the misses was sick," Sadie mumbled.

Getting out of her chair, Lucretia replied, "She had a pretty bad time of it last night. Won't you come up?"

Sadie stood expressionless for a moment then reaching in her apron which she always wore, pulled out a bulging cloth sack and handed it to Lucretia.

"Miss Wilson loves blackberries. The boys picked 'em for her this mawnin'."

With a warm smile, Lucretia replied, "That was sweet of you. Would you like to see Mrs. Wilson?"

Sadie dropped her head. She had never been a visitor in a white person's house and felt uncomfortable about the invitation.

Lucretia reached down and took her hand. It was dark and calloused from hard work.

"She would love to see you," Lucretia said.

Sadie slowly made her way up the steps and upon reaching the hallway turned to the boys who were following her, "You young 'uns stay on d'porch."

They scampered back to the steps and started to play with the hounds that had come out from under the house.

Lucretia took Sadie inside and leaving the two women alone to talk, returned to the porch. One of the boys was petting one of the hounds while the other had wandered over to where Lucretia had been sitting and was thumbing through the pages of Lucretia's book.

"What do you think of it?" Lucretia asked, coming up quickly behind the boy.

Surprised, he dropped the book, ran across the porch, jumped to the ground and ran around the corner of the house.

Lucretia reached down and picked up the book. "It's all right. Come on back," she said.

The boy still on the steps replied, "He's a little skittish. He'll come out directly."

"Well sir, what's your name?"

The boy looked up at Lucretia. "I'se Jacob and the scairt 'un over there is Joshua."

"How old are you boys?" she asked.

Jacob reached up and scratched his head, "I'se 'bout ten and the scairt' one is eight."

Lucretia smiled over to him and eased back unto her chair. "What do you think about this book?"

Jacob pushed the hound aside. "I don't know nothin' 'bout no books. I do know that I'se named after a Bible man. He might be in one of d'books."

Lucretia laughed. "Yes, he might be. I'd like to read you two a story. Now you come on and sit here beside me."

Lucretia opened the book and began to read. Speaking loudly so as to be heard by the other boy, she began. Before long, out of the corner of her eye, she saw Joshua creep from behind the side of the house and slowly sneak on the porch.

But as the story progressed, they edged their way closer to Lucretia until finally they were nudged against her. Listening intently, they took in each word and in time Joshua began to turn the pages for Lucretia when she nodded. When the story ended, the boys began to laugh and Jacob, the spokesman, said, "Did dat really happen?"

"No Jacob, it's just a story. Did you like it?" Lucretia asked.

Jacob smiled up at her and, showing all his white teeth with a wide smile, replied, "It shore was something."

Joshua, spellbound, could not take his eyes from the black figures on the pages. Pointing at an opened page, he said, "Do them black things say dat story?"

Lucretia cleared her throat and pointed down to the words. "Those black marks are letters and when you put them together, they become words and words become the story you just heard."

At that moment, Sadie came out to the porch. "Mrs. Wilson is one fine misses." Then looking over to her boys she said, "Let's get on to da house. Got to feed the men folks."

Grabbing one by each hand, she led the boys down the steps. As they were half way to the trail that led to their house, Jacob turned and called out, "Appreciate the story. Wish I could read dem words."

"Hush yore mouth child. Readin's for da white folks," Sadie said.

Looking back at Lucretia, Joshua muttered, "Is Miss Wilson an angel?"

Sadie replied, "Heavens no child! Why'd you say such a thing?"

"She has that sparkly hair and sweet face," Joshua said, skipping down the path.

"Then what about a good ha'nt? Reckon she's that?" Jacob added.

Reaching out and swatting Jacob on his seat, Sadie replied, "Hush your mouth boy. She ain't one of them things."

Later, remembering the glow on their faces as she read to them, Lucretia made a vow to herself that somehow and someway, those boys would learn to read.

With the sun setting, Lott and John trudged up to the house. Lott called out to Lucretia, "How's my Misses doing?"

"She seems to be getting stronger, Papa," Lucretia answered. "How's your crops doing?"

Brushing some of the dust off his pants legs, Lott replied, "Corn's laid by and we've got some bowls on the cotton. Things look good."

Tired, John sat down on the steps and began removing his socks and shoes. Looking over at Lucretia, he said, "I'll tell you one thing. You're one good looking woman, Lucretia Wilson. I been waiting all afternoon to see that smile of yours."

John got up and put his arms around her and kissed her.

She always has the sweetest kisses, he thought as they embraced.

"Did you tell your Mother about all the things that happened between us while in Gettysburg?" Lucretia asked, thinking about what Sarah had said.

"No, not really. Why?"

"What about the day out on the battlefield and the storm?"

"I didn't say anything about it. " John replied.

"Last night when I was sitting with your mother, she related that instance to me and other things as well."

"Oh," John said. "Mama's doing that again."

"What do you mean?"

"Grandpa was a preacher man and Mama has always been one Holy woman. Sometimes she says she hears things and even claims that angels visit with her. I've told you about her visions."

"It's most unusual, John. She told me everything that happened up there in that rainstorm."

"That is unusual, but this is not the first time she has known about the impossible. Cretia, she's on mighty good terms with the Lord."

After a pause, John continued, "Cretia, we ran across Sadie and the boys down the way. Y'all have a good visit?"

Lucretia glanced over to her book. "John, those children don't even know what a letter is. They know nothing about books."

John reached down to pet one of the hounds that had snuggled up to him and replied. "I told you the Negroes down here are illiterate."

Lucretia was quiet for a moment then reaching down to stroke the hound that was now licking her hand said, "I want you to help me set up a school house. I want to teach those children how to read and write."

"Cretia, it ain't ever been done here."

"What about that room you fixed up for Toby in the barn? It could be cleaned up. It already has an old table and some chairs in it. Wouldn't take much to have it ready."

John thought for a moment. Even though he felt uncomfortable about such an endeavor, he himself had advocated educating the Negro when he was running for office. And here by his side was a woman willing to commit herself to help them.

A feeling of pride moved within him. "I think we could do that. You could start with Andy and Sadie's boys and perhaps we could round up a few more here abouts."

"You really mean that?" Lucretia said.

"Why not, Cretia. I'd like to see how it'll turn out. That is if'n you can get them to come."

Kissing him on the cheek, Lucretia replied, "They'll come. You just wait and see."

Later, Lott fixed a pallet on the floor next to Sarah to give her the full comfort of the bed. When Lucretia went to say goodnight to Sarah she found Lott already sound asleep.

Sarah, still awake, motioned Lucretia to her side. "Sit a spell, child, beside me."

Lucretia eased over to the side of the bed. "You need anything before I retire?"

Sarah shook her head and said, "You take care of 'em, Cretia. That's why the Lord sent you down here. They gonna need you."

At that moment, a breeze brushed through the room causing the lantern to flicker. Sarah took a deep breath and whispered, "He is so merciful. Thank you, Lord." And looking directly at Lucretia continued, "My friend's returned."

Lucretia glanced over at the fireplace. Outside, the lonely cry of a whippoorwill broke the silence.

"You best go on to sleep darling. I'm gonna rest some now," Sarah murmured.

With the early light of dawn, her door screeched open and Lucretia heard a shaken voice say, "John, you best get up. Your mama's gone."

At the funeral, scores of neighbors and friends silently huddled together in support of the family. The Wilsons stood hand in hand comforting each other by the graveside.

Reverend Lucas, the local minister, dressed in a long black robe stood at the head of the grave, book in hand. For several moments, he stared down at his open Bible. Then he closed it and lifted his face upwards. After a moment, he smiled and said, "The Lord has made this world too beautiful. That's what Sarah so often said."

Looking to Lott, he continued. "She loved the early morning. This was her time with God. While you all were sleeping, she was up worshipping with her Lord and Savior."

Then looking over at the woods nearby, he smiled. "Music, have you ever heard such singing. Even the birds pay respect for this lovely woman. No more fitting time to lay this soul to rest than at the time she revered, the first break of morning. Like her life it is fresh, a new beginning, and a promise of good things to come. The good Lord blessed us with this saint of a woman and now has taken her home. Her goodness will live on within the souls she has touched."

Lott then reached down and clasping a hand full of red soil, slowly let the loose soil drop upon the casket. Each family followed him but when Lucretia bent down, the sound of a lone whippoorwill was heard off in the distance reminding her of the same cry she had heard during the night when Sarah was speaking with her. She slowly stood up and, looking skyward, said a short prayer.

When the service ended, throngs of people came by to pay their respect. One by one they filed by the family giving them words of comfort.

A woman dressed in black with a thin vale over her face lifted the covering and reaching out took John in her arms. Her black hair flowing down her shoulders sparkled in the morning sun and tears stained her cheeks. Holding him tightly for a moment their eyes met and John was breathless. For a bleak second, his mind raced to times past.

Before he could speak she whispered, "I'm so sorry." She then quickly lowered the vale and slipped out through the crowd.

As they were about to leave, a tall well dressed man pushed his way through the crowd and approaching John held out his hand. "There was a time when she was like another mother to me. We all are gonna miss her."

"I appreciate you coming, Frankie," John said. "Mama would have liked it."

Turning to Lucretia he said, "Frankie, this is my wife, Lucretia."

Frankie bowed slightly and staring at her, was taken in by her beauty. This was indeed the same woman he had met in Philadelphia, but she was even more beautiful than he remembered.

Lifting and kissing her hand, he said, "It is my pleasure, Mrs. Wilson. John has done well for himself."

An uncomfortable feeling came over Lucretia as she stood there holding his hand. Embarrassed, and feeling she had met him before, she blushed and replied, "Nice to meet you, Sir."

"You can call me Frank, if you like. You and John will have to visit with us sometime. I'd love to show you the plantation."

"We stay pretty busy," John replied. "Please give your mother our regard."

As the family was about to leave, Lott was still standing by the grave, head dropped. John walked out to him and placing his arm around his shoulder whispered, "Papa, you gonna be all right?"

"I just want to stay a spell," he spoke softly.

"You want me to stay with you?"

Lott clasped his son's hand. "Y'all go on to the house. I'll be there soon."

In their bed later that night Lucretia murmured, "She is a beautiful woman, John."

John was silent for a moment. "What do you know about her?"

"Everything and nothing," she replied. Snuggling closer to him she whispered, "It doesn't matter what happened between you two in the past, you're my husband and I love you dearly."

John kissed her passionately. Holding her in his arms, he then realized he had never loved anyone so much in his whole life.

Sleep would not come and Lucretia's mind raced back over everything that had happened that day. Sarah's illness and death seemed like a dream. She could envision herself awakening and finding Sarah busy preparing the morning meal or out on the porch reading her Bible. Then there was the hillside cemetery and the open grave with Lott standing there alone. The image of Suzanne and the tall man, Frank, suddenly flashed in her mind. She is so beautiful. I can see why John was attracted to her, she thought.

Finally drifting off to sleep, Lucretia vaguely remembered the look on Frank's face and again felt she had seen him somewhere before.

24

GOOD HOPE SCHOOL

In the days following Sarah's death, a sense of loneliness filled the Wilson home. Lucretia and John tried to console Lott as much as they could. Lucretia assumed the household duties but knew she was just a substitute for the woman who had held this family together, meeting their every need.

She buried herself in the chores and Lott and John did the same with the farm tasks. John's concern kept him close to his father. The two began each day at first light of morning, caring for the livestock and tending the fields and ended each day at dark.

It was during the dark hours of night that Lott struggled. Sitting alone reading his Bible, he would momentarily forget what had happened and expect Sarah to come bustling into the bedroom. Once, late at night, he felt a warmth next to him. At times when he could not sleep, he would get up and wander outside, walking about the place until exhausted.

On one such night, Lott went down to the barn and upon his return saw a woman dressed in a white nightgown walking toward him. "That you, Sarah?"

A soft voice answered, "It's just me, Papa."

Lott dropped his head for a moment and then warmly embrace his daughter-in-law.

Early morning found them sitting out on the front porch awaiting the break of day. It had been a long night, but Lott was enjoying the company of his daughter-in-law whose face glowed as they talked. He realized that even though he could never bring his Sarah back, life still had a lot to offer. With John and Lucretia's love, he knew all would one day be fine and that he would see better days.

Meridian Train Station.

Hissing, the locomotive screeched to a stop while scores of people hustled about on the walkway. Pushing people aside and staggering through the crowd, Frankie searched the passengers coming off the train. Frustrated, he yelled out, "Tim Johnson! Where in the hell are you?"

Disturbed by the noise, people cleared a path down the sidewalk to get out of his way.

"I know you're here," he called out.

A tall man who had been pushed by Frankie caught him by the arm and whirling him around said, "What's your problem, Young Man?"

"Take yore hands off me! You know who I am?" Frankie loudly replied.

Seeing Frankie's condition, the man shook his head and walking away said. "Don't really care. You just look like a common drunk to me."

Before Frankie could respond, he heard the familiar voice. "You looking for me!"

Tim took Frankie by the arm and escorted him up the street to the hotel where the Ollivers owned a suite. Once inside, Tim helped Frankie remove his boots and ordered some coffee. With much coaxing, Tim finally got Frankie to bed. Lying back on a fluffed pillow, Frankie muttered, "You shore ain't no liar, Boy."

Blowing across his steaming coffee, Tim glanced over at him. "That was nice of you. One good thing about yore drinking, it does clear your tongue."

Closing his eyes, Frankie chuckled, "Naw, you did tell the truth. That woman John married was the one we seen up there in Philadelphia."

He was silent for a moment then blurted out, "That's got to be the most beautiful woman I have ever seen. I can just taste her lips right now as I run my fingers through those curls."

"You best forget about her, Frankie."

Frankie sat up in bed and taking a sip from his cup, burned himself. Spitting the coffee out and ignoring the pain, he exclaimed, "That woman's still got an eye for me. I could tell the way she looked at me the other day. I can just see her with me now, naked and in my arms."

Tim looked over at him, "You up and married Becca. You got the woman he loved. Ain't that enough for you?"

"Hell no! I married her only when she thought he'd been killed. When he showed up, she took to 'em again. You know, that child living up at Mama's. She ain't mine. I know damned well he slept with 'er."

"You the one lying now, Frankie. Ain't no truth to any of it. It's all in your head. John told me he never touched her in that way."

"You know he lied to ya, Tim."

All was quiet for a moment, then Frankie muttered, "Think what you may, Tim Johnson, but I want that woman and I do get what I want."

Tim was silent. In a few hours, Frankie will be sober and probably not even remember any of the conversation, Tim reasoned.

As he drifted off to sleep, Frankie mumbled, "Funny thing about this whole situation is that I want John's wife and my sister wants John. Ain't that something? Looks like we could work something out."

Looking sadly at Frankie, Tim wondered what had happened to the man to cause such hatred. There was a time when the three of them were inseparable. Maybe wealth and the love of a woman had changed all that. There were brief times when Frankie would show glimpses of his youthful nature when he seemed to care for the feelings of others, but those times were becoming rare.

Wilson farm.

The cool brisk winds of fall swept across the hill country and soon frost would settle on the deep orange pumpkins resting in the field. The once green waving leaves of corn had turned to a parched brown and the cotton glistened white in the distance. Harvest season was at hand.

John once again sought the help of the Choctaws to bring in the crops. As they arrived, Lucretia searched for the ones she had met earlier hoping they would come. But they never did.

Holding to his word, John cleaned out the room in the barn, but since it turned out that he needed the room to store the extra corn that had been harvested, he found another location. There was an old laborer's house near the lower part of their farm that was larger than the room in the barn and it had a woodstove.

When Sadie realized that Lucretia was serious about teaching her children, she began to spread the word. Most seemed skeptical, never remembering much help coming from a white person

One day Lucretia was arranging the benches and tables John had built for her and was unaware of a rider approaching. A shadow in the doorway startled her, and looking up, she recognized Professor Hendon.

"Afternoon, Young Lady," he said, removing his hat. "May I come in?"

"You will have to excuse me. This place is horribly dirty," she replied.

Hendon took a sweeping glance around, shook his head and said, "Didn't believe you'd do it."

Lucretia wrinkled her brow as she studied the man in front of her. His reputation as an excellent educator was widely known in these parts, and surely since he was from the North, he would appreciate her efforts.

"Would you teach them," she asked.

Hendon reached up and stroking his face replied, "Children are children, makes no difference to me."

"Then are you saying you would teach them?"

Hendon eased down on one of the benches, took a deep breath and replied, "Not at this time. It's not the right thing to do. You know, this is still Mississippi."

"Then you think I shouldn't."

Hendon dropped his head and thought for a moment. "It's noble of you, but you won't find approval in this community. In fact, there are some white folks around here who don't even educate their own children and will certainly resent an education for the Negroes."

"I'll teach them too if they want to come," Lucretia said.

Hendon chuckled. "There won't be any whites joining you."

"I appreciate your encouragement. Why did you even come down here?" Lucretia said sharply.

A smile broke across Hendon's face as he stood up. "Wanted to see if you were serious about the teaching and wondered if you could use some of my old readers."

Going outside, he reached inside his saddlebags. "And some chalk. I'll bring you out a few old chalkboards tomorrow."

Standing on the porch with her hands on her hips, Lucretia shook her head. "You are an old fox, Mister Hendon. But why are you helping?"

Hendon replied, "I didn't say it was wrong to teach the Negroes, but that it just wasn't the right time. I admire your courage, Young Lady."

Saddling his horse, he peered down at her. "You and John are too much alike. You are living far beyond our times."

He glanced back as he left, "By the way, when do you plan to start this new adventure?"

Beaming at the sight of five well-worn readers and several pieces of chalk, she replied, "Hope to start next week."

Hendon shook his head. "Won't be any darkies here next week."

"And why not?"

Pointing south, he said, "What do you see down yonder?"

"All I see beyond those fields is a tree line in the distance."

"That's correct my dear, and what do you see in those fields?"

"Cotton?" Lucretia answered.

"Correct again, and in a few days those would-be students of yours will be down there from daybreak until dark picking it. Like I said earlier, this is Mississippi."

Lucretia frowned but knew what he said was true.

"No need to fret, Miss Lucretia. You'll just have to wait until the crops are in."

"And when will that be?" she asked.

Hendon thought for a moment and scratching his head replied, "Maybe, late October."

§§

As the days passed Frankie could not keep his mind off Lucretia. He had become obsessed.

The rumor of the school for Negroes repulsed Frankie and he felt sure John would not allow such a thing. But more talk surfaced about the school and driven by a desire to see her, he decided to make a visit. Excited by the thought of seeing Lucretia, he felt that an afternoon ride in the countryside would be just what he needed.

A bright November sun slowly rose over the horizon causing the heavy frost that had formed to glisten as the rays streaked across the grassed countryside. Smoke curled out of the chimney of the Wilson home. Fall had arrived.

John, dressing for the day, called out, "Lucretia, you seen my heavy socks?" Getting no reply, barefooted and boots in hand, John tipped across the open hallway and entered the kitchen.

"This floor is some kind of cold," he exclaimed.

Walking to Lucretia over by the woodstove, John placed his arms around her waist and cuddling her to him said, "Morning love."

Turning, Lucretia kissed him. "Morning to you."

"Did you ask me something a few minutes ago?" she asked.

Having poured himself a cup of coffee and now settled in a chair next to the stove, John held up a bare foot, "They kinda naked ain't they? Can't find any of my wool socks."

"I'm sorry, John," she said with a smile. "Some of my students don't have any socks to wear. In fact, most of them go barefooted, so I kind of borrowed some of yours for this first day of school," she explained. "I hope you don't mind."

"What about Papa? Does he have any?"

The door screeched open and a pair of woolen socks sailed through the air landing on the floor by John's feet.

"Been hiding mine," Lott laughed, pulling up his suspenders. "But you can use those."

Blushing, Lucretia said, "I'm really sorry about this. I'll go down to Walker's store this afternoon and buy some. I feel so sorry for some of my students."

The men laughed and assured her that as long as the rest of their clothing didn't go amiss, they could do without a few socks.

As the men were leaving the house, John called out to Lucretia, "We'll be going by the school. I'll start you a fire."

The old laborer's house with cracks in the sideboards and a leaky roof might have the appearance of a shack, but to Lucretia it was a dream come true. John had put up a bell out front that was rung at the beginning of the day. A sign above the door read "New Hope School."

When she arrived there this morning, Lucretia found a roaring fire in the stove and several children huddled around it.

Joshua hurried to greet his teacher. "Mawn'n Miss Wilson."

Quickly shutting the door, she whisked in. "Good morning to you all. Everyone happy today?"

"Yes ma'am," they all replied in unison.

As the morning went by more children arrived. By noon Lucretia was faced with the challenge of teaching seventeen youngsters. Their ages ranged from one who claimed to be five years old to a tall boy who appeared to be in his teens. Since most of the children were not dressed warmly, Lucretia let the older boys pull the benches near the stove. Since she was limited in slates and chalk, Lucretia decided to divide the class in groups to share.

Lucretia glanced out at the children huddled snuggly together. Some were barefooted and the shoes on the rest were well worn. Their clothing was made of homespun material and close to rags.

One by one, Lucretia had the children introduce themselves. Some of the names, she could recognize, but the southern Negro dialect made it difficult for her to understand them all.

After introductions, the children sat quietly watching as Lucretia handed out the slates. The older boy named Tad spoke up, "Miss Wilson, is you really gonna teach us to read? Folks says us Nigguhs ain't 'spose to."

Startled, Lucretia cleared her throat and answered, "If you children will come here every day, I'll teach you to read and write."

Then she continued, "What did you call yourself?"

Tad looked back at his classmates who staring at him then spoke to Lucretia, "You talking about Nigguh?"

"Yes," Lucretia replied.

"We used to be slaves but most white folks calls us Darkies or Nigguhs," Joshua said.

Lucretia looked the children in the eyes and said, "We won't have either of those words used around here. The proper word is Negroes and that is your first lesson."

A larger number than expected and a mixture of so many different ages made Lucretia a little nervous, but remembering that they all were illiterate and on the same level put her mind at ease.

Eagerly the children worked through the day and before they realized it, it was time to go home. Before leaving, the children had to repeat their full names and to Lucretia's surprise, most had the name Olliver. Realizing that these children must have been the property of Frank Olliver's family made slave ownership a reality to her.

Lucretia did not hear the buggy pull up in front of the school because the children bounded noisily from the room to tell their parents about their exciting new experience.

She hastily straightened the classroom for the next day and wrapping her shawl around her shoulders briskly walked out and closed the door.

"New Hope School. Not a bad name Miss Wilson."

"I thought it appropriate, Mister Olliver," she replied.

Frank, dressed in a charcoal gray suit with a heavy dark blue overcoat draped around his shoulders, resembled some of the federal officers she had seen during the war. He was clean-shaven and his long blond hair was combed neatly. He certainly did not look like the working men she had met here in Little Rock. Even for Sunday services, their dress was not this eloquent.

"What brings you out here, Mister Olliver?"

"Please call me Frank."

With the afternoon sun casting its rays across her face, Lucretia's eyes sparkled in the light making her more beautiful than ever.

Looking at her, Frank felt a tightness in his chest and catching a breath continued, "Wanted to see your school. You know, it's causing quite a stir in the community."

"I don't see why? I'll teach any child who wants to learn, black or white."

Frank shook his head. "You're wasting yore time, Ma'am. Nigguhs can't learn nothing. All they're good for is working the fields and then you have to stay after 'em. They have the tendency to be on the lazy side. And for any Whites, they won't come."

"As I've been told, this is Mississippi," Lucretia said sternly. "But I stand to differ with you on who can learn. From what I've seen today, there's nothing wrong with these children's minds."

Frankie stepped down from the buggy and walked up to the porch. "I surely didn't mean to upset you. I can be outspoken at times. Would you please pardon my lack of manners?"

Uneasy, Lucretia took a step backwards, reached down, and picked up the satchel that contained her books. "I think I need to be getting home."

Making his way up the steps, Frankie eased by Lucretia and pushing the door open, peered inside.

After a moment, he turned back to her. "You could use some better tables and benches."

Walking inside, he looked around and said, "Them walls could be chinked to keep in the warmth."

Lucretia stood watching him in the doorway.

Standing by the stove and shifting his eyes to Lucretia, he shook his head and said quietly, "I must admit, Young Lady, you sure got spunk to do something like this. Nobody else 'round here gives a damn about the Nigguhs. I do admire you for it and if'n you don't mind, I could give you a little support."

Surprised, Lucretia wondered what he meant.

Frankie walked toward her. Here we are together, all alone, he thought. His heart began to pound.

"I'll help you if you'll answer something for me?"

Beginning to feel uneasy in his presence, Lucretia said, "I think I need to be on my way."

"You do remember seeing me there in Philadelphia, don't you?" he asked as he moved closer. "You were attracted to me, weren't you?"

Terrified, Lucretia turned to leave but Frankie caught her around the waist and pulled her to him, "You wanted me then and you still do."

"I don't know what you're talking about," she said trying to get loose.

Freeing herself, she rushed out. Frankie grabbed for her arm, tearing the sleeve of her dress.

"I've got everything a woman could ask for. Come on back inside and let's talk about it."

Bounding down the steps, Lucretia's only thought was to get away. She ran as fast as she could across the schoolyard with Frankie right behind her.

Glancing back, Lucretia suddenly felt a strong set of arms grasp her. Then a deep raspy voice shouted, "Mistuh Olliver, you best get on away from her! If'n you bother this woman again, I'll kill ya with my bare hands."

Seeing Toby, Frankie jerked to a stop and gasping for breath, muttered, "Kill me! You ain't gonna kill nobody, Nigguh!"

Toby took a step toward Frankie and glaring at him said, "I was once yore slave and you sold me away from my family. Hadn't been for the Wilson's buying and freeing me, I don't know what would have happened to me."

Then looking down at Lucretia shaking in fear, he continued, "As the

Lawd is my witness, if'n you ever harm this child, I will kill you."

"I wasn't going to touch her anyways," Frankie said. "You didn't see nothin' happen here, you understand?"

"I understand and I hope for your sakes dat you understand me," Toby replied.

Quickly getting into the buggy, Frankie shouted back, "I'm gonna take care of you! You just wait and see!"

"You ain't man 'nough to do it," Toby shouted back. "You'll pay someone else to do your work for ya, just like always."

After Frankie had left, Toby turned to a sobbing Lucretia. "Gonna be all right, child. He won't hurt you. You'll see."

"Why did he try such a thing?" she cried looking up into the wrinkled face.

"He hates Mister John and I think he hates life itself."

Sniffling, Lucretia muttered, "Because of Rebecca?"

"Prob'ly so child, but to tell you the truth, he ain't ever been the man Mister John is and he knows he never will be. That's what I believes is driving him."

"How do I tell John about this?"

Toby shook his head. "You don't tell 'em a word, Missy."

"He's my husband. I have to."

"Miss Lucretia, I've known John all his life and I know him pretty good. The man's had some mighty hard times. He's tried to make amends with Mister Olliver but right now I'd say he's close to breakin'. If'n you tell 'em 'bout this, I'se afraid Mister John will kill 'em.

"He won't do that, Toby."

"He loves you woman. He'll kill 'em shore as I'm standing here."

Noticing her torn sleeve, he pointed down the road to his house. "We best go down to d'house and fix that dress. Sadie can make it good as new."

25

NOVEMBER FESTIVAL

A BRIGHT HARVEST MOON CAST ITS MILKY LIGHT INTO THE bedroom where Lucretia and John lay. Cuddled under a mountain of quilts, John held Lucretia close as the temperature hovered near the freezing mark. During the past several days John had noticed a certain quietness in Lucretia. He missed her sweet cheerfulness.

Caressing her gently, he whispered, "You feeling all right?"

"I'm fine," she said quietly.

"Thought we might take the train and go up and visit your parents for Christmas. You like that?" John asked, expecting a happy response.

"That's a long way," Lucretia mumbled.

John then thought about their short courtship and hasty marriage and taking a breath said, "You do love me, don't you?"

Nestling closer to him and giving him a kiss, she replied, "You know I've always loved you."

John knew he still had a lot to learn about Lucretia and women in general, but hearing her say she loved him was all he needed for now.

The next day a light rain was falling so John harnessed the horse to the buggy and went to the school to bring Lucretia home. He was surprised to find Toby sitting under the cover of the front porch wrapped in a heavy blanket. Pulling the rig to a stop, John leaned out. "You going to school these days?"

Toby laughed. "You knows me. I don't need no readin'. I kinda hangs round here to help the Misses and the chill'en and keeps a fire going and the place clean."

The fact was, since the incident with Frankie, Toby was now the first to arrive at school and the last to leave. He was determined no one would harm Lucretia.

At that moment the door burst open and children poured from the classroom. Friday brought more excitement than normal as they scampered home for the weekend. In a few moments, Lucretia, buttoning her heavy full-length woolen coat, appeared and seeing John said, "How's my husband today?" She smiled and closed the door.

John stepped down and helped her into the buggy. "Rain kept us inside today. Papa and me is beginning to get on each other's nerves. We need a good lookin' woman around to cheer us up."

"Hush, John! Toby might hear your foolishment."

Waving as they pulled off, Toby shouted with a chuckle, "Didn't hear a word, Miss Wilson!"

Making their way home John marveled at how Toby had taken such an interest in the school but knew that he wanted his grandchildren to learn to read and write, something that would have been impossible during the time of slavery.

John reined the horse to a stop at the house and helped Lucretia down saying, "If'n the weather clears tomorrow, I'm gonna carry you down to Little Rock for the festival."

"What's that?"

"Folk's all around are gonna get together for the day. Mister Estes is gonna be grinding cane and making 'lasses. Gonna be a hawg killing and a cooking. Then come evening, Mister Walker'll clear the front of his store and we'll have some string music and dancing. How's that sound to you?"

Lucretia reached up and hugged him around the neck. "I think it sounds wonderful! But what is 'lasses and I don't know about the hog killing?"

"Don't worry about it, darling. It's all Southern. I promise you, you'll have the time of your life," Lott said, coming out to meet them.

The morning dawned crisp and clear as Lucretia prepared breakfast and laughed to herself picturing men making molasses but cringed at the thought of a pig being killed.

She thought, I have traveled and seen the sights of England, France and Italy and have enjoyed operas in New York and Philadelphia and now in this strange Southland I am excited about a country festival and killing hogs. What a change.

Along muddied roads, John, Lucretia and Lott made their way to Little Rock. At first Lott wanted to stay at home but Lucretia coaxed him into going, promising the first dance of the evening would be his.

Lucretia was surprised at the number of wagons and buggies about the town and the scores of people that were scurrying about . . . Whites, Negroes and to her delight, Choctaws.

Waving and speaking to friends and neighbors, John pulled up to the side of Walker's store. Laughter and talking filled the air and from somewhere, the twang of a banjo could be heard.

On each side of the main street wagons displayed both produce and handcrafted articles. Beautifully stitched quilts, clothing and leatherware dazzled the eye and seemed as finely made as any Lucretia had seen in her travels.

At the front of Walker's store a group of Choctaw women were sitting on the floor of the porch with an array of beautiful cane and split white oak baskets of all sizes. Pulling John by the arm, Lucretia eased through the crowd.

"I want you to see this," she said.

She examined one basket then another, amazed at how they were crafted. Finally finding one that could be used to carry wet clothing to the clothesline, she turned to John. "I would like to have this one."

"Ask her how much it is?" he said with a slight smile.

Lucretia looked down at the two Choctaw women staring up at her and then back to John and whispered in his ear, "I don't speak their language."

The two Choctaws began to snicker and finally one of the women held up two fingers and said, "Two bits."

Realizing the women understood her, Lucretia blushed.

"I didn't know," she apologized.

Lucretia then purchased two more baskets and a handcrafted beaded necklace to send her mother for Christmas.

Looking at the mass of people, Lucretia nudged John, "You think Tim will be here?"

As they walked down to a place where a mule attached to a long sapling was walking in a circular motion around a cane grinder, John replied, "No telling about that boy."

"What about Frank?" she asked quietly.

Seeing Sam Estes, an old family friend, who was supervising the grinding, John replied, "He won't be here."

They moved past the grinder and walked over to a large kettle resting on stones about two feet above a hot oak fire. A thick sweet smelling liquid bubbled in the large cauldron. When Sam approached with a bucket in his hand, John called out, "Mind if'n we try a cup?"

Sam, a tall thin man who appeared to be in his sixties and completely toothless, put the bucket of cane juice down next to the kettle and reaching up on a post nearby took a cup, dipped it into the bucket and handed it to John.

"Best blue cane I ever growed. Sweet as honey," he said.

Lucretia took the cup and slowly brought it to her lips. To her surprise, it was quite tasty and before she realized, she finished the entire cup. John then took the cup and filled it for himself. When he had finished drinking, he dipped the cup into the steaming kettle and captured a small sample. Blowing across the hot syrup for a few moments, he handed it to Lucretia.

"Try this," he said.

Holding the cup up, she brought the thick syrup to her lips.

"Mmm," she exclaimed. "This is wonderful!"

"Best 'lasses in Newton County," Sam blurted out.

All that morning, John and Lucretia went from group to group socializing. Lucretia had met some of the people at church, but there were many new faces and no way to remember all the names.

As noon arrived, people who had brought lunches gathered at their wagons while others lined up at a tent down by the blacksmith shop where barbecued pork was being served. Taking Lucretia by the hand, they headed toward the tent. A delicious aroma filled the air.

Nudging ahead, John said, "You're in for the treat of your life."

As they were standing in line, someone called out, "Hey Johnboy! Hold me a spot!"

Stretching up to look over the heads of the people, John spotted Tim hobbling as fast as he could toward them. As he joined them, he asked permission to break in line from the people waiting. Winded, he took a deep breath and gasped, "Bet you didn't expect me did you? Just got off the train 'bout daybreak and got here as fast as I could."

"There's quiet a few pretty young ladies here today. I'm not surprised at all," Lucretia replied with a smile, giving him a hug.

Before he could answer Sister strolled up and giving Tim an evil look, drawled, "He don't want no ladies. Wouldn't know what to do with 'em."

Frowning over to John, Tim answered, "That's got to be your sister's blabbering mouth or a bellowing old billy goat and to tell you the truth, there ain't much difference between the two."

Lucretia frowned at the remark, but seeing the shock on Sister's face when she realized everyone had heard the remark, Lucretia had to bite her lip to keep from laughing.

Not so for John and Tim as they laughed so hard tears rolled down their cheeks.

Speechless and embarrassed, Sister stood with her hands on her hips for a moment then turned up her nose and stormed away muttering, "Who cares what Tim Johnson says. He always does manage to show his lack of manners."

"Come on back, Sister! I didn't mean nothin' by it. Just got to tease you."

Turning to Lucretia, he continued, "She's right. My manners is sometimes a little lacking. You'll just have to forgive me."

"Your apology is accepted, but maybe you need to apologize to Sister," she replied, trying not to laugh.

"Now that that is over, let's eat," John said, handing Lucretia a plate.

"What about Sister?" Lucretia asked.

"She'll be fine. She ain't as mad as she looks. This is normal banter for the two," John said.

The barbecued pork, hot freshly baked bread and stew were more delicious than Lucretia expected.

During the afternoon with Tim tagging along, they walked from wagon to wagon examining the goods and crafts on display. More introductions were made, and as usual, everyone made Lucretia feel welcomed. Meanwhile, some of the older men, wanting to get away from the crowd, had pulled benches out to the front porch of Walker's and were enjoying a smoke as they recalled tales from the past.

Lott, sitting on one of the few chairs on the porch and leaning with his back resting against the wall of the building, caught Lucretia looking across at him. He took the pipe from his lips, raised it above his head and smiling, nodded to her. From his expression, Lucretia knew he was enjoying the outing.

Noticing several young women near the creek bridge waving to him, Tim excused himself and strolled down to distribute his charm and hoped for a hearty return.

As the afternoon slipped away there was the occasional smell of whiskey in the air. Men could be seen slipping behind the buildings and wagons for an occasional sip, and the longer they stayed, the more boisterous they became.

Concerned, Lucretia nudged John. "There's a lot of drinking going on."

"Some of 'em will get drunk, and I expect we'll have a few fights before the night is over, but this is about normal I'd say," John said.

"You know Cretia, there's two things Southern men like."

"What's that John?" Lucretia asked.

"A good drink of liquor and a fine woman."

Giving John a playful nudge, Lucretia raised her eyebrows and replied, "Then I guess all you need is the drink. At least that better be all."

Around four in the afternoon, John and some other men were called to help Mister Walker set up the front of his store for the dance that would begin at sundown. While John and the other men began moving tables, Lucretia walked over to Mister Walker. "Mister Walker, I'm Lucretia Wilson, John's wife. Can I help?"

Looking around with a smile, he pointed to some bundles of fabric that had fallen off one of the tables. "You can help with that, if'n you will."

Lucretia quickly walked over and began picking up the rolls of cloth and neatly placing them on one of the tables in the back of the room. Mister Walker, unable to take his eyes off her, called out, "Thank you Mrs. Wilson. It's a pleasure to meet you."

Lucretia turned and smiled back to him. "Just call me Cretia."

Suddenly, a loud commotion out front caught their attention.

As John headed for the door, Tim burst in and shouted, "John, you better get out here and fast!"

Shoving his way through the excited crowd, John found Lott standing at the bottom of the steps. Before he could speak, John heard the thunder of hooves coming from the end of the street. As he stepped out in the muddied road, a horse and rider came toward them. The rider was screaming as he charged through town sending people scurrying to safety. The horse almost knocked John down as it raced by, covering him with mud and water.

Lott grabbed John by the arm and pulled him back, shouting, "The fool's got Amanda on that horse!"

As the rider reached the Little Rock Creek Bridge he reined the tall brown stallion to a halt and slung an empty whiskey bottle at a group of Negroes who were working the cane grinding. He then pulled back on the reins and turned the horse around. With a quick lash of a whip, he came back at a gallop.

Rushing to her husband, Lucretia grabbed John by the arm. "What's happening?"

Focused on the horse and rider, John didn't hear her. As the horse stampeded by, fear ripped through John as he saw the terror on the child's face.

Recognizing John, the child screamed out, "Please help me Mister John!"

Mister Walker, recognizing his granddaughter, burst through the crowd and running up to John stammered, "Somebody's got to stop the drunken fool! He'll kill her!"

John turned to his father. "I'm gonna try to stop the horse. If I do, you get the child," he said.

John ripped off his coat and stepped out into the street.

Reaching the end of town, Frankie turned the horse and swaying in the saddle, hit him on the flank. The animal bolted forward.

As the large stallion approached, John tried to remain calm. With muscles bulging and bloody foam spurting from its bit torn mouth, the monster of a horse was headed directly toward him.

When it was only a few yards away, John waved his jacket over his head and shouted as loudly as he could. Startled, the horse slid to a stop and reared up, almost striking John with one of its huge hooves. As soon as the animal's hooves hit the ground, Lott ran over and snatched the child off its back.

Holding tightly to the horse's neck, Frankie who was almost thrown to the ground, regained his balance and seeing John below took his whip and lashed out at him, striking him across the face. He then kicked the horse in the flank and galloping away shouted, "I'll come back for you!"

John wiped the blood trickling from his forehead and started back to where Lott and Lucretia were standing. He then stopped, turned and walked back out into the street.

"Stay out of his way," Lucretia pleaded.

"He's gonna kill you John. Get out of the street," Lott begged taking hold of Lucretia.

Once again, the horse raced toward him with Frankie brutally thrashing him on. Anger overcame fear as John stood there in the mud, waiting.

Once again, as the horse approached, John waved his jacket in the air, slowing the animal. He quickly jumped to the side and with a leap grabbed the stallion by the head. Digging his heels in the mud and twisting as hard as possible, he brought the horse to a stop sending Frankie tumbling to the street. The massive animal with John clinging to its neck rolled over on its side, pinning John under it. A sharp pain shot through John's right arm. Lying in the mud as the horse struggled to its feet, John lay motionless on his back.

For a moment, he heard nothing but the panting of the exhausted horse, then slowly the sound of cheers could be heard as people rushed out to him. Lucretia, the first to reach him, kneeled down and hugging him placed her arm under his head.

With mud and blood on his face and his right arm dangling by his side, John struggled to his feet.

With Lucretia's help he tried to take a step.

"Y'all better help me. I ain't doing too good," he said to Lott and Tim.

"Somebody gonna help me," came a cry from the muddy street as Frankie took hold of one of the stirrups on his wandering horse and tried to pull himself up.

No one came to his aid, but the crowd watched as Frankie straightened himself and stood up.

"Tim, you gonna help me?" he growled.

The crowd just mumbled to themselves and shook their heads. Then someone called out, "We don't help drunken fools!"

Stumbling about in the mud, Frankie shouted, "Who do you think you're talking to? I'm your representative."

Knowing it was over, John motioned to Tim. "You best go check on him. Get him on his horse and take him home."

"What'd you say, John?" blurted out Frankie walking over to John.

"I told Tim to check on you," he replied.

"You told Tim to check on me. You don't need to tell Tim to check on me. I own the boy," he replied, speaking loud enough for all to hear.

With eyes focused on him, Tim dropped his head. Lucretia placed her arm around Tim and hugged him saying softly, "No one owns you. He's just drunk."

Frankie began to laugh insanely and shouted, "I do love my whiskey, don't I, Mrs. Wilson! Too bad you don't allow drinking at yore Nigguh school."

At that John's anger mounted and with fist drawn he walked toward Frankie.

Lott grabbing his son's arm muttered, "Don't do it, Son. He ain't worth it."

John turned back to his family as Frankie, seeing Amanda on the porch crying, walked over and reached out to her. "You come on with me darling. Yore daddy's gonna take care of you."

Suddenly, stepping in front of him, John pushed Frankie backwards.

"You ain't taking her nowhere in your condition. You gonna get on that horse and get out of here 'fore I decide to kill you," John said.

Startled, Frankie stepped back and smiling out at the crowd and then back to Lucretia shouted, "You know why the interest in that so called child up there?"

"Shut your mouth, Frankie. That's enough," John said.

Frankie pointed to Amanda. "Cause that child up there ain't mine. It's his! That's John Wilson's baby up there!"

"Shut your mouth, Frankie Olliver! That's a lie and you know it!" Mister Walker shouted.

Laughing, Frankie staggered over to his horse and after mounting, glared down at John and pointing to Amanda said, "You take the bastard. You can have her. I give her to you."

Unable to restrain himself, John rushed toward Frankie and pulled him from the saddle to the ground. As he tried to stand, John struck him across the face, sending him spinning. Before he could hit him again, several men grabbed John and pulled him away.

Bleeding from his mouth, Frankie pulled himself up. Wobbling toward John with fist clinched, he sputtered, "You don't scare me a damn bit."

Then looking over at Lucretia, he said, "Hadn't been for that Nigguh the other day, me and yore misses would have had us a party."

Breaking free, John rushed at Frankie again this time grabbing him by his jacket. "What'd you say about my wife?"

"I didn't stutter," he replied.

Turning to Lucretia, John asked, "Did he hurt you?"

Lucretia shook her head. "He didn't hurt me. Let's go home John."

Turning to Frankie, John pushed him backwards. "I've had all I can stand of you. If'n you ever bother me or any of my family, I promise you, I'll kill you."

Frankie glared at John for a moment, then said, "That ain't no problem. You meet me at the old race track come morning and we'll see what ole Frankie can do."

Filled with anger, John replied, "I'll be there."

Frankie then motioned to Tim. "You be my second."

Wiping blood from his mouth, he then pointed to Lott. "You can bring him if you want."

Lott stepped up beside John. "This ain't gonna happen. It's fool talking."

"My Daddy's pistols all right with you, John?"

"They'll do," John replied. "I'll be there come sunrise."

A murmur was heard filtering through the crowd as the impending fight stunned those present. Dueling was illegal in Mississippi and anyone involved would be prosecuted.

Lott raised his hand and shouted, "Ain't noth'n to it! Just two hot heads talking!"

With Lucretia clinging to his side, John walked to the porch where Mister Walker was standing. As he approached, Amanda held out her arms to him.

Reaching for her, John said, "Wish I could take her home. She needs a father who cares for her."

John took Amanda and held her in his arms and whispered to her, "You gonna be just fine little lady. Nothin's gonna happen to you."

"I'll take the child, if you please," came a voice from behind them.

Taking Amanda from John, Suzanne continued, "I'm sorry this happened. I didn't know Frankie was drinking, and I certainly didn't know he had Amanda with him. The maid was supposed to be keeping her today."

Seeing John bloodied, and without thinking, Suzanne reached up and gently ran her hand across the side of his battered face. "I'm sorry."

She blushed and glanced over to Lucretia.

"Forgive me," she muttered.

26

AWAITING DAWN

Washington D.C.

Tired from hours of waiting, James strolled over to the window and gazed aimlessly to the grounds below. A cold steady rain beat against the window. Looking out at the storm, the Washington Monument caught his attention. It rose from the ground like a giant spear about to be launched into the sky. James marveled at the massive giant. Enchanted by its appearance, he remembered the Bible story about the tower of Babel and wondered if the people back then were as taken by its presence as he was by the monument.

Feeling lonely, he whispered to himself, "How I wish I was back in Mississippi nestled in front of a roaring fire with my wife. Not a person within a mile that I can really talk to. Oh the dreariness of this rainy day."

Loud voices in the room down the hall brought him back to reality and he and his fellow officers straighten themselves, hoping the long wait was over.

The door slammed opened and a voice called out, "Ten Hut!"

James and the other officers snapped to attention with a full salute.

Several high-ranking officers coming out of the nearby room returned their salute. Behind them walked a short stocky man dressed in a black suit and chewing a cigar stub that protruded from the corner of his mouth. Some of the men dropped their salute as soon as the senior officers had passed and, paying little attention to the man in the plain clothes, began to murmur to themselves.

One of the senior officers, a major, suddenly wheeled around to the group and shouted, "You get that salute back up! You know who that man is in front of you?"

"No Sir," the officers chanted in unison, throwing up their salutes once again.

"That gentleman is the President of the United States," the major barked, walking up to the officer next to James.

Throwing his chest out, James immediately responded, "Pardon us, Mister President."

Walking over to James who was still holding his salute, Grant took the cigar from his lips and, studying him for a moment, said, "Get your hand down."

He started to move on, but returning to James he muttered, "You look familiar."

"Mister President, Sir, I served as one of your aides during the Vicksburg campaign. After that I stayed with General Sherman for the rest of the war," James replied.

Grant nodded.

"Lieutenant Robinson, I believe. Good to see you survived it," he said.

As Grant walked away, James couldn't believe he had met the general again especially since he was now President. There were times in the field when he had worked hard to keep the general sober enough to command. Grant couldn't stand to be away from his home and family and often he found solace in the bottle.

Even though he drank frequently, he was sober in battle. Once the enemy was confronted, his whole attention was on attack and destroy. Bringing Lee to bay at Appomattox was something that no other Union General had been able to do.

Remarkable man, James thought watching him walk away.

"You men come on in," came a voice from inside.

Entering a conference room with a long table that could seat at least twenty people, the officers were ordered to sit. No sooner had they settled themselves than another order was given to stand and salute. A side door opened and two colonels emerged followed by a general.

"At ease! Be seated." barked one of the colonels.

With a short cropped beard and a tired and frustrated expression on his face, he said, "I'm General Ord of the fourth military district made up of Mississippi and Arkansas. I'm going to make it short. I've been brought to

Washington to give Congress an update on how our reconstruction policies are progressing, and to tell you the truth, I'm tired of the whole mess down there."

Seeing the anger on his face, James squirmed in his seat.

"I'm going to put it like this, if I get reprimanded, then I'm going to pass it on to my subordinates," General Ord said.

"All of you here served the United States Government and my fourth district. You're supposed to be the best I have. We drove the Rebel army from the field, took away their self-government and instituted military rule to restore order. Now, you can say what you want, but this war was fought over slavery and you know what I see going on down there in Mississippi and Arkansas?"

James and the other officers eyed each other momentarily, afraid to respond.

"Every year that goes by I see more local, democratic whites elected to government positions and where is the Negro? Some of them left the South and ended up out West or up here in Northern cities. But I'll tell you two things that's for sure. There's fewer and fewer Negroes voting and most of them are back on the plantation. Nothing's changed. The poor souls are still enslaved."

One of the officers across the table raised his hand. "Sir, we can't make them vote if they don't choose to."

"Choose to! Where have you been lately!" Ord shouted.

"They don't vote because they know the Klan will get them! You do know about the Klan, Captain? Don't you?"

"Yes sir, I do."

"What about the rest of you?" Ord asked.

"We know about them, but they aren't easily caught, Sir," James replied.

"Easily caught! Might near the whole Rebel army or what's left of them are Klansmen. You mean you can't catch them. They're out there by the thousands," Ord said sarcastically.

All was quiet as the general looked each man in the face. Finally James spoke out. "What do you want us to do, Sir."

General Ord nodded his head. "It's about time someone asked that question. I'll tell you what you are going to do. You all are going back to your post, and you are going to gain information on the Klan. Then get them out of their hiding if that's not too difficult for you. After that you are going to arrest some of the bastards, and when you do, we will make an example of them. Anyone caught will receive the gallows, and it will be a public hanging for all the South to see. If you do not bring me Klansmen and soon, you will be relieved of duty. In closing gentlemen, Congress wants the Klan crushed, and I know you will not let your country down. You understand me?"

"Yes Sir!" the men replied enthusiastically.

"You get the word out down there. Klansmen will hang," Ord concluded.

Leaving the room, James pondered the orders. Breaking the Klan would be no easy task. These people, these Southerners, had indeed been beaten on the field, but their spirit and determination was deeply embedded. One thing he was sure, sooner or later, the white Southerners would regain political power, no matter the cost.

James shuddered when he thought of those involved in the movement.

What if it were some of his friends and neighbors or one of his own family. Perhaps I should resign my commission he thought to himself.

ॐ

Lucretia carefully took John's right arm and examined it looking for any indication of a break. She then took his wrist and stretched his arm upward. John wrenched in pain.

You think it's broke?" Lott asked, sitting there patiently observing Lucretia .

"Doesn't appear to be," she replied. "Do you have some horse liniment? "

Lott nodded. "Plenty down at the barn."

"Would you please fetch me some?"

Trying to rotate his shoulder to loosen up the muscles, John said, "I ain't no horse. I'm gonna be fine."

Lott soon returned with a can of greasy black substance and handed it to Lucretia. She dipped her fingers into the container and bringing out a blob, began to rub it on John's shoulder.

"It might get a little hot," she warned.

Her fingers and hands massaging his battered muscles relaxed his soreness.

"Whoa," John muttered. "Hot ain't the word for it."

"You're acting like a baby," Lucretia teased, rubbing harder than ever.

Lott began to laugh. "That stuff is sure smelly. The boy might have to sleep in the barn tonight."

Before John could reply, the door burst open.

"Tell me it's all a lie, John Wilson," Sister stammered, storming over to where John and Lucretia were sitting.

"Excuse me," Lucretia said, frowning up at her. "What are you talking about?"

Sister pointed her finger at John and replied, "I'm talking to that fool there. He knows what it's all about."

John rolled his shoulder around again to see if the muscles had relaxed and partially ignoring her, said, "Speak your mind Sister or leave me alone. I don't feel like playing a guessing game with you."

"Tim said that Frankie had challenged you to a shootin' and he was gonna be assisting with it. All Little Rock knows 'bout it."

"It's called a duel, and Tim is a second," John replied, eyeing his father across the room.

Placing her hands on her hips, Sister squinted her eyes and glaring at John muttered, "You know you ain't gonna do it."

Turning to her father, she said, "You're not gonna let him, are you?"

Lucretia got out of her chair and clasping one of Sister's shaking hands said, "They were just angry. It was foolish talk. I was there. I heard it. They didn't mean it. Everyone knows that dueling is illegal. Right, John?"

John dropped his head and made no response.

Lucretia looked angrily at John and repeated, "John, you didn't mean it, did you?"

With a glance at Lott, Lucretia walked over to her husband. "You're not going to do that, John."

"I've got to go," John replied. "If'n I don't stand up to him now, it'll be just another time or place. You don't know Frankie like I do. It'll only get worse."

Taking a deep breath, Lucretia said, "I know one thing. I didn't marry you to see you killed in a senseless shooting."

"Amen," Sister replied. "Only fools would do something like this."

Lott got out of his chair, walked over to the window and peered out into the darkness. "I told the folks there weren't nothin' to it, and as far as Frankie goes, he won't show. He didn't show when John and Tim mustered into the army. We'll go down there in the morning and won't be nobody there, not even Tim," Lott said.

"Well I'm going with you," Lucretia said.

"Me too," Sister agreed.

Lott shook his head. "Neither one of you are going. Y'all best stay at the house."

Lucretia dropped her head for a moment and then slowly lifting it, looked over at John. With tears forming, she said, "John, I love you deeply, but if you don't let me go with you, then don't expect me to be here when you return, that is if you do return. This afternoon you ran in front of a galloping horse and tomorrow . . . I won't live in this kind of fear."

"Everything's gonna be fine tomorrow, Cretia. Nobody's gonna get hurt. Like Papa said, Frankie won't show up," John said getting out of his seat.

Walking over to Lucretia, he took her in his arms and holding her whispered, "Don't ever say you gonna leave me. I couldn't make it without you."

"Then don't go down there in the morning," she begged.

Since it was late and James was away on government duty, Sister decided to stay over for the night. She asked Lucretia to help her make the guest bed.

"Can you lift your arm?" Lott asked after the women left.

Feeling pain shoot down his back, John pursed his lips as he lifted his right arm and extended it as if holding a pistol.

"Maybe we shouldn't go," Lott said. "You think he'll show?"

Lowering his arm, John replied, "He'll show. I ain't never seen Frankie win too many fights, but I shore ain't seen him walk away from none either."

"Son, I'd hoped you were smart enough to drop this notion, but if you plan to go through with this, you better take my advice. First of all, be prepared to die, because that may be exactly what happens. Next, even though you're a good shot, you must let him fire first."

"What do you mean by that?"

Lott rubbed his chin for a moment and then explained, "If he shoots first and misses, then you can walk away from the whole thing, but if you choose to shoot first, you had better plan to kill him with the one shot. If you miss, then the pressure will be off and he can relax and take a better shot at you. Remember, if you shoot first then you better be prepared to kill Frankie."

John shook his head. "You mean you're telling me to stand there and let him take the first shot at me. What if'n he hits me?"

Lott took a deep breath before answering, "If'n one of you kills the other, it's gonna be murder. You could get hanged. Even if they don't hang you, you will still be a murderer. I don't want you to be a murderer."

"I don't want to be dead, either, Papa."

Tired but knowing that sleep would not come easily, the two men retired for the evening neither wanting the dawn to come.

Hours later, a soft tap on the bedroom door aroused John.

"Time to get up, Son. You've got a decision to make," came from the outer hallway.

Partially because of the pain and Lucretia restlessness during the night, John had slept little. Each time he eased off to sleep, either his shoulder would start throbbing or he would have dreadful dreams.

Sitting on the side of the bed, he worked his arm about to see if it had loosened up any during the night. To his surprise, it felt much better. After dressing, he walked out in the open hallway and in the darkness found Lott holding the reigns of two saddled horses. Roosters could be heard crowing from the barnyard. A light on the eastern horizon would soon issue in a new day.

John took a deep breath of the cold morning air and thought, what if this is my last morning here on earth.

In the gray of dawn with fog settled in the low areas, John and Lott made their way to the old racetrack. With daylight quickly approaching, they could see the clearing through the trees and, down in the creek bottom, the old circular track. To their relief, no one was there. A dense fog hovered over the grounds and all was silent with the exception of the sound of crows screeching in the distance.

Lott smiled over to John. "We'll wait a few minutes 'fore we leave."

Hearing John's stomach growl, he chuckled, "Then we'll go fix us some breakfast."

John was feeling more at ease knowing that this confrontation seemed to be nothing but angry talk, as Lucretia had said.

After waiting a while John turned to his father. "I think it's time to go home."

But at that moment, off in the distance, the whiny of a horse was heard and John's heart began to race. Through the fog two horsemen emerged from the upper end of the track.

John sighed, looked over at his father and shook his head.

Frankie and Tim rode up, dismounted and fastened their horses' reigns to an old hitching rail.

"Morning gentlemen," Frankie said, walking over to John.

Tim, standing by the old starting platform dropped his head and kicked aimlessly at the ground.

Extending his hand first to Lott then to John, Frankie said, "Didn't think I'd show, did you?"

John held on to Frankie's hand and replied, "Frankie, I was hoping you wouldn't. We don't have to do this. You know how good I can shoot. You've seen me drill a nail into a tree at twenty steps with them pistols. This is nonsense."

With a smirk, Frankie jerked his hand away, "Practice does help, John. You may be surprised."

He then turned to Tim.

"Load 'em up. I got things to do today," he said.

Frankie then looked over at Lott and said, "You can watch him load, if'n you care. Want it all fair and proper."

John shook his head at his father. "That won't be necessary. We trust him."

"You both are crazier'n hell if'n you go through with this," Tim said. "You two ought to just shake hands and walk away."

"Ain't but one of us gonna do that. Either you load 'em or we will," Frankie grumbled, thinking of his embarrassment the day before and every other day that John came out on top looking to be the best.

Tim walked over to his horse, took a pistol case from his saddlebag and after placing it on the upper step, began loading them, all the time mumbling to himself.

In a few moments he walked over to Frankie and handed him the pistols. The metal was deeply blued with engraved clusters of grapes on each side. The handles were pure ivory. The barrels were twelve inches long and in the right marksman's hand, extremely accurate.

"Take your pick," Frankie said, holding the pistols out to John.

John took one and, glaring directly into Frankie's eyes, said, "I don't want to be killed or to kill you, Frankie."

Frankie smiled. "Looks like you got a problem then. It's time to take our positions."

Looking over to Tim, he said, "Count 'em for us."

John and Frankie stood back to back.

In the quiet of the moment, John's mind raced back to days, boyhood times, when he, Tim and Frankie were inseparable. He could visualize their play in nearby woods, fishing, camping and racing on this same old track. Never had boys been closer. What had the years done to their friendship? How had it been destroyed?

"One! Two! Three!" Tim called out, as the two walked away from each other.

With each count, Lott's heart pounded so hard he could hardly breath.

"Nineteen and Twenty!'

John took a deep breath, painfully lifted his pistol and turned. Suddenly, an explosion erupted in his face and a swirl of smoke rolled out at him. Surprised and shocked, he staggered backwards.

At the same time, Lucretia and Sister, trying to comfort each other, sat huddled together on the front steps holding hands. Hearing the echo of the crack of a pistol, both women cringed at the thought of what had happened. They now could only pray.

Lott rushed toward his son. "John!" he shouted.

John regained his footing and waved his father off. Turning back to Frankie, he slowly lifted and aimed his pistol at Frankie's forehead.

With his smoking pistol still raised, Frankie showed no emotion, but just stood his ground.

John hesitated.

"Take your shot!" Frankie shouted, releasing the grip on his pistol and letting it drop to the ground.

"Shoot me, if'n you got the nerve! Shoot!"

John slowly pulled back the trigger. The sound of the pistol startled the horses causing them to shuffle about nervously. Frankie flinched and then looked down at his jacket. The left side of the collar of his woolen coat was dangling by threads. He knew the shot had been carefully placed.

For a moment the two men stood dazed and finally realizing that no one had been hit, Frankie looked over to Tim and said, "Reload 'em!"

Tim shook his head. "Ain't gonna be no more shootin'."

"Then I'll load 'em," Frankie said.

Lott hurried over to where Frankie was reloading his pistol and placed his hand on his shoulder. "It's over, Frankie. Nobody's gettin' killed today."

Frankie turned to Lott. The man he saw was the man who had always welcomed him into his home, a man who had always treated him like a son. Slowly peace filled his heart.

John tossed the pistol over to Tim and getting Frankie's attention said, "If'n we can't get along, we need to just stay out of each other's life. You hear me?"

As Frankie and Tim went to the horses, Tim looked over at Frankie. "Why'd you shoot first. I bet John wouldn't have shot at all," he whispered.

Mounting, Frankie replied, "If'n he had shot first, I'd be a dead man. I've got to be going. Take care of the pistols for me."

Riding off, he called back to Tim, "You see the way I stood up to him? I could have fought them Yankees as good as y'all did."

Lott walked over to his horse and noticed John struggling to mount. "You all right, Son?" Lott asked.

John rested his head on the side of his horse and called back, "I think I need a little help."

Lott rushed to John and found drops of blood spilling from his jacket.

"Get over her quick, Tim!" Lott called out.

John eased to the ground in a sitting position while Lott unbuttoned his coat. Pulling the jacket back, Lott gasped. John's shirt was completely saturated with blood.

"He's been hit!" Lott shouted.

"Where 'bouts!" Tim asked, hurrying up.

"Here," Lott said, pointing to a jagged hole in John's shirt.

"Is he spitting blood?" Tim muttered, bending down over his friend.

"I ain't spitting blood," John moaned. "But it shore hurts."

Lott grabbed Tim by the arm, "You ride to Little Rock as fast as you can and fetch Doc McLauren. I gotta get this boy home."

Lucretia and Sister were frightened when they heard the second pistol shot ring out.

"They've done it," Lucretia said, falling into Sister's arms.

A short time later, movement was seen through the fog. Letting go of Sister, Lucretia hurried over to the far side of the porch and muttered, "Won't be long now."

"Where are they?" Lucretia said, turning to her.

Sister pointed down the road. "There."

John tried to straighten himself in the saddle before reaching home.

"Don't want to scare them," he muttered. "There will be time 'nough for that when I get there."

"It's two men on horses," Sister shouted, smiling back to Lucretia.

A hint of a smile crossed Lucretia's face.

Recognizing the big bay, Sister said, "It's them, both of 'em."

As the horses approached the house, the women hurried out to meet them. One look at John's face brought fear to Lucretia. His dark tanned face was deathly pale and a look of pain was in his eyes. Reaching up to him, she flinched when she found her hand covered with blood.

Lott dismounted and reached up to help John down. "Gotta get him in the house. I sent Tim for the doctor."

Lucretia turned to Sister. "Get some water boiling, clean cloths and the black leather bag under my bed. I'm not waiting for the doctor."

As soon as they got John into bed, Lucretia took the bag from Sister and opening it pulled out a pair of scissors.

By the location of the hole in his shirt, the ball must have entered the left side of his chest, Lucretia thought. She shook her head and mumbled to herself, "Lung shot, maybe worse."

She then took the scissors and began to cut the shirt away. Once the shirt was removed, she looked over to Sister. "Give me a cloth. Got to clean the blood off," she ordered.

Wiping most of the blood away, she found a jagged hole in his chest oozing dark red blood.

"That's good," she mumbled.

"What do you mean, that's good?" Lot asked.

"Pink blood would mean a lung shot," John explained, gasping for breath. "Now, leave her alone, Papa. She's as good a doctor as any 'round here."

Holding a folded cloth to stop the blood, Lucretia held her hand out to Sister and said, "There are some forceps in there. Hand them to me."

Leaning down to John, she said, "This may hurt a little."

Carefully pushing the torn skin aside, Lucretia edged down through open flesh. She could see that one of his ribs had been shattered and pushing further the forceps suddenly came into contact with a hard object. With a smile, Lucretia pulled the forceps out and held them up to display a bloody lead ball.

"Thank you dear God!" Lott and Sister exclaimed.

Exhausted, John fell into a deep sleep.

Lucretia cleaned John up the best she could, then tearing a sheet apart, bound it around his chest.

Wiping her face, Lucretia said, "He's got a broken rib and a pretty bad laceration, but he should be fine. I've actually seen a lot worse."

Sister then went to the kitchen and soon returned with three steaming cups of coffee.

No one heard the noise outside until the door slammed open and Tim burst into the room.

"Couldn't find 'em, Mister Wilson! He's off on a call!" Tim said, trying to catch his breath.

Lucretia went over to Tim and wrapped her arms around him, "He's going to be fine. Thank you for going for the doctor."

Tim sighed in relief as he walked over to where John was resting.

Lot shook his head and said, "I don't understand it. Those boys were twenty paces apart. That ball should have gone might near clear through him. I guess it's one of God's miracles."

Standing over John, Tim thought for a moment then replied, "You watch me load them pistols?"

"No I didn't," Lott answered. "I trusted you."

"Well, I'm glad you didn't cause I only put a half load of powder in each of 'em."

27

A SPIRIT AT CHRISTMAS

Word ABOUT THE SHOOTING NEVER GOT OUT, AND IN A matter of days, John was up and on his feet.

Meanwhile, James, after coming back from Washington, went to work with his trusted subordinates devising a plan to identify Klan members. To arrest them, he must catch them in an illegal act and then have enough manpower to bring them in.

"Impossible," he murmured to himself, rocking in his favorite chair and warming himself by a crackling fire.

"What's that, dear?" Sister asked.

"Nothing," he replied.

Sister pushed the covers back and sat up in bed.

"Nothing?" she exclaimed. "Ever since you got back, you barely even talk to me and when you do, you don't make sense. Is there something wrong?"

James got up, walked to their bed and sitting on the edge leaned down and kissed her. "When I went to war, they trained me well. I knew the enemy and I knew what to do. Whether I survived or not was a matter of fate."

James paused a moment then continued, "I'm fighting a war now and I don't even know the enemy and to tell you the truth, I don't even know how to fight."

Feeling his frustration, Sister pulled him to her and hugging him whispered, "You can share your problems with me, James."

He shook his head. "That's just it. I can't tell you. It's government business. What I know could jeopardize my life and yours."

Lucretia was an excellent teacher at New Hope School, and each day Negro parents began to encourage others to enroll their children. Each morning Lucretia was sure of two things: Toby would have a warm fire burning in the fireplace and there would be new faces to greet her.

This morning was no different as Lucretia got out of her buggy to find Toby standing under the front porch surrounded by a mass of smiling children. She scanned each face as she entered the school and said, "Good morning."

"Good Mawn'n," the children replied in unison, hustling to assist her with her books and supplies.

Lucretia muttered to Toby, "Thank goodness I didn't see any new ones this morning. We can't accommodate any more."

Toby frowned and replied, "There's two new 'ens inside. Ain't dressed good 'nough for the cold. They's in there by the fire, but the Choctaw is gone."

Lucretia shook her head. "Toby, that makes thirty-two. I have eight readers and almost no chalk left. Every bench in the room is filled. In fact, I don't think we can get another child in here."

Then recalling Toby's words, Lucretia exclaimed, "Where did the little Indian girl go?"

"Don't know. Them Indians come and go like the seasons," he replied. "Wish I could be more help 'round here, but you know I can't. All I can do is keep the place clean and warm."

From the time Lucretia started until she finished, she labored to the point of exhaustion. The majority of the day was spent in teaching reading and writing and if time permitted, math was introduced. She hoped to begin lessons in history and geography, but there was never enough time. Her job was made difficult because some of the children learned quicker than others and the students who enterred late were at the beginner level.

As time passed she was faced with at least seven different reading levels, but one thing that encouraged her to continue was the hunger the children displayed for learning. They were always on time and well behaved.

After one exhausting day, Lucretia collapsed on a bench next to the fireplace and lowered her head resting it in the palms of her hands. Taking deep breaths, she became faint and without thinking, eased down to the floor. The fire warmed her face as she lay there. She quickly dozed off to sleep.

After the last child had left, Toby went back inside and found Lucretia lying on the floor. He stood over her for a moment wringing his hands. Then easing down to her he gently touched her shoulder and whispered, "Miss Wilson, you all right?"

Lucretia opened her eyes momentarily and clearing her mind, realized she had fallen asleep. Looking up at Toby she sighed, "Please forgive me. I know I scared you. Would you help me up?"

Toby helped her to a bench and pointed to the lunch box on her desk. "You didn't eat yore dinner, did you Miss Wilson?"

"I never thought about it," she said.

Easing down on a bench next to her, Toby said, "What you doing is a wonderful thing, Miss Wilson, but I'm not shore this here can go on. I been watching you these past weeks. You can't keep doing this. Yore body won't last."

Lucretia reached over and placed her hand on Toby's. "How can I stop? You see the look on those children's faces when they realize they are beginning to be able to read and write."

Toby placed his other hand over hers and replied, "Then the Good Lord's gonna have to send you some help. Let's get yore things together and I'll drive you home."

At the sound of the buggy, John walked out to meet Lucretia and Toby. Noticing Lucretia's tired face, he took her hand. "You feeling all right?"

"She's just kinda tired, Mister John," Toby answered. "In fact, she's might near give out."

Lucretia smiled at Toby. "I'm fine. I just need a little rest."

On the porch, she turned back to Toby and said, "Thank you for bringing me home. Thank you for everything."

After Lucretia had gone into the house, John walked back out to Toby and rubbing the horse's nose asked, "What's going on Toby? This ain't like her."

Toby scratched his head the way he always did when thinking and replied, "The school is too much fer her. Too many chill'un and noth'n to work with."

"What do I do?" John asked.

"Don't rightly know. I don't know nothin' you can do except pray that the good Lord will bring her some help."

John walked around and shook his hand. "You take the rig home. I'll bring her in the morning. It's a long walk for ya."

Toby eased down from the buggy. "If'n it's the same to you, I'll put the rig up and get on home. Walkin' ain't never done me no harm."

John found Lucretia already asleep on the bed and later as he was about to wake her for supper, Sister and James rode up.

"Getting cold out here," James said. "Got some coffee made?"

John motioned them in and replied, "Naw, but Sister can make some, can't you Sis?"

Brushing them aside Sister hurried back toward the kitchen.

"All women is good for is waitin' on men. Give me a few minutes," she stammered. "Where's Pa?"

John pointing James to a chair answered, "He'll be in directly. He's down in the swamp checking on the hawgs. Might have a hawg killin' Saturday."

"What about Cretia?" called Sister from the kitchen. "I could use some help."

"She's in bed. Worn to a frazzle."

In a few moments, Sister returned with two cups of steaming coffee and while the three sat there, John told them about the school.

"I don't see how Lucretia can keep going," he said. "There's just too many children, nothing much to work with and to tell you the truth, she can't carry the load. It's killing her. Not only is it impossible, it's not really accepted around here. Know what I mean?"

James, reaching over to get a piece of bark from the fireplace to light his smoke, mumbled, "This is a new age. I admire what she's trying to do. Most folks around here don't give a damn about the Negroes. She's a special kind of woman, John."

"I could do it! I'd help her," Sister said. "That is if'n she ask'd me to."

Surprised, John sat his coffee cup down and said, "You don't mean that?"

"I do," she replied with a smile.

"Then Sister, you go in there right now and offer yore services."

When she had gone, John looked over to James. "That's something, ain't it. We fuss and feud at times, but I'm shore 'nough proud of that sister of mine. I only wish Mama was here to see it."

In the weeks that followed, Sister came each morning and rode to school with Lucretia, but the problems only escalated. More children enrolled and to accommodate them, part of the class, those who had warm clothing, would meet out on the open front porch.

Lucretia was determined that no one would be turned away. As the weeks went by it became apparent that with no extra school supplies nor room, they must admit no more children.

One day, with a cold December wind pushing down from the North, a group of children were huddled on the porch shuddering as Sister tried to teach them. Holding up a small chalkboard and chattering as she spoke, Sister asked, "What is this word?"

As the children started to answer, two horsemen down the road caught their attention. As they neared the building one of the men looked up at the sign posted above the door and exclaimed, "Good Hope School. What do you think about that?"

Hearing a northern accent, Sister asked, "Can I help you?"

One of the men removed his hat and replied, "I'm John Gilbert and the gentleman there is Gary Jenkins. Are you Mrs. Wilson?"

"Just a moment," Sister replied as she went inside.

Lucretia soon appeared on the porch, and once again the men introduced themselves. Getting down from their horses, Gilbert remarked, "You teach those children out here in the cold?"

"I don't have room for them inside," Lucretia explained. "What do you gentlemen want?"

"We've heard about the work you're doing here, and we think we can be of help."

"How's that?" Sister asked.

"We're from the Freedmen's Bureau out of Jackson. You ever hear of us?"

Lucretia thought for a moment, "I heard my husband say that it helps Negroes get land to settle and aids them with their medical problems and assists them in the voting process."

Jenkins looked around the small bleak building and said, "We also help to educate them and by what I've observed here you could use some help, that is if you will accept our assistance."

Lucretia looked over to Sister and then to Toby. "What kind of assistance?" she asked.

Scratching his beard, Jenkins said, "Well, we could add a couple of rooms to the place, and I think we can supply you with books, chalk, chalkboards and maybe some pens and paper. We can probably do more later."

"Do you truly mean all those things?" Lucretia asked.

"We can start the first of next week. We can buy the lumber locally and laborers will have to be employed. Your teaching materials can be here by next Wednesday," Jenkins said.

Lucretia reached out her hand to him. "We accept your offer, Sir, and thank you from the depths of our hearts."

That afternoon after the children had been dismissed and Lucretia and Sister were stepping into the buggy, Toby closed the front door and called out to them, "Afternoon Ladies. I guess the Lawd done up and heard our prayers, didn't He?"

Still unable to believe what had happened, Lucretia shook her head and replied, "The Lord works in strange and wondrous ways. He really does."

Two days later, as Jenkins had promised, materials and laborers arrived. In two more days, two rooms had been added. Each contained three windows, and wood stoves were installed in each of the new rooms. Excitement filled Lucretia's moments, especially when crates of books and supplies were delivered.

With word spreading, children were now coming from as far as five miles away. New Hope School was blossoming.

Christmas was now only two weeks away, and the spirit in the Wilson family was running high. The school was going well, the crops were in and everyone was looking forward to the seasonal get togethers. That is everyone except Lott.

As the December days passed, he became despondent and less talkative. Normally he was up at dawn and would be outside by daybreak taking care of farm matters and livestock, but now he seldom went outside and would often spend the entire day in his bedroom reading or simply gazing out the window. John and Lucretia began to worry about him.

One afternoon when John was away, Lucretia went into his room and as usual, he was sitting next to the window looking outside. Lucretia placed her hand on his shoulder and said, "Papa, want to take a walk with me? I need to get outside and get some fresh air."

Lott placed his hand on hers, not taking his eyes off the window. After a few moments of silence, he said, "You know them chickens are a crazy bunch. They have their own pecking order, and it's not always the big ones that get the grain first. Look at them crazy fools out there running around."

Lucretia leaned down and kissed him on the cheek.

"I'm going to get your coat," she said, walking over to the coat rack.

Lott slowly got up from his seat. "Any special place you want to go?" he asked.

"I find the big woods enchanting."

Holding on to his arm, they slowly walked into the magnificent forest with not a word spoken between them.

After finally making the rounds and approaching the house, Lott looked down at Lucretia and clearing his throat murmured, "I'm proud you wanted me to go with you."

Lucretia smiled up at him and squeezed his arm.

"In fact, I'm glad you and John found each other."

"He is very dear to me," Lucretia replied.

Tears began to form in the corner of Lott's eyes and one trickled down his wrinkled face and lost itself in his thick beard.

Lott sniffed a couple of times and sighed, "When I look at you, I think back to the times Sarah and I had together. The walks we had through the woods. All the good times."

With his voice breaking, he muttered, "God knows I miss that woman. You know, she always tried to make Christmas something special."

Lucretia reached up to him and embracing him whispered, "It is difficult to have Christmas when you miss Sarah. But sometimes I just feel her here enjoying every moment with us. You know, we all love you so much."

Later that night as she and John lay together, she whispered to him, "You all ever decorate for Christmas?"

"What do you mean?" he asked.

"Maybe some greenery here and there. You know, perhaps some cedar on the mantle in Papa's room? "

"We never did nothin' like that," John said. "We usually exchange presents and drink a little eggnog. Then Mama would read the Christmas story from the Bible. Always read from Luke."

John thought a moment, then continued, "We did always have a big dinner on Christmas day. I'm shore gonna miss that."

"I'd like to bring in some greenery. Maybe even a small cedar tree, and you know, Sister and I can prepare the meal."

"Why do want a tree in the house?" John said.

"If you would build a stand for it, we could place ribbons and strings of popcorn on it. Then perhaps place a few candles here and about on some of the limbs. I think it would be fun, and to answer your question, it's called a Christmas tree."

"I ain't ever heard of such a thing, Cretia."

"Can I do it?"

"Sounds like fun to me," he replied.

"Can I start tomorrow?"

John whispered back to her, "I know where some small cedars are. You and me will just have to go cut us one come morning."

With Christmas only a week away, Lucretia dismissed school for a brief holiday and then with John's help selected the tree. Since Lott's room was not only his bedroom but the family gathering place, she decided to put the tree there. With a little coaxing, Sister volunteered her help with the decorations, and soon the tree was covered with strings of popcorn, white ribbons tied in bows and finally small red candles attached to the limbs.

While the women worked, Lott sat there patiently watching, amazed at their creativity. He wasn't especially pleased with having a bush, as he called it, in his bedroom, but to see their excitement pleased him.

After the tree was finished, Lucretia placed several cedar branches on the massive oak mantle along with three large candles. When the last candle was placed, Lucretia looked over to Lott and said, "Well, Papa, what do you think?"

Lott scratched his head and replied, "I must say it's kinda different. How 'bout them limbs over the fireplace? You think they might catch on fire?"

Sister thought for a moment. "They're mighty green. I think they'll be fine until after Christmas."

Christmas Eve finally arrived and James and Sister drove up as the sun was setting. As planned, they would exchange presents, sample a little of the spirits and hear the reading of the Christmas story.

Sitting there enjoying the warmth of the fire and sipping eggnog, Lott suddenly got up and went over to a lamp table next to his bed and reaching down picked up the family Bible. Returning, he looked over to Sister and said, "Will you read it?"

Thinking about all the times in years past that her mother had read them the story, Sister, sniffling, glanced over to Lucretia and muttered, "Cretia, will you read it for us?"

"I really shouldn't," she replied.

Lott handed the Bible to Lucretia. "It would please me greatly if'n you'd do it."

As she read, the family sat quietly listening. Almost by memory, they anticipated each word. At times, John could imagine his mother sitting in her favorite rocking chair covering the same lines. Looking over to his father who was staring at the empty rocker, John was saddened by the look on his face.

Some people never get over the loss of a loved one, he thought.

When Lucretia had finished, she closed the Bible and looked into the face of each family member. With a smile she softly said, "Thank you for letting me read and also thank you for accepting me into your family. I've never been more happy."

John smiled back at her and wanting to lift the family spirits, looked over to James and said, "James, you ever been serenading?"

Puzzled, James answered, "Never heard of it."

"What's that?" Lucretia asked.

"Well, when we were young 'uns, we would bundle up on Christmas Eve and go visiting folks around the neighborhood. Some of 'em would have treats for us like cake, cookies, fried pies and all kind of good things. We'd stay out most of the night having loads of fun," John explained.

"That a Southern custom?" James asked.

John shook his head. "Naw, I don't think so. It's something Mrs. Olliver started around here. She said they do it down there in the Bayou country in Louisiana."

"Sounds like fun," Lucretia said. "You sure they still do it?"

Lott grunted, "I ain't heard much about it since the war. Not sure the young 'uns do it no more."

John got up and grabbing his coat said, "Well, we're gonna find out so y'all get your wraps."

Excited about the thought of visiting friends and neighbors, the group quickly bundled up. "Papa, why don't you come with us? It'll be a lot of fun," Lucretia said, turning to Lott.

"I'm comfortable right here by the fireplace. I plan to drink a little more spirits and my old bones tell me it's not far from my bedtime," he said smiling. "Plus you folks will prob'ly be out most near all night. No Ma'am, I'm gonna stay right here thank you."

"Might be daybreak gettin' in," John said with a laugh as he closed the door.

Hearing them laughing and chattering as they drove off, Lott couldn't help but chuckle to himself. It just takes too much energy to be young, he thought. Just give me a toasty fire to warm my feet and a good toddy and I'll be content.

He then got up and walked back to the kitchen where Sister had left a pitcher of eggnog. He took a glass and found it a little weak to his liking. He thought for a moment then went over to the cabinet next to the woodstove and retrieved a bottle of whiskey. Adding a good cup full, he stirred it around then poured himself a glass.

"That's better," he mumbled as he walked back to his bedroom, his glass in one hand and the pitcher in the other.

Watching the fire slowly burn and sipping on his spirits, Lott's mind turned to times past, times when he and his brother Jake had ventured into this wilderness. He remembered how hard they had worked to build the house that had been his home for almost thirty-five years now. Then he remembered a wagon pulling up in front of the place with a preacher and the prettiest girl he had ever seen, all smiles and curls.

"I knew right then I was gonna marry that woman," he muttered to himself as the spirits began taking hold. "And I did marry her and she gave me three sons and a daughter."

Then realizing how much he missed his wife and brother, a deep sense of loneliness crept over him. Feeling chilled, he reached over to the bed and pulled a quilt down to cover himself. The room began to spin and Lott closed his eyes. In his mind he could see Sarah sitting next to him occasionally flipping a smile to him over the rim of her framed glasses. She gently tucked the cover around his shoulders and kissed him goodnight.

"I can't wait 'till morning," she whispered. "Something special's gonna happen."

A banging on the door abruptly awakened Lott. Startled, he looked around and was surprised to find sunlight streaming through the windows.

Just dreaming again, he thought.

Then the knock came again.

Can't be the young 'uns, he reasoned. Never do knock. They just come and go through here as they please. Since they probably got in late, they're still asleep.

Gonna sleep a little more, he thought.

"Anybody home?"

Something about that voice sounds familiar, Lott thought.

Clearing his throat, Lott answered, "Who you want?"

"That you Uncle Lott?"

Lott got up out of his chair.

"Open up! It's cold out here."

Turning the latch, Lott eased the door open and peered outside. Standing in front of him was the largest man he had seen in a long time. The doorway measured six feet and six inches and this man stood taller than that. His skin was olive brown and his eyes were deep set and dark. His hair was thick and golden blond, worn long and braided in the back like a Choctaw. He wore knee boots with pants tucked in and wore a heavy red and black plaid woolen coat.

Quiet an unusual looking man, Lott thought. Mystified, Lott stood glaring at the stranger and when the man smiled at him, it was as if a veil had been lifted.

"Boy, where'd you come from?" Lott gasped.

Holding out his hand, he said, "Been a long time, Uncle."

"Homer," spoke a happy and amazed Lott.

"It's me, Uncle Lott."

Lott held both arms open and Homer stooping down to enter the room embraced his uncle. Tears streamed down both their cheeks as they stood there holding each other. He had been only a young boy when he and his mother left for the reservation in Oklahoma.

What a man he has become, Lott thought as he patted Homer on the back. Looking into his face was like seeing Jake all over again. He had become the very image of his father.

Excited, he pulled away from Homer and rushed out into the open hall. "John! Cretia! We got company. Get on out here!"

Banging on John's door, Lott shouted, "You get out of that bed and get out here! You ain't gonna believe it!"

A rustling sound was heard from inside the room and in a few moments, John, mussed hair and sleepy eyed, peered out from behind the partially opened door.

John looked at his father and then to the man standing next to him. John still half asleep said groggily, "Who are you?"

Homer reached his hand. "I'm your cousin, Homer."

Surprised, John hesitated a moment then clasping his hand, stammered, "You used to be short and skinny."

"And you were nothing but the runt of the litter," Homer responded, squeezing his hand hard.

Lucretia then appeared and was amazed to see such a large man.

Lott, placing his hand on Homer's shoulder, said, "Cretia, this here is Homer Wilson, my brother's boy. This here is Jake's son."

Noting the size of his hand as he gently embraced hers, Lucretia looked up at him and said, "I've heard a lot about your father. It's a pleasure to meet you."

Not expecting the northern accent, Homer winked over to Lott. "He married him a Yankee, didn't he, and a pretty one at that."

Feeling the chill of the morning, Lott motioned toward his bedroom. "It's cold out here. Best come on inside. We got lots of talking to do."

Lucretia hurrying back into their bedroom said, "Give me a minute and I'll get us some breakfast."

Before she could close her door, Homer pointed out front. "I got somebody with me."

Lott took several steps down the hall and saw a woman sitting on the buggy seat. She stepped down from the rig and walked toward them. She was tall and slender and like Homer, had olive complexion. The woman's hair was streaked with gray and flowed down her back, almost reaching her waist. Even with years, she was very attractive.

Lott took several more steps and began to tremble.

Reaching the steps, the woman held out her hand to him.

"Mind giving an old woman some help?" she asked, looking up at Lott.

Taking her hand, the two stood staring at each other. She then reached up and ran her fingers through his hair. "Used to be black as soot."

Embracing her, Lott whispered, "You ain't changed a bit Hatta. I've never forgotten the first time I set eyes on you. The time Jake rode up here with you hanging on to 'em."

"That's Homer's mother, my Uncle Jake's wife," John whispered to Lucretia. "It's hard to believe they're here."

28

PRELUDE TO A STORM

Lott was filled with joy as he looked at his family gathered around the dinner table. He couldn't take his eyes off Hatta and Homer. He never expected to see them again and with the exception of Thomas, his whole family was there.

Clearing his throat, Lott said, "We got a lot to be thankful for. If'n you don't mind I'd like for us to take each other's hand for the blessing."

After a dinner of baked ham and sweet potatoes, black-eyed peas, and hot steaming rolls covered with butter and molasses, the men retired to Lott's bedroom. The women quickly cleared the table and washed the dishes while the men made themselves comfortable in front of a roaring fire.

In a few minutes Sister brought the men a pot of coffee and asked if any wanted apple pie. All raised their hands as the aroma from the oven filtered through the room. The women soon joined the men and for the remainder of the afternoon they sat together reminiscing and sharing their lost years.

Homer reminded Lott of his brother, Jake. Like his father, he had broad, thick shoulders, a slim waist and strong legs. Homer was never without words. Whether it was politics, farming or the state of the economy, he was well informed.

In contrast, Hatta seldom spoke but listened intently as the men talked. When she did speak, it was always in a quiet voice to Lucretia.

At one point, Lott carefully placed two hickory logs on the fire trying to keep the sparks from popping out at them and then settled down in his favorite rocker. Reaching over and placing his hand on Homer's shoulder, Lott chose his words carefully. "We been talking all day and I just wonder."

Homer looked over at his uncle.

"Y'all have come home to stay, ain't you?" Lott asked.

Homer glanced over to his mother. "We came to pay our respects and to see you all."

He paused for a moment then continued, "Mama heard that some of her people are still here. She wants to see them."

"I had one little Choctaw girl in my school. That is before they moved along," Lucretia said.

Surprised, Hatta asked, "You teach Choctaws?"

"I teach any child who wants to learn," Lucretia replied.

"You know you and Hatta's got two sections of land," Lott said. "Homer, one was yore daddy's and the other was Hatta's and her brother's. It's fine land. Ain't touched a limb on it. It's just like you left it."

"Six hundred and forty acres per section. One mile square," Homer said. "For now, we're in no hurry. We'll see."

Realizing that it was getting late, Lott showed Hatta and Homer to the spare room that joined John and Lucretia's. Even though there was no fireplace, it had two single beds where John's two older brothers used to sleep.

Later that night as John and Lucretia lay cuddled together, John said, "I've never enjoyed a Christmas more, and I'll never forget the look on Papa's face when he saw Homer standing there."

John paused for a moment then muttered softly so as not to be heard in the adjoining room, "What do you think of 'em?"

"Well, Hatta's a little different, but she seems so kind. I really like her."

All was quiet for a moment then she whispered, "But I don't know about Homer."

"What do you mean by that?"

"John, he speaks perfect English, appears very knowledgeable and, I would say, seems well educated. I think there's a lot we don't know about your cousin."

All was quiet for a few moments.

"Another thing that puzzles me is that every time you all began talking about the war, he either says nothing or changes the subject."

"Hummm," murmured John. "You know you're right. I was so proud to see 'em, I just didn't pick up on that."

In the weeks that followed, the Wilson household returned to its normal activities. Neighbors wanting to see Hatta and Homer came by for visits and when word got out that they were back in Little Rock, a steady stream of Choctaws began to trickle by.

With no homes of their own, their visits often lasted for several days. Since the nights were cold, they were invited to stay on the open hallway of the house or use the loft of the barn. The Wilsons, accustomed to their presence, went about their farm work. Lucretia found them fascinating. Once they arrived, she seldom left Hatta's side, and after a few weeks, she began to understand some of their native language and customs. One thing that bothered her was that none of them seemed to have a home of their own.

The longer Hatta stayed, the more talkative she became and before long she and Lucretia were inseparable. Learning that Hatta could read and write, Lucretia invited her to come with them to the New Hope School. Before long, Hatta began to take an active roll in working with the children.

Homer, not wanting to be a burden on the family, went to work helping Lott and John with the farm chores, but there were times when he would saddle his horse, ride off and stay gone for days. He never told them he was leaving. He just rode off. No one felt they should pry into his business, but it was puzzling to the whole Wilson family.

One thing that both Lott and John began to notice was the time he was spending with James. From the very beginning, the two seemed to have a lot in common, and before long James was going along with Homer on some of his mysterious ventures.

§§

One day, hearing a horse whinny, Suzanne paused and looked up momentarily before continuing her reading. A cold north wind was blowing fiercely outside sending leaves dancing across the porch while she, with a quilt tucked about her, was snuggled comfortably by the fireplace.

Then a horse whinnied again and after a moment of silence Suzanne heard someone whistling a strange melody. With her mother and Amanda away on a visit to her grandfather's plantation in Louisiana, she was alone.

Probably just her imagination, she thought to herself.

Once she got involved in a good story, she usually lost all sense of time. But then, she heard the strange sound again. A chill of fear ran down her arms. Putting her book down and easing from her chair, she quietly made her way from the parlor to the hallway to bolt the front door.

Feeling more secure, she returned to the parlor and inching the curtain aside, peered outside. To her surprise, there was an unusual looking man sitting on a chestnut stallion out in the front drive. Wrapped in a heavy woolen red plaid coat, with a wide brimmed felt black hat pulled down low on his brow, he straightened himself in the saddle.

As she watched, the man took what appeared to be a short piece of swamp cane and placed it to his lips. Suddenly Suzanne remembered that those were the sounds she had heard as a young girl. Once while visiting a Choctaw campground with her father, she had heard an old white haired Choctaw playing the same melody. Fascinated by the man and his music, she lost all fear and listened intently to the melody. The man then took the cane from his lips, placed it inside his coat pocket and nudged his horse forward up to the front steps.

"Anyone home?" the stranger called out.

Once more fear gripped Suzanne as she moved away from the window.

"Who are you and what do you want?" Suzanne asked.

The man twisted in the saddle and in a deep voice replied, "I'm really nobody special. You must be Suzanne Olliver."

Astonished, Suzanne eased the curtain aside and looked outside again. At that moment, another man with dark complexion and long flowing black hair riding one of the most decrepit horses she had ever seen rode up to the stranger. The two talked for a few moments and then the man with the long hair rode off.

Suzanne hurried over to the desk where her brother kept a double-barreled derringer and easing it from the drawer, tucked in under a shawl that she wrapped around her shoulders. Then cocking the hammers back, she unbolted the door and stepped outside.

The two stared at each other for a moment, then the man nodded to her. "You've made a fine looking woman, Suzanne."

He then pointed toward the fields that ran as far as the eye could see.

"You've got some kind of place here. Lot of land. How much you got?" he asked.

Taking a deep breath, she answered, "Four thousand acres. Maybe more. I don't really know."

"Four thousand, that's a lot. Bet it took a lot of slaves to work the place."

If he makes one move to dismount, I'll shoot him, she thought.

With the sound of leather screeching against leather as he twisted in the saddle, the man turned back to Suzanne. "Used to be Choctaw land, you know."

"I know," Suzanne replied.

"That's not what I meant. Those two lower sections down there belonged to a Choctaw called Tubby. Your father and some of his associates got him drunk one night and while gambling, had him sign it away. Your father stole it."

A flush of anger surged through Suzanne.

"That's a lie! My father worked hard for all this land," she said, dropping her shawl.

A hint of a smile crossed the man's face and with a Scottish accent he said, "Lassie, are ye goin' to shoot me?"

Raising the pistol, she said, "If you don't leave these premises, as God is my witness, I'll shoot you dead. Nobody insults my family or discredits my deceased father. Who are you?"

The stranger removed his hat and swooped it downward in a mock courtesy, mannerly gesture revealing a thick curly head of hair. He then reined his horse about and staring directly at her, replied, "I'm Homer Wilson. Your father did steal the land, and he also had my father murdered."

After a moment of silence, he continued, " I just wanted to see what kind of place he had built for himself, and I must repeat, you are a striking woman and a courageous one at that. Good day, Ma'am."

Suzanne lowered the pistol and shivered as she stood there watching him ride off. It hurt to hear the things Homer had said about her father, but in her heart she knew that it was probably true. To her, her father was a kind and caring man.

As Homer reached the road that ran in front of their property, he reined his horse to a stop, turned in the saddle and looked back at Suzanne before he rode off.

Suzanne remembered the tall skinny boy that barely ever spoke to anyone. This could not be the same one, not the way he had just spoken to her.

In a few moments, Frankie rode up to the house. Once inside, Suzanne told him all that had happened. Frankie was enraged at Homer's accusations against his father. Going to his liquor cabinet, he poured himself a drink of bourbon and stood with his back to the fire. After a couple of swallows, he threw the glass into the blazing fire and with a guttural voice said, "I'm gonna pay that half breed a visit. Who does he think he is coming on my property and belittling my father with lies. No sir, no man does that to an Olliver!"

"Homer is not a skinny little boy any more," Suzanne said. "You need to stay away from the Wilsons. I shouldn't have told you any of this."

"Shouldn't have told me any of it! Damn, Woman. He was talking about our father."

"Damn yourself," Suzanne shouted back, "He didn't tell me anything I ain't heard before. As much as I love Daddy, you and I both know that some of the talk is true. Don't you remember how he treated you?"

⚡

With the sun setting, the Wilsons were sitting down to supper when the hounds began barking outside. Putting on his jacket, Lott opened the door and walked down the hallway to the front porch. In the gray of dusk he saw a rider reigning in his horse.

"Can I help you?" Lott called out, not recognizing the man.

"Is Homer Wilson here?" came an angry reply.

Hearing his name, Homer made his way to the porch.

Towering a full head taller than Lott, Homer stepped in front of his Uncle and stood on the top step only feet away from where Frankie Olliver now sat.

"I'm Homer Wilson."

Surprised at the size of the man standing there, Frankie hesitated for a moment then gaining his thoughts, replied, "Why'd you tell those lies to Suzanne?"

The rest of the family had now left the table and joined Lott and Homer. John nudged his way past his father.

"Stay out of this, Son," Lott said, placing his hand on John's arm.

Homer now made his way down the steps and began running his hand down the shoulder of Frankie's horse never looking up at its rider.

"Fine animal you got here."

"I didn't come here to talk about no horse," Frankie replied, clinching his whip.

Softly Homer said, "I have proof that your father stole the land from Tubby. I have three written statements from the men who were playing cards that night. And as for my father's death, if you would read the court records, you would see that the facts indicate that Frank Olliver, Sr. was the only man who would benefit from my father's death. And one of the men hired to help kill my father was caught by some of my people on the road outside Forest and before they killed him, he also made a statement."

Frankie, enraged, at what he had heard, drew his whip but Homer reached and snatched it from Frankie's hand. Stepping back, Homer said, "You have become one aggressive man, Frankie Olliver, but it doesn't change a thing about what your father did."

Surprised, Frankie reined his horse back a few steps and shouted out, "I won't accept what you've said. Meet me at the racetracks in the morning. Come day break, we'll settle this matter."

Smiling, Homer looked up at Frankie, "Sounds like you have challenged me to a duel. If that's so, I have the choice of weapons."

Reaching inside his coat, he pulled out a knife with a long blade sharpened on both sides and holding it up continued, "I'll fight you with this and we'll fight here and now."

Startled, Frankie sat speechless. Homer's massive size and his easy movement with the knife made Frankie cringe. He drew a deep breath and turning his horse replied, "There'll be another day."

§§

Lucretia had thoroughly enjoyed her first Christmas in Mississippi. She had grown close to the family and the arrival of Hatta and Homer had brought even more joy into their home.

Even though she missed her parents, she knew this was where she belonged. The thoughts of Philadelphia, New York City and all the comfort and luxuries they presented seldom crossed her mind. Being married to the man she loved and adored meant more than anything else.

January the second of 1871 dawned bright and clear. A string of golden clouds streaked across the eastern horizon shading part of the morning sun, and a light frost blanketed the ground. For the past three days heavy rains had fallen, keeping everyone inside, but now the weather was clear and crisp.

Eager to begin school again, Hatta, Sister and Lucretia bundled themselves, and after John had hitched up the rig, headed down the muddied road to New Hope School. Chatting as they went, they faintly heard hounds barking in the swamp bottom and in a few moments caught the sound of gunfire.

"Gracious, what is that?" Lucretia asked, looking off in the direction of the shots.

"Hunters," Sister replied. "Ain't no farming now. I 'spect they's just squirrel huntin'."

As they neared the school, Lucretia, excited about seeing the children again, could hardly contain herself. She could visualize their standing under the front porch with wide grins, waving as hard as they could. Eagerly she stretched to see if she could get a glimpse.

But to her dismay, no one was waiting for them. There were two horses tied to the corner post of the porch that belonged to Jerry and Austin Coulter, two of her older boys, but no one else was to be seen. Normally Toby would have roaring fires burning in the fireplaces sending bellows of smoke swirling from the chimney, but only a trickle of smoke could be seen.

Lucretia quickly got out of the buggy and bounded up the steps. Pushing the door open, she found most of her class huddled near the fireplace watching Jerry, the older Coulter boy, trying to start a fire.

"Children, what in the world is going on?"

The children rushed to greet Lucretia, chattering and laughing as they covered her with hugs.

"I'll have it going 'fore long, Mrs. Wilson," Jerry called out.

Easing the children away, Lucretia asked, "Jerry, where is Mister Toby?"

Blowing his breath as hard as he could into the flames, he glanced back at her. "Don't know Mrs. Wilson. We ain't seen him."

"Might have come down with an ailing, Mrs. Wilson," one of the other children added.

He would have sent me word if he was sick, thought Lucretia, knowing how devoted Toby had always been.

Hatta and Sister were now hanging their wraps on the pegs on the back wall.

"Well, are we gonna have school today, Mrs. Wilson?" Sister said, as she began straightening the students desk.

"Looks like Jerry's got the fire going. It'll be warm 'fore long."

"Children, take you seats," Lucretia said, as she motioned the women to the back of the classroom.

She whispered, "Something's not right. I want you two to take charge while I go down and check on Mister Toby."

Sister shook her head. "Like the children said, he's probably sick."

"Then I'll feel better knowing," Lucretia answered. "Won't take me long. I'll borrow Jerry's horse."

Hurrying, Lucretia pushed the mare down the road that bordered the swamp and passed harvested cornfields where several crows scavenging for loose corn flew away screaming their sharp cries.

Nearing Toby's cabin, Lucretia began to feel how ridiculous it was for her to worry. Reining the horse to a stop in front of the house, Lucretia saw no one. Looking out to the barnyard, the two horses normally corralled there, were nowhere to be seen.

"Anybody home?" Lucretia called out.

Slowly the door opened.

"Dat you Miss Wilson?" came a voice from inside.

"Is anything wrong?" Lucretia asked. "We expected you at school."

The door opened wider and Jacob eased out followed by Joshua. The boys began to look about, scanning up and down the road, and whispered to one another. Lucretia had never seen them act like this.

"What's going on here?" she asked. "Where's Toby?"

The boys dropped their heads and said nothing.

With a sinking feeling in her stomach, Lucretia stepped down from the saddle.

From inside the house, a faint voice called out, "You boys get on in the house. Shut dat door."

The boys glanced up at Lucretia, dropped their heads again and began to ease back inside.

All was quiet as Lucretia made her way up the steps. The boys stepped aside and pushed the door open for her. The house containing only two rooms was cold. There were only a few glowing embers under a layer of ashes in the fireplace. The front room had two beds. Three chairs encircled the fireplace. A doorway to the side opened into another bedroom.

Lucretia edged her way through the doorway and into a darkened bedroom. The heavy oak shutters on the windows had been closed tight.

"Sadie, it's me, Lucretia."

"You best leave us be," came a weak voice in the dark.

Lucretia's eyes, becoming accustomed to the darkness, scanned the room. Over to the left, she made out a figure lying on the bed with the covers pulled up over her face. Only a bit of curly black hair showed. Inching up, Lucretia eased up to the foot of the bed and slowly sat down. The bed sagged, causing Sadie to moan.

"Sadie, what's wrong?" Lucretia asked.

Hearing the flooring creak, Lucretia glanced over toward the doorway and saw Jacob and Joshua standing there watching.

"Boys, you tell me what's going on here right now," Lucretia said.

"Don't you say nothin," Sadie muttered.

Lucretia reached over, trying to uncover Sadie's face and said. "I know something is wrong, and I'm not leaving until you tell me what's happened here."

Sadie pushed Lucretia's hand away again.

"You best not know," Sadie sniffled. "I don't want nothin' to happen to ya."

"What do you mean by that?"

"They'll kill you too, Miss Wilson."

"Kill me!" Lucretia said. "Who's going to kill me?"

"Haunts will git ya," Sadie whispered.

"Them weren't no haunts, Mama! Them were the Klan," Joshua said.

"Klan!" Lucretia said, getting up and moving to the other side of the bed.

Kneeling down, she said, "I'm here to help you. For God's sake talk to me, Sadie."

Sadie eased the cover from her face.

"Who did this to you?" Lucretia gasped.

Both of Sadie's eyes were swollen almost shut, and her lips were torn open in several places. A deep gash ran the length of her face. A piece of bloodied cloth lay by her pillow.

Lucretia gently ran her hand across Sadie's forehead and taking a handkerchief from her front coat pocket began to wipe her face.

"Boys, it's cold in here. Put some wood on the fire and heat me some water," Lucretia said.

Then pointing to Jacob, she continued, "You take my horse, go to the school and get my black medical bag from the buggy and don't waste any time."

Grabbing Lucretia's hand, Sadie muttered, "You don't know what ya gittin' mixed up in, Miss Wilson. Best leave us be and go on home."

Lucretia shook her head. "I'm not leaving until you tell me exactly what has happened."

"Mama, you might as well tell 'er," Joshua said. "If'n the Wilsons can't help us, ain't nobody can."

In a short while Joshua brought Lucretia a steaming pot of water. Taking a bath cloth she squeezed it out and began to wipe the crusted blood from Sadie's eyes and face.

"As soon as Jacob gets back I'll attend to your face. It'll be as pretty as ever."

Feeling comforted, Sadie leaned back on her pillow and taking a deep breath said, "A bunch of men come got Andy. They says theys gonna put 'em in jail. They's gonna hang 'em."

"Hang him!" Lucretia exclaimed. "What did he do?"

Speaking so softly Lucretia could hardly hear, she replied, "He kilt a man."

"Killed a man? Who?"

"I think his name was Harmon. Sam Harmon," Sadie replied.

"Why?" Lucretia asked, startled at such a thought.

Sadie reached up to Lucretia. Holding tightly to her, Sadie cried,

"They walked in on me cooking. I thought it was the chillun coming in. They grabbed me and . . . "

Holding her, Lucretia asked, "Who is they?"

Gasping, Sadie replied, "Sam Harmon and his brother." Sadie then screamed out, "Those men hurt me."

"What happened then?"

Taking deep breaths and forcing her words, Sadie replied, "Andy and Papa heard me screamin'. They was comin' from de swamp where they was checking on de hawgs fer killin'. Andy drug one of 'em off me and kilt him with the ax handle and beat the other near death."

"When did this happen?" Lucretia asked, beginning to feel alarmed.

"Four days ago. Right 'fore the big rain come in. I heard the dawgs barking. I knowed it was hunters. Didn't think much 'bout it. Andy drug de man out to de porch, and Papa took a hoss to Decatur to git the sheriff. Andy, he took the other Harmon off somewheres. Papa never came back. Late that afternoon, the sheriff and some men come to the house. They got the dead man off da porch and took Andy with 'em. Don't know where he is now."

"What about the Klan, Sadie?"

"Two nights ago a bunch of haunts rode up to da house. They shot their guns off and hollered out that they was gonna hang Andy and Papa. They says that ain't no Nigguh gonna murder no white man. We hid under the bed and thank God they didn't come in."

29

PENDULUM OF JUSTICE

"Hurry up," John said as he settled himself in his saddle. "No telling what's happened to Andy."

John knew that four days was a long time and that he couldn't remember any incident since the end of the war where a Negro who killed a white man lived. It just didn't happen in Mississippi.

"There's a chance he didn't even make it to the county jail," John mumbled.

"What was that?" James asked, throwing a saddle blanket over the back of his mount.

"Just worried about what could've happened," John replied. "I'm afraid we'll get down to Decatur and nobody will have seen hide nor hair of 'em."

"Well, he'd better be there or somebody will pay dearly," Homer said, leading his horse out of the barn.

"Hold up a minute," Lott said, making his way down the steps. "With all the rain, the creek's gonna be might near over the banks. Y'all best go down south of Union and try to cross there. It'll be a lot safer."

The men took him up on it and rode west for about seven miles and finding the streams passable, crossed easily and then turned south toward Decatur. By late morning, they had reached the outskirts of the little town that served as the county seat. Only a few people were stirring about on this wintery morning. Several stray dogs ran out to meet them as they rode into town but scurried away when James cracked his whip.

On Saturdays the little village was usually alive with people stocking up on provisions for the next week, but today on Monday the town seemed uninhabited. Rough framed buildings lined the square with a two-story courthouse rising from their midst like an old English fortress.

James remembered that here in Decatur, General Sherman was almost captured by the Confederate Calvary. That would have been some kind of loss to the Union, he thought.

John's fear for Andy increased as they approached the courthouse. They quickly tied their horses and made their way around to the back of the building.

As they turned the corner, a soldier standing guard outside of the entrance way called out, "Halt where you are!"

Recognizing James, the private brought up a salute. "Morning, Sir. I almost didn't recognize you out of uniform."

"At ease, Private. We're here to see the sheriff," James replied, returning the salute.

"What can you tell me about a Negro named Andy?" John asked.

"It's been one heck of a week, Sir. They brought 'em in here might near beat to death and then twice mobs tried to get him out of jail. Drunk as skunks they were."

"Is he all right?" Homer asked, his face grim.

The private straightened himself and nodded. "He's alive, but thank God the military was here. It took twenty of us to fend them off."

"What officer is on duty here, Private?" James asked.

Pointing to a large white house beyond the square, the private answered, "Captain Baker, Sir. If you want to talk with him, he's down at the Taylor house where we are camped."

"I know the captain. He'll have the details of what has happened," James said. "John, you and Homer go see the sheriff."

An open hallway ran the length of the lower floor of the building with a set of double doors at each entrance. At the far end, a small shingle hung over the sheriff's office. Knocking, then entering, John and Homer found the sheriff ruffling through a set of papers.

He was a tall, thin man, his face wrinkled by age. He wore a mustache that was waxed and twisted down both sides of his mouth, making his face appear thinner than normal.

He stopped what he was doing, nodded to them and reaching up to rub his hand across the side of his face said, "Thought I'd see you sooner."

Pointing to a couple of chairs, he continued, "Y'all have a seat. Wonder that Nigguh is still alive. We shore got a murderer on our hands."

"I'm John Wilson and this here is my cousin, Homer," John said as he put his hand out.

"I know who you are," the sheriff replied.

Then getting out of his chair, he glanced over to Homer. "Ain't seen you round these parts. I'm Sheriff Rawlins."

Then, frowning, he twisted his shoulders about and tried to pop his neck.

"Been sittin' too long," he explained. "That boy has made my job some kind of rough these last few days. It shore would've been simpler if'n they'd never brought 'em in. He's gonna hang anyhows."

Homer flushed with anger. "What is the charge?"

"Charge!" Rawlins laughed. "Cold blooded murder."

"I've been told a man's innocent until found guilty," John said quietly.

Rawlins eased back into his chair. "We'll go through the formality, I reckon."

Pulling a pipe from his pocket, he carefully filled it with tobacco and muttered, "There's gonna be a trial, Son. Our justice system requires it. We do try to maintain law and order here."

"We'd like to see him, Sheriff," John said. "He used to work for us."

"I know all about him, Mister Wilson. I also know how you folks has taken care of him. The military is guarding him now."

Rawlins took a pen and scribbled a note and handed it to John, "This will get you in to him."

John took the slip and as he and Homer were leaving, the sheriff called out, "They gonna try him next week. Just wasting our time and taxpayer's money. By the way, not hearing from nobody, we got him a lawyer."

Surprised, John asked, "Who'd you get?"

"Norton Moore will do it," he answered.

Homer shook his head. "Nothing like justice, is there."

The county jail was a two-room brick building across the street from the south entrance to the courthouse. It contained a small fireplace in the front room that helped make life easier in the winter for the jailor, but the back room where the inmates were kept had no heat. It had two small windows with heavy bars and no shutters to keep the cold out. In the winter, it was extremely cold, and the summer brought unbearable heat.

Walking across the street, John and Homer found James and several soldiers standing in front of the jail talking.

One of the soldiers unlocked the heavy oak door that was reinforced with strips of iron, and as it squeaked open, they found Andy wrapped in a blanket sitting on the bricked floor with his back resting against the wall. The tiny room contained no beds or chairs, only a pan for inmates to relieve themselves.

Disgusted, Homer exclaimed, "Deplorable. Is this the best you can do?"

Blinded by the light, Andy raised a hand to cover his eyes.

"You all right?" John asked, looking down at his friend.

"Lord A'mighty, is that you Mister John?" Andy stammered, so cold he could hardly talk. Pushing himself up, he tried to stand.

"Keep your seat, Andy," John said, taking his arm as he eased him back down. "We're here to help you. James and Homer are with me," John added, pointing back to the two men just entering.

"They says they gonna hang me," Andy mumbled.

"I wouldn't bet on it," Homer replied, squatting down to get a better look at Andy.

"They hurt you pretty bad," James said, standing over to the side so as not to block the small amount of light that was filtering into the room.

Andy turned his head up and to the side to reveal several deep bruises and cuts on his cheeks and forehead. Then, reaching down to his side, he said, "They beat on me pretty good, Mister John. Kicked me here in d' side. They thought they was gonna kill me, but my Papa stepped in and stopped it."

"Where's Toby now?" Homer asked, reaching down to examine his wounds.

"They says he's down at d' stables. Probably sleeping in d' loft. He's been staying here with d' soldiers most of d' day looking out for me," Andy replied.

"Well, we're gonna get you out of here as soon as we can, and Lord willing you ain't gonna hang. They are feeding you, ain't they?" John asked.

"They feeds me," Andy nodded.

"He won't be getting out of here with his case being heard next week,"

James said, walking toward the entranceway.

"Corporal, get this man a bed and several blankets. This place isn't fit for hogs. And leave that door open so some heat can come in here. He's not going anywhere."

"Yes Sir," the corporal replied.

"And bring him a chair. He's no animal."

"Yes Sir. Right away, Sir."

Feeling better knowing that Andy was being protected, the men went to find Toby. As they walked to the stable on the outskirts of town, John glanced over to James. "What do you know about the court proceedings?"

"Well, you probably know the prosecuting attorney is Amos Kelly. He's not bad. Tried a lot of cases here and about. He's noted as a fair country lawyer. They assigned Andy a man named Moore."

"We heard about that!" John said. "Norton Moore, ain't it?"

"That's the man," James replied, quickening his step.

"That man's an imbecile. You know why he's a fulltime farmer? He can't make a living lawyering, that's why," John said, disgusted.

"Looks like we got our work cut out for us if we're going to save that boy from the hangman," Homer said, picking up his pace.

"Let's go check on Toby and then we need to get our heads together. There's got to be a way to save him," Homer said.

When the men reached the stables, they found Toby in the back helping the owner of the livery stable shoe a horse. He told them that he had not been sleeping in the barn as thought but was being housed and fed by the military. For some reason, Captain Baker had taken a liking to him. Seeing he was good with horses, and with his top hand out sick, Alex Tanner, the owner, was paying Toby to help out in the stables.

As the sun was setting, the men returned home. Lucretia and Sister rushed out to meet them as they were dismounting. Hearing that Andy was all right gave them all, especially Sadie, a sense of relief. The women then went to the kitchen to prepare a meal while the men warmed themselves by the open fireplace.

It had been a long day for the riders, and they needed the warmth of the fire and the solace of the evening. Trickles of smoke rose from the pipes of James and Lott, making its way to the ceiling where it hovered.

Clearing his voice as he pushed out a funnel of smoke, Lott said,

"Well, what did you boys find out?"

All was quiet as each man expected the other to respond. Finally, John replied, "Andy appears to be all right. They charged him with murder."

"Murder," Lott grunted. "What kind of murder?"

"What do you mean by that? Murder is murder," John replied.

"No it ain't," Lott said. "There's different kinds. There's first degree murder, manslaughter, and self defense manslaughter."

John shook his head. "I'm not sure I understand."

Homer eased out of his chair and reached down to place a couple of hickory logs on the dying fire and said, "They'll go for first degree murder. They plan to hang him. There's been so much insolence from some of the Negroes down in the south end of the county toward the whites, they'll make an example of him."

Lott nodded in agreement. "You're probably right, Homer, but things could go differently."

"What's on your mind," James asked, raising an eyebrow.

"Well, I been sitting here thinking. First thing, there's gonna be a military presence down there that ain't gonna allow no farce of court affairs, and the second thing is that the prosecuting attorney is gonna think this here is a cut and dried case. They won't spend much time preparing. I think the scales could do a little tipping."

With a hint of a smile crossing his lips, James said, "I just remembered, the captain told me they were bringing in Judge Hacker."

"What does that mean?" John asked, shifting in his chair.

"He's not a Southerner," James replied. "He was a major in the United States Army until he retired last month. Having a lawyer's background before the war, they kind of gave him another assignment, temporary, that is. Happened about two weeks ago."

"That may be true, James, but what about Andy's lawyer? You know his reputation," John said.

The men thought for a moment, then Lott muttered, "I think we need to pay the honorable Norton Moore a visit. I've heard tell a lawyer can have an assistant to help him with a case. Maybe a better word would be apprentice. That's how you get to become a lawyer anyhows, ain't it?"

Frowning, John replied, "Are you saying what I think you are, Papa?"

Lott reached over and placed his arm on John's shoulder. "I see three men here who are as smart as any men 'round about. Heck, James here is a West Point graduate. What I'm saying is one of you boys is on the way to lawyering. You know, there's an old saying, if'n there's a will, there's a way. I think if we put our heads together and fatten Mister Moore's pocketbook, there are possibilities. Otherwise, Mister Andy is gonna swing."

After dinner, Lucretia and Sister finished clearing the dining table and left Hatta in the kitchen planning the morning meal. Lucretia eased up behind John and placing her arms around his shoulders said, "Couldn't help but hear you men talking. Sounds like you got work to do. But, tell me one thing? What are the Harmon's like?"

Lott shook his head. "I guess you could say they're kinda neighbors. They live about three miles down the creek. Barely never hunt up this far though."

Feeling the chill of the night, Sister backed up to the fire to warm herself.

"No Papa, that's not what she means. Cretia wants to know what kind of folks they are?" she said.

"Well, I'd say, there ain't much to 'em. Their farming barely keeps 'em fed, and I ain't ever heard of 'em helping nobody in need. I guess the best thing I could say is I've heard tell they make pretty good shine," Lott answered.

Seeing that it was late, James motioned to Sister, "Time to get on home. You all will have to excuse us."

As he was getting up, Lott reached over and shook James's hand. "If you're not busy, you need to come on back in the morning. We've still got a lot of planning to do."

"Do you know everything that happened in Andy's house?" Lucretia asked.

"All we know is what happened to Sadie and that Andy killed the man," John replied.

"I think you need to talk to both of them before the trial. There's a lot more to it than that," Lucretia insisted.

James helped Sister with her wrap and as they were leaving he turned to the group and said, "I think Cretia's right, and by the way, thinking over what Sadie said about the Klan threatening her, we shouldn't bring that up in court."

"I don't understand," John replied.

"Well, let me put it like this. Being in the military, I have orders. I know things that I can't discuss with anyone except with my superiors. You'll just have to trust me."

News of a murder trial involving a Negro killing a white quickly spread through Newton and the adjoining counties during the next three weeks. People flocked in by the hundreds for the trial, flooding the village with wagons, buggies and horses. Women carrying baskets of food indicated that they intended to see it through. The chatter of people talking, laughing and shaking hands resembled a large family reunion.

Pulling up to the town square, Lucretia was amazed at the crowd of people meandering about and the joyous time they seemed to be having at Andy's expense. "A man's life is at stake here. Why are they acting like this?" she said, looking over at John.

"I don't know. Perhaps it's a novelty to some of 'em. They ain't ever seen nothing like this, and you know, being winter, there ain't much farming to do. Some of 'em are here just to have something to do," John replied.

After a moment, he sighed, "And I guess some of 'em don't like the idea of a Negro killing a white man."

Working their way through the crowd, John and his family finally arrived at the Army headquarters where they left their wagon. They hurried to the courthouse and as they approached, John glanced over to James and Homer.

"Sure hope I can do this," John said, taking a nervous breath.

"You can do it, and maybe we'll have a few surprises for them," James replied. "As a Federal officer, the jury won't give me the time of day and as far as Homer goes, he's an outsider. You are the only one they might listen to."

Reaching the entrance, James stepped forward to address a soldier posted at the door. After a few moments, James beckoned to the family, "It's already about full but there are a few spaces reserved."

James and Homer found seats near the back of the room while Lucretia and Lott took seats near the front. Sister had volunteered to stay home with Sadie and her boys. Mister Moore, seated behind a table in front of the judge's bench, recognized John and waved to him.

As John took his seat, a door opened and twelve men began to file in to the juror's box. At the same time, Andy, escorted by two soldiers, entered through a door to the left and made their way to where John and Moore were seated. Barefooted and with chains securing his ankles and wrists, Andy painfully shuffled across the floor. As soon as they all were seated, the sheriff came forward.

"Hear ye, hear ye, the court of Newton County is now in session. Please rise for the Honorable Robert Hacker," he announced loudly.

A large man weighing well over two hundred pounds and wearing a black robe walked in from the doorway where the jurors had just entered. He had practically no hair and his head glistened as the light reflected across it. A set of glasses hung from the tip of his nose.

"Be seated," he said sternly.

For a moment he studied some papers he had brought in with him, then he looked up at the eagerly awaiting crowd.

"Everyone in Newton County must be here," he grunted.

Then he issued a warning, "This is not some kind of a side show. If any of you get out of line, the soldiers in the back will remove you."

Peering down he said, "Mister Prosecutor, are you prepared to present your charge?"

"I am, your Honor," Mister Kelly replied with confidence.

"What about you, Mister Moore. Is the defense ready?"

Moore cleared his voice, "Your Honor, I've been a little sick lately."

He then lifted his hand and pointed over to John, "This man is John Wilson. He's my understudy. He's gonna have to do most of the talking for me, if you don't mind."

Paul Harmon, sitting in the row behind Kelly, leaned forward and whispered to the prosecuting attorney, "What in the hell is on their minds? That Nigguh used to work for the Wilsons."

Kelly snickered, "This thing will be over in less than an hour. Let's have some fun with 'em."

Judge Hacker frowned and pushed his glasses up. "Wilson's your apprentice?"

"Yes, Your Honor."

"Mister Prosecutor, do you object?" the judge asked.

Kelly shook his head. "Your Honor, I have no objection."

Judge Hacker frowned. "Well Sir, I would like to hear the charges, Mister Prosecutor."

Kelly, well groomed and dressed in a dark gray suit, stood up. His hair was neatly cut and he wore a short cropped beard. Known to catch the eye of the ladies, he turned and smiled to a couple of the women behind him, then turned to the Judge.

"Your Honor, this is a simple case of cold-blooded murder. Andy Wilson has admitted to killing Sam Harmon with an ax handle. He didn't have to kill him. He did it in a fit of anger. Down right inexcusable."

"Tell it like it is," hollowed a man in the rear of the building along with other words of support from within the crowd.

Judge Hacker slammed his mallet down on his desk.

"Private," he said, looking back to a soldier posted behind the last row of seats. "See that man back there with the red and black plaid coat. Remove him immediately and if he tries to come back in here, arrest him."

A murmur went over the crowd as the soldier escorted the man out of the courtroom.

When things had settled down, the Judge peered down at the defense team. Hacker's stern look bore down on John, causing sweat to form on his brow as he tried to anticipate what would come next.

"Mister Wilson, you've heard the charge. What can you say in defense of your client?"

Nervously, John rose. His mouth was so dry he reached down and took a sip of water from a glass near his seat. Turning, he looked over at Lucretia. She smiled back to him and gave a slight wink.

Taking a deep breath, he stepped forward. "Your Honor, members of the jury, I've known Andy for most of my life. I don't see this man as a murderer. I see him as a man who tried to protect his wife, family and his own dignity. We plan to prove to you that he is innocent of murder."

As he talked, everyone hung on each word. His deep sincere voice resounded around the room, demanding their attention. Sensing he was in control of the moment, John gained confidence.

Andy, sitting on the edge of his chair nodded his approval as John began his defense.

John looked over to Kelly and continued, "What is murder, anyway?"

Turning to the jury, he said, "Every one of you is thinking, sure I know what murder is, but do you?"

John paused a moment. "I'll tell you what it is. Murder is the malicious or premeditated killing of one human being by another." John paused to let the jury take in the meaning of his definition.

"Did my client plan the killing of Sam Harmon? We'll prove that he did not plan such an act. He did not know the Harmons were going to enter his house and rape his wife."

"I object!" Kelly shouted, rising from his seat. "Nobody has been charged with rape."

Judge Hacker cleared his voice. "Sustained. Jury, disregard Mister Wilson's last statement."

"I'm sorry, Your Honor," John replied. Walking over to the jury, John continued, "Murder is a terrible thing. In the Ten Commandments given to Moses in the Bible, the Lord says thou shalt not kill, but later in Deuteronomy the Lord tells Moses when the taking of life is permissible. Any of you men question that?"

"I object to that. Our law system does not go along with the Bible," Kelly said.

Judge Hacker replied, "Overruled. Continue, Mister Wilson."

"Thank you, Your Honor."

Returning to the jury, John continued, "Men of the jury, our law system evolved from the Common Law of England and the words of the Bible have been the influencing foundation from its very creation. There are times when the killing of another human being is justified."

Enjoying the challenge of an incompetent amateur and the attention he was receiving, Kelly countered each statement John made. He knew he could terminate the debate at any time he desired, but why waste such fun. Time passed. For hours they debated.

Right before noon, Homer and James eased from their seats and left the building quietly. John glanced back and nodded to them as they left.

Tiring, Judge Hacker called for an hour recess for lunch and ordered everyone back by one o'clock.

Back in the courtroom and taking the floor once again, John walked over to the juror's box and placing his hand on the railing that bordered the seating area said, "If murder was simply the taking of another person's life, then some of you here in the jury would be murderers."

Surprised, one of the jurors mumbled, "Ain't no murderers among us."

Judge Hacker pounded his gavel. "Men of the jury, you're not suppose to respond to such statements. You're here to listen, and as for you, Mister Wilson, you best know where you're going with this kind of talk."

Kelly shook his head, smiled to himself and thought, give this fool enough rope and he'll hang himself.

John cleared his throat. "How many of you fought for the Confederacy? Don't answer," he warned the jurors.

His eyes moved from one juror to the next. "Out of the twelve, I know that ten of you served, and I would be willing to bet some of you killed some poor Federal soldier. Are you then a murderer? I think not."

Several of the jurors dropped their heads knowing full well what John was talking about.

"In fact, Mister Kelly, the prosecutor, served with the thirty-sixth Mississippi. Talk is he killed quite a few from that trench at Vicksburg," John said, looking over to where Kelly was sitting.

Knowing that taking of lives is acceptable and legal in the time of war, Kelly swelled with pride at the recognition he felt he was receiving.

"But what about the time when the Yankees tried to blow up a portion of our line. When the smoke cleared, the Union soldiers stormed up the sides of the crater into a hail of gunfire and a massive slaughter took place. Knowing it was hopeless, several Union soldiers raised their musket butts to surrender, only to be shot down. In fact, one of them begged for mercy but was shot in the face with a load of buck and ball. Ain't that right, Mister Kelly. Wouldn't you call that murder?"

"I object to that, Mister Wilson."

Judge Hacker frowned. "Mister Wilson, you better be careful."

John dropped his head in thought and then continued, "Word around here is that Mister Kelly bragged to more than one person about shooting the soldier in the face."

"That's a damned lie!" Kelly shouted, furious over the accusation.

Calmly, John walked over and looked out at the crowd, pointing to a man sitting on the fourth row. "Mister N. F. Smith, or as most of you know him, Doc Smith served with the thirty-sixth. He was three men down from

Mister Kelly when the man was shot. He saw the whole thing. All you have to do is ask him."

Smith nodded his head and the courtroom was silent. John walked back to the jurors.

"What I'm saying is, there is a slim line between taking a man's life and murder and even in the fury of battle, there is still that difference. Jurors, you must agree with me that no matter how slim, there is a definite difference in taking a man's life and murder."

With his point made, John sat down.

Judge Hacker, noting the late hour, struck his gavel, "Court is adjourned for the day. We'll resume promptly at nine in the morning. I want to see Mister Wilson, Moore and Kelly in my chambers immediately."

When the men had gathered, Judge Hacker removed his robe and lighting his pipe said,

"I don't know what in the world you men are up to, but I allowed you to have your say today. Tomorrow, I don't want to hear any more definitions and discussion about what murder is. I, at this point along with the jurors, don't know a damned thing about the particulars of the killing. Come morning, you men will discuss this case and come sundown it had better be closed."

John left the courthouse exhausted but was satisfied that he had accomplished what he had intended. He had held the court at bay until he could talk with Homer and James.

Meanwhile, Kelly realized that he had not had control of the courtroom today, but he still was confident. And he was angry at being classified as a murderer and knew he better complete this case fast before the jury turned against him.

John, Lott, Homer and James talked deep into the night because they knew that come sundown the next day, Andy's fate would be determined.

The morning sun glistened through the dirt-smudged windows as once again people crowded into the courtroom. The court was called to order and after he had taken his seat, Judge Hacker said, "Mister Kelly, are you ready to proceed?"

"Yes, Your Honor. I'd like to call Mister Paul Harmon to the stand."

After Harmon had been sworn in and had taken his seat, Kelly said, "Mister Harmon, I want you to answer a simple question. Did you see Andy Wilson over there kill your brother?"

"I was there."

Then pointing to Andy, Harmon growled, "I saw that son of a bitch kill my brother!"

A mumble spread over the courtroom as people whispered to each other.

"Mister Harmon, there won't be any more of that kind of language in my courtroom. Mister Kelly, you had better control the behavior of your client," Judge Hacker warned, angered by the outburst.

"Yes Sir, Your Honor," Kelly replied. "Uhhh, Mister Harmon, I want you to tell us what transpired on the day your brother was murdered."

"I object, Your Honor. Murder has not been proven," John said.

"Sustained. Jurors disregard the statement about murder."

"Let me restate. Mister Harmon, tell us what happened to your brother?"

Harmon twisted in his seat for a moment, then said, "We were out doing some squirrel huntin' up the swamp bottom. Bout midday we come up on the cabin and was gittin' hungry. Got to smelling some fatback cooking and decided to see if'n we could git us a meal, and it did smell some kind of good. Well, we went on in and shore 'nough dinner was on the way. The nigguh woman welcomed us to the table and shore fed us good. After we got through eating, one thing led to another and 'fore you knowed it, we ended up in the bed."

"You say she was hospitable to you?" Kelly probed.

"Yeah, I'd say that," Harmon said, smiling.

"Then what happened?"

"Well, we was a having a good ole time 'till her old man come in on us. Seeing she was caught in the act, the wench got to screaming and fighting like hell. Then that nigguh over there swung an ax handle, knocking me senseless. When I come to I was at Doctor McLauren's office in Little Rock. They told me that my brother was dead. They said that Andy Wilson had killed him."

"Thank you," Kelly said, eyeing the jurors.

"Mister Wilson, would you like to cross examine the witness," Judge Hacker said.

"Yes, Your Honor," replied John rising from his seat.

"Mister Harmon, I understand you and your brother make some of the best corn liquor here abouts. Is that true?"

"I object to that, Your Honor," Kelly said. "That's got nothing to do with this case."

"Mister Wilson, I hope Mister Moore there is directing you because if you don't relate that statement to this case, your apprenticeship is going to be a short one," the Judge said sternly.

"Overruled. You may continue. Answer the question, Mister Harmon."

A big smile crossed Harmon's face revealing the absence of several front teeth. "Well, folks say our spirits are fitting. I guess you could say we do pretty good."

Edging up closer to Harmon, John continued, "Do you drink the liquor you make?"

An even bigger smile came across his face. "Damn right I drink it."

Then realizing what he had said, he turned to the judge. "Sorry Your Honor, but I do like to drink it. Like they say, it is some kind of good."

Laughter erupted in the courtroom.

Raising his eyebrows, Judge Hacker stared out into the crowd and everyone quieted down.

"Mister Harmon, on the day of the killing, were you drinking?"

Almost snickering, Harmon replied, "Shore we was a drinking. You show me a hunter who don't carry a bottle and I'll show you one that don't ever leave the house."

"Were you and your brother drunk on the day he was killed?"

"Drunk, nay, we weren't drunk. We had a bag full of them damned squirrels. We could still shoot straight."

John turned to the jurors. "Harmon and his brother came by Moore's Mill outside of Little Rock about mid-morning, and Gab Luther who runs the place said they were barely able to walk. Tried to start a fight with him. He'll testify to what I've said."

John paused for a moment. "Your Honor, I'm through for the present but I might want to recall Mister Harmon later today."

Then thinking back, he frowned at Harmon. "Didn't you just say Andy here knocked you senseless and when you came to, you were informed that your brother had been killed?"

"That's about it," Harmon said with a smile.

"Then what you're saying is that you actually didn't see Andy kill your brother," John asked, looking toward the jurors.

"That's all, Your Honor."

"Mister Harmon you may take your seat and we'll take a fifteen minute break," Judge Hacker said.

As soon as the Judge issued his statement, a stranger quietly made his way up to Kelly and whispered, "You need to send this case to the jury. Folks, including the jurors, are beginning to listen to that young man."

John taking his seat, looked over to Moore. "How are we doing so far?"

Moore looked down at the pad where he had been scribbling and answered, "I don't know. I ain't ever defended no one for murder and never witnessed a court case involving it, but we're still here and I'd say you're doing fine."

As soon as the court was back in session, Kelly rose. "Your Honor, at this time, I'm prepared to make my closing statement."

Surprised, Judge Hacker frowned down at Kelly and then looked over to John. "Mister Wilson?"

John shook his head. "Your Honor, we've only heard one witness's account of what happened, and it is a fact that the two Harmons were drinking on that day. I question the truth of Harmon's story. Your Honor, I do have other witnesses."

Kelly nervously rubbed his hand across his beard and glanced back to the man behind him.

"Then I suggest you call your next witness," the Judge directed.

"Your Honor, I call Sadie Wilson to the stand."

The door in the back opened and Sadie and Hatta entered. Sadie wore a plain but well-pressed gray, cotton dress with a high collar, her head covered with a bandana that was neatly tied in the back in the fashion that most Negroes wore. Hatta, standing tall and erect, was dressed in black, her long hair rolled in a bun at the back of her head. Even at her age, she was a very attractive woman.

As they slowly came down the aisle, people mumbled to themselves. It was a strange sight to see a Negro and a Choctaw woman together.

As they approached the bench, Lott motioned for Hatta to come sit with him as John took Sadie by the hand and walked with her to the chair where she would testify.

Trembling, Sadie took her seat, and looking up to John, whispered, "You ain't gonna leave me, is you?"

"I'm right here with you," he replied.

The sheriff came up holding a Bible and extending it to her said, "Do you swear to tell the truth, the whole truth and nothing but the truth, so help you God."

"Yes Suh, I does," Sadie answered in a soft voice.

"Then state your full name?"

"I's Sadie Wilson."

The Judge frowned again. "There appears to be a lot of Wilsons around here. Mister Wilson would you like to shed some light on this?"

"Your Honor, after the war, the slaves, that is the Negroes, had a problem with their last names. During slavery, they took their master's last name but when they were freed, they could choose any last name they wanted. Some of 'em kept their old names but others changed theirs. Sadie took the name Wilson."

"Was she one of your slaves?" the Judge asked.

"No, Your Honor. We didn't believe in holding slaves."

"That's not quite the truth, Your Honor," Kelly said. "They bought this woman's father-in-law off the blocks in Meridian."

"Any truth to that, Mister Wilson?" the Judge asked.

"Your Honor, there was a Negro man named Toby who worked for the Ollivers when I was a boy. Every time we went to the swamp fishing, hunting, and camping, he was sent to take care of us young uns. I guess you'd say he looked after us. Well, when I heard the Ollivers were gonna sell him, I couldn't bear it. I took what money I'd saved to go to college and I went to Meridian to buy him. With what I had and some help from my father, we bought him off the block. When we got home, we wrote him a letter of release. We freed him. It was his choice to stay with us. After the war, his two boys and Sadie joined him."

After a moment of silence, Judge Hacker said, "You may proceed."

Stepping up to Sadie, John began, "Sadie, on the day of the killing, tell the jurors what happened?"

Breathing heavily, she said, "I was in the kitchen cooking when I heard someone come in the house. I figured it was the boys, so I didn't pay no attention. When I turned about I seen two white men looking at me."

With hands quivering, she dropped her head and began to cry.

John handed her his handkerchief and softly said, "It's gonna be fine. Just tell the truth."

"The men ate what viddles I'd cooked up and when they got through, they took a bottle out and got to drinking. They got to lookin' at me kinda funny. I know'd I'd better git out of the house. When I tried to run out d' back, that 'un over there grabbed me and drug me to d' bed."

With her voice breaking, she muttered, "I fought 'em, but they beat me."

"Sadie, hold your head up so the jurors can see what they did," John said.

The courtroom grew deathly quiet as they looked at her battered face. Even after nearly a month, the bruises and cuts were still evident.

"I object, Your Honor. Her old man could have beat her after he walked in on 'em," Kelly said.

"Overruled, Mister Kelly. You will get your chance. Proceed."

"What then, Sadie?" John asked.

"I hated what them two was doing to me. Andy come in. The man on me turned and looked at 'em. That one over there run to the back of the room for some reason. I was so ashamed I covered my face. There was a lot of shouting and racket going on. When I looked up the one on me was on d' flow covered in blood and they was dragging the other one out of d' house."

John patted Sadie on the hand. "Did you see your husband kill Sam Harmon?"

"No Suh, I didn't see it, but I'm glad he's dead. Them men hurt me bad."

"Thank you, Sadie. Mister Kelly."

Kelly straightened his coat as he got up, and as he approached Sadie, an uneasiness came over him. It was apparent to him that John was not an illiterate bumpkin.

At the same time he felt assured. There was no white jury in the South that would rule in favor of a Negro over a white. Facing Sadie, he turned to the jurors as he asked the first question.

"Sadie, what is Andy Wilson to you?"

"He's my husband," she muttered in reply.

"You two married?"

"I object, Your Honor. It has nothing to do with case," John said.

"Overruled," replied Judge Hacker.

"I'll ask you again. Are you married?"

Sadie looked over to John, not knowing what to say. John nodded for her to answer.

"I guess we is. We lives together," she said.

Kelly smiled at the jurors. "I thought you was married to his brother, Caleb. Now you say you live with Andy. Seems like you've had a lot of men in your life. Sounds like you like the men folks."

Once again Sadie looked to John and then over to where Lucretia and Hatta were sitting. Catching her eye, Lucretia eased a Bible from underneath her wrap and held it where Sadie could see it.

Seeing the book, an assuring strength filled her. "Mister Kelly, us colored folk don't git married like the white folks do. Caleb asked the master if'n we could marry and he told 'em we could do so. Then we jumped the broom together. That's how we marry," she said.

"I think we all know about the broom jumping," Kelly said. "What about you taking up with Andy?"

Sadie thought for a moment. "In the Bible, when something happens to yore husband and he gits kilt like mine was, it is the job of the younger brother to take her in. That's what they did. I didn't have nowheres to go. I guess you could say they kept me in the family."

Pleased by the response, John smiled at her.

"Well tell me this? We all know how the Nigguhs sleep around. How many men have you known?" Kelly asked.

"I object, Your Honor!" John said.

"Overruled. Mister Kelly, you are trying my patience. Proceed in caution," the Judge said.

Sadie dropped her head and muttered, "I don't want to answer that."

"You have no choice," Kelly replied. "How many men have you been with?"

John motioned for her to answer.

Barely audible, she murmured, "Only one 'sides Caleb and Andy."

"Only three!" Kelly said, laughing. "Three in all! Pray tell who the other might be?"

"When I was about thirteen. I was down at the barn looking at a new batch of kittens when he come up behind me and grabbed me. I didn't want no part of it, but he forced himself on me. Didn't have no choice," she mumbled.

"No choice," Kelly asked. "Who was the man?"

Sadie raised her head and in a loud voice replied, "It was Master Frank."

"Frank who?" Kelly asked, not clearly understanding her.

"It was young Frank Olliver."

A wave of whispering spread across the courtroom as Sadie continued, " And the only other times were when those men, the Harmons, attacked me."

Kelly, taken by surprise, stood speechless. Olliver, their state representative, was known to spend time with the ladies, but this was not expected. Kelly's mind went blank.

After a moment of no response, Judge Hacker said, "Mister Kelly."

Kelly looked up at him with a blank expression on his face. "That's all, Your Honor."

John then stood. "Your Honor, I'd like to ask Sadie a couple more questions."

Walking over to her, he said, "Did you let Mister Harmon have you?"

"No Suh, I didn't. I fought 'em as hard as I could."

"Sadie, if'n you don't mind, will you ease your collar down and face the jurors."

Several of the juror's mouths sprung open as they stared at her while others shook their heads. A crusty scab ran the width of her lower neck.

After a moment, John said, "Thank you, Sadie."

Then he continued, "What caused that?"

Sadie looked over to Harmon. "That man over there held a knife to me. Said he was tired of fighting me. Ever' time I moved, the blade cut me."

Once again, a murmur filled the room.

John walked over to the jurors. "Gentlemen, when you look at this beaten woman with a slash across her neck, I think that none of you can say she consented. Those two men raped her. That's all, Your Honor."

Judge Hacker looked over to the prosecutor. "Mister Kelly."

"I have no more questions," he said, dropping his head.

John then whispered to Moore and Andy for a few moments before rising from his seat. "Your Honor, I'd like to call Andy Wilson to the stand," he said.

A concerned look crossed Judge Hacker's face. "Mister Wilson, will you approach the bench."

The Judge said, "I'm not convinced that you and Moore know exactly what you are doing. Under the fifth amendment, the Negro does not have to testify against himself. It could prove costly to him."

Speaking softly, John replied, "Sir, I know, but we feel it will prove beneficial."

"I hope you realize that man's life is in your hands. Proceed then."

After Andy had been sworn in, John wasted no time. "Andy, I want you to tell the court exactly what happened on the day of the trouble."

Andy cleared his throat and taking a deep breath began. "Pa and me was coming to the house when we heard Sadie hollering. Skairt me to death. I know'd somp'n was wrong so I picked up an ax handle and run into the house. I saw a man on my wife and I swung my stick and knocked 'em off of her."

Then pointing to Harmon, he stammered, "That other man, that 'un over there, turned and went fer a shotgun that was leaning against the wall. I knocked 'em to d' floor 'fore he could git it. When I looked back to Sadie, the other'n was coming at me with a knife. I hit 'em as hard as I could."

John looked to the jurors. "Andy, why'd you hit them men?"

Andy thought for a moment, then replied, "When I seen what d' man was doing, I knew I had to git 'em off of her. I was afraid they was gonna kill her and when they were not on her no more they was tryin' to kill me. I didn't have no choice. I was just trying to keep them off Sadie and make them leave us alone."

"Andy, was you sorry the man died?"

"Mister John, what they was doing to my woman was wrong. I love my Sadie. But killing don't solve nothin'. I just was tryin' to keep my family safe."

"Thank you. Mister Prosecutor, your witness."

Kelly smiled, knowing now he could get his verdict. Placing his hand on the railing in front of Andy, he stared into his face. "Answer me this. Did you kill Sam Harmon?"

"Yes Suh, but . . . ."

"Just answer the question, yes or no. Did you kill Sam Harmon?"

Andy frowned at Kelly, then answered, "Yes Suh. I guess I did."

"Didn't you take the law in your own hands."

Confused, Andy replied, "I don't know hows to answer that."

"Well let me ask you this. Couldn't you just have beat' em up and let it be at that?" Kelly asked. "But you didn't," he continued, shaking his head in disgust. "You killed one man and almost killed the other'n as well. That's all, Your Honor. I rest my case."

After a brief recess, Judge Hacker directed Kelly to make his closing statement. Kelly confidently approached the jurors and scanning them from left to right said, "This won't take long. The Negro over there admitted to killing Sam Harmon. He could've chosen another alternative, but he didn't. I say it was murder."

Kelly continued, "He hit that poor man so hard he crushed his skull."

Then pointing to a woman seated with several children, he said, "You see that woman back there with them chillun. They ain't got a soul to take care of 'em now. Members of the jury, I ask that you find Andy Wilson guilty of cold blooded murder and I pray to God he hangs."

"Amen!" several men shouted.

At that and without being told, soldiers in the back rushed to quickly remove the unruly from the courtroom.

Judge Hacker slammed his gravel to his bench and exclaimed, "The next one of you that says a word out there will be jailed and that's a fact!"

He then looked over to where John was waiting. "Mister Wilson, Mister Moore, you may close."

Andy, face dripping with perspiration, placed his hand on John's. "May God be with you, Mister John."

John patted his hand, looked back to Lucretia and rose to face the jurors.

"Gentlemen, you all know that a man's life is at stake. Andy, over there, has been accused of murder, but I say he reacted like any of us would."

Looking into their faces, John saw no sympathy, only bitterness. Then moving from one man to the next, he continued, "I want each one of you to forget that man over there and put yourself in his shoes. Let's say you come home and find two Negro men raping your wife. One of 'em holding a knife across her neck while the other'n is doing it."

John paused for a moment as he noticed the expressions on their faces change. Then he walked over and faced one of the jurors and raising his voice said, "Hearing the screaming, your children rush in to see what is happening to their mother. The poor little things witness their mother's rape and in fear, run for their lives. What would you do to those Negroes."

Without thinking, one juror shouted, "I'd kill them."

Another man in the second row instantly added, "I'd cut his throat. That's what I'd do!"

"Members of the jury, silence! Mister Wilson, watch your questions," the judge barked.

"Your Honor, please excuse me. I intended it as a statement, not a question," John answered.

Turning back to the jurors, John continued, "When Andy came in the house and saw what was happening, he did what any man would do, he tried to protect his wife. He struck Paul Harmon when he was reaching for his shotgun, and he hit Sam when he came at him with a knife. If Andy had not fought with 'em, they would have killed him. Gentlemen, in this state that is called self-defense."

"After it was over, Andy put Paul in his wagon and carried him down to Little Rock where Doc McLauren could doctor on 'em, and Toby went to Decatur to get the sheriff. Andy and Toby could've killed both of them and hid their bodies in the swamp, but instead they did what was right. Their actions are certainly not those of a murderer, but are indeed the actions that each of you would take in a similar situation."

"Gentlemen when you retire, I ask you once more to put yourself in Andy's place. What would you have done? You'd do just what Andy did. You'd fight for your wife and you'd fight for your life. I ask you men to search your hearts, pray to God for justice, and do not do what is expected of you, but what you know in your heart is the right and just verdict and that is that Andy Wilson may have killed a man in self-defense of both his wife and his family, but that he is innocent of murder."

Judge Hacker then shrugged his aching shoulders and said, "Members of the jury, as you retire I want you to know a man's life is at stake. Consider all you have heard and may justice be served. It is now four o'clock. At no time will you talk to any outsiders, and if it becomes necessary for you to retire for the night, the military will find accommodations. As far as you people here in the courtroom, you may stay or leave, but strict order will be maintained."

Andy was then taken back to jail as most of the people left to find something to eat and to stretch themselves. John invited Mister Moore to have supper with his family who had prepared a meal earlier.

Grouped together in the corner of the courtroom, John asked, "How'd we do Papa?"

"Son, you did fine," Lott answered.

"Won't make no difference though. They'll convict him anyhow," Moore said, in between bites.

"Not so sure," Homer said. "I saw something in their faces there at the end."

John, placing his arm around Lucretia's shoulder, glanced over to James and Homer. "I appreciate y'all slipping out of here and getting me some information about them jurors. It don't hurt to know something about their nature."

Two hours ticked away. Just when everyone felt that the jurors would probably not reach a verdict that evening, the door opened and they began to file back into the room.

Hearing that the jury had returned, people chaotically rushed back in. Taking his seat, Judge Hacker said," Gentlemen, have you reached a verdict?"

"Yes, Your Honor."

The sheriff took a slip of paper from the foreman of the jury and handed it to the Judge. Judge Hacker studied it for a moment and then handed it back to the sheriff.

"How do you find Andy Wilson?"

The foreman stood, took a breath, paused and replied, "We find Andy Wilson innocent of murder."

A silence came over the courtroom and then everyone in the room began to applaud.

Paul Harmon stood up and screamed, "What's wrong with you fools! They just let that killing Nigguh free!"

A few others joined in the protest, but soldiers rushed down and took charge of the disgruntled men before any violence erupted.

As Harmon was taken from the courtroom, he turned and pointed to Andy, "Boy, you gonna be one dead Nigguh! You just wait and see! You Wilsons gonna git it too!"

Infuriated by his outburst, Judge Hacker stood up and pointed to a nearby soldier. "Arrest that man right now. Get him out of my sight."

"Elated, John and his family flocked down to Andy as his chains were removed. Then over the noise of the crowd, John heard Judge Hacker call his name.

Hacker motioned John to his quarters. Closing the door, he offered John a seat.

For a moment, he sat there frowning at John and finally shaking his head said, "Young man, I ran a pretty loose court these past two days as far as procedure goes, but I did it for the sake of justice. It also became apparent that you and that lawyer Moore don't know a tinker's damn about defending someone, and Kelly's not far ahead of you two."

Embarrassed, John dropped his head.

"Get that head up, Son," the Judge said. "Knowledge or not, you did the damnest thing I've ever seen. You saved a Negro's life while taking on a white Mississippi jury. I'd like to commend you. What do you do for a living?"

John smiled. "I'm a farmer, Your Honor."

As John was leaving, he turned to the judge. "Your Honor, shouldn't Harmon be charged with rape."

The judge cleared his throat. "Mister Wilson, you just saved that man's life, and since this is still Mississippi, I suggest you leave well enough alone. One more thing, Mister Wilson. This state could use some good lawyers. You just might want to consider that."

John found the courtroom almost empty. Lott and Lucretia waved to him from the back of the room. As John was making his way up the aisle, a slender but dignified man sitting there alone rose and approached him.

Reaching out his hand, he said, "I'm Patrick Everett from Meridian. I've just established a law office there. Like most folks, this case interested me. What do you know about law?" he asked.

John shook his head. "Really, not much. We farm and raise horses."

At that moment, Lott and Lucretia joined them. John introduced them to Mister Everett.

"I'll tell you something, Mister Wilson. At first I didn't give you much thought, but as the trial progressed, you captured my attention. As a trial lawyer, I also know the judge gave you a lot of leeway. I also know, you don't know much about trying a case. Putting that Negro on the stand could have been devastating."

"You're absolutely right," John replied. "I just hoped that Andy's true intent would come through more than his color."

"I understand, Mister Wilson, but what I'm trying to say to you is that you have no business farming. Young man, you need to be in the courtroom. You know, you've got a lot of potential. I'm not sure any lawyer in Mississippi, including myself, could have saved that Negro."

"Thank you," John said, shaking his hand again.

"I've got two books out there in my saddle bags that I wish you'd read. One of them is Black's Dictionary of legal terms and from what I observed in the courtroom, you can certainly use that. The other is Blackstone. He was an English judge who wrote his opinions on law. Most of our legal foundation is rooted with the English. What I'm saying is I'd like for you to come work for me as a real apprentice. I think we can go places. How about it?"

John glanced over to his father and then to Lucretia. "I appreciate your compliments and offer, but I can't do that. I'm needed at home."

In serious thought, Lott pursed his lips then looking over at Lucretia said, "Son, we all were proud of you today. Me, Andy and James can run the place. If'n it's all right with your wife, I think you ought to go get them books right now."

30

GHOST WALKERS

RISING EARLY, HOMER PUT ON HIS HEAVY JACKET AND lumbered out to the front porch for a breath of fresh morning air. Dawn had always been his favorite time of day. A light in the east revealed layers of orange and pink clouds settled on the horizon.

Smelling tobacco smoke, he realized he was not alone. Turning he was surprised to see Lott already seated on the porch.

"How long you been out here?" he questioned.

"'Bout fifteen minutes. Pretty, ain't it?"

Homer nodded. "You know, whether you're here or in the Territory, it's the same."

"What's it really like out there?" Lott asked, knocking the spent tobacco from his pipe.

Homer walked over to where Lott was sitting and pulled up a chair next to him.

"It's a lot like it is here," he answered.

Changing the subject, Homer said, "Uncle Lott, they can't afford to let Andy's release go unchecked."

"What do you mean by that?" Lott asked, frowning.

"It's just a feeling, that's all," Homer said. "I think Andy and his family should stay here for a while. You still got that room out in the barn?"

"Needs a little cleaning up though," Lott replied.

"I heard what y'all said but I ain't giving up my place. I ain't scart of 'm," Andy said, having been within earshot.

"You got to think of your family. There were some threats made down at Decatur that we must take seriously," Homer said.

"Well, my cousin Louis is down at the place now. He's kinda looking after things 'till we gets back."

"Is he armed?" Lott asked.

"What does you mean by dat?"

"Does he have a rifle?" Homer replied.

Andy shook his head. "He's shore 'nough armed, and he's got a mean streak in 'em."

Remembering James Earl and Thomas, Homer said, "I hated to hear about James Earl's death. The South lost a lot of good men. Ever hear from Thomas?"

Lott paused for a moment, then replied, "Our nation lost a lot of good men. About Thomas, we got one letter from him. He was somewhere out in Texas."

"Heard he quit the army, walked off. Why'd he do that?"

Lott got up to stretch himself and answered, "Well, Thomas came in here on furlough to raise some troops, and he got to telling those war stories and John got to listening to 'em. Before I know'd it, John had enlisted. I didn't want him to go, but I couldn't stop 'em neither. I told Thomas he was the one that got him into that army and he better be shore he kept an eye on 'em. Well, when they got in that big battle up in Pennsylvania, John was reported killed. Thomas felt responsible. He couldn't take it. He quit and came home."

"Uhhh," Homer grunted. "Does he know John is alive?"

Lott shook his head. "There's no way he could know."

Lott's bedroom door squeaked open and Hatta walked out carrying Lott's heavy coat. "Cold out here. You should be old enough to take care of yourself," she said, wrapping the coat around his shoulders.

Later that morning, James and a Choctaw man came to see Homer. After they talked privately, Homer told Lott that he had to be gone for a few days.

Meridian, Mississippi.

Several coaches that had been unhitched and moved off the main track rested silently down from the station. Wood stoves had been installed and one of the coaches had a steady stream of smoke rising from its ventilation port. Inside a group of men sat talking.

"Can you believe what happened over in Decatur?"

"That ain't suppose to happen here in Miss'sippi," one of the men answered.

"We come too far now with gittin' control of things. This here is a setback. If they'll free that Nigguh, no telling what'll come next. Them Darkies think they run the town of Newton like it is."

"Fred, you rode them tracks all the way from Birmingham. What do you think?"

"Men, I don't know why you're worried. This ain't no problem. Just like General Forrest said, 'put the scare on 'em and keep it on 'em. You gonna have to pay that Nigguh a visit."

"What are you suggesting?"

"I say you gotta keep the scare on 'em. Y'all gotta go down there and issue out some justice. You got anybody who can handle this kind of thing?"

One of the men pointed to a tall, rough looking man with a deep scar down the side of his cheek standing guard at the side door. "That's the meanest white man I've ever met. Rode with Forrest. He weren't no soldier; he was a murderer. Took no prisoners."

"Good," the man from Birmingham said. "He needs to round him up some men and be sure he gits someone who knows where the Nigguh lives."

Leaving, Pierce pulled up the collar of his coat to keep out the cold north wind and began walking down the board walk when suddenly one of the doors of the depot swung open almost knocking him down.

Angered, Pierce lashed out, "What the hell do you think you're doing!"

Startled, Tim answered, "Sorry, I didn't see you."

Then as the early morning light crossed Pierce's face, Tim cringed. Standing before him was the foulest man he had ever known. Late in the war General Forrest finally had dismissed him for conduct unbecoming a soldier when he killed two of the general's aides in a brawl. To most folks, Pierce was nothing but a scoundrel, a murderer.

Flushed with anger, Pierce straightened himself. Then studying Tim closely, his expression changed. "You're Tim Johnson, ain't ya?"

Tim, expecting a fight or worse and not really wanting to tangle with Pierce, welcomed the change in Pierce's manner.

"I'm Johnson," he answered.

"You're from Little Rock, ain't ya?

"That's right."

"You know the country 'round there?" probed Pierce.

"Like the back of my hand," Tim said.

"You want to make some money?" Pierce muttered. "Fifty dollars."

"What do I have to do? " he asked hesitantly.

"Just go show me where someone lives. That's all," Pierce replied.

Afraid not to go along with him, Tim said, "Well I'm on my way to Little Rock to check on my mother. Might as well make a little money."

As the two were walking down to the stables Pierce said, "You know where the Nigguh Andy lives?"

Surprised, Tim replied, "Sure I do. What about it?"

Reaching the stables, Pierce asked, "How far is the closest house to 'em?"

A chill came over Tim. Stammering he replied, "The Wilsons live a couple of miles north of him. Maybe less."

Smiling, Pierce turned his face to the north wind. "If'n this here wind keeps up, it'll be perfect. Won't hear a sound. Let's go to Little Rock."

Then suddenly remembering, he added, "Hold up a minute. I've got to go send a telegram."

The scowl on Pierce's face and the tone of his voice brought fear into Tim's heart. Not since the times he stood in the firing line during battle had he felt this sense of foreboding.

Tim knew it would take all day to cover the thirty odd miles to Little Rock, and they would be lucky to get there before dark.

As they rode together, Pierce made no effort at conversation. It was apparent that his mind was on something else.

About mid-afternoon they approached a small settlement called Duffee where three men rode up and joined them. They were all strangers to Tim and they made no effort to introduce themselves. As dusk was settling in, the group reached the outskirts of Little Rock.

Pulling his mount to a stop, Pierce turned to Tim. "Too early. We don't need to go through town. There's suppose to be a church on the north side. Take us there."

Swinging his horse northward, Tim led the men around Little Rock and soon they reached the Little Rock Baptist Church. It was now dark. Wasting no time, Pierce reined his horse to the back of the building and beckoned the others to follow.

Settled in the saddle, Pierce said, "How far is it to that Nugguh's house?"

"He lives about three miles west," Tim replied.

Knowing wrong was in the making, Tim mustered his nerve and added, "I can tell you exactly where he lives but I need to git on home. You don't owe me no fifty dollars."

Without hesitating, Pierce replied firmly, "You going with us."

Before Tim could respond, he heard horses approaching. Pierce hooted like an owl three times and all was quiet for a moment. Then someone out front made the call back to him. It was so dark Tim could barely see the riders as they turned the corner of the building.

Pierce called out, "Buddy, give us some light."

In the light of a torch, Tim was startled to see four horsemen clothed in white. His first impulse was to kick his horse in the flank and run for his life, but he was afraid he would be shot before the horse could take two steps.

Looking at the men that had joined him in Duffee, Pierce muttered, "Time to git dressed boys. We got work to do."

Then reaching in his saddlebag Pierce pulled out a roll of white clothing and tossed it to Tim.

"Put this on," he ordered.

After pulling a revolver from its holster and carefully checking its cylinders, Pierce said, "Put that torch out. Johnson git up here and show us the way."

A cloudy sky covering a rising full moon cast a twilight glow across the countryside. With a brisk wind blowing in their faces, they turning off the main road leading north out of Little Rock and took a farm road that wound westward. After a couple of miles, they came upon the school.

"What's that?" Pierce asked in a gruff voice.

Tim squinting through the dark replied, "That's New Hope School, I believe."

"That's the Nigguh School, I heard about," Pierce grunted. "We'll burn it on the way out."

Mustering his nerve, Tim said, "I want to know what you want Andy for?"

Pierce reached over and grabbing Tim's horse's reigns, pulled him to a stop.

"Where you been fer the past month? Don't you know what happened?"

"I've been on the train for the past five weeks working the tables. I just got in to Meridian this morning," Tim said.

"Well, I'm gonna make it short. That nigguh Andy killed Sam Harmon and the court set 'em free. It's sentencing time now," Pierce hissed.

Tim cringed knowing what he had in mind and began looking for an escape.

Passing a large open field recently plowed for spring planting, the men topped a rolling hill and Tim halted. To their left was a heavy forest of oak and hickory trees and down at the base of the hill a small cabin was settled snuggly under a stand of barren pin oaks. A stream of smoke trickled from the chimney. A light could be seen through one of the windows.

"Is that it?" Pierce asked Tim.

"That's the place," Tim murmured wishing he could warn Andy.

Turning to the men trailing behind him, Pierce said, "We'll circle the place. If we can't git 'em out, use the torches."

"Burns, when you git to the backside, whistle," Pierce ordered. "Johnson, you stay with me."

Moments seemed like hours as Tim sat waiting. He had known the Negro family all his life and could think of nothing they had ever done to harm anyone. He couldn't believe Andy had been charged with murder. It had to be a mistake, he thought.

A clear whistle in the distance pierced the night.

Pierce clicked his tongue against his cheek and his horse moved forward. Slowly they approached the house. When they reached the outskirts of the yard, Pierce stopped and pulled his revolver from its scabbard and cocked the hammer back.

"Anybody home!" he shouted, sitting still in the saddle.

Enjoying the warmth of the fire, Louis eased out of his chair and walked to the window.

Nobody ever comes by here at night, he thought, except maybe some coon hunters.

Easing the curtain aside, his heart stood still.

"Damned ole haunts," he said to himself easing over to bolt the door.

Pierce called out again, "Andy, you might as well come on out here. I know you's there."

Hearing the sound of a white man's voice, Louis realized it wasn't any Haunt at all.

"What ya want?" he called back.

Pierce shifted in the saddle, "It's time fer justice. Either you come on out or we'll burn you out. We'll kill all of you if need be. Choice is yores, Nigguh."

Louis quietly eased over to his shotgun resting next to the fireplace and moving back to the window, replied, "Andy ain't here. I'se here by myself."

Becoming angry, Pierce pulled his pistol up and leveled it on the window. Seeing the man's upper body appear, he pulled the trigger. A crack exploded through the night as the glass shattered.

As the smoke cleared, the roar of a shotgun erupted sending Pierce reeling in the saddle. His horse stumbled forward and Pierce tumbled to the ground.

Regaining his balance, he stood up and cursed, "Damned fool, shot my horse!"

Feeling a pain in his left arm and noticing a dark blot on his shoulder, he realized he also had been hit. "Light yore torches," he shouted. "Burn 'em out!"

Seeing Pierce down and having a chance to run, Tim reigned his horse and was about to kick him in the flank, when a voice called out, "You're dead Johnson, if'n that horse runs!"

Streams of fire streaked toward the house as torches bashed through windows.

"Git ready men," Pierce said. "The smoke's billowing. They's either gonna be cooked Nigguhs or they's coming out."

Knowing that the end was near, the cloaked Klansmen emerged from the shadows and circled the burning house. Patiently they waited. Flames broke through several places in the roof, lighting up the night.

Tim backed his horse away, horrified at what was transpiring. Suddenly the door burst open, sending a wave of smoke and flames gushing outward and Louis, temporarily blinded, plunged forward, shotgun in hand. Squinting to see, he leveled his shotgun. A cluster of shots rang out and Louis fell to his knees. Four or five more shots pierced the night and all was quiet.

Walking up, Pierce kicked him in the side several times as the other men joined in.

"Dead'rn hell. Justice has been served," Pierce shouted.

The fire, fueled by a strong wind, leaped into the sky sending sparks dancing upward as the Klansmen hovered around their kill. As the men began to remove their masks, crashing thuds filled the air and two of the men collapsed, blood gushing from their heads.

Taken by surprise, the other members of the group grasping their rifles, turned in search of what was happening. A whistling like wind and the sound of something striking flesh brought terror to them as three more fell senseless to the ground. Silhouetted against the flaming house, the remaining men tried to scurry to safety, but to no avail. The attackers were not to be seen. Quickly they fell.

As soon as Tim saw the first man drop, he kicked his horse and galloped away. He had only gone a short distance when he felt a sharp blow to the side of his head and becoming dizzy, fell to the ground in pain.

His mount bolted and Tim, unable to stand, heard screams coming from the burning house. Fearing for his life, he began to crawl toward the woods behind him. Reaching a large oak tree, Tim with his heart beating so fast he could barely breath managed a sitting position. With his back resting on its trunk, he prayed he would not be found. His pain made it dificult for him to stay conscious.

Hearing a twig snap, Tim opened his eyes and in the misty dark he saw the silhouette of a man slowly working his way toward him as if he were tracking fallen game.

Tim hoped all this was just a nightmare, but he knew better. Another stalker joined the other one. Closer and closer they came until one of the men was standing only feet from where he sat.

Taking a deep breath, he stammered, "Kill me if'n you want, but I didn't want any part of what just happened."

The sky cleared for a moment and moonlight streaked across Tim's bloodied face. As the man lifted his arm to strike, the other man grabbed his arm and whispered, "No, not this one."

⚜

Strong night winds had pushed the clouds away and the morning dawned bright. It was Sunday and the Wilsons were late rising. The whinny of a horse outside and someone walking down the planked hallway woke John.

Knocks were heard on his father's door and in a few moments someone tapped on his. "John, this is James. You got to get up and hurry."

"What's the problem?" John replied, sensing the seriousness in the tone of his voice.

"Haven't got time to explain. I got your father up and I'm going to wake Andy. I'll meet you at the barn. I'll be getting the horses saddled."

Lucretia tugged at John's arm. "John, what could have happened?"

"I don't know, but I've never seen James act this way," John replied, pulling on his trousers.

When John, Lott, and Andy came out of the house, James had the horses saddled and waiting.

"Don't ask me anything 'cause I don't have the answers. Just come on," James said.

Galloping as fast as they could, the group headed south. Tipping a rise in the road, a trickle of smoke could be seen in the distance. Bouncing in the saddle, Andy called out, "Dat's coming from our place."

Reining their horses to a stop, the men sat stunned in their saddles. Only smoking simmering coals and a blackened stone chimney remained of what had been Andy's house. At the steps lay the body of a man covered with a blanket. A dead horse lay next to him. Further out was a neat row of bodies dressed in white clothing lined up side by side in perfect order. Each one had his arms folded over his chest and his weapon lying at his feet. Sheriff Rawlins and two of his deputies were standing out near the row of bodies.

"Y'all might as well git down. We got one hell of a mess here," he said.

Andy was the first to dismount. He slowly walked over to the body by the steps, knelt down, and pulled the covering back.

"Shot 'em fourteen times," the sheriff called out. "Didn't have no chance."

Dismounting, John, James and Lott walked over to the sheriff. In the distance, they could hear the sounds of a large number of horsemen approaching.

"I sent for the military," James said.

Looking down at the row of bodies, he turned to the sheriff, "How were these men killed?"

The sheriff shook his head. "Don't know. I was waiting for y'all."

Dazed, John looked over at Andy who was on the ground crying and then back to the spectacle in front of him. Blood had saturated the head coverings.

"Klansmen, ain't they," John said quietly.

Before anyone could reply, the soldiers rode up.

"Got here as fast as we could," a lieutenant called out, saluting.

"Take your men and cover every inch of ground around this place. Go as far as a quarter of a mile if need be," James ordered. "Sheriff, have you identified these bodies?"

"I said I was waitin'. Ain't touched a stitch on 'em," he replied. "I figured y'all would take care of things."

A lump came in John's throat as the sheriff leaned over the first body. The first two he uncovered, no one knew, but both had been struck in the head.

Pulling off the third hood, he called out, "This one is Paul Harmon."

The next one's skull was badly crushed in but the sheriff noticed the scar down his cheek. Shaking his head, he said, "This here is one ugly devil. Ain't ever seen 'em before."

Then looking closer, he added, "He's been shot too. I guess the Nigguh got a piece of 'em."

John glanced down at him. "His name is Pierce."

"How'd you know him?" the sheriff asked.

"Long story," John answered, turning his back and walking away.

Painstakingly, the sheriff, James and Lott moved from body to body.

"John, you better come over here," Lott said.

Peering down, John gasped. "What is he doing here?"

"Who is he?" the sheriff asked.

Lott hesitated, then answered, "It's Professor Hendon."

Off in the woods, a voice shouted out, "You better come down here. We got a live one."

At first John did not recognize the battered man. Crouching down, the sheriff lifted his head.

"It's Tim Johnson," the sheriff called out. "He's breathing."

At that, John mounted his horse and kicked him into a full gallop into the swamp.

Motioning to James, Lott said, "You better go git 'em. He's going to the big woods."

Meanwhile, walking up to the Lieutenant who was left in charge, Sheriff Rawlins said, "You find any more?"

The officer shook his head, "I've never seen nothing like it. We covered every inch of ground around here, and there's nothing except those dead men's horses tied where they left them."

"What do you mean nothing?" the sheriff replied. "Somebody killed eight men then laid 'em out in a straight row. Ain't but one of 'em been shot. The rest got their brains knocked loose. There had to have been one hell of a fight going on. This place should be a mess."

"Just what I said, sheriff. There's no trace that anyone else has been here; not a footprint of any kind. Somebody killed these men but there is nothing here. It's like a ghost killing," stated the officer. "I don't understand it at all."

31

KLAN STRIKES BACK

"Klansmen slaughtered" and "klan on the run" headlines ran in newspapers almost immediately. Had it not been for the unusual circle of events that had occurred, the killing would have gone unnoticed by people outside Mississippi. More than once the military was ordered out to where the bodies were found, and the result was always the same. Nothing was discovered that indicated who killed these men.

§§

The moon had been up for several hours as Lucretia sat waiting for her husband. An owl screamed out in the woods, and in the silence of a winter's night, an uneasiness came over her." Time passed slowly. Thoughts of Tim and Professor Hendon crossed her mind as she sat waiting. It was beyond her comprehension how those two men could be caught up in this disgusting affair.

The owl screeched again and in the distance, a rooster crowed. A lighting of the sky in the east ushered in a new day.

"That you, John," Lucretia whispered hearing footsteps outside the bedroom door.

"It's me, Lucretia," John replied.

After they had held each other for a moment, John said, "I'm sorry. I've been through some hard times, but nothing like this. It makes no sense."

Feeling the pain gripping him she replied, "I love you, John."

John squeezed her tightly. "Help me to bed, please."

Hendon's death brought great sorrow to the Little Rock community. Through the years, he had taught almost all of the young people, and with his bubbling personality, he had been the life of social events. Many could not fathom him as a part of a killing, but others hailed him as a hero of the white movement.

People from all over the northern part of the county flocked to the Little Rock Baptist Church for the funeral. John, along with his father, were selected as pallbearers, and as John sat there looking at the body of the man he had revered, he tried to block out the awful sight he had witnessed.

Two days later as John came in from the fields he found Sister waiting for him.

"Afternoon," he said, pulling his muddy boots off at the porch.

"Here, let me knock them off for you," she said reaching to him.

Surprised, John said, "What's wrong with you?"

"Nothing," she answered. "Come on in. Supper's ready."

John found Homer settled at the table along with James and the family. Since Homer and Hatta had arrived, the family seemed closer than ever and their meals together were a time of enjoyment.

After sitting down at the table, he looked at Homer. "When did you get in?"

"This afternoon. I been all the way up to Winston County. Found one of my uncles up there. Did you ever meet Ofa Tubby?"

"Don't think so," John replied.

After the meal, Sister looked over at John. "Tim's been asking for you."

John shook his head and made no reply.

"He's in the jail down in Decatur. Doctor said even though he took a terrible lick to the head, he should be fine. You need to go see him," Sister said.

"I can't do that," John murmured. "I just helped bury one of my friends. I don't know how to face him."

"Well, he's been the best friend you have and word is they didn't find no gun anywhere about him."

"Sister's right," Lucretia said, but maybe you just need more time."

"Maybe we all need some time," Lott said, looking over to where Homer and James were sitting.

As Hatta began clearing the table, Sister reached over and hugged John. "I'm sorry, John. I know all of this is difficult, but if you don't mind I want to go see Tim."

"I can arrange it," James said, getting up from the table.

"Talk is, there is no way he'll go free. People in Washington mean to stop the Klan movement. I'm afraid they're going to make an example out of him," Homer said.

"You saying it's all over for him? How do you know that?" John asked.

Homer shifted nervously in his seat, then replied, "I've read a lot in the papers about how the government stands in regard to the Klan. To me it's just common sense."

"Mister, I'm here to see Tim Johnson. I'm Mrs. Robinson. I think you know my husband."

"Yes ma'am," the private replied, opening the outer jail door.

Looking inside he called out, "You got another visitor, Johnson."

Tim tilted his head to see his visitor and recognizing Sister, grumbled back, "Don't want to see her. Git her outta here, Yank."

The private turned the key opening the cell door and let Sister enter. Tim moved back against the wall and shut his eyes. A white bloody cloth bandage was wrapped around his head and the left side of his face was purple with bruises. One eye was swollen shut.

Pulling a chair up next to his bed, Sister softly said, "What ya doing in here, Tim? We all are worried about you."

Opening his eyes he replied, "I don't want none of yore lectures. If'n you've come down here to pester me, it ain't the right time."

Sister reached down and placed her hand on his. "Tim, I ain't here to play pranks. I'm here cause my heart is breaking for you. I want to help you."

All was quiet for a few moments. Then he said, "I didn't kill nobody, and I didn't want no part of it."

Then he sputtered, "The fact is I was scared of Pierce. I was afraid he was gonna kill me. Should have took my chances and run."

"Tell me what happened," Sister said.

Slowly and tediously, Tim described all the events the day of the killing. When he finished, he looked over to Sister. "That's the Gospel truth as

God is my witness. But you know what? The way things appear, there ain't a court in this here state that'll believe me."

"Hush that talk, Tim Johnson," Sister said. "You got more fight in you than that."

Hearing a noise outside, Sister glanced toward the doorway. "I thought you wasn't coming," she said.

With the door slamming behind him, John stood there looking at the two and replied, "Well, I'm here."

Tim's face lit up and with a hint of a smile, he reached out his hand. "Been hoping you would come. What took you so long?"

John eased down and took a seat on the foot of his cot.

Gripping his hand, he replied, "Got here as soon as I could. You doing all right?"

Tim pursed his lip and nodded. "I shore got myself in one big mess."

"You sure look pretty bad. That's for sure."

"Tim, I want you to tell John everything you told me and don't leave out one word," Sister said.

When Tim had finished he looked John straight in the face and said, "I may have a lot of faults, but I ain't ever lied to you."

John dropped his head momentarily and taking a deep breath said, "I believe you, Tim. Have you told this to anybody else?"

Raising up on his elbow, he thought for a moment. "I told the sheriff and some military officer. In fact, a couple of newspapermen come in to see me yesterday. I was kinda fuzzy headed though, don't remember too good."

"You mean they let that many people in?" Sister asked.

"I guess," Tim answered, lying back down. "Lot of folks been in here."

"Tim, how did those men get killed?" John asked, running his hand across his brow.

"Everybody asks me the same thing," he replied. "But John, I don't remember. It was dark and things happened I can't explain. Didn't hear nobody come up on us. No shots at all. I know something hit me. Hit me hard. Looking up to John, he added, "You think you can help me. John? You saved poor Andy from the lynching."

John took another deep breath and looking at Tim replied, "That was all luck."

"I don't believe that," Tim said, smiling."Folks said you did a fine job."

Seeing the hope in Tim's eyes, John's mind was flooded with all the times they had had. He remembered school days and Tim's mischievous deeds that always landed him in trouble. He remembered fishing trips and skinny-dipping in the creek. John felt the excitement of their enlisting in the army together and the fear as they stood in the firing line expecting death at any second.

"You can do it, John. You can save me," he pleaded.

John shook his head. "I'll see to it that Everett will represent you. To me, he's the best lawyer in these parts, and I'll do all I can to assist him."

Tim thought for a moment. "John, I know gaming ain't the most acceptable occupation, but I have been trying to make something out of myself. But, you know the truth, I'm just the son of a drunk. What more could be expected?"

"You just hush that talk, Tim Johnson. You've done fine. Even though I don't agree with some of your ways, you are a good man and you also got a fine mama who loves you dearly," Sister said.

"I do have a mama that loves me," Tim replied softly.

"Has yore mama been to see you?" John asked.

"Ain't seen her yet," Tim replied.

As John rose to leave, Tim asked, "You think you could go by and check on her for me?"

"That was already in my plans, Tim," John said smiling.

§§

Two weeks later: Meridian Station

"Good seeing all of you again," Daniel McWorthan said, putting his cigar down in an ashtray. Then pointing to his right he said, "Want y'all to meet Earl Buchanan from Jackson and next to him is Malcolm Tillman from Vicksburg."

The group exchanged handshakes and then took their seats.

"Men, next time you run into Frank Olliver, thank him for the use of the coach. It couldn't be more convenient," McWorthan said, reaching down to retrieve his smoke.

"Now to git down to business, we got a problem on our hands with this here killing. We sent a group down there to take care of that Nigguh, and the whole bunch got themselves butchered."

"What'd you find out about it?" Malcolm asked, tapping nervously on the table.

"Well, I went to the jail myself. Told the fool guard I was from the newspaper and they let me right in to 'em," Worthan answered.

"I talked with Johnson for more than an hour."

What'd he say?" one of the men asked.

"He was out of his head. He didn't know who did the killing," McWorthan replied.

"Well, I'll tell you one thing, until we git some answers, there ain't too many gonna volunteer to go night riding," one of the men said.

"What they gonna do with Johnson?" Buchanan asked.

McWorthan nodded. "I did a lot of listening around the courthouse, and I'll tell you one thing, seems like nobody gives a damn about Johnson. Well, that is except the government. They intend to stop the Klan. Oh they'll have a trial but he aint' got no chance. He'll hang. They'll probably say he is a leader of the Klan or something like that."

"You know the funny thing about this, I'm not sure Johnson is even a member of the Klan. I don't know how Pierce ever hooked up with him," one of the men added.

"Well, I'll tell you one thing," McWorthan said. "We've come too far in taking control to have something like this happen. The Nigguhs may think they's on the rise but it ain't so. We gonna git 'em out of office, and it's gonna be harder than hell for one of 'em to own a single piece of property. That means they are gonna have to move on out or go to sharecropping and that ain't far from puttin 'em back in slavery."

A moment of silence filled the coach as the men sat thinking, then Buchanan said, "It's quite a mystery how those men got killed, but the fact is, they did. But just think about this. Who represented that Nigguh down there in Decatur and got 'em freed? Who gave that Nigguh that piece of land and helped him build his house? Who was running for office a while back and upset some folks with his talk about helping the Nigguh? Men, like a revelation from God, there ain't but one man that can be behind that killing, and that's John Wilson."

"Damn," one of the men said. "Hadn't thought about that. Sure makes sense."

The more they thought about what had been said, the more they became convinced that John had to be the one behind the killings. After several hours of discussion, Tillman stood up and said, "We sent what we thought was a man most capable of taking care of that Nigguh and we know what happened to him. I think it's time to get a professional to take care of this problem. I know a man in New Orleans who for the right amount, will do the job. He won't ask no questions and he's most reliable, but he don't come cheap. If you want, I'll wire him."

"All that agree to this, raise your hand," McWorthan said.

A while later, Tillman returned, "It'll cost three thousand dollars, all up front. If we decide to do this, one of us will have to give him the information."

"Our movement has gone too far to stop now," one of the men said. "I say let's vote."

"All approve," McWorthan said.

All raised their hands and McWorthan stated, "I'll send the money to him and since I know the situation, I'll tell him what he needs to know."

§§

Several weeks later with spring breaking, John went back and forth from his home to Mister Everett's office in Meridian. The first part of the week he spent studying and working with the lawyer as they prepared Tim's defense, and the last few days of the week he would tend to the spring planting.

Early one Sunday morning, John and his family were preparing to attend church services when Homer galloped up. John could tell by the expression on Homer's face there was a problem.

Hastily dismounting, Homer blurted out, "Anybody come by here today?"

"No. Why?" John asked. "Where you been for the last two days?"

"So, you mean you haven't heard about it?" Homer asked.

"I've heard nothing," John replied, reaching out to shake Homer's hand.

"There was an explosion in Meridian last night. Nearly blew the depot away," Homer explained.

"Some private coaches got blown up and it knocked a section of a train off the tracks. Rattled every window in the city."

"Anybody get killed?" John asked.

"From what was left, it appears it killed seven or eight men," Homer replied.

Then getting back on his horse he called out, "One of those coaches was owned by Frankie. I'll tell you more later. John, you all be careful. Things are going on. You might want to carry a pistol."

Tim's case was heard the following week. As hard as Everett and John tried, the jury still found Tim guilty in a conspiracy to murder. In Tim's favor, it was noted that he was found without any weapon. But since he was dressed in a Klan outfit and was obviously with the group, there was no logical defense. When the verdict was handed out, the judge thought for a moment then announced the sentence.

"Members of the jury, I want to thank you for your work. We are going through perilous times here in this country, and it is essential that we uphold law and order. No one or any group can go around the countryside burning homes and killing our citizens. What happened over there in Little Rock is despicable. It cannot be repeated."

Looking at Tim, he said, "Mister Johnson, please rise."

Anxiety stricken, Tim stood with Everett and John at his side.

"Mister Johnson, what you men did is disgusting," the judge said. "The other men with you certainly received their justice, and justice will prevail in this land. Mister Johnson, you are sentenced to death by hanging and may God have mercy on your murderous soul. The time and place I will order, and in the meantime you will be turned over to the military where you will be moved from this locality to insure that there will be no interference from any outside group."

Silence came over the courtroom as Tim sank to his seat. Then a feeble, trembling voice cried, "He's the only child I have. You can't take 'em from me. What will I do?"

Sobs were heard throughout the room as Tim was led away. John slumped down with his hands over his face as the reality of Tim's fate sunk in and that justice today had not been served.

Days slipped into weeks, and spring arrived in the hill country. Many of the children's parents were sharecroppers and would be needed in the fields, so Lucretia dismissed school. As she and Sister, laden with books and materials were closing the door, a man rode up out front. With his dark complexion and long black hair tied in the back, he looked to be part Choctaw but did not dress like the locals. He wore a bright red shirt with puffed sleeves, striped gray pants that were tucked into the tops of his boots and with the exception of long sideburns, was clean shaven.

Taking his wide brim hat off, he wiped the perspiration from his forward and looked up at the sign above the porch.

"Good Hope School," he said in a strange accent. "What kind of school is this?"

Lucretia, placing her books in the back of the buggy and walking out to him, said, "We teach mostly Negroes and occasionally a few Choctaws. I guess you could say we are willing to teach any child no matter what color."

The man put his hat back on and twisting in the saddle replied, "That's certainly noble of you. I think all children need the opportunity."

"Are you new around here?" Sister, always skeptical of strangers, asked.

"Just passing through," he replied. "You ladies live near by?"

"I'm Mrs. Wilson," Lucretia said, and looking over to Sister she added, "This is my sister-in-law, Mrs. Robinson. She helps me here at the school."

The man tipped his hat and looking directly at Lucretia with a surprised expression said, "Mrs. Wilson. I see."

Then tipping his hat, he kicked his horse in the flanks and trotting off said, "Good day, Ladies."

"The end of the war sure brought a lot of strangers down here," Sister said.

Days passed and no more thought was given to the stranger. Spring turned into summer and the fields were once more covered in young corn and cotton green by the steady rains. Pushing himself too hard and not feeling well, John decided to take a few days off.

With a brisk wind swirling the tops of the trees and sending leaves fluttering, a horseman approached. Hatta, hearing hoofbeats, wandered out to the porch to see who it was.

"Morning," she said. "What brings you out on a day like this?"

The rider tipped his hat and replied, "Got a telegram for Mister Wilson. John Wilson, that is."

Hatta took the telegram and carried it in to John who was resting. "It's for you. You feeling better?"

Lucretia smiled from where she was sitting and said, "He's doing much better."

John thanked Hatta and opened the paper.

Noting John's expression, Lucretia put the book she was reading in her lap and softly asked, "What is it, John?"

"It's from Mister Everett. He left some material down at the Decatur courthouse and wants me to pick it up. Says it's urgent," John replied. "I best go right away."

"John, you're not well, and I'm not sure about this weather. Why don't you wait until tomorrow?" Lucretia said.

John thought for a few moments and agreed. As he was lying back down another rider was heard outside. In a few moments, James tapped on the door.

"Feeling better," James asked, taking a seat next to Lucretia.

"He is, if I can keep him in the bed," Lucretia said with a laugh.

They talked for a few moments then John showed James the telegram.

James reached over and patted John on the shoulder. "I need to go down there anyway. I'll be glad to help you out. I'll get the material and bring it to you tomorrow."

"I really appreciate this and I hope that it's not asking too much." John said.

"I'm glad to help out," James said, as he made his way out of the room. As he walked to the porch, James noted dark clouds building in the west. "Looks like rain. Mind if I borrow your oil cloth?"

"Go ahead. Take my hat too. They're out there on the peg."

"My horse seems to be coming up lame. Mind if I borrow yours?"

"Help yourself. You know where he is."

Except for rain dripping from the roof, it was an exceptional quite morning. Then a sound like a light thunder was heard in the distance.

Later that morning, Lott spotted a horse wandering in front of the house with its reins dragging the ground.

"John, there's a loose horse outside. Looks like yours."

"Don't think so," John replied as he got out of bed. "James took 'em."

John hurried out and grabbed the reigns and led the horse to the hitching post. Rushing in out of the rain, he said, "It's my horse all right and look at this."

His hands were now drenched with blood.

32

STORM WALKER

WHEN LUCRETIA JOINED THE MEN ON THE PORCH, SHE was stunned to see blood on John's hands.

"Cretia, that's my horse out there," John muttered. "And it is covered in blood."

John stammered to both of them, "I'm gonna go get dressed. Papa, saddle us up two horses."

John and Lott had no trouble following the horse's tracks. Knowing that time was an essence, Lott told John to go on ahead.

"Remember you are seeing two sets of tracks," Lott said, one south and one returning. If you find him, fire your pistol to let me know."

John's anxiety intensified as his imagination took flight. The blood on the horse led to one conclusion. He just hoped that he could reach him in time. Pushing the horse as fast as possible, he followed the tracks past fields of corn and cotton and down through the swamp bottom clustered with massive oaks and hickories. Nearing the river crossing, John reined his horse in, and from the high banks that overlooked the water, he studied the muddy water. There were no tracks on the opposite bank. Whatever happened must have happened in the middle of the stream, he thought to himself.

Slowly John led his horse down the steep bank and into the water. The river was only a little over a foot in depth at this point. John turned the horse downstream. The horse carefully stepped around the rocks that covered the bottom as they weaved down the middle of the stream. John had gone only a few yards when the river took a sharp turn and his horse suddenly balked.

On the far side of the bank lay the body of a man face down in the water. John recognized the hat and oil cloth. Shaking he pulled out his revolver and fired.

He then dismounted and waded out into the river. He quickly turned the body over. The glazed eyes confirmed what he already knew and a deep sadness settled over him. John felt a hand touch his shoulder.

"Let's get 'em on home, John," said Lott.

John faintly replied, "How do we tell Sister? Papa, you know that bullet was meant for me. I feel like it's my fault."

⸎

Sister was devastated by the death of her husband. He was her life. Even though they were from two distinct cultures, they loved each other dearly.

Several days after the funeral, Homer returned with a stranger and quickly assembled the family in Lott's room.

"This is Mister Lawrence Decker from Washington," Homer said.

Everyone introduced themselves and took seats.

With a pleasant smile, Decker said, "I want to thank you for having me in your home and what I tell you has to be held in confidence. You may or may not know, the government is trying to break up the Klan movement here in the South. We have men all over these southern states infiltrating their units."

Looking to John, he continued, "You know that there are people who feel that you are some way responsible for the killing of the Klansmen down south of here."

Surprised, John replied, "That makes no sense."

"I agree," Decker answered. "But that's what they think and after Pierce had been killed, a group agreed to hire a man, a professional, out of Louisiana to take care of you."

A murmur filled the room.

"We feel when James rode out of here dressed in your oil cloth and riding your horse, the killer thought it was you."

"I felt that way too, but really couldn't figure out why someone would want to kill me," John said.

"Well, we went down to the creek bank and looked for evidence. We found a fifty caliber shell on the west bank and found tracks leading to the spot where James lay."

"What are you trying to tell us?" Lott asked.

"Well, the killer certainly realized he killed the wrong man, and will probably try again. Especially since everyone around here knows that you just buried your relative."

The family sat in silence as Decker continued. "You know that explosion that killed those men in Meridian. Those were some of the top leaders of the Klan. We took care of them.

"With their leaders gone, then this may be over," John said.

"Probably not. These men hired and paid the killer. He's on his own now and as a professional killer, who knows what he will do. He probably enjoys killing."

"What can we do?" Lucretia asked.

"If I were you, I'd pack up and leave until we can get all of this under control," Decker said.

The family sat quietly for a few moments, then Lott said, "This here has been my home for most near forty years. I don't see myself leaving."

"I'm not leaving either. I've never been a runner," John said.

John walked to the window and then turned to Lucretia, "Cretia, I'm sending you back to your parents. Homer, I think you and Hatta need to be gettin' on back to the Territory."

"John, I'm not leaving," Lucretia said firmly.

"We're not leaving either," Homer said, looking over to his mother. "A fight has never scared me, especially when family's involved."

In the days that followed, the family was extremely cautious as they went about the daily chores. The women stayed in or near the house and when the men ventured out to the fields or wherever they needed to go, they went in pairs and were always armed.

Sister, torn by the loss of her husband, moved back in with her family.

Days went by and soon spring turned into summer. Slowly the family began to return to normal, hoping the killer was satisfied.

One morning, a family of Choctaws came by and told Hatta that a group of the Choctaw clan was meeting in Neshoba County for a few days and invited her and Homer to come with them.

Standing on the banks of the Pearl River, Homer looked out over the vast hardwood bottom. The trees had never been cut and the thick foliage provided a natural canopy for a meeting place. Wagons of all sorts were clustered about as the Choctaws made camp. Although the Choctaws were usually working the fields at this time of year, occasionally and without notice, they would leave and gather for meetings and socializing.

Large groups continued to drift in as the day went by. The constant chatter of their native language amused Homer who had been away from his people for years.

Strangely, Homer experienced a bizarre dream for three straight nights. It always started with a thunderstorm and lighting bolts striking the earth. He hovered for safety in the Wilson's barn unable to reach the house. Then out of the darkness, a man appeared as bolts of lighting struck all about him. He showed no fear. Stronger and stronger the storm came, tearing shingles off the barn and shaking its foundation. Homer called out to the man, and at that moment he would awake.

On the fourth night Homer and several older Choctaw men sat around the fire smoking and drinking a little corn liquor, gazing up at peaceful evening sky. The stars were scattered into eternity and occasionally a flash would cross the heavens only to be chased by another.

One of the old men pointed upward and chuckled, "That racing star is your father, Jake, chasing a woman."

The men laughed for a moment, then the man continued, "You remember your father?"

Homer thought for a moment. "I remember him. I remember his strength as he held me in his arms. I remember the tenderness he showed my mother. I can see the peace in his eyes when he held an infant, but also the uncontrollable fury when angered."

All was quiet for a few moments as the men enjoyed their tobacco and spirits, then Homer spoke again, "I see a man who would do anything for someone in need, another man who would without thought, kill a man with no remorse. I see my father lying on the porch of our home bleeding to death, his life evaporating from his body as a fog slowly lifts in the early morning. It pains me to think of his loss, and I hate the men who took him from me."

The old Choctaw shook his head. "I understand most of what you say because I too remember him and feel the pain. I know we killed one of the men who attacked your father. Shilup led us to him."

"Who is Shilup?" questioned Homer.

"Shilup is a ghost of one who dies. It stays around for a while until it departs for hereafter. Your father's shilup led us to the man," he said.

"Shilup," Homer said, smiling.

"I think all of them eventually were killed. It proves what the Bible says, 'Vengeance is mine saith the Lord.'"

"You believe in the Bible and its God," one of the Choctaws asked.

Homer thought for a moment. "Doesn't matter whether you are a Choctaw, White man or any race, there is only one God. One people may call him one name and another something else, but He's the same. He's our Creator."

As the night passed, one by one they left the campfire until only Homer and one old man remained.

He mumbled, "Some of the people call me Nanapesa or Judge, others call me Ishtahulla-chito or Witch because I see things that I shouldn't. In your eyes I see trouble. It speaks in your eyes and it struggles on your lips."

Homer then described the dream that had plagued him the past few nights, and the old man sat quietly for more than an hour in thought.

He finally spoke, "This place you describe is your home with the Wilsons. There will be great danger there, and you will not be able to help them. Someone else, a stranger, but one you know, will walk through the lightning. He's the lightning walker."

Homer grew apprehensive. "Will my family be safe?"

The old man took another draw from his pipe and replied, "Your dream stopped there. That question can't be answered."

That night Homer restlessly tossed as he tried to sleep. He knew it was more than a two day ride by wagon to Little Rock and if the old man was right, danger was imminent. As soon as Hatta woke the next morning, Homer told her of the old man's words.

"What was the man's name?" Hatta asked.

Homer thought for a moment then replied, "I think he is called Ishtahulla-chito."

"Tell me all he said, Son."

After a moment of thought over Homer's account, she said, "The word Mahli Chitto means big storm. He's a dream catcher, a prophet. I think it best for us to go home. There's going to be trouble."

Trusting the word of the old Choctaw, they hurriedly packed their belongings and left.

As the sun was setting, a brisk wind began blowing out of the west and near the horizon a wall of dark clouds began to form. Tired from a day's work, Lott walked out on the front porch to enjoy the sounds of the evening. He looked across the fields of tousling corn and rows of dark green cotton. Down beyond the barn, two young colts playfully chased each other.

God has made the world too beautiful, he said softly to himself, admiring the land carved out of a wilderness.

"You usually talk to yourself," came a voice from behind.

"I do have some interesting conversations at times," he replied.

Sister reached around her father and gave him a light squeeze. Taking her hand, the two walked to the corral to see the new colts. After talking a while, Sister said, "You miss Mama, don't you?"

"Every day of my life," Lott answered.

"I don't see how you can stand it, Papa."

Leaning on the corral rails he replied, "It was hard, but you know, I still have a million memories of her."

The two watched the colts run and play for a moment, then Sister said, "I didn't have the chance to collect many memories, but the ones I do have will always be with me."

Walking back to the house they found John and Lucretia sitting out front waiting for them. To the west, the dark clouds were building, and streaks of lightning filled the skies.

As night fell, the wind picked up and the rumble of thunder could be heard in the distance. Some time after four o'clock the next morning the storm hit. Torrents of rain fell and the lightning was so severe that the sky seemed continuously illuminated by its bolts.

Unable to sleep, Lott listened. The sound of horses whinnying got him out of bed. Lott pulled on his pants and went to the window. Several horses were running around frantically terrorized by the storm.

"How'd them critters get out?" he mumbled, reaching for an oilcloth and hat.

Hurrying to the porch, he made his way down the steps toward the horses. One horse bolted away from him several times, and as he was about to throw a rope around the animal's neck, a sound like thunder erupted in his ear. Something hit him so hard it knocked him to the ground taking his breath. Feeling intense pain, he tried to stand but fell.

Mustering all his strength, he called out for help.

John raised up in his bed.

"That sounds like Papa," he said, reaching over to wake Lucretia.

Dressed only in his underware, John rushed out into the hall. Hurrying to the porch, he stumbled on a loose board and fell. As he fell, a flash of light came from the loft of the barn and a whizzing sound sailed over his head, striking the wall and splintering pieces of wood in all directions.

Recognizing the sound of a bullet, John cringed and quickly crawled up against the wall. It was then when he saw his father lying in the mud.

"Don't come out here," Lott yelled with what little breath he had left.

"Papa's been shot," John shouted to Lucretia as she stood in the bedroom door. "Stay here no matter what. I'm going to get Sister."

Terrified, Lucretia quickly moved back inside and all was quite for a while except for the raging storm. Suddenly John returned, pushing Sister ahead of him.

John whispered, " Sister, I know how well you shoot. Take the double-barreled shotgun and move to the room behind us. Ease open the window and be ready. Papa's out there hurt. I'm going back to the hall and try to draw some fire. The shot came from the barn. If there is another one out there, he will try to come up from behind me. That's when you shoot. Be sure he's close enough and use both barrels. You'll be covering my back."

Hurrying back to the bedroom, he handed Lucretia two revolvers and a rifle. "When I pass my other one to you, give me a loaded one back and don't get near the window," he said.

Sprinting back to the hall in between flashes of lighting, John eased up and taking aim at the opening in the loft, squeezed off a round. No sooner had the ball hit the boards near the opening, another shot rang out taking off pieces of plank above John's head.

Expecting shots from behind the open hallway, John looked quickly back before beginning another round of gunfire. Back and forth the firing went as Lucretia handed the loaded rifle to John.

Just as he was reaching for a new load, he heard the click of a hammer being cocked behind him. As he turned, the eruption of a shotgun shook the hallway, and he saw the figure of a man flying backwards off the back porch.

"Reload it, Sister," he called out. "And stay where you are."

Easing back to the front, he called out to his father.

"I'm alive, Son. Don't come out here," he muttered.

All was quite for a few moments. Then gunshots erupted again. One ball struck the ground next to Lott's head sending mud and water splattering. In a few moments, another shot rang out, landing even closer to Lott's head.

Easing back into the room, John motioned for Sister.

"Good shot," he said. "There ain't but two of 'em and one's dead, thanks to you. The other one is using Papa for bait. His only chance to get me is to lure me out by shootin' at Papa.

Thunder rumbled to the east, and then all was quiet except for the steady dripping of rain from the roof. Dawn was beginning to break.

John turned to his sister. "Take my new shotgun, the one that uses shells and come with me. Fill your bonnet with all the shells I have. When I run for Papa, you start firing at the opening in the loft as fast as you can. Fire one barrel at a time in order to space out the shots."

Then he whispered to Lucretia, "When she is reloading, you take the pistol and fire toward the barn. Even if you don't hit anything, it may keep him pinned down."

Sprinting as hard as he could with the blast of Sister's shotgun to his back, John headed for his father. He grabbed Lott under the shoulder and began to drag him toward the house.

They were almost to the steps when a shot erupted from a stand of oaks forty yards behind him. The force of the ball took John's legs out from under him, and he fell to the ground in pain. At that, Sister fired a round toward the trees as Lucretia rushed toward her husband. Before she reached the steps, another shot rang out.

At that moment, a man stepped out from behind one of the trees. Walking slowly, rifle in hand, he slushed through the water puddled in the yard. Reaching John and Lott, he looked down at them for a moment then up to the porch. Seeing Sister sitting there crying, he said, "Madam, I don't plan to kill you, but if you move, I will."

Lott lay unconscious with a pool of blood about him. John looked at the man standing over him. Never had he seen such a cold look on a person's face. His hair was long and tied behind his head and he wore peculiar striped gray pants.

The man was still staring at Sister. "You killed one of my men back there. I can't believe a woman took him."

Then he lifted his rifle and aimed it at John's head.

At that moment, a shattering roar tore the morning apart and the man stumbled backwards, dropping his rifle to the side. He shook violently and placed his hand on his stomach, blood oozing from between his fingers.

The sound of footsteps sloshing through the water came closer, and John could see a large man with a full graying beard though the dawn's dim light. He wore a large brim hat and sharp-toed boots like none John had ever seen before.

The man cocked the hammer of his revolver and pointed it at the man he had just shot. Squeezing the trigger, he said, "These here are my folks and your killing days are over."

Excitement filled John's heart at the sound of his familiar voice.

The man walked over to them and looking at his father, stooped down and pulled him close. Checking the pulse in Lott's neck, he mumbled, "You too tough to die old timer. I gotta get you in the house."

Looking to John, he studied him for a moment and said, "And who the devil are you?"

A smile crossed John's face.

The men looked closer. "God have mercy, Boy. I thought you was dead. Thought them Yanks got ya."

The two embraced and John stammered, "Lot of folks thought I was killed up there. I guess us Wilsons have seven lives, Big Brother."

John called out, "Sister, get out here to help us. Our brother Thomas is back."

"John, you better get up here," she replied. "It's Cretia."

A numbness came over John and he began to tremble. "Help me up, Thomas."

Reaching his wife, John knelt by her as tears began to stream down his face. Blood covered the front of her nightshirt.

Thomas quickly eased down and placing his finger on her neck took a breath of relief and said, "This woman ain't dead. Sister, take my horse and get a doctor out here."

Doctor McLauren worked as fast as he could. The ball that struck John entered his upper thigh and with some careful probing, was soon removed. Even though Lott had lost a lot of blood, the ball that hit him passed directly through his shoulder leaving a wound that should heal.

But the bullet that struck Lucretia had entered her lower chest and though it appeared not to have hit any vital organs, was lodged near her heart. Even though the bleeding had stopped and her breathing was becoming more regular, Doctor McLauren said there was no way he would attempt to remove the bullet.

John turned to Thomas. "You got to ride down to the station and wire Cretia's father. He's a doctor. Tell him what has happened and tell him to get here as fast as he can. If'n anyone can save her, he can."

33

STATELY VISIT

Washington, March 1877

"ARE YOU MISTER WILSON?"

"Yes, I am," John replied, in his native southern drawl.

Extending his hand, he said, "I'm Jason Atkinson. I'm one of Mister Deven's assistants. He'll see you now."

Walking into the large stately office, John could not believe he had been asked to meet with the Attorney General of the United States. Not only was he shocked by the invitation, but his travel expenses had been paid as well.

"Make yourself comfortable, Mister Wilson. It shouldn't be too long."

"Thank you," John answered, taking a seat.

No sooner had he settled himself in a plush dark red leather upholstered chair, than a door opened and a stout gray haired man dressed in a fashionable dark blue suit came into the room.

He walked over to John, reached out his hand and introduced himself. "I'm Charles Devens, and you are John Wilson."

"Yes Sir, I am," John replied, getting up from his chair.

Devens then told John to take a seat, and he made his way back to a large desk in front of John and sat down.

Sensing John's nervousness, he smiled across to him. "I don't blame you if you're somewhat apprehensive about being asked to come all the way up to Washington, but I believe it could be worth your while."

John straightened himself in his chair. "I have tried to think what I might have done to warrant the invitation."

"Mister Wilson, I've followed your career for quite some time. The first time I saw you, I was a captain in the Union Army assigned to the Meridian area after the war. I was there when you made your political speech, and I must say I was impressed with what you said. You struck me as a man of vision."

John shook his head and smiled. "Didn't do me much good. My vision, as you called it, wasn't well received."

"You should have been elected. The South needs good intelligent men like yourself. They were very foolish in their selection," Devens said. "After that, I really didn't expect to ever hear from you again, but the killing of the Klansmen near your place and the way you defended the Negro and got his acquittal caught my attention. That wasn't supposed to be possible, especially with a local all-white jury."

Embarrassed, John cleared his throat. "Sir, I really didn't know what I was doing. The judge ignored quite a bit of trial procedure," John said.

"You did win the case, didn't you?"

John thought for a moment and replied, "Sir, I guess I did at that."

"You did at that," Mister Devens repeated. "After that, having been a lawyer myself, I have made it a point to keep up with you. You have made quite a name for yourself in Mississippi."

"Thank you Sir," John replied.

"Well, this brings us to the point of why you have been asked to come here. As you may know, our newly elected President of the United States, President Hayes, is making some sweeping changes that the South should welcome. In the process, there has got to be law and order."

"I don't understand," John said.

"The President would like to offer you the position of federal judge," he stated, watching John closely.

"Federal judgeship," John replied with surprise in his voice.

"That's right. You will handle matters that will come to you from the state of Mississippi. During the years to come, Mississippi will need men of your character and intellect. You think you can handle it?"

Astounded, John sat speechless and at that moment there was a knock at the door. Turning, John was shocked to see Homer entering the room. Dressed in a federal officer's uniform, he walked over to John with a sheepish grin and, extending his hand, said, "I guess you could call me Colonel Wilson. I am an 1858 West Point graduate, and I was assigned to the Seventy

First Pennsylvania during the war. In fact, I was behind that stone wall at Gettysburg when you all hit us."

"Now I'm really confused," John said, shaking his hand.

Pulling up a chair beside him, Homer continued, "I was fortunate to have a man tutor me when I arrived in the Territory, and even luckier when I, through the help of the territorial governor, received an appointment to the Academy."

"But, Homer, you fought for the North," John said.

Homer nodded. "I did and that was a difficult decision, but I felt it was the right thing for me to do."

"Knowing that Colonel Wilson was from Mississippi and was part of your family, I was the one who sent him back to try to break up the Klan activity there in East Central Mississippi," Devens said.

"Then all that riding around meeting with the Choctaws was only part the plan?" John asked, looking over at Homer with a smile.

Homer shook his head. "Well, I did want to see how my people were faring, but at the same time I was looking for Klan activity."

Suddenly John's mind cleared. "You were in on the killing of those Klansmen, weren't you?"

Homer looked over to Mister Devens. "Can I tell him that, Sir?"

"Go ahead," Devens answered.

"John, when Andy was released, we knew there had to be a retaliation. Night after night we staked out the place hoping they would show," Homer said.

"Who is we?"

"I had fifteen Choctaws helping me," Homer replied.

"Unbelievable!" John said.

"The night they came, we were a little late getting there and things happened so fast, we could not save the Negro," Homer said.

"How were those men killed?"

"You ever hear of rabbit sticks? They are silent, and the men using them can throw them with deadly accuracy," Homer explained.

"What's a rabbit stick?" Devens asked.

"The Choctaws take a piece of hickory 'bout twelve or fourteen inches long and whittle it down into something like a small club. They usually carry several with them when they go hunting. Believe me, they know how to use them," Homer said.

"But, they could find no signs down there."

Homer smiled. "We brushed away our tracks and when we reached the creek, we waded for a good mile upstream before we climbed out to the bank."

"What about Tim? You know he wasn't part of it. Why'd you let him die?"

"Dead, who said he is dead," Devens said. "No indeed. He's been here in Washington ever since he was removed from Mississippi. How do you think we knew about where the Klan was meeting in Meridian," Homer said.

"After the trial and the bombing in Meridian, we moved him here for his own safety," Homer said.

Devens laughed. "And I think it's time to get him out of Washington before he takes any more of our money. That man is good at poker. I want you to take him home with you when you leave. The President will be issuing him a pardon."

John was elated that Tim was alive, but then a thought dawned on him. "I see now that I was just bait for you. The Klan thought I was behind the killing. My wife was almost killed."

Homer looked over to Devens as silence filled the room. Clearing his throat, Devens replied, "We did not wish that upon you. Things got out of hand. We are truly sorry. How is she now?"

Quietly, John replied, "Thanks to the good Lord and the ability of her father, Doctor Caulder, we were able to save her. She is visiting with parents in Gettysburg while I'm here."

John thought for a moment then continued, "Well, since this seems to be a time of revelation, what did my old friend Frankie have to do with the hiring of the killer?"

"Nothing, nothing at all," Homer answered. "When he ran for the state legislature, he courted the Klan for their support, passed out liquor and cash to those who would take it, but once elected, he began to distance himself from the group. Believe it or not, he became truly engrossed in politics. You two may have your differences, but he's not a murderer."

"That's good to know," John said.

"Growing up, Frankie was always getting over his head in trouble, and you were always there to get him out. You know, I think he still believes you would come to his assistance," Homer said.

John cleared his throat and after a moment of silence replied, "You're probably right at that. I've always been kind of a fool."

Suddenly, the door opened and two soldiers entered followed by a large distinguished looking man with a short-cropped beard. Homer snapped to attention, and John and Mister Devens stood up.

"Good afternoon, Mister President," Devens said.

"Good afternoon, Gentlemen. Please take your seats," President replied.

Devens motioned for the president to take his seat, and he took a chair next to Homer.

Looking directly at John, President Hayes said, "I suppose this must be Mister Wilson."

John quickly got up and shook the President's hand. "It is indeed my pleasure to meet you, Sir. I'm John Wilson."

With a slight grin President Hayes replied, "Take your seat, Mister Wilson. I have heard a lot of good things about you. You know we have a lot in common. I understand you love to read as I do, and at heart, I'm still a backwoods lawyer."

Noting the pleasant expression on the President's face and learning they had common ground, John began to relax. He never dreamed he would meet the President of the United States.

"Now John, if I may call you that, you may have heard that there are going to be sweeping changes coming that will certainly affect the South, and I think you can be an asset to our country."

"Yes Sir," John replied.

The President rubbed his hand across his mustache, "You know, the national election was total chaos and a special electoral commission was appointed to sort it out. In the end a compromise was made, and to make things short, the Federal troops are going to be removed from the South. You Southerners have been wanting self rule. Well, that's going to happen."

"Then the military rule is over?" John asked.

"That's right. And I expect men such as you to help us maintain law and order in the South and provide a smooth transition, that is if you are willing to accept the position I am offering you."

"Yes Sir," John replied. "I'll do all I can."

"Mister Devens has some papers for you to sign and with luck we will be able to get Congress to confirm your judgeship."

"What kind of papers," John asked.

"John, there are still a lot of fire eating, Rebel hating Republicans up here on the hill, and since you technically fought against the federal government, I feel a letter of apology would be beneficial," President Hayes said.

A concerned look crossed John's face. "With all due respect Mister President. What am I apologizing for?"

President Hayes cleared his throat. "For taking up arms against the United States and for being part of a rebellion that tore this country apart and took thousands of lives," he said softly.

John dropped his head and thought for a moment, then said, "Sir, when my state withdrew from the Union, and you being a lawyer know there is no clause in the constitution preventing such, I acted like any good citizen. I helped protect our state's rights."

President Hayes shifted in his chair, "John, think carefully about what's at stake here. There is a clause in our constitution preventing a state's withdrawal."

"Sir, I lost a brother and quite a number of friends fighting for the cause," John said quietly. "Signing such a statement would be a disservice to those men."

"John, there are times when we all have to compromise our principles if it is for the betterment of our country. When I pull those troops out, there will be perilous times in the South unless men such as you step up and assume your duty. The Negro will be one of our first concerns."

"Mister President," John said, sitting on the edge of his chair. "At present it is almost impossible for a Negro to obtain land of their own. In fact, most of them are sharecropping as we speak. If there is no guarantee of their personal and political rights, I see a time when they will not only be unable to buy property, but I'm afraid they will be denied their right to vote and hold office as well. Sir, if you pull those troops out without guaranteeing their rights, they won't be any better off than before the war. In fact, by such an act, they will still be shackled."

"Shackled is a harsh word, Mister Wilson. You Southerners have been wanting to gain your state's rights and your return to self government. Well, this is going to happen. I respect your feelings, but I'm offering you a chance to help the people of Mississippi as you rebuild your state, and if you don't accept this position, the man who does fill this spot may not have the citizens' welfare at heart. And yes, you are going to have a tremendous problem as to what to do with the Southern Negro. You can hold to your ideals and walk away or you can roll up your sleeves and go to work. The pen's there in front of you. It's your decision."

The President walked to the large window overlooking the mall below and looked out, his back to John. "Shackled," he said. "I guess you are saying the South is unconquered."

John then glanced from Homer to Devens. Staring down at the pen and paper, he saw the smoke rising from the firing line and heard the rumble of muskets firing. He saw men drop to the ground all about him and afterwards heard the painful moan of the wounded and dying. As he sat there, the black pen became larger and larger as if it were reshaping itself into a piece of field artillery, an instrument of death.

34

FINAL HORIZON

Little Rock, Mississippi, 1930

THE AFTERNOON SUN SLOWLY MOVED TO THE WEST, sending scorching rays across the porch where the old man sat. Having snoozed off, he awoke and looked down at the young boy lying on the bench, with his head resting on his lap. Even with perspiration trickling down his face, the boy slept peacefully.

Easing his pocket watch out, he murmured to himself, "Good gracious, it's already pass five o'clock."

Nudging the boy, he said, "Time to wake up Andy. We've got to be going."

Andy slowly opened his eyes and looked about aimlessly for a moment. Then glancing up at his great grandfather, he smiled. "Want to go back to the creek?"

The old man laughed.

"No, but I think we need to thank the clerk for having us around," he replied.

Inside the store, the clerk was counting his day's earnings. He looked up as they came in.

"About ready to call it a day?" he asked, hoping that this time the two would go on their way.

The old man held out his hand to the clerk. "I know we were probably a burden to you today, but I want to thank you for your hospitality."

Surprised by the old gent's manners, the clerk felt embarrassed he had not shown the two much courtesy.

Shaking the old man's hand, he replied, "Y'all weren't no trouble at all. You'll have to come back to see me sometime."

Then looking down into the dark blue eyes of the boy below, he reached into his counter drawer and after fumbling for a moment he found what he wanted and handed it to Andy.

Lying in the palm of Andy's hand was a perfectly chipped Choctaw arrowhead. With sparkling eyes and a huge smile, he looked up at his great grandfather and exclaimed, "Is this what I think it is?"

The old man smiled at Andy and then back to the clerk.

"It's got to be the most perfect arrowhead I've ever seen. I think you need to thank this kind man," the old man said.

As they were leaving, another elderly man entered. The expressions on their faces showed that they knew each other. They talked for a while and at times laughed. Finally, the old man and boy left the store.

Motioning, the clerk asked, "Timothy, Timothy Johnson. Who in tarnations is that eccentric old codger? Them two's been 'round here all afternoon."

Surprised, the man replied, "You mean you don't know who he is?"

The clerk shook his head. "Ain't never seen him before. Strange sort though."

"That so-called old codger is none other than the Honorable John Wilson. He was raised right up the road from here. In fact the old house burned about the turn of the century, and the Smiths built another one where it once stood. You know Jim and Nannie Smith, don't you?"

"I know 'em," the clerk answered. "Everybody knows Little Jim."

"Well, Judge Wilson spent more than thirty years on the bench and when the war broke out with Spain, Ole Teddy Roosevelt took 'em with him down there to Cuba. He was something like a secretary for 'em. He kinda wrote up what all happened."

The clerk scratched his head and said, "You know, I have heard of him. You mean that old man is Wilson?"

"That's him, and later when Roosevelt was elected president, he wanted Mister Wilson to work for 'em up there in Washington, but Wilson turned him down. Decided he'd rather remain a judge," Johnson said.

The clerk shook his head. "He's been around here all day, and I ain't said much more than a hello."

Johnson began to chuckle. "You want me to tell you something funnier? My father and him fought in the war together. In fact Papa married his sister. Wilson is actually my uncle. Ain't seen him in ages, not since him and his wife moved up to Pennsylvania. You know, his wife was from up there."

"Didn't he have a cousin, a giant of a man? Folks say he was part Choctaw," the clerk said.

Johnson nodded. "Name was Homer. He came back here in the nineties and after staying a spell, left here with Suzanne Olliver. Word was, the two got married, and he went down to the low country to run her grandfather's plantations. But you know, that was a long time ago."

⚡

Reaching the crest of the hill overlooking the village, the old man stopped the car and resting his arm over the top of the seat turned and looked down to the valley below. Weaving its way among the tall oak and hickory, the stream wasn't more than a trickle. Beyond its banks, Walker's store, now renamed Herrington's General Merchandise stood firmly in the center of town bordered by recently built establishments. A railroad now ran east to west behind the row of stores, and back to the north, the top of the steeple of the Little Rock Baptist Church could be seen.

"So many memories," he murmured.

Seeing the sadness in his eyes, Andy tugged on the old man's sleeve and said, "Popee, is everything all right?"

"Everything's fine, Lad."

"Popee, do you think we'll ever come back here again?"

The old man thought for a moment then replied, "I'm gettin' up in years. I don't think I'll be back, but I have a feeling you will."

EPILOGUE

Like the United States presidential election of 2000, the election of 1876 was filled with chaos and confusion. Four states—Louisiana, Florida, South Carolina and Oregon — submitted two sets of electoral returns, one by the Democrats and one by the Republicans. As a result, both parties claimed victory. On December 6, the Electoral College awarded the disputed votes to Hayes. This gave Hayes, the Republican candidate, 185 Electoral votes to Tilden's, a Democrat, 184. Democrats in Congress accused the Republicans of fraud and challenged the decision.

In January, 1877, Congress appointed a fifteen-man Electoral Commission to decide which electoral votes should count for Hayes and which for Tilden. Its decisions were to be final, unless both houses of Congress voted otherwise. During the debate in Congress, members of both parties threatened to seize the government by force.

As Inauguration Day approached, the leaders of both feared that the country might be left without a president. In a private meeting, Southern Democrats in Congress agreed not to oppose the decision of the Electoral Commission. This gave Hayes the presidency, because the Commission had a Republican majority. In exchange, the Republicans promised to end Reconstruction and withdraw federal troops from the South. Southerners thus regained complete control over their state and local governments for the first time since the Civil War.

The deal made with the South to remove troops and grant them complete control of their state governments stopped what chance the Southern Negro had for political rights. With the return of white supremacy, the Negro had a difficult time purchasing property. With the inability to own land, the only other option was sharecropping or working for low salaries.

In addition, practically every African American in the South lost his right to vote and hold office because of the new poll tax and literacy exams. The system of segregation began isolating the Negro from the White, and the African Americans in the South were again bound to a state of servitude, this time for approximately eighty-five years.

During those years, no one stepped forward to help them gain their due rights. Finally in the nineteen sixties, African Americans began to demonstrate and fight peacefully for their civil rights. Today in the South, there is still a state of segregation, but laws have been passed to grant African Americans their rights, and race barriers have been broken. The African Americans are beginning to assume their rightful position in the American society. There is still a distance to go, but the future is promising.

Little attention was given to the Native Americans residing in Mississippi. In the early nineteen hundreds the Choctaw were basically homeless and destitute. In 1918 the United States Senate established the Bureau of Indian Affairs in Philadelphia, Mississippi, and land was purchased, primarily in Neshoba and Newton counties, for the creation of a reservation.

Under the leadership of the tribal chief of the Mississippi band of Choctaws, Chief Phillip Martin, the tribe has flourished. The investment in casinos has brought tremendous wealth to the tribe, and they are using some of the income to purchase factories and to educate their youth. In the late nineteen fifties not a single Choctaw attended East Central Community College, an institution that serves the area where the Choctaw Reservations are located, but today many are attending colleges and earning advanced degrees.

www.ingramcontent.com/pod-product-compliance
Lightning Source LLC
Chambersburg PA
CBHW011401010726
47495CB00009B/2725